THE CURSED BARON
THE GLORIOUS VICTORIES OF ELEANOR MACLEOD
VOLUME ONE
by Ashley Mayers

First Printing: 2019

ISBN: 978-1-943918-16-4
International Print Edition

Grass Roof Publishing
P.O. Box 14908
San Francisco, California, 94114
www.GloriousVictories.com

Also by Ashley Mayers:
THE SITA CHRONICLES:
    Red Sapphire
    Violet Sapphire
    White Sapphire
    Golden Sapphire
    Cerulean Sapphire
    Green Sapphire
    Black Sapphire
THE GLORIOUS VICTORIES OF ELEANOR MACLEOD:
    The Cursed Baron
    Angels in Disguise
    Damsels and Demons
    Eastward Beyond the Sky
    Before Midnight Ends
THE RIDDLE

Notes from the publisher:

The Glorious Victories of Eleanor MacLeod is a new five-book epic that adds another layer to the rich fantasy world created by Ashley Mayers and first published in 2015-16 in her seven-book modern multicultural epic, *The Sita Chronicles*.

The Cursed Baron, the first book of Eleanor MacLeod's story, begins during the denouement of *The Sita Chronicles*, and quickly brings the reader back to the 1920s, when Eleanor MacLeod's fanciful entrance to the world of Ashley Mayers began. As an homage to the genres that Ashley Mayers found most fascinating as a young reader herself, each book in Eleanor's epic plays with elements of a classic genre. *The Cursed Baron* starts us off with an Agatha Christie style murder mystery, while the subsequent books in the series play on a spy novel (*Angels in Disguise*), a fairy tale (*Damsels and Demons*), a western (*Eastward Beyond the Sky*), and a tragedy (*Before Midnight Ends*), each with a unique Ashley Mayers twist.

Throughout this series, it is the author's intention to give enough background for an uninitiated reader to develop a relationship with the world of *The Sita Chronicles*, while introducing them to several new heroines whose stories haven't yet been told. Both series fit together as puzzle pieces, creating unique insights into characters who are lovingly developed over the combined set of twelve books.

This series, like *The Sita Chronicles*, is a completely original, multicultural saga with roots in Hindu mythology. It exists in a world not dissimilar to ours, where Avatars (deities on Earth), Rakshasas (shapeshifting demons originating on Venus), and Yakshas (shapeshifting nature spirits) are real. While knowledge of Hinduism is not required to enjoy this series, a short glossary is provided in the back of the book to offer readers more context on Hindu cultural references.

TABLE OF CONTENTS

CHAPTER 1 – THE MYSTERY GUESTS

February 12, 2016 – Elphinstone, Scotland

The warm light and happy banter of a celebratory evening emanated into the dark night as soft, fluffy snow drifted up against an ancient stone manor. Out front, illuminated only by the eerie, flickering light of several old-fashioned gas streetlamps along an otherwise deserted rural driveway, a 1926 Rolls Royce remained parked as it had been for several hours, packed with four shivering people who questioned their circumstances more and more vehemently with every gust of icy wind that whistled through the poorly-sealed metal cage of the antique car.

Each of them, regardless of age, showed evidence of the fiery red hair that had run in their family for generations. Their sharp wit and effusive kindness echoed almost as heartily as their thick Scottish brogues as they sat huddled together, dressed in elaborate costumes that matched the vintage of the car impeccably, keeping each other company and watching their white breath fog up and freeze into delicate ice crystals on the windows.

"Aunt Judy, do you think it's true? Do you think the Rakshasas of Venus are really related to us?" A young boy asked as he wiped another patch of ice out of his way to continue his devoted survey of the dark, cloudy sky.

"No one ever said they were related to us, Douggy. Not by blood, at least," Aunt Judy replied through chattering teeth.

"But Ellie looks just like us!" Douggy argued. "Her name is Eleanor MacLeod Marriner, isn't it? The MacLeod is us, isn't it, Da?"

"Aye. It is, Douggy," a middle-aged man with just a few wisps of red hair covering his freckled bald spot agreed. He blew into his frozen hands to warm them up. "But I didn't think they'd leave us out here in the cold for so long. Do you think it's all a wicked prank by the lads down at the pub? They've been teasing us for months about being magical aliens."

"Aye, I've been wondering that myself..." Judy admitted. "But we promised Neha we'd wait for her cue. Let's give it another few minutes. If it's not a prank, it will certainly be worth the wait."

They returned to their quiet vigil, waiting obediently in their uncomfortable position, listening for the cue that their otherworldly hostess had enthusiastically arranged when she'd called them out of the blue just a few days before.

At first they'd thought the entire affair was a joke, just one of many cruel pranks their family had been submitted to for decades by the scores of ruthless ruffians back in their hometown of Elphinstone, which, despite its fairy-inspired name, was, in truth, an unremarkable row of houses that had sprung up in a grassy field outside of Edinburgh roughly a thousand years ago.

But, when Neha Rutherford Patel Vishravan—the interplanetary ambassador of the Rakshasa people of Venus, whose smiling face and bubbly voice were now known to everyone on Earth—insisted over the phone that their presence was absolutely essential for the epic birthday party she was planning,

2

and then sent over a trunk of roaring twenties costumes by courier within only a few *minutes* of their begrudging agreement, they decided that playing along with whatever shenanigans were afoot was worth the risk simply for the story.

You see, the story was worth the risk for one simple reason: The world as they knew it had dissolved. It had been replaced by a reality that was utterly and intensely mad. So many of the truths they had taken for granted their whole lives had been turned upside down that it was hard now for them (and everyone else on Earth) to decide daily which things around them were too absurd to believe.

It had been that way since four months earlier when, as they had gone about their ordinary human business on an unusually sunny Scottish November afternoon, their computers and their televisions lit up with the shocking revelation that the human race was not alone in the universe. Not only had humans overlooked their powerful shapeshifting neighbors on Venus during their exploration of the solar system in the 1970s, their unobservant race had also managed not to notice that for thousands of years, indeed since before human civilization began, many of those powerful beings had been secretly hopping about on Earth.

The revelations themselves were mad enough, but when they heard the names of two of the outed aliens—one Colonel Edmund Marriner, formerly of the British Army (all the way back in World War *One*), and his strikingly familiar daughter, Ellie MacLeod Marriner—they almost collapsed with the shock.

The family legend had persisted for decades: Eleanor MacLeod—their clever and loving firecracker of an aunt, who'd single-handedly saved the family from destitution and shame (a story they only ever recounted amongst themselves), had abandoned her proud choice of spinsterhood to marry an angel in disguise.

She'd produced a beautiful child with the gentle English soldier, and on the night of young Ellie's birth in 1926, Eleanor MacLeod had died. It shouldn't have been surprising. They'd always known that the MacLeods were cursed. Still, the tragedy was overwhelming. They'd hoped that somehow the angel in disguise would manage to save her. He, more than anyone, was destroyed by the ruthless reality that he couldn't.

For years after the tragic night, Edmund Marriner, the kind English soldier who had such an unexpected grasp of the Gaelic language, such an uncanny talent for cricket, and such a beaming love for his daughter who looked so hauntingly like her mother with her porcelain Celtic skin and fiery red hair, would bring young Ellie up to Scotland to be with her family. The older of the MacLeods, and even Gramma Moira, called him Abbi, a name totally unfamiliar in English or Gaelic, but no matter how much the curious wee bairns needled, no one would ever explain why. Even Ellie didn't know. Instead, they'd change the subject with a smile, and thus, the family legend settled down, into a background simmer.

Young Ellie's long summers were spent rolling about the soft, wet grasses of the emerald hills, and her freezing Christmases were spent by the roaring fire in Gramma Moira's cozy townhouse with her loving older cousins, Debbie and Charlie, while year after year, her unusually tall father's posture hunched with the tell-tale signs of human aging, until the war got in the way. By the Christmas of 1946, no one mentioned Abbi again except in hushed whispers, and so life continued until 1966, when Ellie too disappeared.

A veil of sadness resonated in her vibrant voice as she rang on Christmas Eve to inform her cousin Ruth that she wasn't going to make it. They never heard from her again. They wondered amongst themselves what had really happened. They hoped wistfully that perhaps Ellie had gone back to Heaven where Abbi had come from in the first place.

4

And so, when the news of the alien presence on Earth was followed up by a series of videos posted to the internet, including an excessively detailed lecture on the long history of the Rakshasas' meddling on Earth and a speech by a very familiar man by the name of Edmund Marriner, the MacLeods suddenly had their explanation. It seemed sufficiently mad to only discuss after several pints at the pub, until the phone call from Neha brought them straight to attention.

They had to know if the legends were true. If it was a prank, it was a perfectly-executed one worthy of their temporary suffering. If it was not a prank, it would surely be epic, or so they told themselves as they shivered more and more as the evening wore on.

And so, as they awaited Neha's cue, minute by minute rethinking their wisdom on accepting her invitation in the first place, they were ever so relieved when Douggy began bouncing up and down with excitement.

"Aunt Judy, look! It's them! It's really them! Their wings are even bigger in real life than they are on the tele! The lads at school aren't going to believe this!"

They each crooked their necks and wiped away the ice on the windows to watch the fair, rosy-cheeked, surprisingly youthful man with jet-black hair alongside his beautiful Anglo-Indian wife—his *Rakshasa* wife, who was just as alien as he was, or so it seemed on the tele—descend gracefully from the night sky with only their angelic golden falcon wings to carry them.

"It's about time, Abbi," Debbie MacLeod whispered as she watched them hit the ground silently in the soft, drifting snow.

Debbie was an ancient woman by human standards at the age of 102, but she still had a few strands of red persisting in her thick head of frizzy white hair. She was the only MacLeod of her generation left, and she, unlike the rest of them, knew everything. She'd learned long ago how to keep a secret, and so she sat silently with contentment listening to their banter and watching the divine visitors land.

As a violent bluster of snowy wind shook the car, she shivered and pulled her thick fur coat tighter around her thin body, shifting uncomfortably in the beaded flapper costume that Neha had provided for the occasion. She wouldn't have dared wear anything like it, even in the 1920s, but she kept that thought to herself too.

Douggy slammed his small freckled nose against the glass of the car window to get a better look at the alien spectacle.

The Rakshasas stood on the driveway only a few meters away from the car, and they took a moment to observe their surroundings. They both looked decidedly out of place on the frigid evening, as Edmund wore an outfit of white tropical linens, and his wife wore a yellow sundress with a delicate white summer sweater. Their large wings protruded seamlessly from their completely unwrinkled clothing.

Neither of them paid attention to the snow as Edmund pulled his wife into his arms and kissed her softly on the lips.

"Are you alright, my love?" he asked with concern as he noticed the subtle grimace in her expression.

"No. I'm sorry, Edmund. I don't want to ruin Ellie's party, but I'm not alright! I can't get that poor girl out of my mind! I chose not to heal her, and now she's going to die!"

Edmund engulfed her into a supportive embrace and whispered into her ear. "*We* chose not to heal her. I am just as responsible as you are for her fate."

"That doesn't make me feel any better. That child was too young to make her own decisions. Her parents made a terrible choice, and now she will suffer the consequences."

"We did the right thing, Supriya. *You* did the right thing. That girl's parents did not even try to seek medical treatment for her condition. It would never have reached the tragic stage it was at when they found us if they'd done what the doctors told them to do in the first place. Instead, they chased us across the globe in an effort to force our healing hands. If we had given in, others would have followed."

"I guess," she conceded, unconvinced.

He took her hands into his. "My love, you have already had to remind me too many times that if they think they can simply pray for our help, developments in human medicine will cease. They will seek divine intervention that we cannot provide because if we did, we would throw off the delicate balance that has kept Earth moving forward for billions of years. Sometimes for the worlds to be preserved, individuals must perish. It is the nature of the cruel universe, and even we can't change that."

"Logically I agree with you, but their suffering is consuming me." He pulled her tighter into his arms, and she suddenly seemed frustrated with herself for her heightened emotional state. "I'm sorry, Edmund. This is supposed to be a happy night, and here I am ruining it. I just don't know how Neha can put on a fake smile and flit about cheerfully when she feels like this!"

"You needn't be the life of the party tonight, Supriya. Why don't you join me for our hellos, wish Ellie a happy birthday, and then you can sneak upstairs and unwind with a carafe of mulled wine. I'm sure Kuveni or Mélusine will produce one for you, and then I will join you when the party is over."

They embraced reservedly, and then lost themselves in the moment until he pulled away and smiled kindly, wiping the violet tears from her eyes (a thoroughly alien sight to the eavesdropping MacLeods), and absorbing them straight into his skin with a subtle shiver.

"I love you, Edmund."

"I love you, Supriya."

He kissed her gently on the lips, and she melted into the delicious distraction. They almost gave into a more heated frenzy, until a chorus of laughter echoed from inside the manor, wresting them from their indulgence.

"To be perfectly honest, I have never been particularly enthused on Ellie's birthday myself," Edmund admitted as he glanced towards the bright windows. "The day always brings back too many haunting memories. If only I'd had the ability to heal humans back then, everything would have been different…" He trailed off pensively until Supriya squeezed his hands, bringing him back into the present. "I've had ninety years now to practice hiding my feelings from Ellie. I'm sure you will get better at it in time as well."

"I'm sorry. I hadn't even thought about what the day must mean for you. What a wretched irony that the most joyful moment of your life and the most tragic one happened at the same bloody time."

"We mustn't start thinking of it now. I have had many intensely joyful moments in my life since then, and I am sure to have many more to come." He stole a final kiss from her and then pushed forward with a burst of forced cheer.

He rolled his shoulders, and as his wings dissolved into a momentary flash of violet metallic liquid—of his alien Rakshasa plasma that enabled his shapeshifting over the human body he'd inherited from his mother—his light tropical linens morphed into a perfectly-fitted 1920s tuxedo, complete with a dapper white vest and long tails.

Supriya followed his lead, dissolving her wings in exactly the same manner and producing a form-fitting, slinky, beaded silver dress, straight out of *The Great Gatsby*. She closed her eyes and scrunched her nose, and her wild long locks of silky black hair calmed themselves and twirled into an exotic art deco up-do with a matching silver headband.

"You look marvelous, my love." Edmund offered her his arm with the archaic Victorian gesture that he knew she loved.

"As do you, Colonel." She sighed as she began to relax. "I hope Neha appreciates our adherence to her roaring twenties dress code."

"I think your sister's theme is rather a cute idea, actually. Besides, I loved this era, and you, my love, would have felt perfectly at home back then."

"Well then, shall we skedaddle in late and hope no one notices our tardiness?"

"I think we will need divine intervention for no one to notice our entrance," Edmund laughed. "But, we had better hurry inside all the same. I'm rather embarrassed at being late to my own daughter's birthday party."

"Whoa," Douggy whispered as he watched them gracefully make their way towards the slippery stone steps hand in hand. "Da, can you believe their clothes are just an illusion? That angry bloke on the tele says that they're going around naked all the time, but it sure doesn't look like it, does it? They don't even look like they're cold!"

"Sshhh, Douggy. They don't need us to gawk at them. They get enough of that every day from everyone else on Earth," Judy hissed.

The hushed exchange of the otherwise silent MacLeods caught Edmund and Supriya's attention.

With a momentary flash of demonic fury, Edmund's eyes turned black, and he whooshed at superhuman speed to rip open the car door. Douggy fell out into the fluffy snow, while the rest of his family sat in silence at the shocking development.

"The press was not invited tonight!" Edmund boomed. "We have made it clear that paparazzi intrusions into our personal lives are unacceptable! You will leave here now!"

The startled MacLeods shivered as power emanated from his deep baritone voice.

"We're not paparazzi. We're MacLeods," Douggy whispered on behalf of his family from his position in the snowbank.

Edmund stepped back as if the news had attacked him. He looked upon the faces of the shivering visitors, landing on Debbie. She struggled to extricate herself from her position, but with some minor finagling, Judy helped her up out of her seat, and Edmund braced her as she stood up on the snowy ground.

She looked into Edmund's eyes, observing without a hint of fear the black demonic tint brought forth by his anger. "It's been too long, Abbi."

"Debbie?" Edmund asked searchingly as he steadied her. "Good lord, time has gotten away from me."

"I hoped I wasn't too ancient for you to recognize me," she smiled. "And in the dark, no less! I'm glad your vision is back in tip top shape."

Edmund was left momentarily speechless, and Supriya whooshed to his side to help Douggy up out of the snowbank. Edmund reeled with shock at the unexpected reunion, but as he assessed the remaining MacLeods staring back at him from the car, he subverted his black demonic eyes, and a wide smile spread across his face, followed by a deep red blush of thorough embarrassment.

"I'm so sorry! You must forgive my abhorrent outburst. The paparazzi have been dastardly persistent these last few weeks. They've been hounding us across the face of the earth." Debbie nodded her forgiveness while the other two MacLeods began wiggling out of the car. "But what are you doing waiting out here in the snow? This ancient car doesn't even have a heater!"

"Neha invited us," Debbie explained. "She thought it would be a fun surprise for Ellie, but she had some sort of special plan for the revelation. I believe she is intending to present us as a birthday gift."

"Oh Neha..." Supriya shook her head with familial embarrassment at her sister's predictable antics. "I hope you can forgive her. She's a bit... all over the place sometimes."

"I'm just grateful that this wasn't all a cruel joke cooked up by the conniving lads down at the Elphinstone Arms," Judy said graciously as she stood up in the snowbank beside Douggy and shivered.

Supriya and Edmund both blushed with embarrassment.

"Really, it's nothing," Judy insisted as she straightened out the creases that had settled into her wrinkled silk dress during her hours in the car. "Meeting the legendary Abbi in person was worth the wait."

"You are so wonderfully patient with us," Edmund said apologetically as the group gathered themselves into a row before him. "Too patient. It is such a lovely surprise to see you."

He carefully pulled Debbie into a hug, but he pulled away as she shivered. "I reckon you'll need some hot tea to thaw you, Abbi."

"Oh, how I've missed you, Debbie. I'm so glad you came." He smiled and hugged her again. "We've been flying at high altitude for many hours, all the way from South America. It makes us both particularly frigid, and this snow doesn't help."

Debbie smiled. "Don't worry, Abbi. It makes me feel nostalgic. And if it weren't for Neha, I don't know when we might have reunited. I might have made it to my grave without offering you and Ellie a proper goodbye."

He teared up at the reminder of the cruel ticking clock that had already claimed so many of the humans he had loved so much.

"I reckon we haven't been properly introduced to your companion." Debbie changed the subject as she noticed his struggle.

He hesitated with a pang of guilt before introducing them. "Yes, yes, of course. Supriya, these are the MacLeods. The

MacLeods are Ellie's cousins from Eleanor's side of the family. Debbie, this is Supriya Rutherford Patel Marriner. She is my... wife."

Debbie smiled and shook Supriya's hand warmly. "It's about time someone made Abbi whole again. I'm sure Amma would have approved."

Edmund swallowed hard. "You're a good, tidy lass, Debbie MacLeod." He pushed forward, eyeing the rest of the crowd. "I'm afraid I don't recognize any of you."

Debbie patted his hand. "Don't trouble yourself, Abbi. This is my niece, Judy. She's Ruthy's daughter, and this is Arthur, who's Rose's son. Ellie knew him as Arty when he was just a lad, but you'd already made yourself scarce by then."

"Yes... yes, of course. Ellie told me all about you." Edmund shook the man's hand, and then gently finagled his hand back after Arthur held on too long with curiosity.

"I'm Douggy!" Douggy exclaimed.

Arthur blushed. "Douggy's my lad."

Edmund shook the boy's hand, and the boy shivered, giggling with delight as he felt Edmund's alien frigidity.

"Can we see your spikes?" Douggy asked.

"Douggy!" Arthur scolded.

Edmund smiled forgivingly. "Maybe later. Shall we all go inside? We're already dreadfully late."

Arthur and Judy looked conflicted.

"We promised Neha we'd wait until she gave us our cue..." Arthur hedged. "Her driver seemed very insistent that we wait when he left us here a few hours ago."

"But it is rather freezing out here," Judy said as she wrapped her coat tighter around her thin silk dress.

"Nonsense!" Edmund declared. "You have been more than patient with us. Come inside, and we'll get you all sorted. I'm sure that there will be a wide array of hot beverages to warm you from the inside out."

"It does sound rather cheerful in there," Arthur admitted.

"It will be even more cheerful when Ellie realizes you're here," Edmund said excitedly. "I can't thank you enough for coming tonight. There is no better birthday present for her on Earth. She has missed you dearly for decades."

Edmund and Supriya flanked Debbie to help her up the icy steps, but as they reached the top of the stone staircase, the imposing door of the old manor flew right open before them.

Neha, decked out from head to toe in her own elaborate blue and silver beaded flapper costume, complete with a long, slender cigarette holder giving off a subtle stream of white, sweetly-scented smoke, swooned melodramatically.

"Daaaarlings, you look fabulous!!!" Neha swooned with an affected impression of a posh English accent. "And you've already reunited with the illustrious MacLeods! Melly, come greet them!"

In a blur, an ethereal woman in a white, sparkling beaded flapper dress appeared by Neha's side. Instead of her usual medieval-inspired style of copious tendrils of blonde fairy hair, on this special night, Mélusine's hair was gathered into a smooth bun and held in place by an elaborate jeweled comb that sparkled as the lights from the party beyond bounced off of its many diamonds.

"Ma chérie, you didn't tell me there were humans waiting outside!" Mélusine exclaimed. "I never would have made it snow if I'd known!"

"I didn't?!" Neha exclaimed with genuine concern. "Crikey! I'm the worst hostess ever! I thought it would just be a few minutes, but then the clock kept creeping forward! I was waiting for Edmund to arrive for the big reveal, but then, my beloveds," she eyed Edmund and Supriya accusingly, "you were unfashionably late."

"We were detained by an unexpected matter of the utmost solemnity," Edmund said with subtle annoyance at her jab.

"Not something to be discussed right now," Supriya added as she eyed the MacLeods and then threw an authoritative look at her sister.

"Yes, yes, of course." Neha became serious. "I'm sorry. I should've realized you wouldn't be late without a good excuse."

In a blur, Neha and Mélusine joined Edmund and Supriya in escorting their shivering guests inside.

"*Mon dieu*, you are as cold as ice!" Mélusine whisked Arthur and Douggy inside behind the rest of the group and slammed the door behind them. She placed her hands on their wrists, and they shivered as she used one of her many foreign talents to push her warmth right into their bodies.

Douggy held out his hands before him with wonder. "Whoa!" He touched his warm fingers to Judy's freezing hand.

Mélusine repeated her gesture for Debbie and Judy, and when the virtuous MacLeods were sufficiently thawed, Neha kissed Mélusine and whispered her apologetic thanks into her ear.

"Dad?!" a young boy's voice called from the bustling parlor just beyond the cavernous foyer. At the fastest speed the boy could run, he charged straight into Edmund's arms.

"Charlie!" Edmund scooped his adopted human son into his arms and twirled him around. "I see Kuveni got you here in one piece from Cambridge?"

"Yeah! It was wicked! And we stopped at a chocolate factory to get Ellie's birthday present!"

"I hope Kuveni kept you safe from those creepy oompa loompas," Supriya chimed in.

"It was actually kind of boring," Charlie admitted. "But maybe someday she'll make a magical Yaksha chocolate factory, and I can be the boss."

"You should focus on your education for now, I think," Edmund replied with a more fatherly tone than he'd intended. "You're looking quite dapper tonight," he changed the subject.

"Oh yeah, just like James Bond! Kuveni made it for me!" Charlie looked down and straightened the bowtie of his perfectly-fitted tuxedo that looked particularly adorable on his nine-year-old figure. "She said that this is just how the tuxedos were in 1926 when Ellie was born! Did you have a tuxedo like this?"

"I had several. I had to wear one to every dinner party. Such formality is hard to imagine now, isn't it? But I'm quite sure I never looked as fashionable as you do right now."

"Wait till you see Ellie!"

As if on cue, in the crowded room beyond, the birthday girl noticed their arrival.

"I'm so glad you two could make it!" she exclaimed with a thick Scottish brogue.

Ellie smiled and waved, but as she skipped cheerfully into the foyer to greet them, and her emerald green flapper dress jangled in sync with her steps, all of the blood drained from Edmund's face, and he stepped away from her.

"Dad, what is it? What's wrong?" Ellie asked nervously as each Rakshasa in the room took in a whiff of Edmund's spicy fear.

Edmund took a moment to compose himself, and then he gathered his daughter into his arms.

He whispered into her ear. "I'm sorry, Ellie-bean. I thought for a moment that I was looking at a ghost."

CHAPTER 2 – GHOSTS

Edmund squeezed Ellie again, and then he put on a big fake smile and stepped back to assess her. "Happy Birthday, Ellie. You look lovely."

Ellie looked at him searchingly, as she knew better than anyone how rare it was for her powerful father to produce such a fearful reaction without a good reason.

"It's the costume," Edmund whispered, as he looked self-consciously at the MacLeods behind him. His head began swimming as he worked to ignore more reminders of his dead wife than he had faced in ninety years. "Your mother had a dress that was very similar to the one that you're wearing now. It was her favorite for quite some time. You look so much like her tonight, Ellie-bean... more than you ever have, and then when you used the accent, you sounded so much like her..."

"Sorry, Dad. I didn't realize. I've been spending so much time in Edinburgh, the brogue just took over. I suppose that means that

I inherited some form of your clumsy Rakshasa linguistic abilities after all."

"It is I who should apologize. I'm sorry for bringing my melancholy to your happy day. I really am so happy for you, Ellie. Can you believe we've spent ninety years together? Only one more decade, and we'll reach our centennial!" He mustered all of his remaining strength as he saw the glimmer of sadness in her eyes, and he pulled her into another hug. "Now, Neha has concocted quite an elaborate gift for you." He glanced over to the enthralled MacLeods. "We mustn't keep her waiting any longer."

"How could she have another gift?" Ellie asked, as she let her father pull her along back into her birthday cheer. "She already bought us the house!"

"Wait, who's 'us'?" Supriya asked excitedly.

"Don't get your hopes up," Neha whispered as she put her arm over her sister's shoulders as a subtle hello after their many weeks apart.

"Grandpa!" a tall middle-aged man with rosy cheeks and greying mousy brown hair exclaimed as he spied their group in the foyer. "Angus, they're here!"

"Wicked! They made it after all!" Another middle-aged man, much shorter than his brother, but with the same rosy cheeks and greying mousy brown hair exclaimed with childlike excitement.

Ellie's human stepsons, with whom she had only been reunited a few months earlier after decades in exile, raced each other to greet Edmund.

"Where did you fly in from tonight, Gramps?" Angus asked excitedly. "It's nice to see you too, Supriya," he added politely.

"We've been in Venezuela for almost a week," Edmund replied. "We were helping them rebuild a few hospitals. It took a bit of extra authority on our part to make sure the global aid funds were being properly allocated. We'll probably have to go back there in a few weeks to make sure they've complied with our orders."

Edmund pushed back his moment of stress at the mundane problem and smiled as he pulled the two men into his arms for a grandfatherly hug. "I've missed you boys. You look like you're doing well, though?"

Angus and Duncan nodded their agreement.

"The photography gallery is almost ready to open on Princes Street. Mum has been leading the charge, and it's looking really good," Duncan explained.

"I'm glad," Edmund smiled. "Now, what is this I hear about Neha buying you a house? *This* house?"

"We couldn't have Ellie and her lovely sons stuck living in Craig's old Edinburgh flat now, could we? So, I took matters into my own hands, and I bought them this one! Guess whose it was?!" Neha clapped excitedly.

"I don't recognize it," Edmund said as he took a more observant look around the old-fashioned foyer complete with elaborate medieval tapestries hanging down the stone walls.

"I do," Debbie interjected. "It was Robby MacLeod's, before his downfall. This is the first time I've ever been inside."

Neha jumped up and down as her excitement bubbled over. "Ellie, guess who's here to enjoy the return of the MacLeod family estate to its rightful owners?!"

Ellie walked up to Debbie slowly. "Debbie?" she whispered as her heart began racing.

"The one and only, Ells, and I'm still kickin'!" Debbie winked and pulled Ellie into a weak, aged hug.

"Good lord, time flies," Ellie murmured as she took another look at her cousin's aged decline. "I had no idea that you'd gotten so old."

"Older than you, squirt, and I don't mind if I show it."

Ellie looked down at her youthful body, and a pang of melancholy darkened her expression.

Debbie patted her hand. "Don't worry, Ellie, we're all happy for you. It's about time the world knew about all the work the angels have been doing in the shadows all these years."

Ellie pulled Debbie into another hug, and made no effort to quell her violet tears of joy. "I've missed you, Debs."

"Now, now, there's no need to be down on your birthday. We came on over to help you celebrate, not commiserate. Now, you remember Judy and Arthur, but you've never met Arthur's lad, Douggy."

"Can I see your spikes?!" Douggy asked as Ellie shook his hand.

Arthur hissed his disapproval, and Douggy shrugged.

"I don't have any. I got enough humanity from my mother to avoid them," Ellie replied. "I guess it came with the red hair."

"Yer a MacLeod through and through, Ells, and you always have been," Debbie winked.

"Charlie, perhaps you'd like to show Douggy around?" Neha suggested as she noticed Ellie's discomfort.

Charlie's posture deflated at the suggestion. In addition to Douggy being annoying, he was at least two years younger than Charlie, who was already just a few weeks away from the ripe old age of ten, and he had no interest in leaving his father, whom he hadn't seen in several weeks, to entertain an immature brat he'd just met.

"If I have to," Charlie sulked.

With a pleasant breeze, a plump, pink-faced, middle-aged woman in a 1920s maid costume materialized beside them. The younger MacLeods startled at the sight, while Edmund smiled and engulfed the woman into a hug.

"Kuveni! Thank you so much for escorting Charlie here."

"It was my pleasure as always." As their hug loosened, she squeezed him a second time for good measure. "But I think that young Charlie has had enough of me for the time being. I believe, my lord, that your son has been looking forward to seeing you for weeks. Perhaps I will show the MacLeods around, and Charlie can stay here with you."

"What an excellent idea, Kuveni," Edmund said amicably as he put his arm over Charlie's shoulders. Charlie sighed with relief.

A look of momentary guilt crossed Neha's face as she realized her error, but quickly Kuveni's overflowing cheer calmed everyone, and the entire group relaxed and followed the birthday girl into the well-lit banquet hall. Charlie wrapped his arm around his father's waist as they listened to Kuveni's hurried introductions.

"Now, my illustrious MacLeods, I am a Yakshini, and so is Sabrina over there, and our lovely Puck just there. Technically, he's called a Yaksha because he's male, and we are all nature spirits who serve as the sacred guardians of Earth. As you know from the incessant chatter all over the tele, we have many useful talents that we don't need to get into right now. Got it? Good. Let's move on. Mélusine, whom you've already met, is a Rakshini, which means that she's half-Rakshasa and half-Yakshini (a very powerful combination, the *most* powerful, some say), as is young Maya over there, and Lady Neha, who did not start out as a Rakshini, but she became one all the same after her unfortunate decapitation at the hands of her sister, but that is a much longer story (Don't worry, they've made up swimmingly since then). And then there's Master Rahul over there who is a Rakshasa-human hybrid like Ellie and Edmund and Supriya, and the rest of our lovely guests are entirely human, just like you! Come, let me introduce you to the Rutherfords. They are also humans who married into our unusual family."

Despite the many grave thoughts simmering in the back of their tired minds, Edmund and Supriya managed to maintain their happy smiles and gracious banter for several hours as Charlie spent every second glued to his father's side, and Kuveni introduced the

MacLeods personally to each and every guest, until the clock struck midnight, and Ellie could not contain her sleepy yawns.

"I'm sorry, everyone. I'm an old lady now. I must retire to bed. This was such a wonderful birthday—the best I've ever had. Thank you all so much! Especially you, Neha."

Neha whooshed to her side and engulfed her into a hug, and for the first time in her life, Ellie did not wiggle awkwardly out of it. Instead, she squeezed Neha as tightly as her Rakshasa strength would allow.

"I don't know what I did to deserve such thoughtful gifts from you, Neha, but I am grateful all the same," Ellie said tearfully.

"I'm glad you like them. You are my only niece, after all." Neha winked as Ellie guffawed at the realization that had never occurred to her before. "You can call me Auntie Neha from now on." Neha looked serious as Ellie struggled for a response, and then she grinned at her little joke. "Just kidding. I agree. The relationship is weird with you being almost twice my age. We can just say we're cousins, and now that the MacLeods have forgiven me for leaving them in a freezing car for two hours in the snow, we can all be one big happy family!"

Ellie's eyes bulged at the intel that had been strategically withheld from her all night, but the MacLeods only smiled graciously.

"And now, my friends, we must disperse so that the birthday girl does not hear the raucous party continuing without her," Neha declared. She smiled and snapped her fingers. "You will all find steaming pots of hot tea in your rooms and an unlimited supply of hot water in the bathrooms. We will reconvene for breakfast at eight o'clock in the morning, and since Mr. Montero is nowhere to be found, you can all be as late as you'd like. Good night!"

As Neha began assertively herding the party guests to their rooms, Edmund pulled Charlie into a good-night hug.

"We'll be here for four days before we need to leave for Indonesia. Think about what you'd like to do with our time together. Anything you want," Edmund offered.

"Thanks, Dad," Charlie whispered. "Can we…"

"Can we?" Edmund coaxed.

"Can we go sailing? Kuveni said that the Hebrides are beautiful, even in February. She even said she'd make it warm for us if we want."

"What a wonderful idea," Edmund agreed. "I suppose Ellie is too busy to join us?"

"I'll ask her," Charlie said excitedly.

"Perhaps in the morning," Edmund suggested. "You know how soundly Ellie sleeps. She might already be in bed… speaking of which, it is after midnight…"

"Yeah, I get it, Dad. I'll see you in the morning." Charlie leaned in for a slightly awkward hug with Supriya, as they were both still getting used to her position as his stepmother (his hot, alien stepmother, as the lads at school reminded him daily). "Have fun." He winked, and then skipped away before his father's blush could fully materialize.

"I think perhaps my son has been spending too much time with Kuveni and Neha," Edmund said with minor concern.

"He's going to be in the double-digits in a few weeks. You'd better get used to him growing up."

"Good lord, I hadn't even thought about it… Time really does fly, doesn't it?"

"Indeed, it does, Colonel." Supriya took his hand into hers, but as they turned to head up the old stone staircase, Mélusine intercepted them.

"Mes chéris, you did an admirable job tonight of hiding whatever was troubling you, but I think that you could use some mulled wine to relax you before you head to bed?"

"You read my mind," Supriya smiled.

"The rooms are not particularly well-suited to cauldrons. Perhaps you would like to relax in the lounge for a bit?" Mélusine suggested.

Supriya and Edmund followed her into another cavernous room with elaborate tapestries hanging down the old stone walls, to a sitting area with deep, cushy leather couches and a low coffee table. Soft muted light flickered from medieval fire torches along all of the walls and from the delicate candles in the crystal chandelier, reflecting in the mirror over the large roaring fireplace and giving the space the distinct feeling of times long past.

"I have always loved how gentle firelight is," Edmund sighed. "There's something comforting about it."

"I agree completely, mon chéri. Now, if you'd like to sit yourselves down…" Mélusine snapped her fingers, and a large cauldron full of bubbling mulled wine appeared in the center of the coffee table, along with two mugs.

"Aren't you going to join us?" Supriya asked.

"My fiancée is awaiting my arrival in our quarters at this very moment. She has a lot of triumphant energy to work out after the success of tonight's party," Mélusine winked. "When you are ready to retire to bed, your room is the first at the top of the stairs on the right. There aren't any Rakshasa beds in the house, so you'll have to use the bathtub at the end of the hallway to warm yourselves up… although, perhaps the mulled wine will do the trick…" She closed her eyes and shrugged. "I'm being summoned by my impatient beloved. *Bonne nuit.*" Mélusine closed her eyes and disappeared.

Edmund and Supriya slowly meandered to the couch.

"Back then, I would have been itching to get a tuxedo like this off after a long night," Edmund said as he looked down. "It's much more comfortable when it's a part of my form."

"I guess we don't even have to worry about spilling wine on our Rakshasa clothing. Our plasma would probably enjoy it!"

24

Supriya plopped down onto the couch with a melodramatic swoon. She reached forward and began serving up two steaming mugs of mulled wine. She handed one to Edmund and held hers up for a toast.

"To the triumph of light on another hard night."

Edmund clinked her mug, and then together they drank down their mulled wine in one Rakshasa gulp. Immediately, Supriya refilled a second helping.

"I'm rather ashamed of my conduct tonight," Edmund admitted.

"Why?"

With another big gulp, their second helping was gone, and Supriya poured them a third.

"I could not hide my sorrow from Ellie." Edmund stared before him, replaying the memory in his head. "Neha had gone to such lengths to make this a special day for her, and I showed up unfashionably late and reminded her within moments of seeing her that this is also the anniversary of her mother's death. She doesn't need to think of such things on her birthday."

They both drank down their third servings.

"We are what we are, my love," Supriya said gently. "Ellie loves you, and she has known since she was a child how difficult her birthday is for you. She hid her feelings just as you did. But, it is the Age of Truth now. Perhaps Lord Shiva decided that it was time for the truth to reign here too."

"Perhaps..." Edmund murmured.

Distractedly, he poured another serving into their mugs. Supriya kissed him softly on the lips. She took a deep, calming breath and then sighed her contentment.

"These sulfites really do relax us, don't they?" she said with a yawn. They drank down their final servings and then placed their mugs on the table. Supriya took Edmund's hand into hers, intertwining their fingers which were now pulsating with warmth.

"I love you, Edmund. Tomorrow will be better than today. I'm sure of it."

Edmund sighed resignedly and lifted his long legs up onto the coffee table. Supriya lifted her feet up onto the couch, and then nestled into a position with her head in his lap.

"I am complete with you in my arms, Supriya," he whispered as he kissed her hand and then relaxed.

And together, in each other's loving arms, they slept.

The entire household remained silent as the ancient cuckoo clock dinged its four o' clock song. The flickering fire torches continued to burn as Supriya stirred and nestled back into her position on her gentle husband's lap.

But, upstairs in the birthday girl's room, one fiery redhead awoke with a start. She gasped in her awakening Rakshasa breath and held her cold arms out to inspect them. She quickly jumped out of bed and wrapped herself in one of Ellie's flannel robes, and without wasting a moment, she began her search of the house.

As silently as she could manage, she tiptoed down the hallway, enjoying the thoroughly tactile sensation of the biting cold of the stone floors on her bare feet. She listened at each door, and then nervously pushed open the one at the top of the stairs on the right, to the room Ellie had been told would be her father's. It was empty.

She tiptoed down the stairs and wandered by flickering torchlight through the empty hallways until she reached the lounge, where she spotted her target.

She took a deep breath and braced herself for the reaction she knew her unexpected presence would elicit from her oft-tormented husband.

She tiptoed past the low table with the continuously bubbling cauldron of mulled wine, and she couldn't help herself as she stroked his sleeping cheek.

She took another deep breath and paused, using the novel feeling of air in her lungs to calm her nerves.

"Edmund," she whispered. "Edmund, darling, wake up."

He stirred and then settled back into sleep.

"Edmund, darling? Abbi?" she pushed.

Nothing. Her patience was waning. She knew she did not have very much time for her little plan.

"COLONEL!" she hissed. "LORD KALKI!"

Edmund finally opened his eyes half-way. "Ellie? Ellie, what's wrong?"

Suddenly her nerves overtook her, and she couldn't say a word.

Edmund opened his eyes wider, and with one full look at the haunting face of his long-dead wife, Edmund yelped and scrambled up off the couch, leaving his confused living wife to her own rude awakening as he whooshed himself up against the far wall.

"Eleanor?" He asked with a fearful quiver in his voice as she approached.

"One wild Scottish thistle at your service, Colonel," she declared.

CHAPTER 3 – WHAT MUST BE SAID

Edmund's fear quickly morphed into rage. "Neha? This is the cruelest prank you could have ever unleashed. I will never forgive you for this."

"Edmund, my darling, I am not Neha. It's me, Eleanor. *Your* Eleanor, in Ellie's body. I used her Rakshasa plasma to create the effect." She glanced at her reflection in the mirror across the room and stroked the ridge of her angular nose. "I'm so glad that Ellie looks like you. Your mother's human genes did a wonderful job of softening my sharp features." Edmund's heart raced and raced, and Eleanor could not ignore the fresh burst of rich, spicy Rakshasa fear that wafted off of him. "I'm sorry for frightening you, darling, but I couldn't leave it alone anymore."

Edmund was speechless as his brain quickly struggled to comprehend what was happening, and Supriya blurred to their side to intervene. She rubbed her hands together until the glowing silver light of the Guardian of Memories burst forth from her palms, and without any warning, she slammed her hands onto the stranger's temples and held on until she found what she was looking for.

"Shiva's wrath, Edmund. She's not lying," Supriya whispered. "Eleanor has used Ellie's deep sleep to work her way to the surface."

"The surface?" Edmund asked searchingly.

Supriya closed her eyes and struggled to process the confusing intel for herself. "When Eleanor died in childbirth, she didn't enter the natural karmic cycle. Her consciousness went into Ellie instead, and she's been nestled inside of her ever since."

"But that isn't how it works," he argued.

Eleanor sighed. "Darling, I am a singularly unique woman." She reached forward to stroke Edmund's cheek, but he shuddered at her ghostly touch. "Please don't be afraid. There is so much about me that you don't know, but it is the Age of Truth now, and I can't watch silently any longer without intervening. Now, I can't be here for long. Ellie was not sleeping well tonight after all of the commotion, and I do not want her to wake up in the secondary position in her own body. It's a very unpleasant feeling, believe me."

Eleanor took Edmund's hand into hers, and then she smiled reassuringly and took Supriya's hand into the other. She led them assertively back to the couch and sat them down next to each other.

"Do you want me to leave?" Supriya asked awkwardly as she worked hard to hide her own raging anxiety at the extremely complicated prospect of her husband reuniting with the long-dead wife whom he had mourned devotedly for decades before even looking at another woman.

Edmund squeezed Supriya's hand. "Please stay."

"Yes, please do," Eleanor seconded. "I came here for both of you."

Eleanor nudged the boiling cauldron out of the way and sat herself down on the coffee table to face them, positioning herself like a coach, ready to pep up her players before the big game.

"Edmund, my darling, I am happy for you. Supriya, I can't thank you enough for finally bringing my grieving husband back to life. Seeing you together and feeling the joy that Ellie feels at your union makes me feel like I have finally reached the heavenly status that my mother was always so concerned about."

She winked at Edmund, but he remained speechless as he absorbed her confident irreverence. He knew Eleanor too well, and he knew as she gazed lovingly into his eyes with a shadow of sorrow in her expression that this woman sitting before him was her.

"Eleanor?" he asked meekly.

She smiled. "Aye, it's me. I'm glad we can tear the tartan now that we've got the denial out of the way." Eleanor became serious. "The fear in your eyes earlier tonight broke my heart and Ellie's. And so, I came here to tell you what you need to hear."

"Alright..." Edmund could barely squeak out the word.

Eleanor took Edmund's free hand into hers. "My darling, my silent hero, my ruefully tormented husband: My death was *not* your fault. I knew what I was getting into long before you even proposed. From the first moment we met, I could tell that there was something special about you, something divine, and something rather alien. You know that I always had impeccable judgment." She couldn't help but wink again, and then she returned to seriousness. "You were not like anyone else I'd ever met, and I loved you so dearly for it. I loved you for *everything* that you were, even those frightening black eyes that you never noticed in yourself. But, then again, why would you?"

"You saw my demonic eyes when we were married, and you never said a word?"

"Darling, you had enough on your fragile, shell-shocked mind. I knew far more about you than you knew about yourself, and I loved you even more for it."

"Did other people see them?"

"Yes, darling. Many people did, and they loved you anyway."

"Who?! Did Debbie see them? Did the other bairns? Did *your mother*?!"

As Eleanor felt Ellie stir, she rushed the conversation along. "Darling, we don't have time to discuss it now. There is so much that I need to tell you. Too much. But right now, I must tell you again what I know you haven't let yourself believe. You thought I was sparing your feelings, but I meant it then, and I mean it now: I don't have any regrets. I don't regret meeting you, I don't regret loving you, and I don't regret marrying you. Our three years together were the best years of my life, and I wouldn't trade them for anything. *Anything*, Edmund, do you understand?"

"They were the best of mine too, out of almost two hundred years. Until recently..." He trailed off with a grimace.

"Wipe that guilt off of your face right now, Colonel. The great honest love that you have with Supriya is my salvation, and I will not let you ruin it. I had to endure years of torment watching you endure your foolish marriage to that cruel shrew, and now, finally, I can rest in peace again."

"You know about Grace?"

"I know what Ellie knows, darling. Everything that she's seen, I've seen. We were both cheering wildly inside as you signed that annulment paper."

"Why didn't you stop me from marrying her, dearest? I would have listened to you!"

Eleanor sighed with resignation. "I know, darling. Sometimes I regret not stepping in myself, just like I regretted letting Ellie endure all those years with her murderous bastard of a husband." She glanced at Supriya. "I will never be able to thank you enough for punishing him like you did." She returned her attention to Edmund. "But I'm dead, darling. These are not my choices to make, and making mistakes is part of growing up. As hard as it was to watch you both struggle, it was not my place to step in."

"You're here now," he whispered.

"Because you are alive again, Edmund! Fully and completely. *Finally*, after ninety years, you are living again, and I can't keep watching you suffer on my behalf. Your guilt is dastardly counterproductive. Please, Edmund, I beg you. Let go of me."

Eleanor squeezed Edmund's hand entreatingly, and his tears began to flow.

"Eleanor, dearest, if you hadn't been with me, you wouldn't have died in pain. You might have lived forty or fifty more years! I stole that life from you!" Edmund finally vocalized the tragic truth that had haunted him for so long.

She reached forward and wiped his violet tears into her skin, shivering at the odd sensation as they absorbed right into Ellie's body.

"Darling, when we met, I was spending my days wiping madmen's bums and my nights eating stale shortbread in bed. I was happy with my life. I didn't need anything or anyone else. But then destiny threw you into my path, and there was no turning back for either of us. The life we had together was like nothing I could have ever imagined, and if you gave me the choice today to live three years of our life together or thirty of the alternative, I would take the three. I mean it, Edmund." She grabbed Supriya's hand. "Tell him I mean it."

"She means it," Supriya agreed.

Eleanor pulled Edmund into a gentle hug, and then she coaxed Supriya into their bundle. "I am so happy for you both. You have all the blessings I can give."

Eleanor kissed Edmund on the forehead and then Supriya.

"And now, my beloveds, my partners in crime, we must deal with Ellie's birthday present."

Eleanor plopped herself back down into her coaching position.

"I didn't get her anything," Edmund confessed with a fresh burst of guilt.

"I did not transcend the great barrier between life and death to chastise you, darling," Eleanor reiterated. "Even before your miraculous ascension, you carried the weight of the world on your shoulders. I can't even imagine the painful divine choices you've been forced to make in these last many months. Remembering to purchase some tchotchke for your daughter's birthday should not be anywhere on your list of concerns. And, in case Ellie's beaming excitement at your arrival did not make it clear, your presence here alone is enough of a gift for her. But I know that you would never allow yourself to sink to such egotism, regardless of whether or not it is warranted, and so I propose to you, my darlings, that this year we conspire, the three of us, to give our beautiful Ellie something that really matters."

Eleanor smiled reassuringly and reached forward to wipe the last rogue tear from Edmund's cheek.

"I will do whatever you need," Edmund agreed as he composed himself.

"Me too," Supriya seconded.

Eleanor rolled up the sleeves of Ellie's bathrobe and leaned in to begin her proposal. "Our daughter, Edmund, is dreadfully afraid of love now, thanks to that cruel monster that ruined her. Oh, how tempted I was to murder him in the night. I spent years plotting the perfect crime. If it weren't for those two innocent little boys, I probably would have done it. I was impressed by your restraint."

"If I'd known everything he'd done to her, I would not have been able to contain myself, and she knew me well enough to realize that," Edmund admitted. "It kept her away from me, because she was afraid of what I'd do to stop him. If only she could have confided in me…"

"Darling, daughters do not tell their fathers such things, no matter how close they are. Craig's actions were *not* your fault, and

34

Supriya's punishment for him was thoroughly appropriate. My point was that it has been more than twenty years now, and she is no better off than she was then. Poor Ellie does not have the tenacity that I did, and she simply doesn't trust her own judgment anymore. She has collapsed in on herself, and she doesn't have enough experience to know how to pull herself out of it. And so, I need your help. Together, my darlings, we will bring her back to the light."

Eleanor closed her eyes and took a deep breath. "Ellie is stirring. We don't have much time."

"What do you want us to do?" Supriya asked pragmatically.

"Supriya, I would like you to take all of my memories. Use them to help Ellie know me... the real me, not just the enshrined martyr she grew up with. She needs to know who I really was, and..." She glanced at Edmund. "So do you, darling. I loved you as much as any wife has ever loved her husband, but I was not the woman you thought I was."

"What do you mean?" he asked with a burst of anxiety.

"Supriya, once you've seen my memories, you will understand the delicate nature of the task. Please use whatever means you think are best to help them know me."

Supriya nodded her agreement, and Eleanor squeezed her hand in thanks.

"And you, my darling Edmund, must tell Ellie the truth about how we met. I know why you've avoided it, and I don't blame you, but the time has come to tell her the full, unabridged story. Help her understand what it felt like to meet someone with whom you fell so thoroughly in love. It was not like those absurd romance novels that she secretly reads. Give her the story, so that she too can know the great joy of the vibrant life we had together. It must balance the pain of my death that has haunted you both for so long. And above all, my darling, you must finally stop mourning me. I will always be with you in one form or another, and now you have a new life that you must enjoy to its fullest without a hint of guilt. Can you agree to my terms?"

"I love you, Eleanor," Edmund whispered as he kissed her forehead.

"Is that a yes?"

"Yes," he agreed.

She let out a deep sigh of relief. "Oh, how I love you. Now, Supriya, please, we don't have much time."

Supriya rubbed her hands together until the tell-tale silver light of the Guardian of Memories burst forth. She placed her hands on Eleanor's temples, and they shook in unison for almost a minute until an unseen force pushed Supriya away. "I have all of it," she said woozily.

"Thank you, Supriya. Now, please, in my last few minutes, I must write Ellie a note." She glanced around with a sly smile and then called into the air. "Does anyone happen to know where I can get some paper and ink?"

With a pleasant breeze, Kuveni appeared in the middle of the room, holding a leather-bound booklet and an old-fashioned fountain pen. Eleanor was not surprised by her magical Yakshini entrance. Instead, she stood up, and they hugged each other affectionately.

"Thank you, my dearest, most beloved girl. I've been hoping you'd come and sort him out."

Edmund didn't know whether to be more startled by Eleanor's familiar demeanor or Kuveni's.

Eleanor reluctantly tore herself away from Kuveni's tight embrace. She sat herself down on the floor, leaned forward onto the coffee table with the notebook, and began feverishly writing.

"I know what you need!" Kuveni snapped her fingers, and a dusty bottle of very old cognac appeared beside her along with a crystal glass.

36

"You know me too well, Kuveni." Eleanor didn't look up as she continued on with her letter.

Edmund watched Eleanor dazedly, as he struggled to comprehend the implications of their familiarity.

"What is this? What's happening?" he asked bluntly.

"My beautiful boy, I hoped we wouldn't need to explain, but I suppose with all of your distractions over the last many months, it hasn't really come together for you."

Edmund's mind raced as Kuveni closed her eyes and momentarily dissolved, reforming as a tall, thin, dark-haired, middle-aged woman with fair skin and rosy cheeks, clad in a black flapper dress. She looked strikingly similar to a female version of Edmund, and, most importantly, he knew her.

He'd seen her only once since Eleanor's tragic death, and she was right. He hadn't thought about her at all since fate finally forced him to take his reluctant place as an interplanetary leader, and... since he'd met Supriya.

"Kate," Edmund whispered. "*You* were Kate Marriner." He slammed his hand against his head. "God, how foolish can I be! Of course, you were Kate!" He stood up and hugged her. "You've always been there, haven't you? You've helped me more than anyone else in my life, and you never took credit for anything."

Kuveni squeezed him tighter as her eyes teared up. "It has been my pleasure, Master Edmund, every step of the way."

She and Edmund both glanced over to Eleanor, who continued her feverish writing.

"I believed for quite some time that you were my sister, you know. No matter how many times you and the others told me that you weren't..." Edmund trailed off as a series of memories he'd been avoiding rushed into his mind. "I suppose there were quite a few odd characters in our lives back then... Good lord, how many of them were you, Kuveni?"

"Perhaps a few," Kuveni admitted guiltily as Eleanor threw her a knowing side glance. "Certainly more than Lord Vibhishana sanctioned. I had to be especially devious to keep him from discovering my meddling, but I had a number of forgiving allies on my side, including your wife."

Eleanor signed her name and ripped her hand away from the paper with a flourish. "Ellie is waking up," she declared.

She poured herself a taste from the old bottle of cognac and sniffed it lovingly. She downed it in one long, languorous swallow, and then stood up. She kissed Edmund on the forehead one last time, pulled Supriya into a tight hug, and then winked at Kuveni.

"Remember my blessings. Help our daughter. Revel in your joy," Eleanor declared her final orders. "Oh, and don't let Ellie read my letter until *after* you tell her the story of how we met! Oh, and congratulate Mélusine for me! I'm so happy to see her in love!"

Eleanor lay down on the couch and closed her eyes. Her sharp nose melted into Ellie's more gentle contour, and her thinner lips returned to Ellie's full rosy hue. Ellie gasped in her awakening Rakshasa breath and opened her eyes with a start.

"I had the most bizarre dream!" she exclaimed.

She looked around to her father and Supriya, who were still wearing their costumes from the night before, and then to Kuveni's unusual form that looked… strangely familiar.

"Dad? How did I get down here? I didn't sleepwalk, did I?" She pursed her lips. "Did I drink cognac? That's a development I could do without… Dad, are you alright? You look like you've seen a ghost again."

"I did, Ellie," Edmund murmured. "The most beautiful ghost in the world."

CHAPTER 4 – STORYTIME

"Did someone say my name?" Mélusine asked as soon as she materialized beside them in the lounge, clad in her typical white flowing medieval dress. "The voice was familiar, but I couldn't quite place it…" Her gaze fell on Kuveni's unusual form, and she smiled. "Thank god. It's about time."

"Kuveni?" Ellie laughed. "I thought for a minute you were my long-lost aunt!"

"Yes, that was the intent originally, as well," Kuveni admitted. "I created this form to present myself as Edmund's cousin back in the 1920s. I came to like it quite a bit, but after Eleanor left us, I didn't want to use it anymore."

She looked around at her audience and returned herself to the jolly, plump, grandmotherly form that they all knew, just in time to narrowly avoid an effusive reaction from Neha, whose enthusiasm for the development would have certainly derailed the serious nature of the matters at hand.

With a pleasant breeze, Neha was standing beside Mélusine. "It's a tad early for breakfast, isn't it? It's hard to tell up here in the dark north."

"Dad, is everything okay? I thought I heard you scream," Charlie said with a yawn as he clomped down the stairs in his flannel pajamas.

With Charlie's loud declaration, the rest of the household began to stir.

Edmund stammered for an explanation, while Neha's eyes darted about the scene, landing on Eleanor's note and the dusty bottle of cognac.

"What's this?" she asked as she swooped down to pick it up. "Was someone else here?"

Supriya snatched the letter from her sister's grasp and handed it over to Edmund. Neha gasped with melodramatic offense, but Ellie cut her off before she could vocalize her discontent.

"Dad? What's going on?"

Edmund only stammered.

"Your mother paid us a visit," Supriya revealed on behalf of her speechless husband. "She wanted us to help her with your birthday present."

"I'm sorry, who?" Ellie asked confusedly.

Supriya searched for the most tactful description of their encounter while she debated heatedly with herself whether or not she should reveal Ellie's uniquely personal connection to her mother. "Eleanor MacLeod... er... managed to make a temporary leap from her... er... place of rest... to seek our help on your birthday gift. She left you a note and drank a taste of cognac before she disappeared. She asked us to wait to give you the note until Edmund tells you all about how they met."

"I'm sorry, what?" Ellie looked to her father for confirmation.

Edmund finally pulled himself together. "Ellie-bean, Eleanor came to us. She gave us her blessings and asked us not to grieve for her anymore. I gave her my word." As Edmund looked into his daughter's questioning eyes, he couldn't help but see an inkling of Eleanor looking back at him.

"But why wouldn't she want to see me? To talk to me directly?" Ellie asked with a quiver in her voice.

Edmund pulled her into a supportive hug and whispered into her ear. "She is you, Ellie. She used your body to come to us. It was a great gift that you gave us to let her come as she did, and I am certain that if she could have held you in her arms and told you how much she loves you, she would have."

Ellie collapsed onto the couch with the shock of his revelation, and Edmund sat down next to her and took her hand into his.

"I don't feel like I'm her. She was way more comfortable in her own skin than I am... at least that's how you made it seem," Ellie humphed.

"I will admit that the relationship is a strange one," Edmund said gently. "I hardly have a grasp on it myself. You are your own person, Ellie, but she is there in you, sharing your joys and your sorrows, wishing the best for you, and she always has been."

"She gave me her memories to give to you," Supriya added as she sat down on the other side of Ellie, trapping her into a cold Rakshasa sandwich on the cushy couch. "She wanted you to know her... the real her. She was a singularly unique woman."

"What does that mean?" Ellie looked at her father.

"She was a wonderfully unique woman. The most kind, clever, and accepting woman I'd ever met. I didn't know it was possible for a human to be so forgiving of my many foreign traits. But that isn't really what she meant, was it, Supriya? There was something else? Some other story, to which I wasn't entirely privy?"

Supriya debated how much to jump into with the curious audience watching them. The story was fantastic—worthy of its own epic, really—but needed delicacy in the telling, just as Eleanor had warned. Supriya made her choice.

"She wanted us to start with your father telling the story, Ellie. She asked him to tell you the full, unabridged story of how they met."

"But you said that you met at a party? That the only interesting thing about it was that you met each other?" Ellie couldn't temper a hint of annoyance as she addressed her father.

"We did meet at a party of sorts, but it was certainly a lie to say that nothing interesting happened. It was a rather intense experience for both of us, to be honest. I have avoided telling you because of many reasons, although none of them are particularly good excuses now that you're all grown up. I'm sorry, Ellie."

"Your mother asked me to connect you with her memories," Supriya reiterated. "Do you want them now, or do you want to wait until after the story?"

Ellie stared at the crackling fire in the fireplace, contemplating her unexpected choices.

"Ellie, we don't have to do any of this right now," Edmund pointed out. "It's not even five in the morning. You can go back to bed and get some sleep if you'd prefer. We will all be here in the morning."

"No!" Ellie exclaimed. "The story is so wild that you felt the need to lie to me about it for ninety years?! No, I don't want to wait! Do you think I could sleep with a prospect like that looming?!"

Edmund smiled at her youthful passion.

"I was just debating about the order of things. Supriya, you know everything, I assume? I will take your recommendation."

"Then let's leave the storytelling up to Edmund for now," Supriya suggested. He will have to use all of his narrative talents to keep himself from giving away the ending too early. It is a murder mystery, after all."

"A murder mystery?!" Charlie exclaimed.

Neha clapped her hands excitedly. She snapped her fingers and materialized a table in the corner of the room covered in fresh pastries and an enormous samovar of steaming hot coffee.

"I assume the whole household is going to want to hear this," Neha explained as she glanced over to the crowded staircase of politely eavesdropping guests. "Come on in! Eleanor MacLeod came back from the dead to tell Edmund to tell us the heart-thumping story of their first meeting!"

Edmund blushed. "I hadn't planned to make it a public announcement, Neha."

"Aww, come on. We're all family!" Neha argued. "Besides, you were way too much of a Victorian to do anything too scandalous on your first weekend together, even if you were falling head over heels in love. Am I right?"

Edmund's blush intensified. "Are you so certain that you know me, Neha?"

Neha's jaw dropped with delighted surprise. "Edmund, this story is getting better and better every second!"

She snapped her fingers and produced a series of cushy bean bag chairs all across the cavernous lounge's persian carpets.

As the crowd shuffled in to take their seats, Edmund squeezed Supriya's hand, kissed Ellie's forehead, and then stood up and took a deep, calming breath. Charlie skipped to his side, and he guided his son to fill his unoccupied seat between Supriya and Ellie on the couch.

He looked upon the many intrigued faces of his sleepy audience, stood in front of the roaring fire, and leaned against the old stone mantle, readying himself.

"I suppose then, I must start with the day I received an unexpected invitation from a dead man..."

CHAPTER 5 – THE INVITATION

I had returned home late from a meeting at the Albany Street Barracks on a dark, rainy October evening when Mr. Valov, my devoted Czech butler, met me in the foyer of my townhouse just on the opposite side of Regent's Park and presented me with a silver tray of the day's mail. It was a practice that even I found archaic for the modern postwar days of 1922, but Mr. Valov seemed to like the formality of it, and I was not at all interested in arguing with anyone about anything that was not of the utmost importance.

At first, the day's cache of mail seemed perfectly ordinary: a few bills, a few letters from old colleagues and friends, and a few invitations to various military events which I was often obliged to attend as a colonel in His Majesty's army, despite the fact that my work had been rather unimportant for years at that point, ever since the war had ended (I was ever so grateful for the reprieve).

But, as I sifted through the personal letters, leaving the rest to be dealt with in the morning, I noticed one postmark from Hampshire that caught my eye.

It came from Ralph Crowden, second son of the Baron of Heathfield, a bright-eyed young soldier whom I'd commanded for about a year of the wretched war in 1917, until he was injured in one of the countless chemical attacks we were submitted to in those godforsaken trenches, and he disappeared into the medical establishment, never to return to the field. I had assumed that he'd died, and at that point in the war, I no longer had the energy to confirm the grim fates of the thousands of innocent boys who were dying horrific deaths under my command, and so he had remained on the list of unlucky deceased in my mind until that moment.

As I ripped open the envelope like a child on Christmas morning, it felt in some ways not dissimilar to how I've been feeling in these last few minutes, although the circumstances, as it turned out, were not nearly as supernatural as I have come to expect in recent months.

To my utter delight, Ralph Crowden had survived. The chemical burns in his lungs had left him unfit for duty, and so he had managed to escape the hellish frontlines for the rest of the war. He had eventually returned home and married a young lady named Anne, and was currently living at his family's ancestral estate with his wife, making great strides at moving his life along. He was inviting me and a few other friends to visit for a long weekend, the first he was attempting in his postwar married life.

I hadn't known Ralph particularly well—although, I was vaguely familiar with his family who had served as the local gentry in the sleepy village in Hampshire where I'd lived for many decades of the 19th century—but my dearest friend in all the world, the only friend I'd ever had who knew my secret, Edward Rutherford, had taken him on as a bit of a mentoring project, and so I felt perhaps a bit grandfatherly towards him.

And so, although I simply detested the formality of those aristocratic country weekends that I had attended every so often throughout the decades, I felt obliged to accept the invitation, and I sought solace in the relaxing idea that surely Ralph would not be any better off than I was in the dreadfully slow process of recovering from the many symptoms of shell shock that still haunted me on a daily and nightly basis.

At the thought, though, I became rather anxious, as it occurred to me that I had not, in fact, spent such a concentrated period in the company of casual acquaintances since before the war. I was certain to awaken every night screaming with my nightmares of the trenches, as I had every night for over four years. Perhaps whatever shell shock young Ralph was combatting would not be so… loud.

Well, that was that. I would simply decline the invitation. As the doctors had reiterated many times, there was no need to push myself into avoidable situations that triggered my anxieties.

As I sighed with ambivalent relief and frustration, the telephone rang, and Mr. Valov disappeared into the hallway to answer it. As I was not expecting a call from anyone, I waited impatiently for the news of who it was.

"Captain Rutherford for you, sir," Mr. Valov announced with a bow.

I practically flew out of my chair to answer it.

"Edward!!!" I exclaimed. "How are you, old chap?!" Even I was surprised by the desperation for human contact that rang out in my voice. I hadn't realized until that moment that I had been feeling rather lonesome for months… since the last time Edward had escaped from his shrewish wife to pay me a visit in London.

"Oh, I couldn't be better, old man!" Edward replied with his typical jolly enthusiasm.

"You sound like you have some news, Edward!"

I could feel him struggling to contain his excitement. "Margaret is going to have another baby! She's already eight months in!"

"Oh Edward, congratulations!" I could not have been happier that despite Margaret's cruel temperament, Edward was getting what he had always wanted most in his life, and that despite the fact that he had so enthusiastically, without any qualms, taken on Margaret's first child as his own, he would now have a biological child to continue on his legacy. I hoped, above all, that the development indicated that Margaret had finally stopped wishing for poor Edward to be her dead fiancé with whom she had produced her first child back in 1918.

"Yes, yes, I couldn't be happier. And Sabrina is so adorable, Edmund. She is waiting so patiently for her baby brother or sister to come. She has been helping Margaret knit some booties!"

"I can't believe she's old enough to knit!" I exclaimed. It seemed like only weeks before that Edward had hastily married his secretly pregnant bride on behalf of our dead comrade.

"I can't either, old man. I can't either. Speaking of which, did you get an invitation from young Ralphy?! Who would've thought? I thought for sure he was a goner, and now he's gone and gotten married!"

"Yes, in fact, I received the invitation in the mail today. I haven't decided yet whether to accept. I don't know him particularly well."

"Oh, he was a good boy," Edward sighed nostalgically. "I was devastated when he went down. I simply don't understand why he waited so long to reconnect! You should go! Say hello for both of us!" Edward suddenly became self-conscious. "I mean, only if you'd like it, Colonel, of course. I'm sure you have many more important things to keep you occupied…"

"Quite honestly, Edward, I don't know if I will be able to conduct myself appropriately. I haven't been able to shake the nightmares, and I would rather not awaken an entire household of strangers with my screams."

"Hrm…" Edward was at a loss.

"I don't suppose you're interested in going with me?" I proposed hopefully.

48

Edward paused for a long thoughtful moment. "I wish so dearly I could, old man, but Margaret is in a rather delicate condition."

"Yes, yes, of course. Please forget I suggested it." I was not surprised by his response, but it disappointed me all the same.

"But, Edmund, why don't you go? Everyone these days is used to the eccentricities that those wretched trenches instilled in us. I'm sure that they won't mind whatever evidence you produce of your veteran status. And who knows, maybe there will be a lovely lady there to take your mind off of your troubles."

"Ha!" I let out a loud chuckle. "You have always been a dreamer, haven't you?"

"Stranger things have happened, *old man*." Edward drew out his favorite moniker for me as a subtle reminder that he knew of quite a few far-fetched truths, all of which involved me. Suddenly, I was bewitched by the prospect of discussing the problem that had plagued me for almost a century with a knowing friend.

I looked around to make sure that Mr. Valov was not lurking and lowered my voice. "Edward, I have had very bad luck with women. My unique... er... 'condition' means that I can never get too close. Whenever I do, sooner or later they run away screaming. Women can't tolerate unexpected truths like mine, and I've never been interested in using them only for... er... pleasure. I need a woman with whom I can be honest, and I have not, as of yet, ever found one."

Edward paused, I'm sure because he was surprised by the unexpected honesty of my confession.

"I'm sorry, old man. I will admit I've never thought about the odd difficulties you must face... but surely there must be some women you can confide in? I hear these days that there's a whole batch of VAD girls who are quite worldly. They all had jobs during the war, and now they don't have any interest in getting married! *Modern* girls, they call themselves. Margaret says that the war ruined them as much as it ruined us." He paused so that we could silently roll our eyes in unison. "Perhaps a modern girl is what you need?"

"Yes, perhaps." The thought had not occurred to me. "Thank you, Edward. I will keep your idea under advisement."

"Any time, old man, any time," he said with a sigh of satisfaction. "Now, I had better get moving before Margaret realizes I'm on the telephone. Enjoy yourself, old man! And perhaps in the new year, when the baby has come, we can all get together in London?"

"I'm looking forward to it," I agreed.

He hung up, and then reluctantly, I hung up.

"Mr. Valov, please call the number on this invitation and let them know that I will be joining them next week. And please, can you call my tailor and tell him I will come in for a fitting? I need some civilian clothing."

"Yes, sir," Mr. Valov agreed.

I breathed in a deep, anxious sigh. It was time to re-enter the world of the living.

CHAPTER 6 – THE ILLUSTRIOUS CROWDENS

I arrived late at the train station in Basingstoke still clad in my standard daily uniform. It had been so long since I'd packed for a weekend at a country estate that I had no sense of how long it would take, and therefore, I had not even thought twice about scheduling myself into meetings until the very last minute of the working day.

By the time I returned home to a beautiful spread of new clothing, collected from the tailor earlier that day by Mr. Valov and thoughtfully spread out across the divan in my sitting room for my perusal, I realized that I didn't even own a large enough suitcase to hold all of it. The idea of packing an entire trunk for a three-day trip seemed positively ludicrous, but as I inspected the fine fabric and careful pressing of the items, I quickly gave in, and attempted (unsuccessfully) to help Mr. Valov gather it up into a trunk that had been gathering dust in my library since long before the war began.

And so, I was rather sheepish (and unsurprised), when an annoyed chauffeur greeted me in the dark station as my train, two trains later than the one I'd planned, arrived in the pouring rain.

I looked around, taking in the quaint Victorian styling of the space that I knew well, as I had lived at my own country estate just outside of Basingstoke for over forty years in the late 19th century, before I'd returned to my robust youthful state and joined the Colonial Army in India. I had carefully avoided returning, despite my deep love of the place and my curiosity as to how the town had changed in the decades of my absence, in the off-chance that one of the nosy villagers might notice my unusual height, and then the rest of my familiar features. The village had always been rather small, and I was quite sure that everyone who lived there until 1895 knew me. At the thought, I gathered my own trunk, and with a few words of apology, I followed the chauffeur hastily out of the empty station to the lone waiting car.

We drove in silence for about twenty minutes of paved roads, followed by another fifteen minutes on muddy dirt roads, until we pulled up to an estate (far grander than my country home on the other side of town) that looked as if it had been built at the height of aristocratic grandeur—my guess was about the 1760s, just before the revolution in France had made such ostentation fall temporarily out of style.

"You have arrived at the Baron of Heathfield's estate, sir," the chauffer informed me as if he were a train conductor.

I thought momentarily about usurping his position in the driver's seat for a hasty return to the station, but the front door of the stone manor swung open, and a regal Sikh butler commanded the chauffeur with silent authority to escort me to the door. The chauffeur shrugged, and then begrudgingly stepped out of the car into the rain to hold an umbrella for me as I exited the back seat and scampered over to the covered stoop.

The butler wore a meticulously folded black turban, and his black beard and mustache were thick and youthful despite the crevices of advanced age that lined his good-natured face. He was clad in a Punjabi-style uniform, worthy of a maharaja's guard, that I had not seen since living in India, including a gilded karpan tucked into a sheath that hung from his crimson silk belt. As I took a nostalgic moment, remembering back fondly to the days many decades earlier when I'd commanded a Sikh regiment in the Indian Army, two teenaged boys dressed in muddy, wet traditional English servant's uniforms appeared from around the dark side of the house and rushed to gather my heavy trunk out of the boot of the car.

Without a word (only annoyed glances at me and the butler), they dragged the item inside, scratching it on the floor as they went. When they reached a grand staircase, they muttered some epithets and began clomping my trunk up each and every step, but before I could jump in to help them (or my poor old overstuffed trunk), the butler shook his head with unspoken disapproval and maneuvered himself to stand in my way, blocking my view of them. He nodded dismissal to the chauffeur, who waited awkwardly with his hand out beside me until I realized he was requesting a tip, and I handed him a few coins from my pocket.

He sighed with disappointment at my miserly offering, and slinked back to his car without a word, while I scratched my head at how much the world had changed since the last time I'd attended an aristocratic weekend getaway. Back in my day (an elderly phrase that had crossed my mind on too many occasions since the wretched war), a member of the house staff wouldn't have dared to ask for a tip, and if they'd been offered one, they would have been required to steadfastly refuse it. I sighed with annoyance at my embarrassing lack of awareness of modern manners, and returned my attention to the butler, who was watching me with minor curiosity.

I greeted him with a friendly, apologetic smile.

"I'm terribly sorry for my tardiness. I do hope that I haven't caused too much trouble for you."

"You speak Punjabi, sir?" the butler asked with surprise. "Your accent is flawless."

I closed my eyes and shook my head with silent personal castigation. I hadn't even noticed that I was speaking Punjabi. Simply his appearance had prompted my addled brain to switch into the tongue. I focused all of my mental capacity on returning to English.

"Yes, I grew up in India, and I served in His Majesty's army there for many years," I explained. "Am I speaking English now?"

I hoped my odd question would not raise his suspicion.

"Yes, sir, you are. I am Mr. Rana. I am Lord Crowden's butler. I have served him for thirty years, since he was in the civil service in India."

I smiled with relief as he moved the discussion along.

"I am Colonel Marriner," I introduced myself. "And I realize that I am shamefully late. It has been too long since I've attended an event such as this one, and I will admit that I'm a bit unpracticed in my etiquette. I would be most grateful if you could instruct me, if ever I run amiss."

Mr. Rana bowed his gracious agreement and gestured for me to enter the cavernous foyer. I reached into my pocket to offer him the last of my coins, as I wasn't sure when the appropriate time would be to tip him, but as I attempted to hand him a shilling, he only looked at it confusedly. I felt the blood rush to my cheeks in one of the embarrassed blushes that plagued me often as I realized that I had chosen the wrong option.

"I'm sorry. When is the appropriate time to tip the house staff? If I'd known I should tip, I would have brought more coins, but the last time I attended a gathering like this, it wasn't expected."

"It is not expected here," Mr. Rana replied.

"But the chauffeur?"

Mr. Rana relegated a look of annoyance, whether at me or the chauffeur, I wasn't certain. "He wasn't a regular member of the house staff. We will not be contracting him again."

My blush only grew, as I processed just how much my late arrival was inconveniencing them.

"I'm terribly sorry that I was so late. Please send his bill to me. I will be glad to pay it in full."

"That will not be necessary, Colonel." He closed the door behind me and changed the subject. "Dinner has already begun. I will announce your arrival."

As he left me alone, I took in a deep, calming breath and looked around. The space was dripping with the exact ostentation I expected from the outside. Every floor and wall were covered in Italian marble, and the domed ceilings were adorned with elaborate murals that had surely taken an army of artisans years to complete. My initial estimate as to the home's age had clearly been wrong— the paintings were certainly mid-seventeenth century Italian baroque. I'd been forced to memorize the garish nuances of the style when I'd studied painting in London in the 1840s.

"Major!" A raspy voice distracted me from my observations. "Or, I suppose I should call you Colonel now!"

A young man with sandy blond hair and light grey eyes, clad in a formal dinner tuxedo, rushed to greet me. While he stopped to catch his breath after the minor exercise, I took a moment to appreciate my brilliant foresight in garnering an appropriate wardrobe for the occasion.

"Lieutenant Crowden?" I asked questioningly, as I hardly even recognized the poor chap.

"Indeed," he confirmed. "But you can call me Ralph, just as long as you don't call me Ralphy—that privilege is reserved for Captain Rutherford. I was so sorry to hear that he couldn't join us, although I'm not sorry to hear the cause. What wonderful news, don't you think?"

"Yes, indeed," I agreed.

"Every time I hear about another soldier making his way, I think that perhaps I will make it too. But, come. We have quite an audience already. Mr. Rana will make sure that your luggage is taken up to your room. Oh, and I must beg your forgiveness. My brother, John, managed to invite himself to what was otherwise going to be a relaxed occasion. You see, I don't go out much these days… the various noises of the modern world still startle me. But Anne has been so incredibly patient, and the doctors suggested that as a starting point, perhaps I might bring the world to me. I wasn't even going to attempt it until Anne encouraged me by suggesting that perhaps a few other veterans might take some of the pressure off. But, the best laid plans…" He sighed with disappointment. "As it turns out, you and I are the only ones."

"Well, I'm sure we will manage." I hoped it wasn't a lie.

"Yes, well, you were always so encouraging…"

Booming laughter echoed in from the dining room, and a fresh burst of spicy fear wafted off of Ralph.

"What's wrong?" I asked as his anxiety triggered my own.

"You mustn't take anything that my brother says seriously, Colonel. I thought about cancelling the whole do when he showed up, but it was too late. Some guests were already on their way. My brother has always been a bit… er… overly opinionated, and our father has been dreadfully ill for several months now. He is bedridden in his chambers upstairs, so he won't be around to chaperone, and I have never had the required sway to rein in my brother's conduct."

Ralph's genuine fear at the prospect of his brother's behavior filled me with dread, as I hadn't even been confident in maintaining my own appropriate conduct with perfect circumstances. I honestly did not know how I might react when provoked, as I had spent four years solidly avoiding even the most minor of confrontations. The shameful Rakshasa symptoms of the trauma I'd developed towards the end of the war had slowly died down, but as I had no idea what exactly had caused them in the first place, I was especially concerned about facing anything that might encourage them to return.

But, my stomach made the decision for me, and as it growled loudly enough for Ralph to hear, I knew that there was no polite way for me to make my exit.

"Please come," he reiterated. "We've only started the first course."

"Oh, but I'm not dressed appropriately," I protested as I looked down upon my drab, damp uniform.

"Nothing is more appropriate than a colonel's uniform, I reckon," Ralph said with a supportive smile. I thought back upon my trunk of new clothing and shrugged my concession. Surely the only thing I could do that would be ruder than arriving late would be to make the entire party wait while I vainly dressed myself in a starched tuxedo. I knew I'd be lucky if I could even remember how to tie the bowtie. Ralph pulled me from my momentary distraction. "I don't see your Victoria Cross, Colonel. I suppose you don't wear your medals every day, or else you'd be too top heavy."

"No, no. I only wear them with my dress uniform," I said as I fought back a bout of melancholy. Every medal I'd earned only reminded me of the many men I hadn't been able to save. Secretly, I'd hidden every medal away in the desk of my library in London, only to bring them out when absolutely required by my job.

"Yes, of course," Ralph said politely. "Please come with me, Colonel. I'll introduce you to our party. They're not all as overwhelming as my brother, I promise."

He gestured for me to follow him into the dining room, and with one last deep, calming breath, I readied myself to head into the lion's den.

CHAPTER 7 – UNFIT

The look of utter disgust painted across the faces of the two young women at the table filled me with another burst of guilty anxiety as I made my tardy entrance, but it did not take long for me to pinpoint the real source of their anger, which wasn't me.

"What?" a red-faced man with dull, glossy eyes, greying brown hair, and an owl-like nose asked with feigned indignation from his position at the head of the table. "You know I'm right. What's wrong? Cat's got your tongues? Quick Rana, call *The Guardian*. It's the first time in history these modern women have nothing to say. We should make a national holiday of it!"

Another red-faced man, this one fat and repulsively sweaty with hardly a few wisps of blond hair on his bald head, burst into loud hyena laughter, while a grotesquely thin, sharp-featured woman with short platinum blonde hair that did not at all disguise her advanced age sat furiously holding her tongue beside him.

The instigator at the head of the table, whom I assumed must be John (although his company seemed equally unappealing), took a long swig, finishing off half of the wine in his glass, and then silently gestured to the staff for a refill. A young footman reached forward and began to pour, but as he pulled the bottle away, the red-faced drunkard violently gestured for him to continue pouring. The poor footman looked to Ralph, who shrugged his concession, and then followed his orders.

Ralph looked pained as he took in the train wreck before him, and then he muttered a calming phrase, given to him undoubtedly by the doctors who were managing his recovery, and introduced me to the unamused group.

"Everyone, this is Colonel Edmund Marriner. He was my commanding officer in the war. Colonel, this is Anne, my wife."

One of the two unamused young women, a rather plain but kind-looking girl with short brown hair held back from her pale face by a distractingly ostentatious head band, stood up and shook my hand. "It is a pleasure to meet you, Colonel. Ralph has sung your praises for years now." Her accent gave away that she hailed from the north, perhaps a rural area in the moors outside of York.

I smiled, hoping that my typical blush at minor praise would not show itself. "The pleasure is all mine." I reached forward to kiss her hand, as was the etiquette for such introductions many decades earlier (the last time I'd been to such an affair), but as I caught the look of surprise in her eye, I abruptly updated my gesture into an exceptionally awkward handshake.

"Right, and, Colonel, this is Harry and Mrs. Fitzgerald." He couldn't hide his lack of enthusiasm as he pointed to the ugly, red-faced couple. "Harry is an old acquaintance of my father's. He is here at John's invitation."

I worked hard to hide my distaste for their sweaty palms as I shook their hands.

"And this is my brother, John," Ralph said nervously, as he conspicuously avoided eye contact.

"Jolly good of you to finally join us, Colonel!" John exclaimed with an exaggerated salute. "Is there another war on yet? I daresay that's the only excuse for an army man like yourself to show up so late to a dinner party." He exploded into drunken laughter at his facetious jab and drank down his entire glass of wine.

"Right," Ralph pushed forward quickly. "And this is Miss Ellie MacLeod, Anne's best friend. They were VAD nurses together in France during the war. Anne has put all of her nursing talents into my recovery these days, but Miss MacLeod has continued her career as a nurse at the veteran's hospital in Edinburgh."

"It's Eleanor," the beautiful, porcelain-skinned, Scottish redhead corrected him as she stood up politely to greet me. "Only Annie can call me Ellie. Otherwise I think it sounds like a name for a perfectly behaved little girl, don't you? I wouldn't want to give anyone a false impression."

She winked as she shook my hand, and I couldn't tear my eyes away from her. Her long, flowing, fiery hair was twisted into a complicated hairdo of braids and plaits that appeared to be magically held together by a headband with a set of delicate peacock feathers. Her emerald silk dress that was covered in subtle peacock feathers embroidered into the fabric clung to her fair skin, giving her the distinct look of an ethereal nymph. I had never, in over one hundred years, seen anyone whose beauty could even be compared, but her beauty was not the only aspect of her that I found instantly bewitching. She had a sort of energy about her, a vivacity that emanated from her and stirred something deep inside of me that I had never known before, even while the brute at the end of the table did his best to squelch everyone's attempt at cheer. Eleanor simply seemed beyond him, as if she could outrun his meddling purely with her own tenacity.

I realized, after an awkward pause, that I was shaking Eleanor's hand for far too long.

"Colonel, I think perhaps you need something to warm you up," she said with a shiver as she gently confiscated her hand from my grip.

I felt the heat of an intense blush rushing into my face. "Er… I suppose I do. It is quite chilly outside tonight." I cringed as I offered my tried and true excuse for my Rakshasa frigidity, and I worked hard to hide the devastating realization that popped into my head to compete with Edward Rutherford's optimism: There was no way I could hide my unique condition from an educated modern woman. Sooner or later, probably far sooner than any of the less worldly women in my past, she would figure it out, and I would be left to a stuttering explanation of truths that I myself had no desire to think about.

"There's some steaming water in the wash basin in the powder room," Eleanor suggested helpfully. "Perhaps that would be a good start."

"Why, Ellie here is just a regular working girl, isn't she?" John interjected with a loud guffaw at his double entendre. "Eddy, maybe you can get her to show you all of her many talents. Annie here must have told her how delightful a wounded soldier's gratitude is in the sack, because she has no interest in wasting her talents on me."

Eleanor threw him an expression of distinct hatred and then looked pained as she glanced at Ralph and Anne, and then politely decided to hold her tongue. I turned to Ralph, who looked down at the floor with silent defeat, and as I observed the group and contemplated the unpleasant truth that no one there felt able to challenge this worthless drunkard, I decided that the honor would have to fall on me, for there was no way I would be able to spend three days in such aggravating company without doing anything to mitigate the problem. It needed to be done while it could still be managed civilly—I knew if I wasn't careful, I'd end up killing the bastard.

"You may call me Colonel Marriner, Mr. Crowden," I said sternly. "And no woman in her right mind would waste her talents on a drunkard like you."

I was shocked by the aggressive nature of the words the moment they came out of my mouth, and I felt another hot blush take over my entire face with my well-deserved embarrassment, but Eleanor looked up at me with a flash of fresh respect in her eyes, and I took the opportunity to sit down beside her and remove myself from the limelight.

After a moment of shock at my audacity, a mischievous grin spread across John's face, and I realized, to my great anxiety, that I had perhaps just picked a battle that I was not willing to fight.

"You may call me *Lord* Crowden then," John declared. "I am the heir apparent, after all. Unless Ralphy here has intentions upon my life."

"He will do no such thing!" Ralph finally intervened. "Our father could not have been clearer that you are not to use the title until he's dead!"

"It won't be long," John chuckled.

"How can you be so callous? Our father is on his deathbed!" Ralph's exclamation died off as he bent over and began wheezing, violently struggling to inhale and exhale with his damaged lungs.

Anne jumped out of her seat to rub his back as his face turned white and then a dangerous color of grey.

"Mr. Rana, get his inhaler! Please!" she called in a panic.

Mr. Rana appeared, bearing a small inhaler on a silver platter. The formality of the sight was absurd to my unaccustomed temperament, but Anne didn't blink. She gathered the inhaler and helped her suffocating husband use it, while the rest of us watched helplessly.

"In and out, slowly, darling, yes, that's it," Anne whispered into Ralph's ear.

As Ralph stood up and finally took in a full, belabored breath, Anne helped him into his seat and then looked straight at her antagonizing brother-in-law.

"John, may I see you for a moment in the hallway?" she asked too politely.

"Uh oh, Ralphy, did your little spell of weakness arouse your wife?" John cooed. "We wouldn't want to tire you out in your delicate condition. I'll help you out with your husbandly duties just this once."

"Now," Anne hissed.

John shrugged melodramatically as if he had no idea what could have possibly set her off, and then screeched his chair out, clumsily kicked the table leg, barely caught himself before keeling over in a drunken stupor, and then straightened his bowtie and followed her out of the dining room.

Ralph only stared into the distance, inhaling slowly and counting under his breath.

"If I'd known he'd be here, I never would have come," Eleanor whispered into my ear. "I've never met a more sadistic bastard in my life."

"What is wrong with you?" Anne's livid voice echoed into the dining room from the hallway. The servants threw each other nervous looks, but said nothing. "You will stop this atrocious behavior this instant!"

"Who's going to make me?" John fought back like a cheeky child.

"If you don't stop acting like a beastly brute, I will go right up to your father's room, and I will tell him why Mr. and Mrs. Fitzgerald have graced us with their presence this weekend."

"You wouldn't dare," John shot back. "The moment the old man croaks this will all be mine. I am the eldest son. I am the future

Baron of Heathfield. And you will be out on the street if you do anything to cross me. Got it?"

"Perhaps it won't all be yours. Have you seen the Baron's will recently? What makes you think that he will leave you everything? Or *anything*, for that matter. This isn't a Jane Austen novel. This is the twentieth century!"

The floor creaked, and Anne let out a muffled whimper as their conversation dissolved into hushed hisses. I stood up and almost knocked my chair straight into the lap of the attentive footman as I prepared myself to intervene.

"I have worked before, and I will work again." Anne's voice quivered as the volume increased. "I am not afraid of your threats, John, and neither is Ralph. I will not let you abuse him like this for your entertainment. Mark my words, I will tell the Baron *everything*, and you'll be lucky to walk out of here with the shirt on your back."

Anne returned to the dining room in a hurry, repositioning her headband and avoiding eye contact with everyone but Ralph.

"Sweetheart, how are you feeling?" she asked as she sat back down next to him and performed a perfunctory examination of his returning color.

"Fine," Ralph whispered as he threw me an apologetic glance and then watched his brother stumble back towards his seat.

"So, Colonel, tell us: What exactly do you do now that there aren't any Krauts around for target practice?" John turned his attentions unwisely on me.

As Anne's face turned red with rage, I decided to use a different tactic by ignoring his insolence completely. "I work with the management of the Household Cavalry."

"The cavalry?!" John exclaimed. "How quaint! We should go for a hunt tomorrow! We have some pups that need broken in, don't we, Rana? They could use a cub hunt!"

"I have no interest whatsoever in teaching innocent puppies to hunt and kill baby foxes," I replied calmly.

"You'd better not share that opinion with the generals," Mr. Fitzgerald laughed. "They'd declare you unfit for duty!"

John exploded into laughter at the prospect. "Unfit for duty! What a worthy club! Colonel, let me assure you, it is highly underrated."

Ralph shook his head with silent embarrassment.

"Is that how you managed to avoid the godforsaken trenches, Mr. Crowden?" I simply couldn't stop myself from taking the bait, as the question had already been needling me since the moment I arrived. The travesty that such a worthless braggart would have avoided the hellish fate that so many honorable men were submitted to stirred a dark rage deep within me.

John held up his hands proudly to show the group. "There, you see? My thumbs don't even bend!" He winked and then set about using his perfectly capable hands to drink down the glass of wine in front of Anne's place setting.

"Avoiding conscription under false pretenses is a serious crime, Mr. Crowden." I worked hard to keep my growing anger at his flippant attitude at bay.

"Ha! Tell that to the doctor who diagnosed me!" John replied without a hint of guilt. "Doctors these days can hardly tell the difference between a hand and a foot. Don't you think, Ellie?"

"Only the crooked ones, Mr. Crowden. Like those who are paid to make a false diagnosis," Eleanor shot back. "Their wanton morals do not remove the blame or the liability from those who illegally hire their services."

"You really are a spineless bastard, aren't you, Mr. Crowden?" Mrs. Fitzgerald interjected.

Everyone's shocked attention landed straight on her. Despite the sudden awkward silence, she gave no hint of apology, and John suddenly became serious, *genuinely* serious, for the first time since I'd arrived. He stood up and knocked his chair over, while his footman rushed to catch it.

"I'm finding this dinner tiresome," he declared with an exaggerated yawn. "Rana, have them bring up the rest of my meal to my sitting room." He offered me another exaggerated salute and then looked down at Ralph with disgust. Without a word to his brother, he let his glassy eyes wander over to his red-faced guest. "Fitzy, perhaps you'd like to join me later tonight for a nightcap in my sitting room. We can discuss men's business."

Mr. Fitzgerald nodded his agreement, although he too appeared to have been touched by the obvious nature of John's outstanding crime. I wondered if perhaps the comparison between Ralph's involuntary state of permanent illness and John's self-imposed drunken malady had impressed upon Mr. Fitzgerald the lack of humor in the situation. I could only hope so.

"Well then, until tomorrow," John murmured as he stumbled out of the dining room.

"Mr. Rana, please ask Mrs. Murray in the kitchen to send along the next course," Anne asked quietly.

"Yes, madame," Mr. Rana agreed.

And so, like the good Brits that we were, we continued our meal in somber silence, punctuated by a polite and rather uninformative discussion of the weather.

Good lord, this is going to be a long weekend, I thought. The prospect terrified me.

CHAPTER 8 – ARS AMATORIA

By the time we were finished with dessert, Ralph looked like he was ready to collapse with fatigue.

"If you'll forgive us, it's been a rather trying day." Anne helped Ralph to his feet as she offered their apologies. "We do hope that tomorrow will be more relaxing, once everyone has had a chance to settle in."

I almost laughed at the absurdity of the idea, but I managed to hold in my reaction. "Indeed. May we all hope for the best," I said politely instead.

"Thank you for your patience, Colonel," Ralph rasped.

I nodded my acknowledgment, and Anne escorted him to bed.

"Well, I had better go join John for that nightcap..." Mr. Fitzgerald said as he stood up. His wife threw him a distinct look of disdain, which he ignored, and then he nodded to me, barely looked at Eleanor, and waddled confidently out of the dining room.

Eleanor pulled a small watch out of a perfectly camouflaged pocket in her dress and sighed. "It's hardly even half past nine."

"I'm not particularly tired myself," I admitted. "I don't usually retire until after midnight."

The idea of going to bed early in this uncomfortable foreign place, only to be left with my inevitable nightmares of the trenches was especially unappealing. My mind wandered to contemplating whether I could avoid sleeping entirely for the rest of the weekend.

"I work the evening shift at the hospital," Eleanor commiserated. "I don't usually get home until two in the morning. My sleeping schedule is rather off from the rest of society's."

Suddenly, a thought more rash than any that had crossed my mind in decades consumed me. "Mr. Rana, is there a room where Miss MacLeod and I might enjoy an evening drink?"

Eleanor looked at me with surprise, and I suddenly worried that I'd overstepped my gentlemanly bounds.

"Yes, sir. There is a ladies' parlor and a gentlemen's parlor, as well as a library. You may retire to any of those rooms, and I will be happy to serve you. Will it be a gin and tonic, sir?"

I looked to Eleanor, whose expression had transitioned from surprised to enamored. "I would prefer cognac, actually. If there is any? I don't want to be any trouble. Although, I suppose I should drink whatever the lady is having." I looked to Eleanor, expecting her to join in the conversation, but she only remained watching us with silent fascination. "Would you like to join me for an evening drink in the library?" I asked as I remembered my manners and turned towards her to offer my official invitation.

As the intensely shy person that I was, I realized that I should have been feeling rather intimidated by the prospect of asking the beautiful stranger for a drink, but something about her quelled my raging timidity and replaced it with a sense of calm confidence that I had never in my life ever experienced before. But, as she remained silent, I secretly chastised myself for being so utterly out of practice in my etiquette for engaging with ladies—I could not, for my life, understand her reaction. She did not seem offended, and yet she was not accepting my invitation…

"Oh, were you talking to me?" Eleanor finally asked with puzzlement. I looked over to Mrs. Fitzgerald who had been watching our exchange with a blank expression, and suddenly I worried that the sour woman might have thought I was extending the invitation to her.

Mr. Rana gallantly stepped up to my aid, addressing Eleanor. "The colonel was asking if you would like to share an evening drink with him in the library. Perhaps a fine cognac? We have several from which to choose," he translated on my behalf. My heart began racing as I realized that I had already made the same sloppy linguistic error again. I'd been speaking with him (and apparently, Eleanor) only in Punjabi for the entirety of the conversation.

I closed my eyes and concentrated all of my willpower on returning to English.

"Yes, I'm terribly sorry…" I waited to make sure that she was understanding me. "Sometimes I forget which language I'm speaking. I grew up in India, you see, and Mr. Rana's presence here seems to have triggered some sort of linguistic memory." I hoped that my vague explanation would be enough.

"What a fascinating phenomenon," Eleanor said with genuine interest. "I did find that my Scots gave way to a rather British intonation when I was surrounded by Brits, working as a VAD nurse in France. I even picked up some ridiculous American phrases once they joined up. I was tending to the wounded for almost four years among a sea of English dialects far stranger than anything I'd ever heard in Scotland, and when I got home, what did my mother say? 'Eleanor Mary MacLeod, what happened to you? You're talking like a drunken sassanack!'" Eleanor rolled her eyes. "I told her I'd married a direly wounded Catholic French Canadian widower and that I was just up to collect my things before returning to my new role as the homemaker for his adorable nine children in the backwoods of Québec." She smiled at the mischievous memory.

"Did you really?" I asked as her enthusiasm seemed to infuse me.

Eleanor grinned. "These old curmudgeons sometimes need things to be put into perspective for them. Don't you think?"

"Yes, I suppose they do." I suddenly hoped deep down to the bottom of my heart that she would never realize how much of an old curmudgeon I secretly was myself.

She must have sensed my concern, or perhaps she noticed that I was, in comparison to her, already an old curmudgeon, as I looked like I was in my fifties, and she could not have been much older than thirty.

"Don't worry, Colonel," she corrected herself quickly. "It turns out there was a limit to my daughterly cheek. I only lasted a few seconds of observing her genuine horror before I gave in and revealed that I was still just her incorrigible spinster daughter. Have you ever noticed how much better the term 'bachelor' sounds for men than 'spinster' does for women?"

"You know, bachelors were often punished in the ancient world. In Sparta, they were forced to parade naked through the streets and sing about their dishonor." I basked in the unusual pleasure of being able to share one of the decidedly trivial facts I'd picked up during my decade of reading in the library of Kuveni's household in Bath.

"It's a good thing you're not a Spartan then," she winked. "Somehow you don't strike me as the type to enjoy the fanfare of a naked stroll through the Grecian streets."

I blushed again. Her audacity was so shocking, and yet, with every brazen comment, I felt her bewitching me more.

"Anyway, my original point, Colonel, was that when I returned to my family's village for a few months of rest after the war, my native Scots language popped right back into my head. I lost the odd collection of accents and returned completely to the language of my youth. But now and then, when a sassanack soldier comes into my ward, I still slip in and out of whatever accent he's using. So, I can only imagine how strong the effect would be if I had been hopping back and forth between languages as different as English and Hindi my whole life! I assume your nanny must have been Indian, then? It's no wonder you speak the language so fluently if it is the language you were first exposed to."

"I am an orphan, actually... I grew up in an orphanage in India." I paused as soon as the words came out of my mouth. I had never in my life ever admitted that truth to anyone, not even Alice, my first wife back in the 1830s. "And... er... Mr. Rana and I were actually speaking Punjabi, although it shares many similarities with Hindi." I hoped that the diversion would move us along past the scandalous implications of my origins... and the dubious timeline of the events.

"An orphanage in India?" Eleanor did not let me get away with my revelation so easily. "But your English is so posh! I thought when you said you'd been raised in India that your father must have been the viceroy himself!"

I felt another hot blush in my cheeks. "I came to England as a young man... to Bath, actually. A thoughtful relative, the only one I've ever known, arranged quite a few tutors for me. It is from them that I learned my *posh* English, as you put it."

It was Eleanor's turn to blush. "I put my foot in my mouth with that one, didn't I? I know the English don't like to comment on the obvious differences that their variety of accents convey. I mean, you're all thinking about it constantly, and yet you pretend that you have no bloody clue that Annie is from somewhere rather dreary in the Yorkshire moors!" I smiled as she accurately pointed out a conclusion I had made myself (and kept to myself, like the good Brit that I was) immediately upon meeting Anne. "It's all a bit much for my Scottish temperament, to be honest. I've never been particularly good at hiding what I'm thinking."

"As you probably noticed, neither am I." I winked, and as a wide smile spread across her face, I gathered up my courage. "Shall we continue this discussion in the library?"

"I would love to," Eleanor agreed. I stood up and offered her my arm with an archaic Victorian gesture that puzzled her.

"Follow me," Mr. Rana suggested helpfully.

"These modern women throwing themselves at desperate soldiers left and right… it sickens me…" Mrs. Fitzgerald muttered disapprovingly, and rather passive-aggressively.

Eleanor and I barely controlled our inclinations to engage her as we left her alone in the dining room to follow Mr. Rana through a long, cavernous marble hallway, into the grandest library I had ever seen. The sight stirred a great excitement deep within me, and all unpleasant feelings evoked by Mrs. Fitzgerald's snide remarks dissolved.

"Good lord, how extraordinary," I murmured. "I've never seen anything so marvelous in my life."

"Perhaps John should have opened one of these books at some point. He might have learned something useful," Eleanor muttered. She startled, as if she hadn't meant to voice the words out loud, and looked to Mr. Rana and then to me with a moment of embarrassment at her rude comment. But, as I burst into giddy laughter, she followed suit gratefully, while Mr. Rana smiled and dutifully held his tongue.

"I'm not convinced the man can read at all. Thinking is required for reading, you know, and I haven't seen much evidence of that."

"Colonel, you are just a bundle of surprises," Eleanor said as she wiped her tears of laughter from her eyes. "I've never met a career military man with one ounce of the sense of humor that you have."

"It has been a long time since I've been able to enjoy it myself," I confided. "And please, call me Edmund."

A mischievous smile spread across Eleanor's face, and she offered me her hand to kiss with an exaggerated impression of the Victorian gesture I'd attempted earlier in the evening with Anne. But, with her gauntlet dropped, I simply couldn't resist, and I dropped into an elaborate bow that I hadn't used since 1854 when, through a series of surprising events, I'd managed to find myself at Windsor Castle for the celebration of Prince Leopold's first birthday, presenting myself to Queen Victoria herself.

"My lady MacLeod," I declared melodramatically as I reached the apex of my bow.

Eleanor was stunned, stuck in position with her wide, giddy grin, and I winked at my triumph in our little game.

"Please, call me Eleanor," she said. I secretly hoped that I heard a bit of a swoon in her voice, although she never told me so explicitly.

I kissed her hand, grateful that the coffee from dinner seemed to be continuing its work in keeping me warm, and then returned to a standing position.

Mr. Rana indicated that we should seat ourselves in two deep leather chairs, but I simply could not keep myself from pausing to peruse one of the many shelves of books that covered the walls, floor to ceiling, to at least thirty feet in height.

"Ah!" I said excitedly as I spotted a thick, dusty, ancient printing of one of my utmost favorites. "Mr. Rana, might I take a look at this?"

Mr. Rana looked towards the empty hallway, indicating subtly that the proper answer was 'no,' and then he nodded his agreement.

I carefully took the book from the shelf and opened it, preparing to savor my first whiff of the old pages—a smell that I hadn't experienced in decades, but that still got my heart racing with excitement all the same, as I had associated it with the adventure of a new intellectual journey since my adolescence in Bath when I had systematically read through many thousands of books left for me by my guardians for my education.

As I observed exactly how delicate the yellow, flaking pages were, I carried the book carefully to an imposing mahogany desk and placed it on the clean blotter.

Eleanor followed me, to my great excitement, and leaned in, rubbing up against my arm ever so subtly as she squinted to read the title page.

"It's in Latin," she said with surprise.

"Is it?" I asked, as I had never paid particularly close attention to which language the books I read were in. "Yes, I suppose it is. It is the complete works of Ovid. He was a rather canonical Roman writer during the reign of Augustus. His poetry was somewhat bawdy in the beginning, but it became rather heart-wrenching after he was exiled to the Black Sea from Rome."

I gently flipped through the pages, landing on one section that I had found particularly interesting (and somewhat confounding) in my youth. I couldn't help but laugh.

"What is it?" Eleanor asked. I could feel the burning curiosity in her voice.

"*Ars Amatoria*—It's basically an ancient textbook for relationships. I found many passages quite informative in my youth. It was, in fact, perhaps my first exposure to the idea of relationships at all. Up until that point, I had hardly met a handful of women."

"You were reading Ovid in your youth? In the Indian orphanage?"

"No, with my tutors in Bath, after I left the orphanage," I explained, hoping once again that our discussion would not become detailed enough to reveal the dubious timeline of events. I swiftly moved the conversation along. "*Odi concubitus, qui non utrumque resolvunt.*" I read the first passage on which my eyes landed out loud, and then focused all of my mental energy on translating it into English. "It says: I abhor intercourse that does not relieve both... er... I suppose both parties involved. It is a statement about the importance of mutual... er... pleasure." I paused as I noticed the second half of the couplet. The first half was certainly shocking enough, and I blushed as I realized how absurdly inappropriate the passage was to read to a woman I had just met. But, before I had a chance to apologize, Eleanor put my mind at ease.

"How modern!" she exclaimed. "*This* is considered great classical poetry? It seems rather practical to me."

I smiled. "The language has more of a ring to it in the original. Ovid was using elegiac couplets that sound better in Latin, I think."

"Perhaps D.H. Lawrence should consider switching to Latin," Eleanor laughed. "Although, I'm not sure a modern writer could abide by the restraints of ancient meter."

"I've never tried writing poetry myself, so I cannot offer an opinion. Overall, though, I too find Ovid's writings rather practical." I turned to another page. "Here he is reminding men not to forget their lover's birthday... Ha! And here he reminds us not to ask about a lady's age."

"Wise man," Eleanor winked. "Well, Edmund, shall we continue our conversation over that drink you promised me?"

"Certainly," I agreed excitedly.

I had never, in my entire life, felt so comfortable with a woman. I followed her back to the chairs Mr. Rana had suggested sometime earlier, and as she plopped herself down, somewhat awkwardly in the low chair, Mr. Rana approached with a cart bearing several crystal decanters of various brandies and a set of elaborate crystal glasses.

"Mr. Rana was being quite kind earlier," I admitted. "He suggested cognac because I requested it during our exchange in

Punjabi, but I am quite certain that Ovid would advise for you to make the selection on behalf of us both."

"I would very much like to try whichever cognac you suggest. I came to love it when I was in France during the war, but it is not considered a proper lady's drink, especially not in Scotland. I rarely have a chance to enjoy it."

"We have an 1847 Chateau Léonie and an 1886 Hine," Mr. Rana said as he pointed to two of the crystal decanters.

"Are you sure it's alright that we drink them?" I asked, as the ages and producers alone made it obvious that the offerings were rare and extremely expensive.

"They will be best suited to those who drink slowly enough to enjoy them," Mr. Rana replied as he subtly glanced into the hallway towards John's room.

"Indeed." I was grateful that he not only made the offer genuinely, but that his logic, I had to agree, was sound enough to remove all guilt I might have felt in consuming the Crowden's finest cognacs. "Perhaps we might each have a taste of both?" I asked hopefully.

Mr. Rana nodded and obliged my inconvenient request by gathering two extra glasses from the bottom shelf of the cart and pouring four small tastes. He presented the first two glasses to Eleanor and me. "This is the Chateau Léonie. The prior Baron of Heathfield acquired it while this baron was already in the civil service in India. I am afraid that the collection will not last very long into the next Baron of Heathfield's reign. Please, enjoy it. I must go see to the Baron's nightly medicines. Colonel Marriner, when you are finished in here, please ring for me using the bell there by the door, and I will show you to your room."

"Thank you, Mr. Rana. You have been of great help."

"It is my pleasure, sir," Mr. Rana said with a bow. "Enjoy your evening." He offered Eleanor a polite nod, and left us alone.

Eleanor and I both took in deep whiffs of the cognac, swirled it around in our glasses, and then slowly took sips, savoring the unusually delicate flavors of rich caramel and smoky vanilla.

"Thank you, Edmund," Eleanor said as she finished up her first sip and let out a long, satisfied sigh.

"For what?" I asked, glad that I had done anything that elicited her gratitude.

"I did not think three hours ago that I'd make it through the weekend. I was considering how quickly I might catch a train out of here in the morning," Eleanor confessed. "And now, despite everything, I feel more relaxed than I've felt in years."

"I know exactly what you mean."

We both paused to take in our next savoring sips.

"So you work with the Household Cavalry now?" Eleanor asked casually. "That must be interesting."

"Yes, in London," I replied. "I primarily work on creating and enforcing policies around the treatment of the military's horses. Their role has changed quite a bit in the last few decades. They were gruesomely treated during the war, just like the men, but now that they aren't on the frontlines, I am working on improving their circumstances."

"How fascinating. I suppose they could use an advocate. I wouldn't expect them to get much mind from anyone when our struggles are still so great to undo the great wrong done to so many wounded soldiers."

"Indeed. I'm sure that I should be using my talents to advocate on behalf of veterans, but I don't have the wherewithal. My own shell shock is still unbearable at times, and I simply can't bear being faced with the gruesome results of the battles I was forced to fight for so long. It took me some time to admit it to myself, but it is what it is."

"Ralph mentioned that you were awarded the Victoria Cross. I assumed you must have seen quite a bit of brutality to be in a position for such heroism."

"I saw as much brutality as a man could possibly see." I had spent four years avidly avoiding the memories, but something about Eleanor, about her strength and the calm confidence she brought out in me pushed me forward. "I was reassigned from India the moment the war began, and I spent the next four hellish years as a commander in the trenches."

"Good lord, how horrific. You don't show it."

I shrugged. "My wounds are on the inside."

"You are not the only one," she murmured.

We both took in another sip of our cognac as we sat in silent contemplation.

"Might I ask, Edmund, why you stayed in the army after the war ended? You are the only ranking officer I have met who saw so much action on the frontlines and still chose to stick around afterwards. Most of the colonels and generals I've met never really saw action themselves—certainly not years in the trenches."

I thought about her question for the first time since I'd made the decision four years earlier. "At the end of the war, I planned to retire from military service and hide myself away as a hermit, but the generals decided to promote me instead. They offered me whatever commission I wanted if I was willing to stay, and so I chose the horses. They offer me a peace that I haven't been able to find any other way."

Eleanor paused thoughtfully before she spoke. "It is probably best for you to keep working. It will keep your mind occupied. I work with shell-shocked veterans every day in the mental ward of the hospital, and the ones who are the worst off are typically the ones who have nothing in their lives but the memories to haunt them… That is, perhaps, one reason that I keep working myself. How can I possibly be expected to flit about doing housework when there are millions of soldiers who still need help? I got used to the pace of working fifteen hour days, six days a week. I think I'd go mad if I stopped."

"I have no doubt that you are doing a great service with your work. Many of my men spoke about how the nurses saved them, not just physically."

"You speak as if you've never had an encounter yourself," Eleanor pointed out.

A pang of anxiety went off inside of me at the direction of the question. "I interacted with VAD nurses from time to time, mostly after the war. I never required treatment myself."

"Never?! In four years in the trenches?!"

"I'd rather not discuss it." I hoped that she would take my resistance however she needed to take it to drop the subject.

"I'm sorry," Eleanor said quietly as she realized how aggressive her tone had become. "I didn't mean to push. I'm grateful that you never needed treatment. The injuries I saw still haunt me."

"Me too," I whispered.

"Shall we try our other cognac?" Eleanor mercifully changed the subject.

"I don't know how it could possibly be better than the last, but there is only one way to find out." I worked hard to quell the burgeoning pain of our prior discussion as I handed her the other crystal glass.

"Cheers," I smiled as I held up my glass in a toast.

"Slainte," she winked.

We both sipped our tastes slowly.

"It is hard to compare. They are quite different. I think this one is less sweet, but it has a fresh component that the other lacked," I said as soon as I swallowed.

"The other's character changed quite a bit while I held the glass in my hand. I think the warmth brought out the caramel notes. Perhaps this one will change over time as well," Eleanor suggested.

I smiled, as I had never met a woman in my life who seemed remotely interested in discussing the nuanced flavors of fine cognacs with me.

"What?" Eleanor asked self-consciously as she noticed my attention.

"You are unlike any woman I've ever met," I admitted.

"And you, Colonel, are unlike any man I've ever met," she countered amicably. "Have I shocked you with my modernity?"

"I can't say," I confessed. "Shock is not the right word…"

"If we weren't surrounded by ancient books, I'd suggest we smoke some cigars together. Then I'd really shock you," she winked.

"Do ladies not smoke cigars?" I had spent so little time with women in recent decades that I had lost track of the various taboos for their gender. I myself had often found it confounding why they were willing to submit themselves to most of the uncomfortable fashions and activities that were often touted as "ideally feminine," but as I'd been avoiding the heartbreak of another dismal break-up for almost a century at that point, I had paid particularly little attention to women's topics of any kind.

Eleanor smiled at my question, assuming, I'm sure, that I was teasing her. "I'm quite sure that most men I meet these days think that I'm putting on some act as a modern woman, that secretly I wish I were married. They think that because I've reached the ripe old age of thirty-seven (Ovid would be ever so proud that you didn't ask), I'm simply putting a good spin on my dismal marital prospects. What they don't realize is that I am perfectly content with my life as it is. I have no desire to indenture myself as a housewife. I've always been terrible at household chores, anyway." She threw me an assessing look and waited for my response.

"Was that a question?" I asked innocently.

Eleanor laughed. "I suppose it wasn't. What is your opinion of marriage in these modern postwar times, Edmund?"

In retrospect, I realize that the question should not have been so surprising, given the trend of our conversation and the obvious magnetism that was growing between us, but something about the overt nature of it still shocked me.

"I've been such a hopeless bachelor for so long that I haven't given it any thought at all," I said truthfully. "I haven't courted a woman in a very long time. Longer even than you would believe."

"Clearly," Eleanor smiled, "you haven't courted a woman since the word 'courted' was in common use… and since kissing a lady's hand upon meeting was in fashion."

I shifted uncomfortably at the reality that she had already started noticing my anachronisms. My fears that her sharp wit would uncover my secret began to slowly churn.

"I'm sorry, I shouldn't tease you like that." Eleanor must have noticed my concern. "You are constantly surprising me, Colonel, which is a rare quality indeed. Please don't stop."

"I'm sure that I couldn't, even if I wanted to."

"So, no housewife for you, Edmund Marriner?" Eleanor pushed.

I thought carefully about the question, unclear as to her motive. It was obvious that she did not want to be a housewife, whatever that entailed, but as a 'modern' woman, I was unsure whether her interest in my opinion on the topic was philosophical or personal. I decided to hedge my response with what turned out to be a rather honest representation of my utter lack of awareness on the topic of modern marital households.

"I will admit that I'm puzzled by the relationship between marriage and housework. Why would a married woman do housework at all? Is that not what the staff is for? Certainly, one does not dismiss the house staff upon marriage?"

I could tell by the look on her face that I had succeeded in fulfilling her request for constant surprises with great haste.

"I believe that the average household these days does not keep a large house staff. Therefore, the woman is expected to stay at home and do the chores," she replied, clearly working hard at diplomatic phrasing.

What she obviously meant to say was: "Colonel, what kind of sheltered aristocratic life have you lived that you don't realize that most people live without a house staff? How on earth could you have been raised in an *orphanage* and not realize the hardships that define most ordinary people's lives?" And she would, of course, have been right. During the year of my marriage to Alice in the 1830s, under Kuveni's magical Yakshini roof, I had never witnessed my wife do one smidgeon of work, and so, I suddenly realized, my frame of reference must have been inaccurate. But, I still, even then, was not the worldliest of men, and so I found Eleanor's assertion genuinely shocking.

"Are you saying that even women who have been working at skilled jobs are expected to stop what they are doing upon marriage and replace their worldly endeavors with cooking and laundry? Why?!"

Eleanor paused for a moment to assess whether my utterly naïve question was intended to be sarcastic, but I must have exuded such a sense of childlike passion that she managed to accept my question with every bit of authenticity that I intended.

"Colonel, you are asking the question that every modern woman has been desperately asking the world. You are the first man I've ever met who seems to agree with us."

"Well, I think it's a travesty," I scoffed. "In every sense of the word."

"I think so too," she agreed, but then her tone gathered more intrigue. "So, are you saying, Edmund, that if you got married, you would not expect your wife to stop working?"

"I have never thought about the question before, but now that you mention it, I most certainly would not! I can't believe anyone would! I suppose I would enjoy taking some time off together to travel… perhaps hop back over to India, as I have missed it dearly since I left… but no, I can't think of anything more absurd than removing a woman from a position in which she creates great value for society to do mundane chores that can easily be hired out." I realized as I spoke that suddenly, as if by magic, an entire imaginary world of my married life with Eleanor had materialized in my head. I was fantasizing about my future for the first time in decades, and it filled me with a great sense of optimism that I hadn't known in so long that I could hardly remember the last time I'd felt it… perhaps back in 1895 when I'd re-set myself and returned to India. But even then, it had been adventurous but not… but not complete. This feeling now was entirely new, and it ignited me.

"You continue to delight me, Colonel," Eleanor said simply.

"Nothing about the economy you described makes any sense," I continued on with growing enthusiasm. "The world needs skilled workers in many capacities, and nurses?! That role doesn't just require skill, it requires empathy, maturity, the heartiness to deal with gruesome sights not fit for most humans to endure. Think of what a state we'd be in without nurses! And if all of those nurses became housewives, they'd put the servants out of a job. Those servants would then… what? Beg? Work in factories? But those dismal circumstances are not worthy of their talents! Great servants are one in a million. They would be replaced by women who should remain nurses, and no one in this scenario would be the least bit satisfied, nor would they be particularly efficient in their ill-fitted roles. Are you telling me that this travesty of wasted talent is happening commonly in England as we speak?"

"It is indeed the most common scenario," Eleanor confirmed. "You were not lying, Colonel, were you? You have not given any thought to women at all in a very long time."

"I have been completely surrounded by men for decades," I admitted. "And marriage has not even crossed my mind. I have too many complicated secrets in my past. Secrets that have made marriage rather unrealistic…" I stopped myself, shocked that I'd stumbled into revealing far more already than I had ever shared willingly with anyone in my life. Edward Rutherford knew what he knew because he had caught me, red-handed, in the midst of a rather alien moment on the front. But to reveal so casually that my life was littered with shocking secrets was completely uncharacteristic of me—I hardly recognized myself, and I found the feeling exhilarating.

"The world is not so backward now, Colonel," Eleanor reassured me.

"I'm sorry?" I asked with puzzlement as to what she might be referring.

"Whatever your family scandal was that left you in an orphanage to be followed up by private tutorials on Roman philosophy doesn't matter now, Edmund. The world is different than it used to be. The war made it that way. It is, perhaps, the only benefit of the entire wretched folly."

I was completely taken aback by her shrewd assessment of my circumstances. I suddenly had an urge to come clean, to tell her *everything* that I'd never told anyone before, but I took a deep breath and managed to control myself. She had offered me a mundane excuse that I would be able to call upon to explain many of my eccentricities. Regardless of the details, she knew now that my upbringing had been very abnormal, and still she was interested in learning more. I would not ruin it by revealing unpleasant truths.

I took a long swig of the cognac, finishing up the last sip in my glass, and then assessed the remaining options on the cart.

"Shall we try another?" I proposed.

Eleanor finished her last swallow and nodded her agreement. I sniffed several of our options, landing on a particularly rich, silky-scented brandy.

"I suppose we'll have to judge this entirely by its flavors. None of these bottles are labelled," I said as I poured us each a taste.

I stood up to present the fresh glass to Eleanor, and she stood up to take it. But rather than sitting back down, she sniffed it, took a small sip, and then gathered my glass into her other hand and placed both of them on a small side table.

My heart began racing as she stood on her tiptoes to reach her arms around my neck. I carefully placed my hands on her waist, as my brain hardly processed the shocking escalation. She looked up into my eyes and smiled.

"Somehow I just can't stop myself, Edmund," she confessed. "I have to judge you without any labels."

All of my incapacitating timidity, my years of shell-shocked torment, and my decades of fear at repeating my traumatizing experience with Alice dissolved, and without another thought, I leaned in and kissed the beautiful woman in my arms.

After many minutes of an increasingly passionate embrace, she pulled away to catch her breath.

"Did I pass?" I asked.

"With flying colors," she murmured.

But, as I leaned in for another round of the most thrilling sensations I'd ever felt in my life, heavy footsteps in the hallway distracted me, and I pulled away.

"Someone's coming," I whispered. I wiped her bright red lipstick off of my mouth guiltily, but as I spied Mr. Rana, my raging anxiety dissolved into minor concern.

Mr. Rana approached us with an apologetic look on his face as he noticed the evidence of our recent intimacy. "Colonel, if you wouldn't mind, I would like to show you to your room now. I must wake up rather early tomorrow morning to prepare for the day's theatrics."

"Yes, yes. Of course," I agreed, slightly ashamed that I'd kept Mr. Rana up for too long.

"I will head to bed now too," Eleanor declared. She followed us swiftly out of the library and joined me to follow Mr. Rana up the main staircase. As we reached the top, she stopped and pointed down a dark hallway. "This is my direction. Sleep well, Colonel. It was a delight getting to know you this evening."

"Likewise," I said in a daze.

She smiled and nodded a goodnight to Mr. Rana.

"Be careful, Colonel," Mr. Rana warned in Punjabi. I silently congratulated myself for recognizing the transition in language. "That there is a modern woman. She will always have a mind of her own."

"That, Mr. Rana, is *exactly* what I need."

CHAPTER 9 – SIR PERCY BLAKENEY ARRIVES

After Mr. Rana escorted me to my palatial room (that was a bit too shabby, even for my lax, miserly taste on the matter), I sat on the edge of the canopied bed staring at the tattered, moth-eaten curtains for hours ruminating on the many shocking developments of the evening.

I could not remember a time when more had happened in just a few hours…. more drama, that is. Certainly, I'd been shot at for longer than that—I had plenty of experience staying awake all night dodging artillery fire—but for so many passionate personal interactions to unfold at once was completely foreign to me, and not only in my postwar shell-shocked state.

Perhaps the last time I'd felt anything similar had been the day when Mr. Hanley had confronted me in the town center over Alice's virtue, almost eighty years earlier. In that instance, I'd ended up married by the end of the week. Somehow, this time around, the idea of being forced into a marriage to Eleanor didn't seem frightening at all. My mind remained focused on my odd lack of anxiety about her for quite some time, until I wrested myself from my daydreaming and assessed my surroundings more soberly.

I was on the opposite side of the house from Eleanor, which, despite our burgeoning affection was still a blessing in my mind— she was least likely to hear my shameful nightmarish screams with our current positioning. But still, I didn't know who was situated in the rooms adjacent to mine. The idea of the brutish Fitzgeralds getting an earful of my trauma filled me with dread; although, why exactly I disliked them so strongly, I wasn't entirely certain yet.

And so, after I perused the room and assessed the ancient bed that was decidedly smaller than the one I'd used in the 1830s in Bath, I decided to scamper back to the library to spend the night with Ovid. As I had been too distracted to change out of my military uniform, I was not worried about being caught by Mr. Rana in the morning in my pajamas.

I sprawled myself out on a leather couch that was ten times more comfortable than the creaky bed I'd been assigned, and used my Rakshasa strength to carefully hold the flaking text up for hours and hours while I re-read (in meticulous Latin verse) the relationship advice that I'd found so foreign in my youth. It was less foreign after a century of experience, although perhaps still *more* foreign than I wanted to admit.

"Let her miss you, but not for too long…" What games the Romans played! I thought back fondly on the heated debate I'd had with my tutor on the topic, Signore Foscarelli, an Italian classicist who had been employed in Bath (no doubt, at great expense) to challenge me on the fundamental principles that were being touted throughout the Roman literary oeuvre. I didn't believe then in the virtue of instilling false anxiety into one's dearest companions, and still, many decades later, I refused to accept the validity of the assertion.

I contemplated Ovid's wisdom with less and less scrutiny until sleep became inevitable, and I carefully placed the delicate book on the floor beside me...

I awoke to the sound of the doorbell reverberating off of the old grandfather clock's chimes in the dim, early-morning light. It was the first time I could remember since the war that I hadn't awoken with mad screams to dreams of being trapped in the trenches.

Mr. Rana's footsteps sounded belabored as he warily approached the door. After a muffled exchange, another figure entered the house, and Mr. Rana escorted him to the dining room. I dragged myself up, out of my position on the couch, and flattened the creases in my uniform. I hoped that I didn't have the cushions I had slept on imprinted on my face.

I carefully collected the works of Ovid and returned the book to the bookshelf, noting its exact position in case the opportunity to finish it presented itself in the coming days. The prospect of spending several days at the house was, as I had noticed the night before with Eleanor, surprisingly pleasant. I pushed all of my anxiety at John's beastly behavior from my mind as I envisioned my beautiful Eleanor sleeping peacefully in her bed. My heart raced at the delightful thought.

As Mr. Rana and the visitor's exchange became more heated, I rushed to the closest powder room to inspect my appearance. The imprints from the cushions on my face were still visible. I considered returning upstairs to my room to embark upon a proper morning ritual, but as I listened to the footsteps of the mysterious guest pacing back and forth impatiently, I decided instead to bathe myself in the style I had known in my youth with only the water from the wash basin.

I let myself give into the relaxing pleasures of the hot water for more time than I'd intended until I heard a door slam upstairs.

Then I took a deep, calming breath, hastily hopped back into my uniform, and then headed to the dining room to greet the new visitor.

As I entered the room, a middle-aged man whom I could only describe as a dandy, clad in the most ostentatious of current fashions with a purple velvet suit and absurdly fluffy cravat complemented by beautiful tufts of perfectly placed golden blond hair, stood to address me. He left his matching hat and elaborate ivory walking stick on the table and dropped into a flourished bow.

"Sir Percival Blakeney at your service, but you may call me Percy." He spoke with a deep baritone voice and a decidedly affected British accent that matched perfectly what I expected him to sound like based on his colorful appearance.

I burst into laughter, but he only looked at me with confusion.

"I'm sorry." I worked hard to control my reaction. "Weren't you joking?"

"I don't understand."

"Sir Percy Blakeney? *The Scarlet Pimpernel?* Surely you're aware of the literary reference?" I eyed his particularly flamboyant suit.

An expression of intense annoyance crossed his face as he muttered something under his breath.

"No, I am not aware of the literary reference," he said flatly.

"'*They seek him here; they seek him there... those Frenchies seek him everywhere...*'" I quoted the famous foppish poem for him in an affected accent that didn't sound particularly different from his, but he only stared at me blankly. "It is a series of books about an English aristocrat in disguise who rescues French aristocrats from the guillotine during the French Revolution."

He muttered something else under his breath, shrugged, glanced around the room, and then pushed on.

"Colonel Marriner, I presume? I was hired by the Baron of Heathfield to come here and manage the situation with John Crowden. Clearly, I will need to update my secret identity."

"It would be advisable," I suggested amicably. "Despite his wanton intellect, the reference is popular enough that he will probably recognize it."

"Yes, very sage advice." He reached out his gloved hand in greeting. "I suppose I'll have to choose another name before we can be properly introduced."

"Well…" I thought about the problem. "If John Crowden believes himself to be an imminent baron, you should probably outrank him if you want to have the authority to manage his conduct. Although, he is probably aware of most of the landed gentry of Britain, and he is of the personality who would not respect any foreign title."

"Quite right," Sir Percy Blakeney agreed.

"Perhaps… Lord George Blakeney, Viscount Cornbury? I believe that incorporates several real titles into nonsense, which should be sufficient for an adversary as vapid as John Crowden."

"Colonel Marriner, you are a valuable ally," he replied. "You may call me *Lord* Blakeney from now on."

"As you wish, my *lord*," I winked. "I'm grateful for the reprieve. John Crowden has been an antagonistic brute so far, riling up trouble for his ailing brother. It's taken all of my restraint to keep myself from challenging him. I'm still struggling with shell shock from the war, you see, and it's a bad idea for everyone if I lose myself in a confrontation."

Lord Blakeney's expression turned somber. "I cannot express to you, Colonel Marriner, how deeply I regret that human societies were not able to extricate themselves from their war-mongering enthusiasm before it was too late. The casualties of that worthless war were enough to make the gods weep."

"Lord Blakeney, you must be well-educated in the classics to use such a plural," I smiled, trying to keep myself from giving into my common malaise.

"Oh yes," he said as an odd expression crossed his face. "I am very educated in the classics. The Romans were a fascinating people. Very complex. Very diverse. I have never seen such a combination of those who seek to elevate their virtue and those who seek to thwart it."

"Oh really? I would have thought the British would qualify," I said jokingly.

He paused as he thought seriously about my statement. "You know, perhaps you're right, Colonel Marriner. I will have to think more about it."

"Good morning," Eleanor said as she entered the room. She tightened the belt on her silk kimono as she observed Lord Blakeney. "I thought I heard someone arrive."

"Lord Blakeney, Viscount Cornbury." Our mysterious dandy introduced himself with another flourished bow, and then offered Eleanor an even more flamboyant version of the archaic Victorian gesture that I had used the previous night in an effort to kiss her hand.

She looked at him skeptically, and then looked to me with puzzlement, no doubt putting together the extremely odd coincidence that she was now in the presence of two anachronistic gentlemen.

"Do you know each other?" Eleanor cleverly proposed the most likely scenario.

"Lord Blakeney is here on behalf of the Baron to help keep John Crowden in line," I explained.

"Good luck with that one," Eleanor guffawed. "You must have the patience of Job."

"I believe that Mr. Crowden has already been shown far too much patience," Lord Blakeney said as his ears perked up. I heard it too. Footsteps were approaching from the upstairs bedrooms.

"You are certainly right about that," Eleanor agreed as her demeanor softened. "I'm glad someone will be here to help us out.

His behavior was utterly ludicrous yesterday. I've seen far better behaved maniacs in lunatic asylums."

"Have you spent much time in lunatic asylums?" Lord Blakeney asked as he raised his eyebrows with intrigue.

"Too much," Eleanor replied. Lord Blakeney looked ignited by the intel, but as Eleanor realized his scandalous interpretation of her statement, she rushed to clarify. "When I was first a nurse, before the war, I had to work in a lunatic asylum. It was the only institution I could find that was willing to hire an inexperienced nurse. I worked there until the VAD formed, and then I hopped over to France as soon as I could muster up the money for the passage."

I offered her a supportive smile, and to my great relief, she offered one back. My heart fluttered at the beautiful truth that the unexpected intimacy we'd shared the night before had not been forgotten in the long hours of our separation.

"And so I meant my statement literally, Lord Blakeney," she continued. "If John were not from a prominent family, I wouldn't be surprised to see him in a lunatic asylum in his current state. His sadism is certainly equal to that of many criminally insane patients I've dealt with over the years. His utter lack of remorse regarding his antagonism against his injured brother is not dissimilar to what I've seen in many maniacal murderers."

Lord Blakeney looked overwhelmed by the assertion. "Then it is a good thing that I'm here."

"Good morning," Anne said with feigned cheer as she escorted Ralph into the dining room. They both observed Lord Blakeney with immediate suspicion.

"I am Lord Blakeney, Viscount Cornbury," he introduced himself again. "I am here on the Baron's request to help rein in Mr. John Crowden's behavior."

Anne looked relieved, but Ralph's suspicion only grew. "How could you possibly be here on my father's orders? He hasn't been able to speak in weeks, and John only arrived on Wednesday."

"Yes, but your father is still capable of writing, is he not?" Lord Blakeney countered. "Your father sent for me yesterday. I came as soon as I could."

"Mr. Rana, did you send out letters from my father yesterday?" Ralph asked, his suspicion unabated.

Mr. Rana seemed flustered as he entered the room from the hallway, but his movements were sluggish. A pang of guilt went off deep inside of me for having thoughtlessly kept him awake late into the night. With glassy eyes, he observed the large group. "I did, sir." He leaned himself up against the wall.

"Are you alright?" Eleanor asked concernedly.

"I'm perfectly fine." Mr. Rana insisted unconvincingly as he gestured for her to leave him alone. He returned his attention to Ralph. "There was one letter in the morning to Mr. Banning, and the other I found on his desk yesterday night addressed to Sir Blakeney. I sent it out via a special courier, as it seemed rather urgent."

"Mr. Banning?" Anne said with a quiver in her voice. I couldn't tell if it was anxiety or excitement. "What would your father want to talk to his solicitor about, Ralph? You don't think..." She trailed off and looked nervously around the room.

"Mr. Rana, did Mr. Banning respond to my father's letter yesterday?" Ralph asked calmly.

"Not yet, sir. I didn't send it out using the special courier because it was early enough that I could get it into the regular post. Would you like me to telephone his office to inquire about it?"

"No... thank you, Mr. Rana. I will telephone him myself after breakfast." Ralph squeezed Anne's hand in solidarity, obviously sharing some sort of secret communication between them.

96

"Please, everyone, let's be seated for breakfast," Anne suggested with a new hint of genuine cheer in her voice.

Eleanor led the way, and I followed swiftly to ensure my position next to her, while Lord Blakeney took the liberty of commandeering John's former position at the head of the table. Ralph observed the uncouth move, but shrugged and said nothing. Because he didn't have the energy to argue, or because he had some secret idea about why the mysterious spy was really there, I couldn't say.

"So, Lord Blakeney, how do you know my father?" Ralph asked as soon as we were all seated.

"I have known him for many years," Lord Blakeney replied. "A man of your father's stature has many acquaintances to which he can turn in a time of need. I am one of them."

"And my father is aware enough of the challenges we've been having with John to have sent for you to join us as a glorified nanny for my middle-aged brother?" Ralph asked. I was surprised by the sharpness of his tone. "Why didn't he send for you years ago? John's behavior is hardly unusual. He's been a brute for as long as I can remember."

"We all do what we can, Mr. Crowden," Lord Blakeney replied. "Perhaps you should focus on the fact that he sent for me now."

"Yes, perhaps," Ralph conceded.

"It looks like today will be a lovely sunny day," Anne attempted to move the conversation along.

"It is still very cold," Ralph countered. "Too cold, I think, for October. Did you see the frost on the lawn? This will do a number on the orchards."

"Do you harvest the fruit yourselves?" Eleanor asked.

"No. Mr. Kauter does. He's a farmer from the village who rents the fields. We buy his best fruit, and then he sells the rest at the market," Ralph replied.

"Mr. Kauter?" Eleanor asked astutely. "Is he German? Life must be rather unpleasant for him now."

"He's bloody *Swiss*," Ralph replied with more passion than the question deserved. He noticed his own demeanor and cleared his throat, continuing more calmly. "I believe he's from the Bernese Alps originally, although he's lived here almost as long as I've been alive. You're right that his situation has become unpleasant. His accent sounds distinctly German, as does his name."

"Since he returned from the war, Ralph has made sure to clarify for everyone in the village whenever the topic comes up, which is sadly still rather often, that Mr. Kauter is not a Kraut... er... I mean a German," Anne added.

"That is very kind of you," Eleanor said genuinely.

"For what good it does..." Ralph muttered. "Everyone is looking for someone they can let their anger out on. If you ask me, they should blame the bloody king for letting the whole thing happen at all. We didn't see him out fighting in the bloody trenches, did we? Or bloody Asquith? Or bloody Lloyd George?"

"Ralph," Anne hissed as she glanced nervously to me, but Ralph's simmering passion on the topic had been ignited.

"Millions of lives were brutally sacrificed, all over the assassination of some worthless Austrian prince in a country that still doesn't matter one smack to Britain! If the leaders had been out there living in Hell like we were, the wretched war would not have still been going in 1917 when my life was ruined."

Ralph began wheezing, and Anne rubbed his back.

"Ralph, we mustn't speak of such things. The war is over. We won. We must make what we can of it and not let it keep defeating us," Anne whispered into his ear. Then she looked apologetically to me, assuming, I believe, that I might have been offended by his lack of patriotism on the matter.

I looked to Eleanor and took in a deep breath of the calm confidence she'd instilled in me the night before. "I agree with you,

Lieutenant. The war should never have happened. I would have been far better off myself if I'd remained in India, fulfilling my mundane duties to the Empire there. I watched too many innocent boys die. So many that I lost count…" I trailed off as the faces of my dead men bombarded my mind. I shivered, and Eleanor reached down secretly under the table to squeeze my leg. The shocking gesture wrested me from my spiral, and I gathered my wits, hoping that no one had noticed my momentary descent into darkness. "The only solace I have is that the World War showed us what kind of destruction we are capable of. I can only hope that our sacrifices will be used to ensure that there will never be such a hell on Earth again."

Eleanor offered me a sad smile, and I offered her a silent thank-you, and then we all sat stoically as the servants presented generous platefuls of a traditional English breakfast. The contrast between the shameful rations we'd suffered through on the front and the excess before us now was hard for my addled brain to comprehend, but as the delicious scents wafted off of the hot plate, I took a deep breath and forced myself with all my might to relegate the dark past back to its position just over the precipice in my mind, to focus on the beautiful reality before me.

The eggs were perfectly cooked with the yolks soft enough to ooze out onto the buttered toast. The bacon was crisp but not overdone, and the tomato subtly salted and blackened. The sausage was rich and smoky, but with far more spice than any I'd tasted in England before. I wondered if I might have the opportunity to sneak into the kitchen in the later morning to procure a second helping, and I let myself take in a deep, calming breath at the reality that such a fancy was entirely plausible. I had before me everything I needed, everything I had gone so long without. I was safe, and the war really was over. I paused to let the thought sink in truly and completely for the first time.

I worked hard to pace my coffee consumption such that I didn't draw attention to my unusual thirst, and my gratitude went out to the attentive footman who didn't raise an eyebrow as he served me at a rate far faster than everyone else. I made a mental note to thank him later.

As I finished off my last sausage, the simple pleasures of the delicious meal had filled the gaping hole in my soul with the pulsating warmth of human digestion for the first time in years, and I could not contain my enthusiasm. "This sausage is simply the best I've ever tasted. It reminds me of something quite deliciously foreign… almost Indian."

"My father developed a taste for Indian spices when he lived there," Ralph explained. "He brought his chef back with him, along with Mr. Rana when he returned to England, and his chef trained Mrs. Murray in how to use the spices."

"I will have to offer both of them my congratulations," I said amicably.

"I'm sure they will be glad to hear it, Colonel," Anne replied, obviously grateful that our conversation had officially moved along.

"So, Annie, what autumnal activities did you have planned for us today?" Eleanor asked cheerfully. "I brought my riding clothes, like you suggested."

"Riding clothes?!" Ralph exclaimed. He exploded into a coughing fit, and Anne suddenly looked concerned as she rubbed his back.

"Yes, I had hoped that we could all go riding together," Anne said distractedly. "But Ralph and I have some unexpected business with the Baron's solicitor. Perhaps you and Colonel Marriner can go riding? I assume, Colonel, that you must be quite the expert?"

"Yes, I suppose I am," I agreed. The idea of going for a ride with Eleanor set off a flurry of butterflies in my stomach.

"Perfect!" Eleanor exclaimed. "Finally someone who can keep up with me!"

Anne laughed. "You were always too much of a speed demon for me, Ellie."

"What do you say, Colonel?" Eleanor asked. "Do you think you can keep up with a modern woman?"

"There's only one way to find out." I smiled suavely, hiding my nervous excitement at the idea, but the butterflies in my stomach burgeoned into a flock of squawking geese as Eleanor winked at me.

Anne and Ralph threw each other a distinct look of pride at our exchange, and suddenly it occurred to me that perhaps... just perhaps... there had been a tad bit of meddling involved in Eleanor and my introduction.

Boom.

Boom.

Ralph threw himself under the table and then grabbed Anne and pulled her down with him, while my adrenaline exploded, and I pulled Eleanor into my arms protectively.

"What in the bloody hell is that?!" Eleanor exclaimed as she wiggled out of my grip to look around the room herself.

Boom.

Boom.

Boom.

Ralph whimpered.

"Those are gunshots," I said as I looked around in an attempt to pinpoint the source.

Boom.

Boom.

Boom.

Familiar muffled laughter echoed in through the closed windows.

"You monstrous little toads," Lord Blakeney muttered as he stood up. "John and Mr. Fitzgerald are on the roof shooting at fowl. I will go deal with them now. You are all perfectly safe here. The noise will desist shortly."

Without another word, Lord Blakeney rushed out of the dining room and disappeared down the dark hallway.

Boom.

Boom.

Boom.

Ralph began wheezing, and Mr. Rana appeared from the kitchen door, bearing the silver platter with his inhaler. Anne silently set about helping him breathe, while I took breath after calming breath myself.

"Are you alright?" Eleanor whispered to me.

I closed my eyes and worked to slow my racing heart. After a minute of silence, I opened my eyes and looked around the room, reminding myself of the peace I had felt only minutes before. *The war is over…* I repeated the mantra in my head.

I finally looked to Eleanor, and a distinct puff of fear wafted off of her. I chastised myself for not being able to focus more on comforting her, and I redoubled my efforts to get myself back under control. I closed my eyes, took many deep breaths, and then reopened them.

"I'm sorry," I whispered. "It was too unexpected… It brought up too many memories…"

"You heard what Lord Blakeney said," Eleanor reminded me as she soothingly stroked my back. "We're safe here."

Two hunting rifles fell past the window and landed with a loud clank in the craggy rose bushes just outside. John's angry shouts morphed into surprised yelps, matched by pained squeals from Mr. Fitzgerald.

"Well, it sounds like Lord Blakeney is earning his keep," Eleanor quipped.

She smiled, and finally, with her calm confidence, I smiled. My heart slowed, and a wave of relief washed over me. Her smile only grew, and she patted my shoulder.

"Come on, Colonel, let's go for a ride." She hopped up and offered me her hand. "Nothing relaxes me like feeling the wind on my face."

I gave no thought whatsoever to Ralph and Anne as I let her guide me into the hallway. As soon as we were out of public view, she reached her arms around my neck, stood on her tiptoes, and kissed me gently on the lips.

"You'll be alright, Edmund. I am sure of it now."

I was puzzled by the source of her new confidence after my shameful demonstration of shell-shocked weakness.

"How do you know?" I asked, hoping she could convince me.

"If you can recover from unexpected gunfire with just a few minutes of deep breathing, you will learn to move on from the rest of the trauma. I've seen it thousands of times now."

"Thank you," I whispered as I leaned down and kissed her more deeply.

"For what?" She kissed me again.

"For telling me things I wouldn't believe without the opinion of an experienced medical professional."

"It's my pleasure, Colonel," Eleanor smiled. "Now, shall we go to the stables and meet our companions for the day?"

"I can't think of anything I'd rather do."

"Me neither."

And together, hand in hand, we left the Crowden's familial drama for a peaceful afternoon with the horses.

CHAPTER 10 – JUST BEYOND VIEW

My giddiness and Eleanor's managed to distract us so thoroughly that neither of us noticed that she was still wearing a silk kimono until we opened the door to the backyard, and a blast of freezing air engulfed us. As Eleanor's kimono fluttered in the cold wind, we slammed shut the door and burst into laughter.

"I suppose I brought my riding clothes for a reason," Eleanor giggled.

"I should change too. I actually slept in my uniform in the library last night."

"Why?!"

"Well, the bed was about a foot too short," I lied. I hated the feeling more than I ever had in my life.

"That must be a common problem for you, mustn't it?" She stood on her tiptoes and reached her arms around my neck, and suddenly I noticed how incredibly sensual the soft silk of her kimono was as I spied her lovely subtle curves through the thin fabric.

I pulled away from her before I gave away any evidence of my newfound appreciation.

"I'm sorry," she said, assuming that my gesture was a sign of offense. "It's rude to point out someone's height, I know. But you are rather tall."

"Six foot seven to be precise," I replied. "Quite noticeably tall, I agree." Suddenly my rash desire to be more honest with her began to work its way back up to the surface. "I actually slept in the library to avoid awakening the household with my screams. Last night was the first night since the war that I slept without dreaming of the trenches."

A pang of sadness crossed Eleanor's face, and she reached up and softly stroked my cheek. "It is a triumph, Colonel. May it be the first night of many."

I leaned down and kissed her until the shuffle of fabric as someone entered the hallway distracted us, and we quickly pulled away from each other.

"Fifteen minutes, Colonel. I will be ready in fifteen minutes on the dot!" Eleanor declared. "Don't be late!"

She held tightly onto her flowing kimono and dashed down the hallway and up the stairs. I took a moment to compose myself, and as I noticed Mr. Rana muttering to himself down the hallway, I considered asking him what was bothering him, but as Eleanor's door slammed, I realized that I might need more than fifteen minutes to figure out how to put on my new riding clothes, as it had been several decades since I'd ridden in anything other than a military uniform, and the fashions had changed so drastically in only the prior few years. At the thought, I rushed down the hallway, past Mr. Rana who, with subtle confusion, was now organizing the spot where I'd slept in the library, and up the stairs to my bedroom.

Upon entering my room, I thought momentarily of taking a quick bath to fill myself with warmth before my day with Eleanor, as I wasn't sure how long the coffee would stay in my system on such a cold day, but pragmatism rushed to squelch my fancy, as I realized that there was simply no way I would be able to rip myself from the enticing pleasures of the hot water in time to meet Eleanor's aggressive deadline. And so, I skipped straight to laying out my uniform on the bed and then hopping about the room, awkwardly pulling on my new riding trousers for the first time.

After a few minutes of battling with the new clothes, I rushed down the stairs, making a beeline for the kitchen in the hope that I might sneak my extra helping of the delicious breakfast before Eleanor was ready to leave, but as I charged down the hallway at my fastest dignified speed, I stopped to observe a large painting gathering dust in the corner by the kitchen door. There, in all its glory, was one of the many thousands of waterfall paintings I had churned out during my prior career as a painter of bucolic landscapes in the 19th century. My signature mocked me unmistakably from the bottom right corner.

I stared at the uneven lines and sloppy brush strokes. The trees in the background were hardly distinguishable from the dark horizon in a rather amateurish faux-pas that I knew was not at all intentional. The work was undoubtedly one of my later ones, perhaps painted between the time that my aged eyesight had dreadfully degenerated, but before I had given in and submitted myself to the atrocities of Victorian optometry.

I stood back a few feet to observe the subject. It was a local waterfall of the most ordinary variety in the woods by my house on the other side of the village, one that I had painted many hundreds of times throughout my many decades living in the community. I racked my brain as I contemplated the odd coincidence.

I supposed that it shouldn't have been so surprising that the local baron of the village in which I'd resided had come across one of my highly generic wall-fillers. But I had no memory of selling my work to the Baron of Heathfield. I remembered him being a rather well-known personality who would have announced himself, or, more likely, he would have had his valet announce him. No. I was almost certain that I had never had a face-to-face encounter with the man, but I had seen him out and about every so often on the streets of the village, and surely my memory couldn't have been so bad... surely?

I closed my eyes and did some quick calculations, as a pang of anxiety rushed through me at the prospect that I had thoughtlessly just walked into a dangerous situation in which an old acquaintance might recognize me... If I had sold the painting directly, it would have been to the father of the current Baron of Heathfield. *This* Baron, who lay dying in his bed upstairs, must have already been in the civil service in India by that time...

I took in a deep, calming breath as my anxiety dissolved. If I had met the man who purchased the painting, the encounter had happened long enough ago that every witness was now dead. I worked hard not to let myself contemplate what that meant about my outrageously advanced age in relation to Eleanor's.

I refocused on my original quest for spiced Indian sausage. As my mouth watered at the exciting prospect of entering the kitchen, a new, even more unpleasant anxiety took hold as the stumbling gait of the sadistic brute approached my position.

"Shopping for rubbish?" I cringed as John Crowden's grating voice echoed through the hallway. "I'll give you a mighty fine deal, Colonel. If I weren't such a venerable businessman, I might consider giving that wretched painting away. I think the artist must have been blind."

He slapped me harshly on the back, and I straightened my posture, working hard to hold onto the calming image of Eleanor in my mind.

"I daresay you might be right about that," I said politely, as I forced myself to acknowledge that his uncouth observation was unfortunately correct and could not have been knowingly aimed at me. "Those sloppy brushstrokes are inexcusable."

John was genuinely surprised by my agreement. "An art critic and a soldier, Colonel? You are a veritable renaissance man, aren't you?"

"I wouldn't describe myself as such," I replied flatly, as my stomach growled, and I contemplated the new unpleasant fact that the brute's distraction might keep me from my second helping.

"No wonder Ellie's all over you. I'd watch myself, if I were you, Colonel. Desperate girls are a dime a dozen, and when they get a bun in the oven, they become a prickly thorn in the side, if you know what I mean." He winked.

I channeled all of my energy into containing the demonic rage that burst forth from the core of my being at his multi-tiered insult against Eleanor and his flippant admission of his own wanton exploits.

"Mr. Crowden!" Lord Blakeney's voice boomed from the hallway beyond. "You were ordered to go straight to your room! You will not disobey my orders again. Do you understand?!"

John Crowden's face turned red with some combination of embarrassment and anger at Lord Blakeney's parental castigation. Lord Blakeney ignored me as he approached our position, grabbed ahold of John Crowden's collar, and just as if he were leading an incorrigible toddler to his place of punishment, he dragged the brute down the dark hallway and up the stairs.

"What was that about?" Eleanor asked as she approached me.

"Mr. Crowden and I were just discussing the art," I said distractedly as I took in the vision of Eleanor in her sleek riding clothes. Her fiery hair was gathered up into a bulging bun underneath her diagonally-positioned riding hat, and the fitted coat and baggy trousers looked intriguingly novel on her petite feminine figure. She had meticulously replaced the red lipstick that I had already tasted twice, and I couldn't help but fantasize about helping her remove it again at the soonest appropriate opportunity.

Eleanor burst into laughter. "Really, Edmund, I'm glad to see that you've regained your delightful sense of humor. Discussing art with John Crowden? I'd sooner eat glass."

I smiled. "I wasn't joking, actually. It wasn't the most intellectual of encounters, but we were discussing this shameful piece of art here that has been rightfully relegated to the dark corner by the kitchen door."

Eleanor leaned forward to take in a more serious assessment. "I don't know... I wouldn't call it shameful... It's not the most inspiring piece I've ever seen, but it emotes a certain sense of longing that I find quite jarring. Great art is more about the emotion it evokes than it is the perfection of the technique, don't you think?"

I was utterly speechless at her supportive reaction. She had just unknowingly given me an entire outlook on my decades of work that had never even crossed my mind. I had been so focused on the precision of the strokes and the mundanity of the subject-matter that the emotional impact had completely escaped me.

"And, in fact... look here..." She pointed at my sloppy horizon. "The scene is blurry, but the strokes are not imprecise, as if there is something the artist wants to see, but he simply can't... You know, I think... I think this is the work of a highly skilled painter who was losing his sight! How incredibly sad. No wonder it feels so lonely."

I remained speechless. Without even knowing that she was describing *me*, she had pinpointed more about my emotional state than *I* had when I'd painted the damned painting myself...

"I'm sorry, Colonel. I didn't mean to go on and on."

"I've never thought of it that way before... never..." I murmured.

"Never thought of what?"

"I've never thought of how the emotions that go into making a painting manage to come out... to infuse the viewer..."

"Have you thought much about making paintings?" she asked curiously.

My heart skipped a beat. Surely more admissions of my many exploits would start adding up in the astute timeline of my life that she was already keeping in her head.

"Yes, I studied art a bit in my youth," I admitted vaguely.

"Don't tell me you lived a secret life as a painter?" Eleanor teased. "Was that before your Roman philosophical tutorials or after?"

"Both, actually..." I squirmed uncomfortably. I simply couldn't bring myself to lie openly to her. The best I could do was to protect my secrets with half-truths.

"Both!" Eleanor exclaimed.

"I was a painter's apprentice in India before I moved to England, and then I studied painting in London for some time before I joined the army..." I immediately regretted speaking the words out loud. "Shall we go for our ride now while the sun is high in the sky?" I hoped she wouldn't hear the desperation in my voice as I changed the subject.

"Yes, yes, of course..." Eleanor looked me up and down, and then smiled and nodded her agreement. "You look very dapper in your riding clothes, Edmund. You look almost like an average civilian."

"Don't let it fool you." I laughed, although I meant the statement genuinely.

"Oh, don't worry. I'm never fooled," she winked.

Our joviality morphed into a simultaneous shiver as I opened the door to the outside, and a blast of freezing air bombarded us.

"I'm not sure my tweed is sufficient for such a wintery day!" Eleanor exclaimed. "If I'd known, I'd have brought my tartan!"

I looked into the sky as a high layer of wintery clouds covered the last hint of morning sun.

"Do you want to stay inside?" I asked.

"Never!" Eleanor declared. "Let's see how far we can get before we need a warm respite, shall we?"

I smiled at her tenacious enthusiasm as I offered her my arm. "We shall."

Eleanor took it, and together, we headed into the wicked wintery wind.

CHAPTER 11 – SPOOKED

The vast stables had seen better days. Even in comparison to my shabby room in the grand manor, the condition of the building was disgraceful. Boards were cracking, the door hinges were rusty, and as we entered the space, the stench of rotting refuse bombarded us.

"Good lord," I murmured.

"Annie, why didn't you say anything…" Eleanor whispered to herself.

Most of the stalls were empty but still dirty, offering evidence of their former residents. The only horses who remained were two black and white spotted thoroughbreds, a mare and a stallion, each with matted manes and tails. They kicked belligerently against the backs of their filthy stalls as we approached.

I ran my hand along the edge of the first stall, feeling the deep, uneven grooves that the poor animal had chewed into the wood. I moved along to the second stall, and as I caught the stallion's eye, he calmed down. The wooden walls of his box showed ample evidence of scratching, kicking, and chewing.

"These horses have been neglected," I whispered. "These thoroughbreds were bred to run. They have obviously not been out of these stalls in weeks… possibly months. It's driving them mad." Eleanor reached her hand forward towards the mare, and I reached up and gently stopped her. "She might be dangerous. Both of these horses have been suffering from severe emotional distress."

"I think I can handle myself, Colonel," Eleanor protested with a hint of annoyance. "If you haven't noticed, I deal with emotionally distressed victims every day."

I let go of her arm and watched as she slowly reached her hand towards the mare's mouth. The mare whinnied and bucked, but Eleanor didn't flinch. Instead, she waited for the mare to calm down and continued her movement until she had her hand positioned gently under the mare's chin. She held it there calmly for almost a minute until the mare relaxed, and Eleanor smiled triumphantly. She slowly moved her hand to pet the mare's mangled mane.

"Annie warned me that they've been struggling," Eleanor said with a calm, even tone, keeping her eyes locked on the horse. "When the Baron's health declined, he locked his estate into trusts to keep John from destroying the family's fortune with his dubious business exploits. I think that's why the Fitzgeralds are here, although Annie won't confirm my suspicions. But with the money locked away, Ralph and Annie have used every penny of their own savings to pay for the upkeep of this place. Annie told me that they ran out weeks ago, but the Baron has steadfastly refused to reveal who is named in the will, undoubtedly because he fears for his life if John finds out. It's a wretched situation for everyone, including the horses, it would seem…"

"These horses are not starving. Someone is feeding them, although they don't look healthy," I said as I reached forward to stroke the stallion's mane. "Why would they tell us to bring our riding clothes if there were only two sickly horses to ride?"

"The number of horses is not entirely surprising to me. It was clear from Annie's invitation that this weekend was one of her common plots to end my spinsterhood. I almost said no, except that she sounded genuinely desperate for my company this time around… But how she could let the horses be neglected like this is a different question. It does not take money to clean out their stalls and give them exercise and attention. Annie could have done it herself. She grew up with horses in Yorkshire… How could she possibly be okay with us witnessing these horrific conditions? And yet, she didn't try to keep us away…"

"If Anne knew she wasn't going to ride with us, then her disappointment at breakfast at having to decline was not genuine," I pointed out.

"No. It wasn't. But Annie can be good at putting on a good show," Eleanor said sharply before she caught herself. "Don't get me wrong, Edmund. She's always well-intentioned. But she does have a tendency to cross the line when she thinks she has a good excuse. But *this*. I can't explain this. It's shameful."

"Well, we're not going to go for a leisurely ride," I sighed with disappointment. "Perhaps we should invest our time in improving their circumstances."

I grabbed a shovel, and Eleanor collected a rake that was leaning up against the wall.

"Perhaps you should focus on this area here, and I will do the stalls. It's dangerous to be in there when the horses are in such a state," I suggested.

Eleanor stopped steadfastly in position with a look of obvious displeasure painted across her face, and a burst of anxiety rushed through me at the realization that I had offended her.

"Colonel, I practically grew up in the stables. My father was a thoroughbred trainer. He couldn't keep me away from them, and neither can you."

I was taken aback by her assertiveness. "As you wish, Miss MacLeod," I said with a small bow.

"How about I take the mare, and you take the stallion?" Eleanor suggested with a gentler tone. "I wish we knew their names."

I watched nervously as she opened the door to the mare's stall and entered. She whispered soothingly into the horse's ears and leaned her rake up against the wall in favor of the brush. Starting with small strokes, she began brushing the horse. I decided to follow her lead with the stallion, and together we began the slow process of re-socializing the neglected creatures.

For hours, we fed and watered the horses, shoveled manure, swept out the stalls, replaced the hay, and groomed our wards until finally the stables had returned to a semblance of reasonable condition. At the turn of events, the grateful horses exuded a new sense of cheer, and we let their improved attitudes infuse us.

"Colonel, you are a force to be reckoned with!" Eleanor declared. "I've never seen a more expert approach to stable-cleaning."

"Well, I am a professional," I said as I brushed the last of the hay off of my dirty hands.

"Is that what the army has its colonels up to now?" she teased.

"Only the most senior leaders get the privilege," I quipped as I pulled her into my arms and stole the kiss I'd been fantasizing about for hours.

Eleanor melted into my arms, and we stood for many moments of unadulterated bliss until the stallion interrupted us with a loud humph.

"I think he's telling us to get a room," Eleanor laughed.

"That is a very dangerous proposition," I said as excitement and nerves rushed through me at the delightfully sinful prospect.

"I've always lived on the edge, Colonel." Eleanor winked, and my heart began pumping. "But I believe that we still have some duties to attend to here. Shall we give them some exercise? They seem keen on it, don't you think?"

"Yes, I believe they are," I agreed as I took a deep, calming breath. "We should trot gently or else they might injure themselves after so many sedentary weeks."

"Of course," Eleanor agreed. "Despite my reputation with Annie, I'm not *always* a speed demon."

The horses whinnied happily as we saddled them up, and I worked hard to quell my irrational fear that Eleanor might be in danger as she skillfully lifted herself right up onto the mare's back.

As we trotted into the yard, silent snowflakes fluttered gracefully to the ground where a thick layer of snow had already gathered while we'd been duly occupied inside. The subtle crunch of the horses' hooves on the fresh snow awakened a great nostalgia deep within me for the many cozy winters I'd enjoyed decades earlier, back when my life had been far simpler... and far lonelier. I paused momentarily to contemplate the odd truth that despite my incessant battle against the darkness that the wretched war had unleashed inside of me, my honest friendship with Edward Rutherford, and now my burgeoning affection for Eleanor, were filling a hole in my soul that I hadn't even realized was there.

"How extraordinary!" Eleanor exclaimed. "A snow storm? In October? In Hampshire?!"

"It has snowed here a few times in autumn, but it is very rare."

"How do you know?" Eleanor asked. "Did you memorize the farmer's almanac alongside your Roman verses?"

Now she really had me. In my haphazard web of half-truths, I had barely woven a believable timeline without the four decades I'd spent living just a stone's throw away.

"Ha!" I laughed awkwardly and then launched into my first overt lie. "I meant in England... It snowed a few times in autumn when I was living in Bath in my youth."

"Right..." Eleanor sounded skeptical.

"We'd better get their exercise in before they get too cold."

"You're right. Shall we ride out into the orchards?" Eleanor suggested. "They aren't far. We can inspect the damage that the weather is causing to the fruit."

"I suppose we could harvest some of it for Mr. Kauter. Then we will both be fully qualified to take on new agricultural careers," I suggested jokingly.

"I'll clean out the stables, and you can harvest the fruit," Eleanor winked. "Perhaps we can settle a homestead in New Zealand. I hear they're just giving away the land."

The idea sounded overwhelmingly wonderful. I worked hard to remind myself that she was not suggesting the option seriously.

"I will follow your lead," I offered, eager to make up for my earlier error.

Eleanor smiled, and together we set off at a gentle trot straight towards the freshly frozen orchards.

Despite the steady increase in snowfall, the horses continued enthusiastically and obediently through field after field of bright orange autumnal leaves peeking out from underneath their new layers of white frosting. Eleanor and I rode side by side, taking in the peaceful silence that only ever comes when fresh snow dampens the natural sounds of the crackling earth, until we reached the edge of a grove of withered summer plums.

Both of the horses stopped abruptly and refused to move. I felt the stallion tense with anxiety, and I held the reins with calm authority as he worked hard to follow my command against his primal instincts to run.

"Hold her steady," I whispered to Eleanor with the calmest voice I could muster. "Something's wrong."

"Do you think they're too cold?" Eleanor asked concernedly, completely unaware of the gravity of whatever had silently spooked the stallion. "I suppose we shouldn't have kept them out for so long in this weather. I was enjoying the ride so much that I lost track of time."

Before I could answer her, my stallion bucked. I held on with all of my might, whispering disingenuous reassurances to him as I channeled all of my energy into bringing him back under control. After a moment of resistance, he reluctantly gave in, and I trotted him around Eleanor in a circle.

"Colonel, what's wrong?" Eleanor asked as his fearful outburst demonstrated what I had been unwilling to say.

"He's spooked," I said with an even tone. "There's certainly something wrong here, but I don't know what." I looked around again and took in a deep whiff of the crisp air. There was a faint scent on the wind that I knew only too well... My heart began racing. "Eleanor, I think you should go back to the stables before the mare loses control."

"I most certainly will not!" Eleanor exclaimed. Her mare neighed nervously.

I whispered into my stallion's ear as I carefully disembarked with the intention of tying him up as I investigated the scene, but as soon as my feet hit the ground, he bolted back towards the stables.

At the development, Eleanor's mare bucked, and I rushed to catch her as she barely held on long enough for the mare to return to the ground. Eleanor scrambled off and watched with bewilderment as the mare ran at her top speed to catch up with the stallion.

"They wouldn't do that just because they're cold," she said as they disappeared into the snowy mist.

A subtle puff of her fear infused my nasal cavity, pushing my precarious nerves a dangerous step further.

"No, they wouldn't."

I took her hand into mine, but as both of our hearts began pumping in unison, she stopped and reached up to brace both of my shoulders.

"Colonel, we're safe here. This is England. The war is over. Whatever's wrong, we'll deal with it together. Got it?"

I nodded my reluctant agreement and worked to ignore the nagging feeling that she was managing me with as much feigned confidence as I had used to manage the stallion. I hoped that she would be more successful than I'd been.

We walked slowly into the orchard in the exact direction where the horses had refused to go, when a burst of the dastardly familiar scent bombarded me.

My heart exploded with adrenaline. I looked down and spotted a drop of fresh red blood in the snow.

Eleanor followed my attention until she spotted it too. "Bloody hell, the horses were right! HELLO?" I startled as she began shouting. "Hello? Are you alright? Are you injured? Mr. Kauter?"

Yes! Eleanor was right. Mr. Kauter was surely in the fields trying to save his crops. Perhaps he had injured himself. I forced the mundane explanation—the *benevolent* explanation—to blossom and push out the horrific images of malicious intent that had flooded into my mind.

"Mr. Kauter, I'm a nurse!" Eleanor called. "If you can hear me, please call out!"

"Mr. Kauter?!" I followed her lead. "Mr. Kauter, are you alright? We're here to help!"

Eleanor looked at me with another expression of surprise, but I was fully distracted as a different, more sinister scent worked its way into my nasal cavity: the scent of death. "I think he's very bad off…" I murmured.

"Mr. Kauter!" Eleanor shouted more emphatically.

"Mr. Kauter!" I called.

If he wasn't already dead, I knew that he would be soon.

Against my greatest instincts for avoidance, Eleanor kept my hand glued tightly in hers as we followed the trail of blood. The scent of death taunted me more and more every step until a burst of the disgustingly appetizing aroma knocked me back.

I looked around frantically until I spotted the horrific sight. Many meters beyond us, leaned up against a tree, was the body of a golden-haired young woman in a blood-soaked white nightgown. The frozen soil around the trunk of the tree was entirely red, and beside her, a sparkling karpan stained red with sticky blood shimmered in the muted light.

"Good lord," I murmured. "It tastes like the trenches."

I ripped my hand from her grasp and keeled over, hyperventilating. My stomach growled as the wretched hunger that I had avoided for so long burst forth from deep within me.

"Edmund? Colonel? Are you alright?" Eleanor could not hide her panic.

I closed my eyes. I couldn't look at her. I stumbled away as a fresh burst of her rich spicy fear combined with the ghoulish scent of death to taunt my wretched demon more.

"Death is here." I barely got the words out as I pointed towards the body.

"Good lord," she murmured as her eyes followed my cue. She took a moment to debate between helping me and inspecting the gruesome murder scene. She chose the murder.

Every fiber of my rational being begged me to run, while my demon demanded that I follow her towards the delicious destruction. As my two instincts battled fiercely, I stumbled over to a neighboring tree and sat down, crouching up against it with my face buried in my knees. I worked hard not to listen to her shocked utterances as I took in breath after calming breath to no avail.

Don't lose control. Don't lose control. The war is over. The war is over.
I repeated the mantras religiously in my mind.

After some incalculable amount of time, I smelled Eleanor approach. "It was definitely a murder, and a gory one at that. The poor girl's throat was slashed, and her feet were red with ice burns. She must have been running through the snow barefoot for quite some distance before she was killed," she reported. "The killer appears to have left the murder weapon, so I suppose that means it's probably not a rampage. I wish there were footprints, but the snow has covered everything."

As I looked up at her bloody hands and tasted a fresh mouthful of her fear, I lost my battle. I jumped up and backed away from her.

"Edmund?" she asked nervously.

"I'm sorry," I whispered. "I can't. I just can't!"

And with my shameful admission of utter defeat, I turned away from my beautiful Eleanor and ran.

CHAPTER 12 – IN THE STABLES

My mind raced as I ran faster than I ever had all the way back to the stables, where I found the good horses waiting patiently to be let back into their stalls. Without a coherent thought in my mind, I let them each in and then hid myself away in the empty stall next to the stallion, burying my face in my knees as I leaned up against a bale of fresh hay that I'd placed there during our cleaning session earlier in the day.

I mulled over the gruesome images of the murder scene, while the wicked hunger taunted me. The demon deep inside of me beckoned me to return to the scene of the crime, while the rest of my consciousness screamed and screamed to stay away. My dark voice cackled with delight.

How could you possibly be so stupid to think that you could be with a beautiful creature like Eleanor? With anyone? You do not deserve one hint of love, you worthless, whimpering fiend!

Minutes passed, and then hours, as the frigid air in the stables became so cold that I began to shiver despite my Rakshasa temperament, until my self-flagellation was interrupted by the sound of footsteps crunching in the snow outside.

"Colonel? Edmund? Are you in here?" My heart raced as Eleanor called my name.

I couldn't bring myself to respond, but my shivering body gave me away. I listened to her dainty footsteps as she made her way towards my position, stopping momentarily in each stall to cover each horse with a thick wool blanket.

"Edmund?" she called with her gentlest tone. "Everything is going to be alright. Didn't I say we'd deal with it together?"

She peeked over the stall door, and I finally looked up to face her. She was no longer wearing her riding clothes. I'd been languishing in my own misery for so long that she'd managed to make her way without me from the orchard to the house, deal with whatever copious unpleasantries were required to report the grisly murder, wash off the blood from her hands, and change her clothes into a flattering wintery outfit of grey wool trousers and a loose ivory cashmere sweater, with a thick white rabbit fur collar and a stylish matching coat and hat.

A fresh burst of her spicy fear bombarded my overtaxed senses, but she did not let her emotion show on her face at all. She slowly opened the stall door and approached me with similar care to how she had approached the mare. She removed her sleek leather gloves and placed them in an oversized pocket in her coat, and then reached her slender hands forward to gently brush my disheveled hair out of my eyes.

"You're shaking like a leaf," she said with a feigned calm tone as she felt my forehead and then my neck with her warm hands. I shuddered at the sensation of her soft touch and then returned to my incessant shivering. "Edmund, we must get you back inside. Have you been hiding out here for hours in the freezing cold?" I nodded as my shivers became more violent. "Oh dear..." She furrowed her brow. "You're in shock, and you're hypothermic. We must get you warmed up before this becomes more serious."

I nodded my disagreement. There was no way I could endure John Crowden's antics in my fragile mental state. There had already been one gruesome murder on the property, and I would not let myself be responsible for another.

"I... must... stay... away from them... right now..." I forced the words out through my chattering teeth.

"Why? Why must you stay away? Talk to me, Edmund." She looked straight into my eyes as she took my hands into hers. I shuddered again as her warmth shot through me. "You can tell me anything. I swear to you, whatever it is, I won't tell a soul."

A violent internal debate erupted as my overwhelming desire to be honest with her battled against my gut-wrenching fear of losing her.

"I... don't... know... what I might do in this state..." I admitted. The moment the words came out of my mouth I felt a wave of relief wash over me. I had revealed a truth that I had never once spoken out loud to anyone. "The shell shock... the body... the blood... it brought up too many memories... too many grotesque feelings... I must get myself under control... if John Crowden does something else... I might not have enough restraint..."

"Edmund, darling, you must not let John Crowden's brutish behavior endanger your life."

"I... promise you... you needn't worry... about my health..."

"Your symptoms indicate otherwise, Colonel. Didn't I tell you that I'm not easily fooled?"

I looked searchingly into her kind eyes, and she smiled reassuringly and stroked my cheek. I closed my eyes and breathed in her calm confidence, and when I reopened them, her smile morphed into genuine relief.

"I'm seeing some good progress, Colonel," she said as she squeezed my hands encouragingly.

I took in another deep breath and focused all of my willpower on bringing my shivering under control.

"It is some progress," I conceded. "But I'm not ready to go inside yet."

Eleanor nodded and stood up. My heart skipped as I thought that she might be leaving me alone. Suddenly, the prospect seemed utterly dire.

"Please stay with me," I whispered desperately. "I promise you, Eleanor, I will not freeze out here."

She assessed me skeptically, undoubtedly observing that my chattering teeth and uncontrollable shivering had abated. "As you wish."

She tiptoed out of the stall and then returned with another wool blanket and two dusty bottles of cognac. She wrapped the blanket around my shoulders, bundling me up. She pulled the cork out of one of the bottles and handed it to me. Despite her perfectly-pressed, stylish outfit, she sat down next to me on the dirty ground and leaned back onto the bale of hay. She brought her knees up to match my position.

"We'll start warming you up out here, and when you're ready, we'll go inside."

"How did you find me?" I asked as her sheer presence began to calm my raging nerves.

"When I returned to the house and you weren't inside, I assumed you'd run off to catch your breath. I thought I'd find you with the horses, and lo and behold, I was right. I'm an excellent judge of these things, you know."

"I believe, Miss MacLeod, that you are the cleverest person I've ever met."

I let the novelty of her supportive presence slowly work its way into my tormented soul, and then I took a long swig of the cognac. *Too* long of a swig. Her expression of bemusement morphed into concern as I finished off the entire bottle in one Rakshasa gulp.

"I didn't mean to awaken the beast," she said nervously as I put the empty bottle down next to me on the ground. Her reference threw me straight back into my panic.

"What do you mean by that?" I asked heatedly, unable to rein in my wild emotions.

"Nothing," Eleanor sighed.

I wouldn't let her get away with her unbelievable answer, and I stared her down until she gave in.

"I meant the drink," she said as she reached over me to collect the empty bottle. She held it upside down in front of her to demonstrate her point. "You showed such restraint last night that it didn't occur to me that you'd have a problem with it..." She looked angry at herself as she put it aside. "I shouldn't have brought it."

I breathed in a deep sigh of relief that she was not referring to the true beast that I'd been battling for hours. "I promise you, Eleanor, that you will find me the soberest man in all of England."

"Oh, really? And how might that be, Colonel?"

"Alcohol has never affected me. I have never once been drunk. I don't even know what it feels like."

"Perhaps that was because you were too drunk to remember."

"It wasn't."

She thought long and hard about her response. Then, she opened the second bottle and took a small sip herself.

"We will warm ourselves here while I assess your unlikely assertion with my professional medical perspective," she decided.

"As you wish," I agreed.

We sat side by side in silence for many minutes. The horses whinnied every so often, and Eleanor took several more sips of her cognac.

"My behavior today was shameful." I finally broached my confession. "You should not have had to chase me down like a spooked horse."

"The scene was gruesome, Edmund. I found it overwhelming myself, and I deal with bloody sights every day. It is not at all shameful that you had such a strong reaction. Have you seen anything like it since the war?"

"No."

"I didn't think so. Most men haven't. It's very common to have a relapse of shell shock when faced with such a blatant reminder of your trauma."

I tried my hardest to believe her assertion. Shell shock. It was entirely shell shock. The hunger. The urges. The grotesquely delicious aromas. I had simply been starving in the bloody trenches for too long...

One of the many truths that had been tormenting me for hours worked its way to the surface. "I left you there. I left you alone where a young woman had just been brutally murdered. There was a homicidal maniac on the loose, and I left you there, where no one would hear your screams, to face him without my protection."

Eleanor gave away a subtle sigh of frustration. "Edmund, darling, I've spent thirty-seven fruitful years taking care of myself, and I have far more experience managing homicidal maniacs than I care to think about. Your old-fashioned sense of chivalry is rather endearing, but I assure you that it isn't necessary. We've known each other for less than twenty-four hours. I don't suddenly need you to protect me from the big bad world."

I had no response for her. She put down her bottle and took my hand gently into hers. "Edmund, you focused on protecting yourself. That is exactly what you should have done. You did what you needed to do to get yourself out of a wretched situation. You helped me! You got yourself out of the way so that I could do what

I needed to do. And now, when you're ready, together we have important work to do."

"What do you mean?"

"Are you sure you're ready to dive into our next stressful endeavor?" Eleanor asked seriously. "We have unpleasant tasks ahead of us."

I shifted uncomfortably at the idea of admitting my shameful weakness, but my raw emotions would not let me avoid it. "I can't go back to the scene of the crime. I can't bear the scent of death or blood. I'm quite certain it will send me into another... er... fit."

Eleanor squeezed my hand supportively. "Knowing and respecting one's limitations is an important step to recovery. I'm glad that you're aware of yours. I will be sure to keep you away from the gory evidence. But, Colonel, I do need your help. We need to get to the bottom of this before it's too late."

"This is a matter for the police," I protested.

"The snow has made the roads impassable, and the phone lines are down. We haven't even been able to report the crime yet. We're alone here until the storm clears up, and it's clear to me that we must solve this murder before the police come, or else an innocent man is going to hang for it."

"I didn't do it."

"I didn't mean you, darling. I know you didn't do it."

"How? You've known me for less than twenty-four hours."

"I have impeccable judgment, remember? I don't go around kissing every dashing soldier I meet, you know. You are actually the first who's had the pleasure in many years."

I offered her a weak smile. "I'm grateful for the privilege, although, I don't believe that it's particularly warranted."

"I think you should let me be the judge of that," she countered. "In any case, I'm entirely certain that you are not capable of committing a crime like this. Now, murdering John Crowden on the other hand... anyone is capable of that..." She smiled to indicate her facetious joke, but I didn't find her humor amusing in the slightest. She took my cue and returned to seriousness. "Edmund, my impeccable judgment aside, you couldn't have committed this murder. You and I were certainly together when it happened. The body was still warm when we arrived at the scene of the crime. The poor girl could not have been dead for more than ten or twenty minutes in the freezing weather. Remember how fresh the blood was?"

"I can't forget," I whispered.

"Yes… yes, I suppose you can't…" Eleanor thought more carefully about her next revelation. "After you ran away, I inspected the scene again for more physical evidence, in case the murderer were to return in my absence to clean up after himself. When I had all that I could glean, I ran back to the house to report the crime. Mr. Banning, Lord Crowden's solicitor, was there, along with the rest of this weekend's illustrious party, and I was unable to prevent a macabre fanfare as they all insisted on joining Mr. Banning and me to inspect the scene again. Well, except for Ralph. I believe he locked himself in his bedroom, rather wisely, I suspect, given your reaction… In any event… the scene was untouched when we returned, although several inches of more snow had fallen. It took all of Lord Blakeney's authority to keep the group from contaminating the evidence."

"Did they know who the girl was?"

"Yes. Her name was Ingrid Kauter, Mr. Kauter's only child. She was a scullery maid in the house. She was only eighteen."

"Good lord," I murmured.

"It gets worse." Eleanor took another sip of her cognac. "She was pregnant, Edmund. About four months, maybe four and a half. She was at just the point at which it would have become impossible to hide it."

"John Crowden…" I closed my eyes and took a deep, calming breath as I worked to control my base urge to rush straight back to the house to kill the worthless bastard with my bare hands.

Eleanor sensed my struggle and squeezed my hand. "It's not that simple. As of yet, there is no evidence to link John Crowden to the crime. Mr. Rana's sword was found covered in the victim's blood at the scene. Mr. Banning insisted that we keep him locked in the library for further questioning, and John and Mr. Fitzgerald were only too willing to oblige."

"Bloody hell. Mr. Rana did not murder that girl." I was certain of my conclusion, despite having no evidence but my hundred years of intuition about men's characters to go on.

"I agree. All of the rational evidence points against it. He is not a stupid man, nor is he a sociopath, and it would make no logical sense for him to leave a weapon that every person in the household knows is his right next to the body of his victim."

"He is a good man," I added less scientifically. "He wouldn't do anything of the sort."

"He also has a solid alibi for the time of the murder. He was in the house, seen by many people during the time that it must have been committed."

"Then why is he locked up? This was obviously an attempt to frame him." I worked hard to curtail my burgeoning anger at the nefarious plot.

"I will give you one guess, Colonel. They have his weapon and his race to wield against him, and they will not take my feminine word on the forensic evidence. They want a doctor to confirm the time of death, and until one can get here, they will not accept my assertion about his alibi."

"Fools," I muttered.

"Even the best of men prove themselves to be fools in the face of a scandal like this one," Eleanor shrugged. "I can't say I'm surprised by their reactions, but it's frustrating all the same."

"The blood was fresh," I reiterated. "That corpse had not been rotting for half a day. The scent of fresh death is completely unique, and I know it far too well."

"I agree. I know the nuances well myself from my years in the trauma hospital in France. But the victim was wearing a nightgown, so even Mr. Banning is rather insistent that she must have been murdered in the middle of the night, when almost none of us have good alibis, including Mr. Rana. We have a loud chorus of unfounded speculation to combat, Colonel. And only you can take control of the situation."

"Me?!" I exclaimed. "I can't!"

"Someone on this property right now *murdered* that girl, Edmund. We have to find out who it was! You are an active colonel in the British Army. You have a lot of authority here. Take it. Use it before it's too late."

"I can't just declare martial law," I argued.

Eleanor couldn't contain her passion. "But, Edmund, you know how these inquests go! Especially in a gruesome case like this one! The public will demand justice, and if we don't offer them the real murderer, Mr. Rana will hang for the crime. You don't have to declare martial law. Mr. Banning, Ralph, Anne, and that odd Lord Blakeney will surely defer to your judgment because of your rank. With their support, you will have enough authority to override John Crowden's shenanigans! And, Edmund, it is a likely possibility that he is the murderer! We must prove it! You know as well as I do that the local police will not dare to accuse the next Baron of Heathfield of anything, let alone a scandalous murder like this, unless there is indisputable evidence!"

"I don't have the faintest idea how to investigate a crime like this. I don't want to make things worse."

Eleanor's patience was waning. "Colonel, if we don't do anything, the murderer will win, and an innocent man will die. I'm not going to let that happen, and I believe that you won't either.

132

Either way, I'm going to get to the bottom of this. You can help me or not."

I paused for a long moment before giving in. "I will help you."

Eleanor smiled and hopped up. She held out her hand to me, and I took it and pulled myself up.

"Walk a straight line for me, Colonel," Eleanor ordered. "We can't have any drunken incidents sullying our impeccable investigatory record."

I obliged her request and walked my straight line.

"Have I proven my unlikely assertion to be true?" I asked cheekily.

"You have," Eleanor smiled, but then she became serious. "You must be a leader now, Edmund. An innocent man's life is in your hands. I will stand by your side and so will everyone else who's reasonable. You must be steadfast when John tries to thwart you."

I nodded my agreement, pushing back a fresh burst of raging nerves at the prospect of returning to command. I'd lost so many innocent lives under my command already… their faces threatened to overwhelm my mind's eye, but Eleanor grabbed my hand and yanked me out of it.

"We will solve it together, Edmund. One step at a time."

CHAPTER 13 – THE INVESTIGATION BEGINS

Eleanor gently removed her hand from mine as we approached the front steps of the manor house.

"I will be by your side every step of the way," she reminded me with a reassuring smile.

Despite her kind support, my rage at the injustice of the situation mixed dangerously with my virulent anxiety as I pushed open the front door. As several sets of footsteps stirred from various disparate locations inside the house, I straightened my posture and focused all of my remaining energy on exuding a false sense of calm authority, just as I had done so many times throughout my many years of command.

"Colonel!" Anne exclaimed as she escorted Ralph to greet us. "We were worried sick about you!"

Ralph looked distinctly ill. His face was a deathly color of white and his lips were an ashen grey, similar to the color they had turned the night before when his coughing fit had suffocated him.

"Colonel Marriner went back to the stables to tend to the horses. They were spooked when we came upon the body, and it took him some effort to wrangle them," Eleanor lied on my behalf.

"That took a long time," Ralph observed.

I worked hard to keep a calm demeanor as I responded. "Yes, well, I needed a bit of time to gather my wits about me. The gruesome scene brought back... er... unpleasant memories that I've been working to forget."

"Yes... I suppose it must have..." Ralph conceded. "I'm sorry, Colonel."

"Well, I've taken the time I needed, and now I'm here. Where is Mr. Banning? It sounds like we have a murder to solve." I pushed forward confidently.

"Didn't Eleanor tell you?" Anne asked with surprise. "We already caught the murderer! Mr. Rana is locked away in the library until we can get the police here."

"Yes, Eleanor did tell me that, but I fear, Mrs. Crowden, that the situation is not so simple."

A door at the very end of the dark hallway screeched open and slammed closed, and an elderly gentleman in a very proper suit with a full head of thick white hair and a pair of atrociously thick spectacles clipped to his nose rushed to greet me.

"Mr. Banning, I presume?" I reached out my hand for a friendly shake as he looked up at me. I was almost two feet taller than his diminutive stature.

"Colonel Marriner!" He shook my hand excitedly. "I've been wanting to meet you for a long time!"

I was puzzled. "Has Ralph been talking about me all over the village?"

Mr. Banning exploded into jovial laughter. I tried to embrace his cheer, although under the circumstances it felt particularly inappropriate.

"No, no. I had no idea I'd have the pleasure of meeting you in person when Mr. Crowden called me over this morning. No, I've been wanting to meet the heroic native son of Basingstoke who earned the Victoria Cross for years now. We all have! It was on the front page of *The Hampshire Register* when the king gave you your medal."

I was at an utter loss.

"Native son?" Eleanor asked curiously on my behalf. I was too confused about the misunderstanding to be appropriately concerned at the imminent revelation.

"Oh, no need to be coy, Colonel. I knew your grandfather! Mr. Marriner was a wonderful man. So kind and charitable. I did work on his property as a boy, and he paid me in books! Can you imagine? They must have been worth a small fortune! It's a good thing I didn't realize that at the time, or else I might have sold them instead of reading them. Because of him I became a solicitor instead of a butcher! I see you inherited his height. You look very similar to him, in fact..." He exploded into awkward laughter. "That's how these things go in families, I suppose. Why, my niece is just the spitting image of her mother..."

"Colonel, I didn't know you were from Basingstoke!" Anne exclaimed. "What an extraordinary coincidence!"

My mind raced. My 'grandfather' to which Mr. Banning was referring was certainly me in my decrepit aged state. I assessed his age quickly. He looked to be in his late sixties, which would have put his childhood in about the 1860s... when I would have appeared to be in my fifties...

I squinted in a vain effort to recognize him. Over the years I had solicited the help of many village children for various odd jobs, and I had paid all of them in books that were worth far more than the shillings they'd requested in the idealistic hope of encouraging their educations... It seemed in his case that perhaps my plan had worked. My delight at the development mixed strangely with my discomfort at the precarious situation. I realized suddenly that this man must have known me when I looked exactly the same as I did at that moment...

I shifted uncomfortably as I glanced from face to beaming face of my thrilled audience, and then to Eleanor who looked far more puzzled than the rest of them. The timeline of half-truths I'd spun for her did not accommodate this scenario in the slightest.

"I... er... didn't know my grandfather very well. I spent my childhood in India... but I hear he was a good man... a painter, I believe?"

"Oh yes. He was a wonderful painter. He even presented at the Royal Academy!" Mr. Banning said excitedly. "He tried to teach me how to paint once. I was useless at it, but he was very patient."

"Did he?" I had not taught very many of the village children how to paint. Perhaps three or four in the many years I'd lived there. "Might I ask your first name, Mr. Banning?" I simply couldn't resist. I realized as my tone gave away too much enthusiasm that I was entering very dangerous territory. It would be unreasonable for me to know the first name of a child who had spent time with my estranged grandfather sixty years earlier.

"Thomas," he said with a friendly smile. "Thomas Banning."

"It's nice to meet you, Tommy." I shook his hand again. I did remember him. The idea that the slightly daft but tenacious young boy whom I'd mentored for a bit was the old man standing before me reiterated once again the gravity of my real age difference with the youngsters around me. Once again, I worked hard to push the lonely thought from my mind.

"I did go by Tommy as a boy..." he contemplated out loud.

"I think many a boy named Thomas has gone by Tommy over the years." I winked and then plowed forward, changing the subject. "Now, Mr. Banning, we have serious matters to attend to."

"Yes... yes, of course," he agreed.

"There has been a gruesome murder of a young woman on this property, and Miss MacLeod tells me that we are unable to call the police."

"Yes, the phone lines have been down for hours. We haven't seen this kind of snow in decades."

I nodded my acknowledgment. "I reckon that the snow is a blessing and a curse. While it will delay the arrival of the official investigators, it will also keep the murderer in our midst. Time is of the essence."

"Oh, we've already caught him!" Mr. Banning reported eagerly. "He's locked in the library!"

"Who is locked in the library?" My game was about to begin.

"Why, Mr. Rana, of course!"

"I see." I took in my audience again, and then made my first move. "Miss MacLeod tells me that Mr. Rana was seen tending to his duties inside the house by numerous people at the time of the murder."

Mr. Banning threw an annoyed look at Eleanor. She gazed back at him indignantly.

"Well, was Mr. Rana seen inside the house this afternoon?" I pressed.

"He was, Colonel," Ralph said quietly. "He was tending to our meeting with Mr. Banning all afternoon. He wasn't away from us for longer than ten minutes."

"You saw him too?" I raised my eyebrows as I addressed Mr. Banning.

"I saw him this afternoon," Mr. Banning conceded. "But the girl was in her nightgown! No one saw Mr. Rana in the middle of the night! That was when he must have killed her!"

"I see. Did Miss MacLeod walk you through the physical evidence at the crime scene? I was under the impression that she informed you that the body was fresh when we found it in late afternoon. Miss MacLeod was a trauma nurse in the VAD. She has extensive professional experience assessing these things."

Eleanor threw me a grateful smile, and I worked hard to hide my thrill at her appreciation.

"Well, surely we need a *doctor* to make that official determination," Mr. Banning scoffed, as his enthusiasm dissolved.

"Mr. Banning, Miss MacLeod and I were out riding in the orchards when we came upon the body. The blood was fresh in the new fallen snow. The corpse was still warm. Do you think that after four years as a commander in the trenches, I would not be able to tell the difference between a freshly dead corpse and one that had been rotting for at least ten hours? That is how long it would have had to be there for the murder to have been committed before anyone stirred in the morning. Correct?"

He humphed.

"And if we are talking about a murder in the middle of the night, it would have been there for at least twelve hours, maybe even fifteen or sixteen. I don't think that we need to wait for a doctor to confirm these basic details of the timeline before we continue on with our wider investigation, do you?"

"But... but... the murder weapon, Colonel! That bloody oriental sword was right next to the body! Mr. Rana admitted it was his!"

I could sense that poor Tommy was slipping into a defensive position. "Yes... yes, it is curious. I agree. Certainly it is a detail that warrants further investigation. But tell me this, Mr. Banning: If you were the murderer, and everyone in this house knew that you carried that unique sword, would you have left it there next to your handiwork for all the world to see?"

"I wouldn't, but these foreigners always do bizarre things. They have no logic!" Mr. Banning exclaimed. "Maybe he *wanted* us to know that he did it! I read once about a Hindustani man who killed three women in one day just for the fun of it! He hung them outside his house!"

I was stunned and saddened by the extent of young Tommy's ignorance, and I worked extra hard to keep my tone from demonstrating the condescension I was feeling.

"Remind me, Mr. Banning, how many women do they believe Jack the Ripper killed in the streets of London?"

"I don't see how that is related to this conversation at all," Mr. Banning replied haughtily.

My sadness at his response intensified. "Mr. Banning, I've commanded scores of 'foreigners' in India over the years. I can assure you that their logic or lack thereof is just as diverse as that of any population, including Britain's. I have found Mr. Rana to be a thoroughly logical person, and I intend to treat him as such. Now, I will be taking charge of this investigation until the storm passes and we can call in the police. There is a murderer on this property as we speak, and there is a strong possibility that he is not Mr. Rana. I will interview Mr. Rana and everyone else in due course."

"Let me help you then, Colonel!" Tommy exclaimed. "I've read every single Sherlock Holmes story!"

I was surprised by his quick change in tenor, and completely torn. I had admired Tommy's tenacity so much in his youth that I'd taken him on as a bit of a project, but this man before me, after fifty more years of living in the complicated real world, had clearly lost the drive for finding the truth that I'd worked so hard to instill in him. A deep desire to help him tap into his inner intelligence battled with the pragmatic reality of the situation. This was not about helping young Tommy. It was about finding the evidence necessary to prosecute a brutal and conniving murderer. I did not need him meddling in an investigation that would determine the life or death of an innocent man.

"Thank you for your generous offer, Mr. Banning, but Miss MacLeod will assist me."

Tommy snorted with laughter until he realized I was serious. "Surely, Colonel, you need the help of a level-headed man by your side." An air of disbelief at my rejection rang through loud and clear in his voice.

"Mr. Banning, I need the help of a level-headed *person* for this, and Miss MacLeod has already proven herself on that front many times over. Now, if I'm not mistaken, you came here for a reason? Have you completed your business with the Baron's estate?"

"I can't discuss it," Mr. Banning said with a distinct pout.

"Please come, Mr. Banning," Anne said quietly. "Colonel Marriner is right. We weren't finished with our important business when Eleanor interrupted us with the horrible news, and time is of the utmost essence." She took ahold of Ralph's arm and indicated for Mr. Banning to follow her. "Let us know when you need us for our interviews, Colonel. Thank you for helping us. It's a shame, just a crying shame, what happened to that poor girl."

I caught a distinct eye roll from Eleanor.

"Mr. Banning, I would be grateful if you could provide me with the key to the library," I called before they disappeared down the hallway. Mr. Banning muttered to himself and then looked to Anne and Ralph. Ralph offered a weak nod. Mr. Banning shrugged and pulled the old-fashioned key from his pocket.

"Thank you, Tommy," I said as I took the key and mustered a half-hearted polite smile. "Do you remember what my grandfather always used to say?"

Mr. Banning was startled by the question.

"When the voice of reason remains silent..." I prompted him with the first half of the quote that the man I thought was my father had told to me on the fateful day of my first re-set in 1840. I had spouted the quote incessantly for decades to every child who crossed my path.

"It creates a void for others to fill," he whispered.

142

I smiled genuinely. "Let us be the voice of reason together, Mr. Banning. Shall we?"

"Yes, yes, I suppose," he finally agreed. Then he turned away from me and sulked his way back to the office where Ralph and Anne were waiting.

As soon as he was out of sight, I held up the key in my hand and smiled at my first small triumph. "Now, Miss MacLeod, shall we talk to Mr. Rana?"

"The surprises never end with you, do they, Edmund?" Eleanor asked with wonder.

"No, they really don't," I confessed simply.

"I can't wait for the next one," Eleanor smiled. "Now, let's go rescue an innocent man from the gallows. Shall we?"

CHAPTER 14 – MR. RANA

Mr. Rana was seated in one of the deep leather chairs where Eleanor and I had enjoyed our cognac on the prior evening. He didn't move as we entered the library, but he slowly looked up and offered us a defeated smile.

"Have they come for me yet?" His voice was husky and belabored.

"I am taking over the investigation until further notice," I informed him. "I am committed to discovering the real murderer before the police arrive, and I do not believe that it is you."

"You are in the minority, Colonel. The others are eagerly awaiting my execution." He closed his eyes and his head dropped down, as if he had suddenly fallen asleep.

"Mr. Rana?" Eleanor asked as she approached his position. He looked up at her with wide, glassy eyes. "Mr. Rana, what's wrong? You look ill."

She kneeled down and waved her hand in front of his face, observing his heavily dilated pupils as he struggled to follow her movement with his eyes.

"I feel… odd," he said with a look of subtle confusion in his expression. "I've felt odd all day. Since Lord Blakeney arrived. When he rang at the front door this morning, I couldn't get up. I was paralyzed for many minutes, and when I finally got my body up out of bed, my limbs were too heavy. They are still too heavy now."

Eleanor felt his forehead and then his neck, and then moved on to his wrist. She grimaced. "Your pulse is dangerously slow. Your pupils are dilated. Have you taken any medication in the last twenty-four hours?"

"None."

Eleanor lifted up his arm and let go. It dropped with a thud back into his lap. "Well, something unnatural has happened to you. You should lie down at once."

She nodded to me, and I took her cue and helped Mr. Rana up and over to the couch where I'd slept all night. He protested weakly as I helped him lie down, but without the energy to fight me on it, he quickly gave in.

"Have you eaten anything today?" Eleanor asked.

"Nothing. I didn't have the time."

"Well, that is certainly not helping the situation. You need to get something into your stomach. Where can we get something for you to eat?"

"You can ask Mrs. Murray."

Eleanor hopped up and scurried to the bells by the door, but Mr. Rana nodded his disagreement. "Do you think that Mrs. Murray will answer the call of a murderer? They all know that I'm in here."

"Right. Edmund, you stay here and question Mr. Rana. I will get some tea and digestives from the kitchen." Eleanor did not wait for our approval or acknowledgement before rushing out of the room and slamming the door behind her.

"You were right, Colonel," Mr. Rana said with a sleepy smile.

"About what?" I took a seat in the chair beside him.

"I have never appreciated the tenacity of a modern woman more than I appreciated Miss MacLeod's today. If I manage to escape the gallows, I will have her to thank for it."

I looked towards the door where Eleanor had exited and then concentrated on switching our conversation into Punjabi. "That woman has helped me more in twenty-four hours than scores of doctors have been able to in four years." I sighed lovingly. "She has an exceptional strength about her, doesn't she? As if absolutely nothing fazes her."

"She is very strong. You are right. But you must protect her, Colonel. John Crowden has no moral fiber, and he never has. I have watched that boy reap sadistic pleasure from tormenting those weaker than him for thirty years. If he thinks that he isn't winning this ghoulish game and that she is at fault, she will be in grave danger."

"So you think that John Crowden is our man?"

"Yes. He has threatened to ruin me since he was a boy, and John Crowden often fulfills his threats. I've been waiting for the axe to drop for decades."

I imagined the extreme annoyance the poor man must have felt enduring the abuse of an unworthy child without any reasonable recourse. "You are free to speak candidly, Mr. Rana. I will not share what you say with a soul."

Mr. Rana nodded his agreement.

"Why did you stay with the Baron after it was clear that his heir was a monster? Surely he would have supported you with a strong reference if you'd wanted to return to India."

Mr. Rana sighed and closed his eyes. "I thought about it from time to time. But the Baron was a good man, Colonel. He was one of the best *firangs* I ever encountered—so concerned with justice and truth. Not dissimilar to you in many ways. He was the only British judge in India who would give an Indian the benefit of the doubt. People like that need to be supported, for they are the warriors who will combat the armies of ignorance. He earned my loyalty, and I wasn't willing to let John Crowden ruin that. Perhaps I shouldn't have been so idealistic, but I'm old enough now. I've lived a good life."

"What a shame that John Crowden turned out as he did," I murmured.

Mr. Rana glanced towards the door and then lowered his voice, despite our cloak of the foreign tongue. "John Crowden was a shame to all of us, including the Baron. He was such a monster that his mother refused to have another child. Ralph, I do believe, was an accident. His mother was quite old when he was born. Almost forty. She died the next day, leaving the Baron with a baby and a bully. The tragedy was overwhelming."

"Do you think that affected his treatment of Ralph? Did John blame him for her death? That would certainly explain his antagonistic behavior."

Mr. Rana considered the idea. "It certainly didn't help, but it was not so simple. John Crowden was rotten the moment he came out of the womb, to his mother and to everyone else. He tormented the household with incessant colic for months. The family went through scores of nannies. By the time he could walk and think, he was the cleverest of little boys, but he put all of his intelligence towards nefarious ends. Nothing is different about him today, except that the drugs and alcohol have slowed him down a bit. It's horrible to say, but I have hoped to find him dead from an overdose for years now."

"Do you think that he drugged you and stole your karpan while you were sleeping?" As soon as the idea entered my head, it seemed like the most likely scenario.

"I am certain that he stole my karpan in the night. It was in my room with the rest of my uniform when I went to bed, and it was missing this morning when I woke up."

148

I thought back to his odd demeanor earlier in the morning, and suddenly it made perfect sense. "You were looking for your karpan in the library earlier today…"

"Yes, I looked everywhere to no avail. I feel naked without it, Colonel. I assumed, given his exceptionally childish behavior this week, that John had stolen it as a prank, which he has been known to do over the years. Once, when he was a teenager, he snuck into my room and cut my hair."

My eyes bulged at the horrific image. I knew from my many years commanding Sikh regiments how sacred they considered their unshorn hair. Certainly, growing up in a household with a father who valued Mr. Rana's culture, John Crowden would have known it too.

"I had never felt burning rage like that before. I would have killed him that night if I'd gotten my hands on him. I was extremely lucky that the Baron was such a forgiving man. As I chased that little fiend down the hallway, the Baron interrupted us, demanding to know what had happened. John laughed and threw my stolen hair into the air. I don't think I have ever seen the Baron more outraged." Mr. Rana smiled. "I waited in the yard as right then, in the dead of night, the Baron himself strapped John up in the stables and whipped him. I relished every pained scream that resonated from that boy's terrified being. His hatred for me has been tenfold ever since."

"And you think his hatred for you is strong enough that he would frame you for murder?"

"Yes. Although, I did not think him courageous enough to commit a murder until today. He is usually just an antagonistic coward. That's why I was not so concerned when my karpan was missing. I didn't think he had it in him to do something so gory."

"Do you have any evidence that John was the one who stole the karpan?"

Mr. Rana sighed with disappointment. "Nothing that would matter to a jury. I didn't see him steal it. Although, even if I did, I'm certain they wouldn't take my word against his."

"Yes, you're right," I agreed. I worked hard to not be discouraged. Our conversation, while interesting, had provided nothing useful for clearing Mr. Rana's name. As I mulled over the situation in my head, a scratch at the door brought me straight to attention, and I hopped up to investigate.

When I opened the door, Eleanor was there, bearing a large silver tea service with two enormous steaming pots of tea. Pain was written across her face as her arms shook with the weight of the tray.

"Let me help you!" I exclaimed as she handed it over gratefully.

She shivered as her hand brushed against mine. "Thank you, Colonel. Mrs. Murray wasn't in the kitchen, so I helped myself. I didn't realize how heavy the silver would be."

I whisked it over to the coffee table and then helped Mr. Rana sit up. The steam enticed me as I poured him the first cup.

"One of these teapots is for you, Edmund. We were distracted from our important task of warming you up," Eleanor said as she kneeled down beside me.

She poured me a cup of tea, and I couldn't stop myself from drinking it down in one Rakshasa gulp.

"That's a good start." She smiled as she poured me another. As the warmth shot through my frigid limbs, I couldn't resist, and I quickly drank down my next serving.

Eleanor poured herself a cup, but as her hand brushed up against mine again, she startled.

"How extraordinary!" she exclaimed. "You're warmed through and through, Edmund!" She felt my neck and then my forehead. "I've never seen anything like it!"

"How are you feeling, Mr. Rana?" I quickly changed the subject.

"A bit better. Thank you," he said as he took a small sip.

Eleanor looked into his eyes. "Your pupils are still dilated. You've certainly been drugged. You said that you haven't taken any medications in the last twenty-four hours?"

"I don't take any medications," Mr. Rana replied as his color began to return.

"You're already looking better, but you're still severely dehydrated. You should drink water when you're finished with the tea." Eleanor felt his pulse again and relaxed slightly. "The drugs must have been slipped into something you ate or drank. Recount for me, please, everything you've consumed in the last twenty-four hours."

"Last night I ate a mutton korma in the kitchen after I saw to the Baron's nightly medications and before I escorted the colonel to bed. Mrs. Murray always saves a bit for me from the batches she makes for the Baron—he has only been willing to eat creamy Punjabi curries for months now, ever since he became bedridden. When I was finished, I drank my nightly chai, and that was it."

"Who prepares your nightly chai? Where is it kept?" Eleanor's tone became sharp as she strengthened her investigation.

"Mrs. Murray leaves it on the stove for me to drink after my supper. I always eat after the Baron has gone to bed, and usually Mrs. Murray has retired by that time as well. Last night was no different."

"Did the korma or the chai taste any different last night?" Eleanor pushed.

"Come to think of it, the chai tasted a bit off. I assumed that the cream had gone off and that Mrs. Murray had used it anyway due to the... er... financial difficulties facing the household at the moment."

"Well, that seems like a good lead!" Eleanor said encouragingly. "Where is your cup now? It's not in your room, is it?"

"No. I washed my own dishes after I finished my meal so that Mrs. Murray wouldn't be left with them. I always do it that way."

Eleanor's enthusiasm deflated.

"Does anyone know this ritual of yours?" I asked. "Does John know it?"

"I don't think so," Mr. Rana said disappointedly. "I don't think John has entered the kitchen in decades."

"Perhaps we need to pinpoint the source of the drugs," Eleanor thought out loud. "Do you know what kinds of medication John takes? Could he have fed you his own medication to knock you out?"

"I don't think so. The only drug John uses is cocaine." I raised my eyebrows at his nonchalant revelation of the scandalous detail. "You will find the evidence in his watch—that is where he keeps his supply for immediate use. Sometimes he keeps a back-up supply in a cigar box in the back of his wardrobe. But from my observations of his behavior, cocaine makes one wild and frenetic. Whatever has been done to me is rather the opposite."

"Yes, you're right," Eleanor agreed. "This is not cocaine… It seems more like a sleeping tonic. Does anyone in the household use sleeping drugs?"

"The Baron does. I give him his medications myself. But I locked his door after I left him for the night. He and I are the only ones with the keys to his room."

I was finding the path of questioning discouraging. "What if the keys were stolen in the middle of the night? Was your door locked and bolted?"

"It was neither. I never keep my door locked, in case someone needs me in the night."

"That means that anyone in the household could have easily stolen your karpan..." I whispered. His situation was sounding more dire with every answer.

"You said that you didn't consume anything after your supper and chai, right?" Eleanor interjected. "You must have been drugged before you went to bed. Someone stealing the keys to the Baron's room after you were drugged wouldn't have done any good. That means that some form of subterfuge must have happened earlier in the evening."

"Yes... yes, you're right..." I conceded.

Eleanor nodded and continued on with her theorizing. "So, the most likely scenario is that someone drugged your chai, you went to bed on an unreasonably high dose of sleeping medication with which you have since been struggling all day, and while you were knocked out, they snuck into your room and stole your karpan, with the explicit plan of framing you for the premeditated murder of Miss Ingrid Kauter. Tell me this, Mr. Rana: What is your relationship like with Mrs. Murray?"

"Cordial. We have worked together for twenty years," Mr. Rana replied. "We show each other all the due respect."

"Do you like her?" Eleanor pushed.

"We do not socialize," Mr. Rana replied. "I like her as much as anyone likes their colleagues."

"In my experience, that depends on the colleague," Eleanor winked.

Mr. Rana sighed his concession. "Mrs. Murray is a typical Brit. She finds me frighteningly foreign, as do almost all of them. She has done an admirable job of ignoring her discomfort over the years. I do not believe that she drugged me and framed me for murder, if that is what you are contemplating."

"She did have the most obvious means," Eleanor countered. "But you're certain that she didn't have a motive? What was her relationship with John? Could they have been working together?

Or perhaps, might he have pressured her to do something that she otherwise wouldn't do?"

Mr. Rana thought more carefully about her question. "She detests John as much as the rest of the staff does. I do not know of anything that she is hiding, but she and I do not discuss our personal lives. I suppose it is possible that John learned of something he could use to blackmail her. Although, that would have required more mental acuity on his part than I have seen in recent years."

"Hrm… so it is possible that Mrs. Murray was involved, but we are still missing the motive…" Eleanor whispered to herself. "What about Ingrid? How did she interact with the household?"

Mr. Rana looked pained. "She was a nice girl. A tragic girl. I'm sorry that she's dead."

"What do you mean by tragic?" Eleanor asked with piqued interest.

Mr. Rana shifted uncomfortably.

"Please, Mr. Rana. We must give her justice," Eleanor implored.

He lowered his voice. "She was very beautiful. Too beautiful. Every man who came across her appreciated her physicality. But she had no prospects, even before the war. Her family was destitute and decidedly foreign. After the war, her life was very difficult. Everyone in the village still believes that the Kauters are German."

"Why do you think they didn't move back to Switzerland?" I chimed in.

"I don't know. Mr. Kauter has been here for almost twenty years. All that he has is here." At the thought of Mr. Kauter, Mr. Rana suddenly panicked. "Colonel, you must go to Mr. Kauter. He lives in a cottage on the other side of the orchards. It is the only one, so you can't miss it. No one has informed him of the tragedy. Someone must go before he discovers the body for himself."

"Yes… we must go," Eleanor agreed as she stood up. She leaned forward and assessed Mr. Rana's condition. "Your color is returning. Drink the rest of the tea and eat all of the digestives you can stomach. Your body must have some fodder for battling the effects of the sleeping drugs."

He nodded his agreement as she drank down her last sip of tea, and I quickly poured myself the remnants from my teapot and gulped them down.

At the prospect of re-entering the orchards, a sudden bout of paralyzing fear overwhelmed me. "I don't know if we should leave the house. We must make sure that John does not escape."

"Lord Blakeney is already taking care of that," Eleanor reassured me. "While you were away in the stables, he agreed with my assessment of Mr. Rana's alibi and offered to guard John on our behalf. He's done a surprisingly skillful job of it all day."

"I'm glad he came," I agreed. "Although, we should interview him as well. I don't even know his real name. There is a story there that might be relevant to our investigation."

"Is his name not Lord Blakeney?" Eleanor asked with surprise. "I thought you knew him!"

"When he arrived he said his name was Sir Percy Blakeney." I waited for her to laugh, but instead she took in the intel seriously. "He was thrown off when I pointed out that his secret identity is the name of the Scarlet Pimpernel. He seemed completely unaware of the reference. I suggested that he change his name to Lord Blakeney so that John would be more likely to mind him."

"Why didn't you demand to know his real name? He could be anyone!" Eleanor exclaimed. "He's been guarding John all day! What if they're in it together?!"

I paused to contemplate my grave error. Eleanor was right. I'd been so eager to accept the mysterious stranger's help in managing John Crowden that I hadn't demanded even the slightest evidence of his true identity.

"But the letter from the Baron that Mr. Rana sent out…" I trailed off. "Good lord. John could have planted that letter… You're right. It is possible they're in it together… But earlier today, when I was in the hallway with John and Lord Blakeney interceded, John was genuinely surprised by Lord Blakeney's strict punishment…" I turned to Mr. Rana. "Do you think his surprise was an act? Is John Crowden capable of such skilled deception?"

"No. He never has been. He has never felt the need to hide his misbehavior. He prefers to taut it," Mr. Rana replied.

"That was my impression as well…" My mind worked to incorporate the mystery of Lord Blakeney into the bigger picture of our investigation.

"Well, first things first," Eleanor pushed forward. "We must talk to Mr. Kauter. He must know what has happened, and we must get his intel. If Ingrid had a young man, maybe her father knew about it. That person, in the household or not, would be a prime suspect given the circumstances. You did not know of a young man in her life, did you, Mr. Rana?"

He shifted uncomfortably again. "Not one specifically, no."

I could tell that he was holding something back. "Mr. Rana?"

"No. I did not know of a young man." This was the first time since I'd met Mr. Rana that he'd told a lie in my presence. I debated how to proceed, and decided to leave it. The man had been so open, his quick change indicated that he was certainly protecting someone, and I believed that an overt approach would only lead him into a more defensive position.

"Alright. Let's go talk to Mr. Kauter," I said as I indicated for Eleanor to follow me to the door.

"Thank you both for your help," Mr. Rana said as he looked to each of us. "My life is in your hands."

"We will do what we can," Eleanor smiled. I worked hard to let her pull me along into her calm confidence again.

156

"Protect her, Colonel. Remember what I said," Mr. Rana addressed me in Punjabi.

"I will do what I can," I replied stealthily in the foreign tongue. "Protect yourself, as well, Mr. Rana. Do you have anywhere to go if John attempts a violent attack against you? When he learns that I've released you from the library, there's no telling what he might do. He could begin to panic, which could make him very dangerous."

"I have nowhere to go," Mr. Rana replied. "But this isn't America. I'm grateful to live in a country without lynch mobs."

"Yes... I suppose... Still, the murder was brutal. Someone who did that to an innocent girl could certainly do something similar again, especially if threatened..." I could not rid my mind of the horrific images of the murder scene. In a rash move, certainly brought on by my heightened emotions, I reached into my pocket and pulled out a small, archaic keyring that I always kept with me. Eleanor watched curiously as I took the smallest key off and closed it into Mr. Rana's hand. "You know the big stone manor on the hill overlooking the village?" Mr. Rana nodded his agreement. "It's mine. This is the key. It hasn't been opened in many years, but you can go there if you need to hide. I will help you when I can."

Mr. Rana took the key and carefully placed it in his pocket. "Thank you, Colonel. I don't know what to say. It has been a very long time since I've met anyone with such exceptional virtue."

"May it not be the last," I winked. I closed my eyes and concentrated on returning to English to address Eleanor. "Let's take the horses to find Mr. Kauter. Time is of the essence."

"Indeed it is, Colonel," Eleanor agreed as she eyed Mr. Rana and dropped into a whisper. "Are you going to tell me what that was about?"

"Time is of the essence," I refused.

"Alright, Colonel. Let's go," she shrugged. "Just remember, I'm not easily fooled."

I took in a deep, calming breath, and for the first time I realized that I was hoping that Eleanor would figure me out.

"I'm counting on it, Eleanor."

CHAPTER 15 – MR. KAUTER

By the time we reached the stables, the night was dark and the warmth from my tea was already waning, but Eleanor was singularly focused on our unpleasant task as she charged forward through the deep snow in her stylish trousers and high-heeled boots without a hint of complaint.

"You take the stallion, and I'll take the mare. We'll ride around the edge of the orchard to avoid the crime scene. I think with the exercise earlier, the horses should be able to go faster than a trot, don't you?" She didn't wait for my response before removing the wool blanket and pulling herself right up onto the mare. "Hya!"

I scrambled up onto the stallion. My desire to keep up with her overwhelmed my raging nerves, and my horse did an admirable job of following her into the knee-deep snow.

Eleanor's desire for speed was quickly squelched as our horses struggled to move forward in the soft powder.

"Edmund, I think that when we get there, you should speak to him in German. Perhaps he will trust you more," Eleanor suggested as we rode side by side.

I was taken aback by her suggestion. "What makes you think that I speak German?"

She was, of course, correct. I could speak German. Bernese Swiss German when I so desired, along with every other language I had ever encountered. Remembering to pay attention to the difference between them was the problem… a problem that I had demonstrated more in one day in front of her than I had in many years.

"You were speaking it earlier, when we were calling out to Mr. Kauter. The accent was a bit odd. Quite different from the German I heard during the war, but recognizable all the same. Perhaps… a Swiss dialect?" Eleanor couldn't hide her pleased grin as she baited me.

I had no desire to spin any more of my web of lies. "Yes, I suppose I do speak German. Bernese Swiss German, and many other dialects. I have always had an unusual knack for languages." I took a deep breath, basking in the novelty of the honest statement.

"And how did you come to learn all of these dialects?" Eleanor asked.

"They have always come to me quite naturally," I said truthfully.

"Is that true for other languages as well? Let's see… You have your posh English, Punjabi, I think you mentioned Hindi? Latin, of course, and now Swiss German… and perhaps… Gaelic?"

"I've never spoken Gaelic before. It's a rather obscure language by most standards, is it not? Do you speak it?" I knew I was falling right into some sort of trap, and I didn't care. The thrill of our game ignited me.

"Oh yes. My grandmother was from the Hebrides. She insisted on speaking Gaelic to me and my sisters when we were children. She preached constantly about the importance of maintaining our Scottish cultural autonomy."

"Do you have many siblings?" I realized as I asked the question that I could not picture Eleanor as a child at all. She seemed so thoroughly grown up, as if she had always been that way.

"Only two. I'm the eldest. I have two younger sisters, Mary and Martha. I'm the only one who can actually speak Gaelic, though. My grandmother died when my sisters were too young to really remember her."

"Can you speak it to me? I'd like to hear how it sounds."

Eleanor looked at me skeptically. "Edmund, can you really not tell that we're speaking it now together?"

"Are we?" I asked innocently. I had suspected as much, as my traumatized brain had apparently gone off the linguistic deep end, but at this point, in retrospect, I was rather blatantly hoping that she would uncover all of the secrets that I still couldn't bear to tell her directly.

"Well, I thought I'd see if I could ensnare you with my tongue, Colonel, and I succeeded swimmingly." I guffawed at her scandalous double entendre, and Eleanor's grin widened. "It really is a wonderfully bizarre phenomenon you have going on. I've never encountered anything like it. You don't even have an accent. It sounds as if you are a native highlander, but I'm quite sure that you're not. Now, a native Basingstoker... that is still open for debate, if I'm not mistaken?"

"I'm glad you're enjoying my little mystery." I smiled coyly.

"Oh yes. Very much," Eleanor agreed. "You fascinate me, Edmund. I have never in my life been so fascinated."

As we reached the edge of the orchards, we both fell into contemplative silence as we followed the lone light shimmering in the distance through the falling snow to Mr. Kauter's modest home.

When we arrived, the aroma of sizzling sausage emanated from the cozy cottage, and a wave of anxiety sprang forth from deep within me at the painful reality that we were going to invade the poor man's peaceful evening with the worst news he would ever hear in his life. My stomach growled with hunger as I realized I hadn't eaten anything since breakfast, and I shuddered with disgust at my body's selfish lack of control in the face of such tragedy.

We disembarked the horses and left them tied up loosely by the front door of the cottage.

"You're late!" Mr. Kauter called from inside. "I had to make dinner myself! You promised me that if I agreed to let you stay in the manor with Mrs. Murray that you would be home promptly at six o'clock!"

"What did he say?" Eleanor whispered.

I concentrated on remaining in English. "He says that she's late. I think he's annoyed that she wasn't home in time to cook dinner."

The tragedy threatened to overwhelm me, and Eleanor grabbed my hand and squeezed it tightly. "We're in this together, Edmund."

I knocked briskly in the hope that my demeanor would alert Mr. Kauter that we were not his tardy daughter.

He muttered under his breath as he approached the door, and then peeked out the window beside it to observe us.

I decided to begin our conversation in English. "Mr. Kauter, we have come from the manor house. We must talk to you about some grave news."

He opened the door.

"May we come in?" I asked as I glanced past him to the dingy old living room.

He eyed the horses and then nodded his begrudging agreement.

"The house is dirty. Ingrid has not had enough time to clean it." He collected some soiled rags that were strewn across an old divan and threw them into the corner. "If you're here about our deal, it's off. You can tell Mr. Crowden that he can send every agent from here to kingdom come, and I won't change my mind."

Eleanor and I threw each other a glance of intrigue.

"And what deal might that be?" I asked.

Mr. Kauter eyed us suspiciously. "You know perfectly well what my terms are, and I know that you can't meet them. Don't you dare try to manipulate me with false promises again. Ingrid will be here any minute, and I will thank you to be gone by the time she arrives."

I cringed at his reference. The moment I had been dreading throughout our snowy ride had finally come. "Mr. Kauter, Ingrid won't be able to come home tonight…"

My momentary pause made room for Mr. Kauter's premature response.

"She most certainly will! We're not indentured servants! We're not slaves! We have rights as free citizens!" he exclaimed.

Eleanor placed her hand subtly on my arm, and I took her cue and switched into Mr. Kauter's native dialect. "Mr. Kauter, I am not an agent of the Crowdens." He stepped back with shock at the development and observed my well-tailored, if a bit stable-scented, riding clothes. "I live in London, and I am a weekend guest at their home. I met Ralph during the war."

"You are Bernese?" he asked with puzzlement at the coincidence.

"My… er… mother is Bernese," I lied. "My father is British."

"You must meet Ingrid!" he exclaimed. "She is the most beautiful girl in England! Smart, too! And she works hard! She would be a wonderful wife!"

I threw Eleanor a pained look, but she only watched us with intense curiosity, as I realized that she didn't understand what we were saying.

"Mr. Kauter, I'm sure that Ingrid was a lovely girl, but I am actually here because something horrible has happened…" I took a deep, calming breath. "When Miss MacLeod here and I were out riding in the orchards earlier today, we came across… we came across Ingrid. She was dead. She had been… murdered."

Mr. Kauter stumbled backward and assessed us again.

"It's true," Eleanor seconded, based purely on his body language. "I am a nurse, Mr. Kauter. Ingrid was killed sometime this afternoon. She was stabbed to death with a sword that was stolen from Mr. Rana's room last night while he was drugged."

"Where is she?" he hissed. "Where is she now?"

"She is still in the orchard." A wave of regret washed over me as I delivered the harsh news.

"What?!" Mr. Kauter's shock turned to rage. "Why?! They left her to the beasts like a bloody pagan?! She must have a Christian funeral!"

"Mr. Kauter, the police haven't been able to investigate due to the snow," Eleanor attempted to explain.

"The snow?!" Mr. Kauter shouted angrily. "It snows like this for eight months every year in the Jungfrau and every bloody train runs on time! No excuse!!! This is because those ignorant villagers think that we're bloody Krauts!"

I stepped forward and placed my hand on his arm. I looked straight into his eyes and returned to Bernese. "The phone lines are down, Mr. Kauter. No one in the village even knows this has happened yet. We left Ingrid's body at the scene of the crime because there is evidence there. It must remain undisturbed until we can identify her murderer. In the frozen weather, she should remain intact for some time…" I cringed again at the horrific idea.

Mr. Kauter sat himself down in a shabby wooden chair and stared forward as tears worked their way into the corners of his eyes.

"Ingrid… my Ingrid…" he murmured.

Eleanor and I watched helplessly for many minutes as he wept. Finally, he looked up at me.

"Mr. Kauter, do you have any idea who could have done this?" I asked delicately.

His expression darkened. "Mr. Crowden."

"Did Ingrid have a relationship with him?" I asked.

"She was a virtuous girl!" he exclaimed, conspicuously avoiding a direct answer to the question.

Eleanor stepped forward. "Mr. Kauter, did you know that Ingrid was pregnant? She was about four months in."

His eyes turned wild as he contemplated her statement. He obviously didn't know.

Without a word, he sprung up from his seat and grabbed a shotgun that was hanging over the door.

"Mr. Kauter, no!" Eleanor exclaimed.

I rushed to intercept him, and with one swift movement, I confiscated his shotgun. He stared at me, dumbstruck. "You are a seasoned soldier."

"I am a colonel in the British Army," I agreed. "My name is Colonel Marriner. Mr. Kauter, we're here because we're seeking justice for Ingrid. I've taken over the investigation until the police arrive, and I am committed to finding the real culprit and bringing him to justice. Do not let Ingrid's tragedy ruin you too."

"I was already ruined," he murmured. "Now I have nothing."

Eleanor escorted him back to his seat as I removed the shells from his shotgun and returned it to its position above the door. "You were going to shoot John Crowden?" she asked calmly. "Are you certain that he did it?"

"That bloody bastard," he hissed. "If she was pregnant, it was not her fault. He has been chasing after her for years, since she was far too young for any man's attention. If she was pregnant, he must have raped her. He stole the goods that she wouldn't give him willingly without a ring on her finger, and I will avenge her!"

"The law will avenge her," I countered. "But we have to give it what it needs. We must find indisputable evidence."

"Take me…" Mr. Kauter whispered. "Take me to her."

"I'm not sure that's a good idea…" Eleanor hedged.

"Take me!" he demanded. "I need to see her for myself!"

Eleanor threw me a searching look.

"I cannot go there," I reiterated.

Eleanor nodded her acknowledgment. "I will escort Mr. Kauter. Edmund, you stay here or go back to the manor, and I will join you when we're finished."

Anger rumbled deep within me at my uselessness. This man could certainly overpower Eleanor, and Mr. Rana's warnings echoed heartily through my mind. If John Crowden, or John Crowden *and* Lord Blakeney, were caught meddling with the crime scene, then Eleanor and Mr. Kauter would both be in grave danger…

"I will escort you," I decided nervously. "I will wait at the edge of the orchard for you to do what you need to do."

Eleanor slipped into Gaelic, and I praised myself silently for recognizing her transition. "Edmund, I've already told you that I don't need you to protect me."

"Eleanor, this man you are planning to escort into the orchards alone is in a desperate state. His only child was brutally murdered. He just tried to chase down John Crowden with a shotgun, and if he sees her body and has a stronger reaction, he could easily overpower you. It is in everyone's best interest that Mr. Kauter is not given the opportunity to make things worse."

Eleanor moved to protest, and then gave in. She looked at Mr. Kauter and switched back into English. "Fine. We will go now."

I helped Mr. Kauter up, and we both followed Eleanor out into the snowy night.

"We'd best leave the horses," I whispered. "We don't need the scent to spook them again."

"I know someone else who should avoid being spooked," Eleanor muttered. I ignored her comment.

The snow had finally stopped falling as we trudged into the freezing night, but with the clear skies, the temperature was dropping even lower. Eleanor shivered, and I debated offering her my coat, but I decided against it. I hoped I was starting to really understand her.

When we reached the edge of the summer plum orchard, Eleanor squeezed my hand and let go. "Mr. Kauter, Ingrid is about a hundred meters in. I will lead you, and Edmund will wait here."

Without waiting for a reaction from either of us, she disappeared straight into the eerie dark night. My heart raced as I watched Mr. Kauter follow her.

I stood there uselessly pacing, chastising myself while I fought off a bout of shivers for what felt like hours, until a heated shouting match between Eleanor and Mr. Kauter ignited me. I simply could not let Eleanor be in danger. With only that one thought in my mind, I followed the sound of their row.

"I told you not to touch anything!" Eleanor exclaimed angrily as I approached. "Edmund?! You didn't need to come to our aid! See what you did, Mr. Kauter!"

"I will not leave Ingrid's locket for disrespectful looters!" Mr. Kauter argued as he stashed a golden chain in his pocket.

The scent of death had transitioned from fresh to rotten. The putrid odor infused my senses, and aroused the hungry demon I had worked so hard to subdue throughout the evening. Without a word, I grabbed Eleanor and Mr. Kauter and assertively escorted them out of the orchard.

"Edmund, I'm really alright," Eleanor protested as we reached Mr. Kauter's cottage. She broke away from me and looked up into my eyes. The scent of death still lingered in my nasal cavity, and as a fresh burst of her spicy fear interacted with it, I fought back a wave of nausea.

"We're sorry for your loss, Mr. Kauter. We'll let you know what we learn!" Eleanor called as she grabbed my arm and pulled me towards the house. "Come, Edmund, let's get you back inside."

"What about the horses?" I asked in a daze.

"They aren't here."

I turned my head to look, but she yanked me away from Mr. Kauter's presence, into the dark night. "I'm sure they went back to the stables, just like they did earlier." Eleanor's prior annoyance had been replaced by determination. "I will see to them later. But you, Edmund, need to get yourself back under control. Tell me what you need from me."

I was too overwhelmed by my inner battle to fully appreciate how perceptive she was about my fragile moods.

"I don't know," I murmured.

Eleanor squeezed my hand and shivered at my intense frigidity, but said nothing. "We will get you back to the house to a nice warm bath. I will ask Mrs. Murray to prepare us a quick supper, and perhaps while she prepares it, we can interview her."

"Thank you, Eleanor." I fought back a sudden ball in my throat.

"For what?"

"For saving me from myself."

She squeezed my hand in solidarity, and together we increased our pace.

By the time we reached the house, I was stumbling about in a stupor. Eleanor whisked me into the foyer and looked up at me in the dim light. She held out her index finger and moved it around, watching carefully as I followed it with my eyes. "Fascinating," she murmured. She looked around at the empty hallways, and then grabbed my hand. "Come with me, Edmund. You need to rest and relax a bit before we continue on. I think you should take that bath now."

As I followed her up the stairs, Lord Blakeney approached us from the dark hallway. "Colonel? Miss MacLeod? What's happened?"

Eleanor fell into a distinct panic. "Close your eyes, Edmund. I will explain later," she whispered into my ear. She stood in front of me to address Lord Blakeney. "The colonel has been outside for too long. He's freezing. I will discuss our progress in the investigation with you in a few minutes." She shoved me into the bathroom and slammed the door. "The colonel needs his privacy right now."

She slipped into the bathroom and closed the door behind her.

"Edmund, remember earlier today in the stables? You took deep, calming breaths, closed your eyes, and slowly you got yourself under control. You must do that again. Do you need to sit down? I will start the bath for you."

I watched dumbly as she leaned forward and twisted the faucets. When she was finished, she observed my stupor again and shrugged.

"Darling, I would rather not undress you in a nursing fashion. I'd like to save that privilege for a more pleasurable moment. I will leave you to yourself for now. Stay in here until I return, alright? Remember, deep, calming breaths."

I nodded my agreement, and Eleanor smiled and kissed me gently on the cheek. "I'll be back soon. Bolt the door behind me."

She tiptoed out of the room, leaving me to my disoriented communion with the steaming hot water.

Edmund paused as he took in his enraptured audience. The late-morning sun reflected off of the sparkling spring snow and streamed in through the tall windows, while the scent of fresh coffee emanated from Neha's continuously refreshing samovar. Charlie nodded encouragingly, and Ellie offered her father a supportive smile.

"That was the first time in my life that I truly felt like I wasn't alone. Eleanor made me feel that way." He sighed lovingly. "I have no idea what transpired between her and Lord Blakeney while I was in the bath. In our entire married life, she refused to tell me."

"I can tell you what happened," Supriya offered. "That was Eleanor's wish, after all. For you to really know her. I can use her memories, if you'd like. I guarantee you will find the truth shocking, and you will love her even more when you know it."

"Oh, tell us! Please!" Neha exclaimed.

"Please," Ellie seconded.

Supriya stood up and took her place next to her gentle husband in front of the group. "Do you want to know, Edmund?"

He took her hand tightly into his. "I hand the story over to you, my love."

CHAPTER 16 – LORD BLAKENEY'S SURPRISE

When Eleanor exited the bathroom into the dark hallway, Lord Blakeney was gone. She took in a deep sigh of relief and scampered to her bedroom, grateful for a few moments of reprieve after the most taxing day of her life. She had nursed thousands of wounded soldiers back to health over the years, but she had never encountered an enigma like Edmund. She had never cared so much. She had never *loved* one before…

She fought back the idea with all her might. *You've known him for a day! You know nothing about him! You are not a starry-eyed romantic heroine! You are a MODERN woman!!!*

There was just something about him, something far beyond his delightful mysteries and the adorable look on his face when she stumbled upon each new clue… as if he was both pleased and frightened at the same time. But what was it? What was it that had derailed her from her decades of intense pessimism about love? What exactly was it about this wounded soldier that was bewitching her? She had vowed so many times not to let herself fall into Annie's position, as a glorified nurse-wife, devoting herself to the care of one invalid man... So, what was it?

He was witty, yes, and ever so kind... and certainly she couldn't underappreciate his utterly shocking support of modern women's rights. He was one of the most intelligent men she'd ever met, and yet, his childlike wonder at the complexities of ordinary life was so confounding for a man of his age and experience... How had he possibly managed decades in the British Army without ever realizing that everyone did not have a personal staff at their beck and call?! And yet, just that morning, he had enthusiastically rolled up his sleeves and shoveled manure for hours by her side. His skill at the mundane stable-hand tasks had rightfully impressed her. He was not the spoiled child of a sheltered aristocratic upbringing; he was something else entirely... But what? He exuded such intense quiet power, and yet, it was so overshadowed by humility that he didn't even seem to know that it was there. But she had already seen many tantalizing glimpses of it. She wondered if they were glimpses of who he had been before his torment in the trenches, or if they were glimpses of who he could have been if the wretched war hadn't ruined him... the tragic thought overwhelmed her.

As Eleanor's mind continued to mull over Edmund's mysteries, she distractedly took off the wet coat of the stylish winter outfit that Annie had loaned her and slammed closed her bedroom door with her foot. But, as she switched on the electric lights, her heart jumped into her throat. There, in the corner, stood Lord Blakeney.

"This is my private room, and I will thank you to leave it now," Eleanor declared as she swallowed hard, working to hide her explosion of fear.

"I'm not here to hurt you, Miss MacLeod," Lord Blakeney said calmly. "But we must speak privately."

"There are plenty of private rooms in this house. There was no need for you to invade mine without my permission." Eleanor backed towards the door.

"Why are you helping Edmund?" Lord Blakeney asked bluntly. "Why aren't you scared of him?"

Eleanor was taken aback. "I don't know what you're talking about."

"Don't be coy with me, Miss MacLeod. You know very well what I'm talking about."

"I have no idea," Eleanor lied.

"I will pay you any sum of money you want to tell me everything you know about Edmund Marriner. What will it take? Thousands? Millions? Name your price." Eleanor looked at him with silent disgust, and Lord Blakeney changed his tactic. "I have friends in high places, Miss MacLeod. Tell me what it is you want. Anything at all that will change your life, and you will have it."

"I know nothing about Edmund Marriner. He was a complete stranger to me until last night, and I have hardly learned anything since." Eleanor looked straight into his eyes as she told her lie. "I know only what I have observed in the last twenty-four hours, which is surely no more interesting than what you have observed."

"I have observed many interesting things," Lord Blakeney countered. "Now you have one chance to take my offer. Tell me what you know, and I will reward you."

"I know nothing," Eleanor reiterated as she opened the door. "Now, you had best leave before I start asking you questions that you don't want to answer, *Lord Blakeney*. Isn't that the false name that Edmund helped you concoct this morning upon your mysterious arrival? Or would you prefer Sir Percy Blakeney? Wouldn't Ralph and Anne love to know that you are here under false pretenses to spy on their household? I bet that you don't even know the Baron of Heathfield. That letter that Mr. Rana sent was a hoax. It was part of a bigger plot to help John Crowden, and I will not let you get away with it."

"Is that what you think? You are quite the lady detective, aren't you?" Lord Blakeney laughed.

"Your presence here has something to do with that poor girl's murder, and I'm going to figure out how. Now get out of my room." Eleanor swung the door open as wide as it would go, and Lord Blakeney watched her assessingly from his position in the corner.

They stood, eyeing each other in a silent stand-off, while Eleanor's heart pumped faster and faster. She knew realistically that she would not be able to forcibly evict him from her room, and she glanced into the empty hallway, evaluating her options for escape.

Suddenly, a powerful draft ripped the door right out of her hand and slammed it closed with a commanding crash.

Eleanor was trapped in the room with her mysterious adversary. He rushed towards her and put his hand over her mouth, thrusting her up against the wall.

"Will you tell me now? Or will you let me hurt you to protect a man you just met?" He hissed into her ear as he held her pinned by the neck.

Eleanor whimpered, and then with a sudden powerful knee to Lord Blakeney's groin followed by a kick of her heel straight against his shin, Lord Blakeney was on the floor. Eleanor rushed to the door, but as she threw her weight up against it, the handle wouldn't budge.

Completely uninjured, Lord Blakeney stood up calmly and approached her. She struggled momentarily as he put his hand gently on hers, but suddenly, she was infused with a sense of peaceful well-being unlike anything she had ever felt before.

"You passed my test, Eleanor. Do you have any idea how rare such virtue is in this world?" Lord Blakeney smiled as he brushed a wisp of rogue hair out of her eyes.

Despite her fresh infusion of euphoria, Eleanor was singularly focused on escaping from her brutish attacker. She took a deep breath and threw all of her weight against the door handle again.

"That won't do you any good," Lord Blakeney informed her. "No matter what you do, you won't be able to leave until I release you."

"You did it then? You murdered poor Ingrid? And now you're going to murder me? Did you play with her like this before you slashed her throat with that sword?"

"*Mon dieu, c'est un disastre incroyable…*" Lord Blakeney muttered. "I am not the murderer, Miss MacLeod, and you were never in any real danger. You are *not* in danger right now." Lord Blakeney gestured for her to sit on the bed.

"Are you going to rape me first then?" Eleanor's cheeky tone did not give away a hint of the spicy fear that wafted off of her in increasingly powerful waves.

"I will do nothing of the sort," Lord Blakeney said simply. He held out his hands to his sides in an unthreatening stance and backed into the corner of the room. "Does this position make you more comfortable?"

Eleanor stood stock still in place as she scanned the room for alternative escape options, and as Lord Blakeney caught her eyeing the window, he rolled his eyes with annoyance. "There is no need to take a flight out the window. I am here to protect Edmund."

"He is a colonel in the British Army. He is hardly in need of protection," Eleanor countered.

"Do you really think so? I think we both know that he has been in dire need of protection all day. I was glad to have your help."

Lord Blakeney took in a deep, calming breath, and his eyes turned black.

"Good lord," Eleanor whispered as she backed up against the door.

Lord Blakeney's eyes were the same color of black that Edmund's had turned three times already in the short time Eleanor had known him: first, during John's outrageous shooting session on the roof; second, in the stables as he hid himself away after discovering poor Ingrid's body; and third, after returning to the bloody scene with Mr. Kauter. His eyes had been stuck in their inhuman black state all the way back to the house, and yet, he did not even seem to be aware of his thoroughly alien trait.

Lord Blakeney returned his eyes to their original green. "So, you see, I have a vested interest in Edmund's affairs. We are related, in a matter of speaking, although not by blood. I'm sorry I frightened you, but I had to be sure that you would protect his secrets at all costs."

"Good lord," Eleanor repeated.

"What do you make of us, Eleanor?" he asked curiously.

She stared at him for a long moment as he looked back at her with a kind smile until she relaxed slightly and sat herself down in an antique wooden chair by a small vanity in the corner closest to the door.

"I don't know what to say..." she murmured.

"You just went to great lengths to hide Edmund's condition from me. Surely you must have some explanation for our demonic eyes that leads you to believe that we are not innately evil," Lord Blakeney pushed. "You are, in fact, the first person I have ever encountered who became less frightened rather than more when I revealed this inhuman trait of ours."

"I did not consider it in those terms at all..." Eleanor's mind began racing through a series of bizarre alternative scenarios that she had not allowed herself to consider until Lord Blakeney's revelation.

Lord Blakeney muttered angrily at himself. "And in which terms did you consider it?"

Eleanor chose her words carefully as she observed him with fresh eyes. "I assumed it was a manifestation of adrenaline, brought on by acute shell shock. The black eyes were a result of some sort of chemical reaction. I've seen many inhuman iterations of chemical wounds… Never this precisely, but it wasn't so far off."

Lord Blakeney slowly left his corner and sat himself down on the edge of the bed across from Eleanor. "If you thought that Edmund's condition was simply a manifestation of shell shock, why did you turn down an infinite sum of money to protect his secret?"

"I suppose… I suppose I sensed that there was more to it." Eleanor finally admitted the truth to herself as she admitted it to him. "His eyes are not his only unusual quality… but his secrets are not mine to tell, even to you, with whatever mysterious ailment you two have in common."

"You are an exceptionally wise woman, Miss MacLeod," Lord Blakeney smiled.

"His eccentricities are not just a result of shell shock, though. Are they? There is something much bigger going on. You do not look like you spent any time in the trenches." Eleanor glanced down at Lord Blakeney's perfectly groomed presence.

Lord Blakeney followed her attention to look down at himself. "Looks can be deceiving, Miss MacLeod."

"That might be true, but I have excellent judgment on these matters. I tend to be able to see past the lies I'm told, and you, Lord Blakeney, are not a soldier."

Lord Blakeney smiled with a hint of intrigue in his expression. "Why do you want to know our secrets, Miss MacLeod? What's in it for you?"

Eleanor thought for an extended moment about her response. "I suppose a girl wants to know what she's getting herself into."

"You haven't been scared off yet, it seems? Even after every imperfection you've seen today?"

Eleanor gave into a loving smile. "No. Not yet."

"Are you willing to keep other secrets that are not yours to tell? Bigger secrets?"

"It depends what they are. I will not keep useful intel related to this murder investigation a secret. Ingrid's killer must be brought to justice."

"Quite a reasonable exception," Lord Blakeney agreed.

Eleanor watched with anxious curiosity as Lord Blakeney closed his eyes, but her interest transitioned into utter disbelief as his elaborate suit morphed into a flowing white silk medieval dress, his flamboyant hat disappeared, and his tufts of golden hair grew out into long, fairy-like locks. His kind green eyes with his beautiful long lashes remained intact, while the rest of his masculine features dissolved into more delicate feminine ones.

"Good lord!" Eleanor exclaimed. "I didn't see that one coming! Edmund can't do that, can he?"

"No, he can't. Not yet, at least." Lord Blakeney stood up and approached Eleanor with his hand out for a friendly shake. "My real name is Mélusine." As she introduced herself, her affected British accent dissolved into a more relaxed, lyrical tone with subtle French intonation.

Eleanor dazedly shook her hand, and Mélusine looked down and grimaced. "You must be going mad in these damp human clothes, and in the snow?! I told Kuveni she was taking it too far with the blizzard. Let me help you."

Mélusine kneeled down and touched the cuff of Eleanor's grey wool trousers. In only seconds, the fabric straightened out, fresh and dry as ever, and Mélusine stood back up and smiled triumphantly. "That's better, isn't it?"

"I'm asleep, aren't I? This is usually the point when I realize I'm dreaming." Eleanor pinched her own arm to no avail.

"You may tell yourself that later. Many humans have, but I'm quite sure you're more interesting than that, Eleanor. You are one of the most interesting humans I've encountered in many centuries."

"You're not human, then?" Eleanor already knew the answer.

"Most certainly not. Not one drop," Mélusine scoffed.

"What are you then?" Eleanor felt her curiosity exploding, despite the fact that she was not completely convinced that she was awake.

"All in good time, ma chérie," Mélusine demurred. "What you need to know now is that Edmund and I are not the same. He is half human, and I am much, much older than he is. He doesn't know what he is yet, and it is pivotal that he remains in ignorance. Do you understand? The fate of the world depends on it."

"Oh, just the fate of the world?" Eleanor quipped.

Mélusine did not acknowledge her sarcasm. "I've already revealed to you far more than he knows about his own origins. He does not even know that beings like me exist."

"Why on earth would you reveal yourself to me then?" Eleanor exclaimed. "I just met him last night!"

"I am taking a great risk. A greater risk than you can possibly comprehend..." Mélusine became momentarily pensive before she wrested herself back to her point. "You're right that you're moving far too fast. Kissing him within three hours of meeting him?! Why do you think I came?! We had to make sure he wasn't being seduced by another wanton hussy!"

"So I was right! You did fabricate the letter from the Baron!" Eleanor exclaimed.

"Excellent detective work," Mélusine winked. "I left the letter on the Baron's desk by the end of your session in the library with Edmund. But you were thoroughly wrong that I was in league with

John Crowden. I came here to make sure that you and he didn't undo Edmund's four years of progress since the wretched war."

"I'm glad you were here to help," Eleanor said more seriously. "I can feel how much Edmund is struggling."

"Yes. He's battling more demons than he ever has in his life. I haven't seen him struggle so much since the war, but it's different now. He has devoted himself to avoidance for so long that he's forgotten how to manage his primal reactions to negative stimuli, and even the best of us are not very good at controlling ourselves when faced with a horrendous example of human injustice. A situation like this one can easily push us over the edge…" Mélusine trailed off in thought, and then caught herself and returned to the point. "Young Edmund is straddling darkness and light in a particularly unhealthy manner right now, and he does not have the resources for dealing with his struggle that the rest of us have."

"Why not? Why can't you just tell him everything and help him?" Eleanor asked with a passion that surprised her.

"It is more complicated than your thirty-seven years on Earth allows you to appreciate," Mélusine shrugged. "I will reveal, though, what you already know: The black eyes are a sign that the darkness unlocked by his torment in the trenches is working its way to the surface. He has the strength to overcome it, but he does not have the confidence yet. That wicked war was, by far, the bloodiest mess that the human race has ever unleashed. The fact that after all he endured, he is still one of the gentlest men on Earth is a wonder so great that it gives all of us old pessimists hope for the future."

"I wish you could have spared him."

"So do I. It was sheer torture to have to watch him suffer like he did," Mélusine agreed. "But Edmund had to learn for himself what the darkness of war truly meant. And now, he must start to move on to become the leader that he is destined to be. And you, Eleanor, are in a perfect position to help him, if you so choose."

"I don't think he needs a wanton hussy..."

"Neither do I," Mélusine smiled. "And I will admit that you were very hard to figure out, ma chérie. Even with my two thousand years of experience. But you have proven yourself now, which is why we're having this conversation."

"Two thousand years..." Eleanor murmured. "I don't know what to say. I'm grateful for the privilege, but I do not understand why you've chosen me if you don't even see fit to disclose these details to Edmund."

"We need an ally." Mélusine sat back down on the edge of the bed, leaned in, and lowered her voice. "Edmund is very special. Far more special than he realizes. But he must discover who he is on his own, without our help. The prophecies could not be clearer about that. But he still has many guardians—beings like me who watch over him and look out for his best interests. It is a wicked game for us, deciding when to get involved."

"So he has a team of guardian angels?" Eleanor asked with a combination of wonder and skepticism.

"That's a very Christian way of putting it. Are you Christian, Eleanor?" Mélusine asked curiously. "I didn't see much evidence of your religion in my observations today."

"I was baptized in the Church of Scotland as a child, but I am not particularly religious. Like every institution, churches are as corrupt as the humans who make them," Eleanor shrugged. "I suppose I shouldn't tell you that if you're an angel."

"Ha! That's probably true, although angels are supposed to be forgiving, are they not?"

"All Christians are, aren't they?" Eleanor countered. "I haven't seen much evidence of forgiving Christians in my life, so I see no reason why angels would be any better."

Mélusine smiled widely. "I like you, Eleanor. I like you a lot. Do you know how many humans I've liked in the last two thousand years? Seven. You are the eighth. Congratulations."

"Thank you?" Eleanor asked at the back-handed compliment.

Mélusine was unfazed. "You and Edmund are a very good match. He made many similar conclusions when I was tutoring him in Bath."

"On Ovid?!" Eleanor asked excitedly.

Mélusine's smile only widened more, and she morphed herself into a dark and handsome Italianate man in a very old-fashioned Victorian suit. "You are very clever, ma chérie. Very clever, indeed."

Eleanor reached forward to touch Mélusine's updated wardrobe.

"Yes, please feel free to inspect my form. You will find everything about me to be as real as anything else in this world," Mélusine offered as she held out her arm.

"How extraordinary," Eleanor whispered as she handled the convincingly starched cuff of Mélusine's suit and then poked the warm flesh of her hand.

"I was young Edmund's tutor on many topics in Bath, including Roman philosophy. This is the form I used. He didn't know that he was debating a Roman on the topic, and still he won almost every argument. He was particularly passionate about Ovid, actually. I found his reaction strange, given that he had no experience with love. But Edmund has been a joyful bundle of surprises since the day he was born."

"I said almost that exact phrase last night..." Eleanor murmured.

Mélusine shifted uncomfortably. "I know. A friend of mine was watching you."

"Watching us? In the library? I didn't see anyone." Eleanor was so overwhelmed with the entire situation that she didn't have the wherewithal to be properly offended by the intrusion.

Mélusine shrugged. "She was invisible, in a matter of speaking, anyway. Non-corporeal is a more accurate term to describe her physical state… but, in any event, she was recounting for me in great detail what transpired between you… too much detail, really. But our people, and she, in particular, tend to view privacy as an unnatural human concept."

"I see…" Eleanor said pensively. "And you were there when Edmund was born? Did Edmund's mother know you were there?"

"I was there, as were many others. She knew we were all there… but it is best not to go into too much detail."

"Did the angels sing and the wise men gather?" Eleanor cracked a smile at her irreverent joke.

"Ha!" Mélusine exploded into laughter. "God, how I like you, Eleanor!"

"I'm glad I'm making a good impression." Eleanor's casual tone did not give away her increasing bewilderment at Mélusine's fantastical revelations.

After a slightly awkward pause, Mélusine closed her eyes and returned to her natural feminine form. "We are not angels, but the concept is not entirely wrong either. We are more like a meddling family that has far too much power for our own good… at least when it comes to him. We've meddled far too much in poor Edmund's life, and every time we've tried it, something horrible has happened. After several unacceptable mistakes, we were ordered not to interfere anymore, but this time around, we simply couldn't leave it alone."

"You are surely meddling now," Eleanor pointed out.

"You're right, I am. I am heinously disobeying direct orders from our very wise leader, whom you will probably meet at some point if things work out between you and Edmund. I came today because Kuveni, the woman who was spying on you and also happens to be the woman who raised Edmund in Bath, went raving mad when she saw what you, ma chérie, were up to last night in the library. She called in a very old favor and demanded that I intervene. *Et voila.* Here I am, meddling on her behalf."

"I hope something horrible doesn't happen this time!" Eleanor exclaimed.

"So do I," Mélusine agreed stoically. "But, ma chérie, that is an important transition in our conversation. I can see the way you two are looking at each other. Your selfless protection of him just a few minutes ago reiterated what I already knew was true. There is a very rare and beautiful love growing between you, but you must understand what it truly means for you. Being with Edmund will be distinctly different from being with anyone else on Earth."

"I'm counting on it," Eleanor sighed lovingly. "He is so much better than every other man. So gentle and strong at the same time… So much stronger than he realizes…"

"Yes, yes, he's very loveable…" Mélusine curtly interrupted Eleanor's swoon. "But it's more than that, ma chérie. Loving Edmund comes with risks. There are members of our race who are not good like he and I are. They might try to hurt him, or *you*. You must be prepared to protect yourself."

"I have always protected myself."

"Yes, I can tell that you have. That move you pulled on me earlier was thoroughly brilliant. The weak woman sigh right before the kick? Genius, through and through. Keep that one ready. John Crowden is just waiting for a good kick in the groin."

"Thanks," Eleanor smiled.

"I shouldn't distract myself," Mélusine returned to seriousness. "There are other risks to you… Risks that I probably shouldn't tell you, but I will anyway from one woman to another."

For the first time since Mélusine revealed herself, Eleanor felt genuine anxiety. "Tell me," she decided. "Tell me what it is I'm signing up for."

"There are not a lot of examples from which we can learn…" Mélusine hedged. Eleanor nodded impatiently for her to continue. "I don't know if you and Edmund would even be able to have children, most of our people can't procreate with humans at all,

184

but when they do manage it… the human mother always dies in childbirth. Always, Eleanor. I do not know of a single example in which she hasn't."

"Blimey," Eleanor whispered.

"He is half human. It is possible you could be the first to survive."

"I don't like those odds," Eleanor murmured.

"Neither do I. That's why I'm telling you." Mélusine reached forward and stroked Eleanor affectionately on the cheek. "I do not want to see you die in pain, ma chérie. Humans with virtue as pure as yours should live as long as nature allows."

"My virtue isn't so pure," Eleanor confessed.

"That is not the kind of virtue I meant. I've been around long enough to have no delusions about a woman who kisses a man within three hours of meeting him."

"You should try it sometime," Eleanor winked. "But only with someone worthy, of course."

"I will keep your advice under advisement. I am, perhaps, the opposite of a modern woman."

"You seem pretty modern to me."

"It is one of our natural skills to deceive humans," Mélusine countered amicably.

"You could have fooled me, Sir Percy Blakeney," Eleanor teased. "You seemed out of place the moment you arrived this morning."

"Don't get me started." Mélusine rolled her eyes. "For the record, I *was* Sir Percy Blakeney. I rescued thousands of innocent humans from the guillotine in two years. How was I to know that some worthless writer would get her grubby hands on my story *again*? I hate writers! They make my life so bloody difficult! It took me decades to fine tune that persona, and poof! Useless."

"So I take it you don't follow English literature?" Eleanor asked curiously. "Edmund seems to follow every form of literature."

"He has always been a very avid reader. We loved watching him voraciously devour every book we presented to him as a child, in every language, by the way. He speaks all of them, but I think you've probably noticed that already. He has yet to finesse his ability to transition between them."

"Yes, yes, that one he really couldn't hide," Eleanor agreed. "Although, he is so bloody cute about it, I don't know how anyone could point it out to him!"

"Edmund has always puzzled us. He is so surprisingly at home in the human world, much more than any of us expected. He has overcome so, so much… He really is a great inspiration… I, on the other hand, don't keep up with human affairs much. I mostly meditate in my secret refuge in France. It makes these little farces harder and harder to execute believably when I hop into the human world without enough recent practice."

Their joviality dissolved as they both sat for a moment of contemplative silence.

"I've already thought of myself as too old to have children for a while…" Eleanor murmured. "But I will admit that in the last twenty-four hours with Edmund, the fantasy came alive."

"It is possible that it could work," Mélusine reiterated. "Edmund is only half Rakshasa. There aren't very many examples, even in my two thousand years, especially with hybrids."

"Rakshasa?" Eleanor asked astutely.

"That is the name of our race—of Edmund's father and my mother. Edmund doesn't know it. I trust you to keep it that way."

"I thought you might be fairies," Eleanor admitted. "There is something ethereal about him… and you."

"We are *not* fairies," Mélusine said snippily. "No human word properly describes us. We are very different from humans and

186

much more powerful, but we struggle to find a balance between darkness and light, just as humans do. We've been on Earth longer than the human race has existed, and there aren't very many of us left. That's all that you really need to know."

"You sound almost like gods," Eleanor observed.

"Almost, ma chérie. Almost."

Suddenly, the gravity of the task began weighing on Eleanor. "I don't know how I can keep all of this a secret from him."

Mélusine looked genuinely nervous for the first time since their conversation began. "It is a most profound act of love to keep important truths secret until their appropriate time, Eleanor. It is easy to share everything with those you love. It is much harder to protect them with lies. We are all entrenched now in protecting Edmund with lies, because every time we've given in to our base desires to the contrary, he has suffered dearly."

"I'm not very good at lying," Eleanor admitted.

"Edmund is not very tenacious at seeking the truth, if you haven't noticed. His affability makes it easier for us to keep secrets from him. He almost never asks invasive questions. Many of us have wished that he would be more inquisitive, that perhaps if he were, we could end our unenviable farce. But alas, we must wait for him to develop on his own."

"I have noticed that, actually. I couldn't believe that it didn't even occur to him to ask who you really were when you showed up here today with an obviously false identity."

"*Précisement, ma chérie. Précisement.* He is very similar to his mother in that way. She never realized that Edmund's father wasn't human, and he could not have been more flagrant about showcasing his foreign talents—it was a wonder he didn't give us all away... I shouldn't say anything else about him, I think... Edmund is nothing like him, and he is unaware of Edmund's existence. We have worked exceptionally hard to keep it that way."

"The orphanage…" Eleanor murmured. "That is how the orphanage fits in, isn't it?"

"He told you about the orphanage?" Mélusine asked with surprise. "Oh, ma chérie, it is exactly as I thought. Edmund has never told anyone about the orphanage! This is a very good sign… a very good sign, indeed… He is opening up more than he ever has… *Mon dieu*, destiny is in motion…"

"I've never believed in destiny."

Mélusine took both of Eleanor's hands into hers. "Ma chérie, I have revealed myself to you for a reason. You are worthy of this knowledge, and you can be a powerful ally for us in helping Edmund recover. But this is a great burden on you. It will require many personal sacrifices. You are not required to continue on this path. But, please, if you don't want to continue, break it off with him quickly and gently as soon as you get out of the drama of this horrific weekend. He is still recovering from the trauma of his wife learning his secret. She was a cruel, selfish little tart, not by any definition remotely comparable to you, and her foolish reaction to his secrets scarred him for longer than you would believe."

"He's not still married to her, is he?" Eleanor suddenly panicked.

"She is long dead, but not by his hand," Mélusine reassured her. "He sacrificed himself to save her life, and still she accused him of being a demon. She died alone in a convent in a karmic fate of her own making. That was one of the tragic results of our early meddling. But you and he both have the chance for a very different fate. For a love affair of epic proportions."

Eleanor let out an involuntary overwhelmed sigh.

"Have I told you too much?" Mélusine asked concernedly. "More than you wanted to hear?"

"I appreciate knowing the truth, but it's a lot to take in," Eleanor admitted.

"Good. It should be. It means that you are appropriately considering the gravity of what I've told you. But there is a saving grace…" Mélusine squeezed Eleanor's hands encouragingly. "The kind of soulful love that you have before you enables unique pleasures that I can't properly describe with words. I think that you already have a sense of the possibilities." Eleanor smiled her agreement. "And I'm sure that you will be relieved to know that mutual consent is required for our people to procreate. It means that unless you both wish for a baby while you're enjoying yourselves, it isn't going to happen. That knowledge, perhaps, can give you some reassurance, and some uniquely unburdened pleasure."

"Yes, I suppose," Eleanor said pensively.

"Edmund doesn't know any of this, by the way," Mélusine added quickly. "I am telling you so that you can make your own informed decisions."

"I appreciate it."

Mélusine pulled Eleanor up out of her seat and into a motherly hug. "Think about it. You don't need to decide right now. I would have preferred to wait much longer for this heart to heart, but you chose the speed, ma chérie, and now you are reaping the results."

"Annie always did call me a speed demon…"

Mélusine reached into a hidden pocket in her dress and pulled out a sparkling green sapphire pendant with a delicate golden chain. She closed it into Eleanor's hand. "Use this to summon me if you're in danger, or if you just want to talk. Hold it in your hand, think my name, and I will join you in the blink of an eye."

Eleanor held up the gem to the dim light to observe its otherworldly sparkles. "Dare I ask how the science of this process works?"

"I couldn't explain it even if I wanted to, but you can trust that it will work."

"I have no doubt."

"But you and Edmund must solve your own problems unless the circumstances are truly dire. We must avoid the pitfalls of meddling as much as we can."

"Indeed."

"Now, you have a gentle half-human soldier to check in on, and I have a sadistic human brute to manage."

"You don't know who killed Ingrid, do you?" Eleanor asked suddenly as the thought occurred to her.

"We aren't omniscient," Mélusine shrugged. "What I can tell you is that I was watching John Crowden all day, and he didn't do it. He was locked in his room all afternoon snorting cocaine. I'm sure he's your top suspect, given what a bastard he is, but you'll have to find your killer elsewhere."

"Blimey," Eleanor muttered. "That takes away all of our leads."

"I take it that you don't think our virtuous Sikh butler did it?"

"I'm quite sure that someone is trying to frame him. Although, I do think he's hiding something."

"Follow your instincts, ma chérie. They have done you well so far."

"Not quite. I thought that you were the murderer," Eleanor reminded her.

"I attacked you, ma chérie. You were sensing that something was dangerously amiss, and you were correct. I could have easily killed you if I'd wanted to. If ever you feel the same way again, do whatever you need to do to escape. Humans and Rakshasas alike can be dangerous adversaries, especially to those rare individuals whose loyalty cannot be bought or blackmailed."

Eleanor pulled Mélusine into a tight hug. "Thank you," she whispered into her ear. "For everything."

Mélusine smiled reassuringly as Eleanor pulled away.

"I suppose it's back to work for me then," Eleanor said as she unenthusiastically made her way to the door.

"*Attendez!*" Mélusine snapped her fingers, and a plate of French baguette sandwiches appeared on the small vanity.

"How extraordinary!" Eleanor picked up one of the sandwiches and sniffed it.

"Bon appetit," Mélusine winked. "Your rumbling stomach has been bothering me throughout our little chat. Don't get your hopes up, though. Edmund can't do that. That talent comes from the similarly foreign race of my father."

Eleanor took a small bite, and then the hunger that she had been ignoring for hours erupted, and she quickly gobbled down the rest of the sandwich. Mélusine smiled and snapped her fingers, producing a dusty bottle of red wine and two glasses. Eleanor watched curiously as she pulled a dainty corkscrew from her pocket, opened the wine, sniffed the bottle, and poured Eleanor a taste. Eleanor took a small sip, and her eyes widened at the shockingly robust flavor. Mélusine smiled and poured them each a full glass.

"Did you somehow make this wine? Just now? With the snap of your fingers?" Eleanor asked with wonder.

"Oh no. None of us can make anything as delicious as this. I summoned that bottle from our cellars in France. It is a Château Margaux 1778."

"It must be expensive," Eleanor said as she politely took another small sip.

"Money means nothing to us for many reasons, but the rarity of the vintage is something to be appreciated. Beings who live a long time have the unique opportunity to compile an enviable wine collection." Mélusine drank down her serving in one Rakshasa gulp.

"I knew it!" Eleanor exclaimed. "I knew that was one of his oddities! He drank an entire bottle of cognac in one swallow earlier today! I thought I'd awakened his inner alcoholic!"

Mélusine laughed. "We are always very thirsty, and alcohol never makes us drunk. Red wine will calm us, though, and warm baths... mmm... there is nothing quite as invigorating as a long soak in fresh water. Keep that in mind for the future."

Mélusine became momentarily pensive while Eleanor sipped her wine.

"I must ask a small favor of you, ma chérie..."

Eleanor nodded her agreement.

"Edmund has never once in his life had the privilege of revealing his secrets on his own to a worthy recipient. The only people who have ever learned them stumbled upon him in moments of vulnerability, just as you have today. If you can muster the patience, please, let him share his secrets with you in his own time. It is a rare and beautiful gift for us."

"I will do what I can," Eleanor agreed.

Mélusine pulled her into a final hug and kissed her on both cheeks, and then Eleanor watched as she closed her eyes and morphed back into the foppish form of Lord Blakeney.

"Welcome to the fold," Mélusine winked. "I will help you however I can without giving myself away to Edmund."

And with a final tip of her flamboyant hat, Mélusine left Eleanor alone.

"How extraordinary..." Eleanor whispered.

She pinched herself to make sure she was awake, and then looked around the room. She grabbed the half-empty bottle of wine and the two glasses, and made her way straight to the bath where her gentle half-human soldier awaited.

CHAPTER 17 – THE NEXT STEP

"She knew…" Edmund murmured. "She knew everything…"

"I'm sorry, mon chéri." Mélusine morphed into the form of Percy Blakeney that neither of them had seen in ninety years and approached Edmund, pulling him into a motherly hug. "You cannot imagine how hard it was for us to keep the truth from you for all of those years. But Vibhi was right. We shouldn't have meddled. Eleanor's death broke my heart."

Edmund looked around the room again, struggling for words, until Supriya gently took his hand into hers. "We are what we are, my love. Sometimes the best of intentions just aren't enough."

Edmund swallowed hard, pushing back the aggressive ball in his throat. "I wanted to have children as soon as we were married, and she told me she wasn't ready. If it weren't for your meddling, I might have lost her sooner. You gave us the three beautiful years we had together before she died." He hugged her again. "Thank you. I will never be able to thank you enough for giving her a choice."

"I love you, Edmund," Mélusine whispered back as she wiped a violet tear from her eye. She morphed back into her preferred female form, squeezed his hand, and returned to her seat.

As an awkward silence fell upon the room, Neha snapped her fingers, producing a steaming hot English breakfast in the lap of every member of the audience.

Edmund looked around and spotted Ellie sitting on the couch with violet tears streaming down her face. With one swift Rakshasa movement, he pulled her out of her position and into a hug.

"I love you, Ellie. You are the greatest gift anyone could have ever given me."

"Thanks, Dad," she whispered.

After many minutes of catharsis followed by silent chomping, the crowd settled back in, Supriya rejoined Ellie and Charlie on the couch, and Edmund took a deep, calming breath.

"I suspect then, that you all want to know who killed poor Ingrid Kauter?"

They nodded their agreement.

"I will warn you, the investigation became more heated and… er… more violent… as we continued on." Edmund eyed Charlie and Ellie, and they nodded encouragingly.

"Then I suppose we must continue our story when Eleanor greeted me in the bathroom, bearing the most delicious bottle of wine I had ever tasted in my life…

I awoke in the warm bathtub from a more peaceful slumber than I had known in many years to Eleanor's lilting voice.

"Edmund, darling? It's Eleanor. Can I come in?"

She tapped lightly on the door.

I took a disoriented moment, looking down at my naked body and letting the memories of the eventful day return to my consciousness, and then I scrambled up out of the water.

"Just one minute!" I called.

I watched with secret satisfaction as the last remnants of the warm water absorbed into my skin. My clothes were folded neatly on a small table by the bath. I looked at them confusedly. I didn't remember putting them there. It was possible, I supposed, that I had done it without remembering; After all, I had been in a daze after Eleanor had left me, when I'd undressed myself and slipped into the sinfully hot tub…

I let the emergency of Eleanor's imminent arrival distract me from the minor mystery, and I hopped about the room, ungracefully wiggling on my riding trousers. I smelled the shirt and jacket before putting them on, and to my great relief, there was no evidence of the hours of work I'd done in the stables earlier in the day.

I looked around the room for a mirror, but there was none, and so I fluffed my hair with my hand, took a deep breath, and opened the door.

"You're looking much better!" she exclaimed.

I was feeling better. The delicious warmth of the bath water had infused me, and my body and my soul were now ready to fully appreciate all of Eleanor's beauty, inside and out.

She held up a half-empty bottle of wine and two glasses. "Would you like to join me for a quick drink before we continue on with our quest for justice? I think we could use some time to gather our thoughts."

"I can't think of anything I'd rather do," I agreed. I coaxed the glasses from Eleanor's left hand and then snuck a kiss I'd been dreaming about for hours.

"You're so warm!" Eleanor exclaimed. "The bath must have thawed you through and through!"

I kissed her deeper, and every last sleeping part of me awakened as Eleanor leaned into my arms. When she finally pulled away to catch her breath, she took my free hand into hers. "Come on. There is a table in my room where we can pour the wine."

My heart raced as she led me to her room and closed the door behind us.

"Lord Blakeney confiscated this wine from John's collection," she explained as I placed the glasses on the vanity. She poured what was left of the bottle to the very brim of each glass, and then giggled as she struggled to keep her wine from spilling as she held up her glass in a toast.

"To justice," she declared.

She took a long sip, longer than I expected, and I followed her lead, finishing half my serving in one gulp. I hoped she wouldn't worry as she had earlier in the stables, but as I had proven my sobriety once already, and she seemed to be willing to pour me another drink, I decided that she must have gained some confidence in me that for once I felt like I deserved.

"How extraordinary!" I exclaimed. "This might be the best wine I've ever tasted! I'm glad it wasn't wasted on John!"

"Me too," Eleanor smiled. With her glass down to a manageable volume, she sat down on the bed and gestured for me to join her. My heart raced as I sat down beside her.

She put her hand on my leg, but then pulled back with a grimace.

"Are you alright?" I asked nervously. I felt my hand to my cheek. It was pulsing with warmth.

"Oh yes, I'm perfectly fine. Sorry," she said nonchalantly as she reached up and began pulling the pins from underneath her stylish hat. "I've just had these pins in my hair all day. It's already past eight o'clock, and my scalp is starting to rebel." She quickly collected an entire handful of pins, and then grinned with satisfaction as she pulled off her hat and tossed it across the room. "That's better!" She pulled a few remaining pins out of her large bun, releasing her hair into its natural fiery tendrils.

I was speechless. She looked like a John William Waterhouse siren. Her ethereal Celtic beauty that I had found so alluring the night before was multiplied tenfold by her long, flowing hair.

"It's long, I know, and far too wild. I might as well audition to play *Rapunzel*," she said self-consciously. "I know it's all the rage to cut it short these days, especially for a modern woman. But I loved riding the thoroughbreds with my hair flowing in the wind when I was a lass. I couldn't bring myself to cut it. So, I've had to become creative about making it stylish."

I reached forward and felt one of her silky tendrils. "It is the most beautiful hair I've ever seen."

She reached forward and ran her fingers through my short tufts of greying black hair. "You have a nice head of hair yourself, Colonel. Especially for a man of your age."

"Indeed," I agreed. She had no idea what an understatement she had just made.

"I've always preferred being with experienced lovers. It makes the delights of learning about each other more interesting. I believe Ovid would agree with me, don't you?"

"Yes, I believe he would." I felt a hot blush return to my cheeks, but as she caressed my face with her dainty fingers, I leaned in and kissed her.

As our embrace became more and more frenzied, I ran my fingers through her hair, and she let out a loud moan that startled me.

As soon as I pulled away, she exploded into embarrassed giggles. "The spots where the pins have been pulling my hair are always very sensitive after I take them out," she explained. "Even a gentle touch causes a strange tingling sensation that you just managed to aggravate. A head massage in this state would be utterly scandalous."

"I'll have to keep that in mind," I said as I felt my hot red blush quickly dissolve.

We both took polite sips of our wine, and then I leaned in to reinitiate our delicious intimacy, but the sound of footsteps in the hallway wrested us both from our pleasant distraction.

"We shouldn't be doing this right now," I admitted. "We have a murder to solve and very little time to solve it."

Eleanor nodded her agreement stoically. "I have some bad news on the investigation front, actually. I interviewed Lord Blakeney, and he said that he was watching John Crowden all day, and that John was locked away in his room snorting cocaine when the murder was committed."

"Good lord," I whispered.

"It means that John Crowden isn't our man. So, if it wasn't John Crowden or Mr. Rana, it has to be someone else."

"Do you think we can trust Lord Blakeney? Didn't you have a theory earlier today that he might be in league with John Crowden? If that's the case, then surely we can't trust anything he says." I was rather proud of myself for making the conclusion.

"You're right..." Eleanor seemed troubled. "But I think we were wrong. I'm quite sure we can trust him."

I was surprised by Eleanor's change in attitude. She did not strike me as a person who would change her mind so easily. "Did he tell you more about himself during your interview then? Did he tell you why he's really here?"

"Yes, he did. We were right that he is a spy of sorts. He told me his exact mission and provided proof of his claims under the strict condition that I do not reveal his true identity, even to you. He said that it would cause problems far greater than anything we are facing this weekend."

"It seems hard to believe that there are problems greater than solving a murder," I scoffed.

"He was very convincing," Eleanor reiterated. "But he did pledge to help us however he can without giving away his bigger plot."

"I suppose that's something," I sighed. I was feeling rather useless. "So who does that leave us then? The Baron is bedridden, so it wasn't him, which leaves Ralph and Anne, Mrs. Murray the cook, and... the Fitzgeralds!" Eleanor chimed in as we blurted their name in unison.

"It has to be them! Harry Fitzgerald is almost as unscrupulous as John! Annie had something on them, I'm sure of it. They are here on some sort of nefarious business. They must have something to do with it!" Eleanor exclaimed.

She finished off her wine in one long gulp and then jumped up. She pulled me into her arms and crushed her mouth onto mine, offering me a tantalizing lick of her tongue before she pulled away. "Edmund, my darling, I didn't mean to lead you on. Really, I can hardly stop myself from ripping off your clothes right now and throwing you onto the bed, but we have a murder to solve!"

I stood still for a moment, shocked and thrilled by her forwardness.

"We should talk to Annie and Ralph first," Eleanor strategized as she gathered her hair into a loose ponytail and tied it up with a ribbon from the vanity. "Maybe with our new intel, we can get them to tell us why the Fitzgeralds are really here, and then we can use that information to pressure the Fitzgeralds into revealing their cards when we talk to them... Yes... We should go to them fully armed."

I drank down the rest of my wine in one Rakshasa gulp and then placed both of our glasses on the vanity. "I suppose we drank that at the same speed as John Crowden would have," I said guiltily. "We should have appreciated it more."

"I appreciated it," Eleanor winked.

"Yes, come to think of it, I did too," I agreed.

Eleanor took my hand, and with a vivacity I had never felt before in my life, I followed her into the dark hallway, towards our imminent conversation with a murderer.

CHAPTER 18 – MRS. MURRAY

Eleanor and I wandered about the house hand in hand, listening to the subtle creaks of the old building settling under the weight of the fresh snow, until we reached the bottom floor, and the conspicuous absence of our party and the staff, including Mr. Rana, became concerning.

"You don't think they ran away, out into the snowy night, do you? Is it possible they were all in it together?" I posited the unlikely theory out loud.

"That seems like a far-fetched plot, doesn't it? All of these disparate people conspiring together to kill one person? Think of the effort it would take!" Eleanor exclaimed. "Besides, what motive could they all possibly have to murder an innocent scullery maid?"

"Yes... yes, I suppose the motive is the key to everything..." I conceded. "Surely her delicate condition was a factor, but I still don't understand why. If Ingrid was pregnant, and John Crowden was the father, who would possibly have a motive to kill her, other than him? And we have established that he has an alibi."

"I suppose we should not discount Mr. Kauter as a suspect. It is possible that Mr. Kauter found out about an affair between John and Ingrid and killed her out of rage."

I thought carefully about Eleanor's assertion. "If Mr. Kauter were the murderer, he would have to be exceptionally devious to have acted so surprised when we visited him earlier."

"This murderer was devious. Perhaps we need to entertain the possibility that he has already deceived us in some way," Eleanor reminded me.

"But if Mr. Kauter killed Ingrid out of rage, why would he have gone to the trouble of framing Mr. Rana for it? It couldn't have been a crime of passion. He would have had to plan it for at least a whole day in order to drug Mr. Rana on the prior evening, and surely someone would have noticed him lingering about in the kitchen." I felt like I was finally getting used to the investigative line of inquiry.

Eleanor looked at me with surprise. "You're starting to sound like a detective, Colonel!" I couldn't help but smile at her praise. "You're probably right, but we shouldn't jump to conclusions without asking the witnesses. Mr. Kauter and Ingrid have both been associated with the household for years and years. Perhaps if Ingrid was working in the kitchen, it wouldn't have been suspicious to the rest of the staff to see Mr. Kauter lingering. Now Mr. Kauter's motive to frame Mr. Rana is the bigger question for me..."

I tried to channel my energy into an intelligent response. "Perhaps there was some sort of altercation or rivalry between them that they didn't share with us. Or, perhaps Mr. Kauter found out about Ingrid's pregnancy, set out to kill her, and then framed Mr. Rana because he knew that the only person in the household a jury would trust less than him with his German name was Mr. Rana."

"If we'd known John had an alibi, and Mr. Rana's sword hadn't been at the crime scene, who would have been our top suspect?" Eleanor posited.

I forced myself to consider the dark variations that my mind had been working to avoid. "Mr. Kauter… It would have been Mr. Kauter. Her body was not very far from his cottage, actually. And we knew he must have been out in the fields dealing with the storm. We certainly would have wanted to search his cottage for a murder weapon."

"He did make several references to some 'deal' with the Crowdens…" Eleanor thought out loud. "He did not give us a sufficient answer when we pressed him to explain… perhaps that has something to do with it as well…"

"Perhaps…" I couldn't argue with her sound logic, but there was something wrong with the conclusion. "Still, his grief and his surprise at the news felt genuine. Didn't it? He even proposed that *I* marry Ingrid."

"He did what?!" Eleanor exclaimed. "When?!"

"When I switched into Bernese. I think he decided that I might be Ingrid's only good marital prospect in England. He probably thought that I would not discount their Germanic heritage like the English did. I told him I was half Bernese to explain my fluency in the obscure dialect."

"You must have to tell a lot of white lies, mustn't you?" Eleanor looked as startled as I was as she voiced the thought. "You know, to keep things easier, with your unusual linguistic eccentricities."

"Yes… yes, I do, as a matter of fact…"

Another urge to unload all of my secrets washed over me, but Eleanor mercifully brought us back to the point before I had my chance.

"Thinking back on it, I agree with you, Edmund. I believe Mr. Kauter's grief and his surprise were genuine when we visited his cottage... Still, it is possible that he is an exceptional liar. If he was capable of killing his own daughter, he would likely have maniacal tendencies that might make such a farce easier for him to pull off."

We both paused to mull over the possibilities.

"There is something that has been bothering me the whole time..." Eleanor finally spoke. "Why was Ingrid in her nightgown? How does that fit in? No one reported her missing all day, and then she was stabbed in the middle of the afternoon in her sleeping clothes. Doesn't that strike you as odd?"

"Yes... yes, now that you mention it, it does."

"I am certain about the time of death, but Mr. Banning was right that something must have happened in the middle of the night as well, or else she would have been wearing normal clothing."

"What if she was ill? Perhaps no one expected to see her at the house today, and that is why no one noticed she was missing. Doesn't pregnancy make women feel sick? Perhaps she was in her nightgown because she was resting in bed all day."

"You're a genius, Edmund! Yes, that would explain a lot of the inconsistencies!"

I melted into her arms as she pulled me into a thrilling victorious kiss.

Eleanor pulled away, and her expression returned to solemnity. "That would certainly make Mr. Kauter the top suspect, though."

As we reached the end of the hallway, the loud clanking of pots and pans punctuated a tirade of angry muttering that echoed from inside the kitchen door. At the idea of food, I realized that I hadn't eaten anything since breakfast, and my stomach let out a loud groan of hunger.

204

"I think we'd better interview Mrs. Murray!" Eleanor exclaimed. "Ingrid worked for her. Perhaps she can fill in all of the missing gaps! And perhaps she has some food for you…"

"Are you not hungry?" I asked with subtle embarrassment at my body's loud declaration of my desires.

"I had a wee bite earlier while you were in the bath. I could probably eat more, though. We've been out and about all day."

As we entered the kitchen, Mrs. Murray was staring at a large cauldron of simmering curry. A heaping pile of crusty dishes filled the sink, and sticky stains of earlier cooking experiments blanketed the dusty stone floors. Upon a closer look, the kitchen looked rather dreadful, as if no one had actively cleaned it in days, possibly weeks.

"Mrs. Murray, are you alright?" Eleanor asked concernedly.

Mrs. Murray took one long look at us, and then burst into tears. Eleanor rushed over to her, helped her sit down in a dusty chair, and then pulled up a seat beside her.

"Now, now, Mrs. Murray, tell us what is troubling you," Eleanor said as she stroked her back soothingly.

Mrs. Murray wept for many minutes, wiping her copious tears and mucus onto the skirt of her dirty apron, while Eleanor comforted her without a hint of judgment. With every sob, my love for Eleanor's kind patience in the face of others' pain grew stronger.

Finally, Mrs. Murray took in a deep, snorting breath and looked up to both of us with her red, tired eyes.

"Everything is topsy turvy!" she exclaimed. "Forty years, I've been here! Forty years! Cooked for Lord Crowden's father, I did. I started here when I was nothing but a lass! And when the Baron came back from India with his oriental spices in tow, did I offer a hint of complaint?! No! None! I spent years with that Hindustani chef learning his mystic cooking practices, all to accommodate the Baron's foreign palate. My life I devoted to them, to these Barons of Heathfield, and now what thanks do I get? A boot out the door!"

"What do you mean?" Eleanor asked sweetly.

"They've given me my notice!" Mrs. Murray wailed.

"Really?" Eleanor could not hide the surprise in her voice as she threw me a glance of intrigue. "Did they say why?"

"They said I'm too old to keep up!" Mrs. Murray exclaimed. I glanced around the filthy kitchen but said nothing. "Oh, don't give me that look, Colonel." A hot blush rushed into my cheeks at her reprimand. "It is not the cook's job in any distinguished household to clean the floors and wash the dishes. It is not my fault that this generation of Crowdens couldn't keep their finances in order! They let go of the entire backhouse staff, while they wasted their money on troops of footmen! It's all about keeping up appearances, it is. None of the hoity-toity visitors pay any mind to the filthy kitchen, as long as the supper comes out on time on its silver platter."

"Mrs. Murray, are you certain that they gave you notice?" I asked. "Are you sure that it wasn't a temporary measure? I understand that the Baron's finances are locked up at the moment until they can get things settled. Perhaps they can't afford to keep you until things are worked out?"

"They didn't say that, did they? No, they blamed *me*, they did! After all I've done for them!"

"She is right about that. There was no reason for them to degrade her in that manner if they were simply waiting out a storm…" Eleanor addressed me in Gaelic.

I was grateful that my addled brain was finally noticing the transition in language more actively.

"Perhaps they didn't want to discuss their financial difficulties with the staff. Many households don't," I replied in Gaelic.

Mrs. Murray eyed me with silent curiosity.

"What if there is another reason they want her out of here?" Eleanor posited.

My stomach growled, and they both looked straight at me.

"Er... sorry... I haven't eaten since breakfast," I said sheepishly as I felt my hot blush return.

"Help yourself, Colonel. There will be no dinner for the rest of the house tonight, anyway. They told me not to bother, but I'd already put the curry on. Two hours before dinner they cancelled. Two hours! Do they think the food just appears by magic? Of course I'd already started! And with the Baron's favorite spices just for you, Colonel! They said you liked the sausage at breakfast."

"It was the most delicious sausage I've ever tasted," I agreed.

"Not delicious enough," she humphed. "They gave me my notice a few hours later."

My stomach growled again, and I couldn't resist. I collected a large porcelain bowl, certainly intended for serving rather than eating, and filled it to the brim with the burbling concoction.

"There isn't turmeric in this, is there? There wasn't any in the sausage earlier... I'm intensely allergic." I took a moment to appreciate how lucky I'd been that the sausage did not have turmeric in it. I'd been eating drab English food for so long that I had gotten out of the habit of asking.

"No sir," Mrs. Murray confirmed. "The Baron never liked turmeric. He said it made the food too yellow."

"I share his sentiments," I agreed.

A very human hunger exploded in my gut at the rich, spicy scent wafting off of the steaming bowl in front of me, and I suddenly had to focus all of my energy on eating politely with the British table manners I had always detested when eating Indian food. I felt their eyes bearing down on me as I ate the entire serving without looking up at them, and when I was finished, I guiltily served myself a second helping.

When I finally made eye contact with Eleanor, she was watching my spectacle with enraptured curiosity, while Mrs.

Murray looked rather pleased with my enthusiastic response to her cooking.

"This is the most delicious curry I've tasted in years, Mrs. Murray. Utterly superb."

"Thank you very much, indeed, Colonel!" she said with her first moment of cheer since I'd met the poor woman. "Do you need a cook?"

"Ha! I suppose maybe I do!" The thought of expanding my household staff suddenly seemed reasonable as I envisioned Eleanor joining me in London. I took a moment to relish the fantasy. "I have been taking my meals at the barracks for years. Let me think on that intriguing proposal, Mrs. Murray. It is very intriguing indeed…"

Eleanor cleared her throat, and I suddenly felt rather sheepish about my enthusiasm in the face of the serious tragedy before us.

"Sorry," I muttered as I finished up eating my second helping and eyed the rest of the cauldron covetously. "We must focus on the most important matters at hand." I managed to control my urge to serve myself up a third portion.

"Mrs. Murray, can you tell us about Ingrid?" Eleanor asked as she leaned in. "Please tell us everything you know. We must get to the bottom of her murder."

"Oh, Ingrid," Mrs. Murray's eyes teared up again. "She was a good girl… a tragic girl…"

"Mr. Rana said almost exactly the same thing," Eleanor pointed out.

"Yes, he and I talked about her sometimes," Mrs. Murray agreed. "She was the last scullery maid left in the kitchen… But even she was ordered to stop working last month. Ever since then, they've expected me to do everything!"

"I'm sorry, are you saying that they made Ingrid redundant over a month ago?" Eleanor asked with surprise. "No one has mentioned that to us in our interviews today—neither Mr. Rana nor Mr. Kauter, and surely both of them should have known."

Mrs. Murray looked nervously to me, as if we'd caught her in a lie.

"Are you sure that they let her go?" I asked her encouragingly.

"Well, it wasn't so permanent, I think." Mrs. Murray regained some confidence. "She seemed to think she'd be back to work soon. She wasn't very pleased about it either. She always talked about skipping off to Switzerland, but she never had enough money for the passage. Her father demanded that she give him all her wages, you see, to help pay for their household here. That girl had no hope. She was trapped, the poor thing."

"Poor Ingrid…" Eleanor murmured. "She was a tragic girl…"

Mrs. Murray nodded her agreement. "Ingrid was such a beautiful girl, so much more beautiful than I ever was. And she was kind. She shouldn't have been a scullery maid. If I'd been her mother, I'd have taken her right back to Switzerland when she was a lass, but Mr. Kauter was so bloody stubborn. Ingrid's mother had died back in Switzerland, you see, and he'd go on and on about how he'd given up everything to move here, but I don't know why that should've mattered! I don't see how Switzerland could have possibly been worse than what poor Ingrid endured with John Crowden chasing after her… And then with the war?! Their lives were so miserable! That poor girl should have had better prospects. I'm sorry for her that she didn't."

"Mrs. Murray, if Ingrid wasn't working in the house in the last month, then where was she staying? When we went to Mr. Kauter's cottage, he seemed to think that she was late coming home from work. Did she perhaps have a young man with whom she might have been staying?" Eleanor threw me a look of impressed surprise as I mounted my question, and I couldn't help but smile at her support.

An odd expression crossed Mrs. Murray's face, and she leaned in and lowered her voice. "She was staying in the house. Mrs. Crowden offered her the room across from the kitchen. It was a very odd thing to do, if you ask me. They didn't have the money to pay her for her work, but they had the money to put her up in the house? In the guest quarters? To feed her my food like she was a member of the household? When I've worked here for forty years, and I'm still sleeping in the attic!"

"Did you resent Ingrid for it?" Eleanor asked astutely.

Mrs. Murray gasped with offense. "Most certainly not! I was glad that Ingrid finally had something nice in her life! I resented the Crowdens for it! There are fifteen empty bedrooms in this bloody house! If they were going to tide over the staff in luxurious accommodation until their financial difficulties were resolved, surely they should have let me stay in one too! Mr. Rana has had his own bedroom in the manor since he moved here from India! Now it's just me, Mrs. Murray, alone in the dark, cold servants' quarters like Cinderella!"

"Where do the footmen live?" I asked. "And the chauffer? And the boys who carried my luggage inside last night?"

Mrs. Murray rolled her eyes. "They come in from the village. They only work here when there are guests in the house. Putting on appearances, if you know what I mean."

"If none of the extra staff were staying in the house last night, that reduces our list of suspects even more," I whispered to Eleanor. "None of them would have had the opportunity to steal Mr. Rana's karpan."

"I'm still stuck on why poor Ingrid was staying in the house," Eleanor whispered back to me in Gaelic. "If she wasn't even working, I can't think of a good reason why Annie would have set her up in the house. Can you?"

I desperately wanted to offer Eleanor a useful answer. As I eyed Mrs. Murray, a horrific thought occurred to me, and I joined

Eleanor in Gaelic. "What if... What if Ingrid confessed something about her home life with her father that Annie wanted to mitigate. Perhaps Annie was trying to protect Ingrid from her father." The idea sickened me, but I could not ignore the possibility that it was true. "Good lord, if that were the case, then perhaps Mr. Kauter had an even stronger motive for murder..."

"How awful..." Eleanor murmured. "But you could be right, Edmund. That is, in fact, the strongest motive we've stumbled upon in our investigations."

"Mrs. Murray, did you have any idea that Ingrid was pregnant?" Eleanor asked bluntly.

A look of genuine shock crossed her face, and then her expression darkened. "I did not."

"Do you have any ideas about who could be the father of the child?" Eleanor pushed with her sweetest tone.

Mrs. Murray thought for a long while before answering.

"Please, Mrs. Murray, don't hold anything back, no matter how shameful it is for those you might want to protect," Eleanor implored.

Mrs. Murray glanced nervously at the door and then lowered her voice. "Ingrid and Mrs. Crowden had a row on Wednesday."

"Do you know about what?" Eleanor was clearly ignited by the intel.

"Ingrid did not want to stay in the house when John Crowden arrived. She's been terrified of that brute since she was a lass, with good reason. But Mrs. Crowden did not want to let Ingrid leave the house. In the end, Ingrid locked herself in her bedroom and cried for hours."

"How often does John Crowden visit the house?" I asked.

"It depends... He is not predictable, Colonel, except that he always comes when he needs money from his father. This time, I'm sure, it is no different, except that the Baron's health is failing, so John is even more brutish than he normally is."

"Was John Crowden here… er… four months ago?" Eleanor asked awkwardly.

Mrs. Murray scrunched her nose as she added up the timeline in her head. "That would have been about July, I think… No… No, Mr. Crowden wasn't here in June or July. He arrived in the middle of August to terrorize the household for a few weeks, and then he skipped off to London again."

I felt a rumble of anxiety in the pit of my stomach as her response reiterated even more potential evidence for Mr. Kauter's multi-faceted guilt.

"Mrs. Murray, do you think… do you think that Ingrid was afraid of her father? Of Mr. Kauter?" I hoped she wouldn't fully understand the implications of the question.

A distinct sadness darkened her expression. "Yes, Colonel, I think she was. Sometimes she had bruises when she'd come to work in the morning, even when she was a little girl."

Eleanor and I threw each other a knowing glance. Neither of us were remotely happy that the evidence was pointing to an even more nefarious plot than any we had already had in mind.

"Mrs. Murray, did you see Mr. Kauter around the manor any time yesterday or today?" I asked, hoping that the answer would seal our case.

"No, I can't say that I did."

My posture deflated.

"Mr. Rana was drugged last night," Eleanor revealed. "Someone stole his sword from his room while he was trapped in an unnatural sleep."

"Oh my!" Mrs. Murray exclaimed. "Does that mean you're certain that he didn't do it?"

"It does," Eleanor confirmed.

"Thank god!" Mrs. Murray exclaimed. "I've spent twenty years working with that man. God forbid I wasted my life standing side by side with a murderer!"

I found her simplicity endearing. "We believe that someone's sleeping medication was placed in Mr. Rana's chai sometime in the evening. Were you in the kitchen all evening?"

"No. Mr. Crowden insisted that I serve the rest of his dinner to him personally." She made no effort to hide a look of distinct disdain on her face. "It took me at least twenty minutes to carry that bloody silver tray up the stairs, serve up his majesty's place setting in his sitting room to his satisfaction, and carry it back down again. Anyone could have come into the kitchen while I was gone. That was about half past nine, perhaps slightly later."

"That was almost an hour after John's abrupt exit from the dining room," I whispered.

"Perhaps he drank a bottle of cognac before he called for the rest of his dinner," Eleanor suggested. "There are many reasons he might have waited to call her."

"Yes, yes, I suppose…"

"Mrs. Murray, do you know anyone else who takes sleeping medications? Anyone other than the Baron? Do you know if Mr. Kauter had any?"

"I doubt it," Mrs. Murray scoffed. "A working horse like that surely doesn't need any. Besides, he's preached about how Swiss herbs are all anyone needs for any ailment ever since I've known him."

I began to feel the strain of the difficult task before us weighing on me. We were making some progress in the investigation, but every answer created more questions… I wasn't sure if I was really the investigatory type.

Eleanor leaned in and whispered in my ear. "Mrs. Murray's account creates a problem for Mr. Kauter's opportunity to drug Mr. Rana… it creates two problems, actually: Mrs. Murray didn't see him anywhere near the house all evening, even though she was in the kitchen except for the twenty minutes she was in John's room, and Mr. Kauter probably did not have his own sleeping medications to use… that means he would have had to steal them from someone else without being seen by anyone in the household."

"Perhaps someone did see him," I proposed. "We still need to talk to Ralph and Anne and the Fitzgeralds. Perhaps one of them saw Mr. Kauter."

Eleanor smiled. "You're right, Edmund. You're absolutely right. We should continue on with great haste. We have a lot of good leads now to go on, though."

"You might want to wait until morning to interview poor Mrs. Fitzgerald," Mrs. Murray suggested.

"And why is that?" Eleanor asked with piqued interest.

"Oh, that poor woman looked like death itself earlier today. She came by the kitchen at about two o'clock, only a few hours before Mr. Crowden gave me my notice, asking for some soup. She had a dreadful cough, and she looked quite feverish."

"Good lord, you don't think she might have been poisoned, do you?" I blurted. I regretted my wild speculation as soon as the words came out of my mouth.

Mrs. Murray was startled by the assertion. "Why… why… I don't think so, Colonel! I've seen my fair share of flus over the years. She seemed perfectly sick to me! Does poison cause fever and coughing? She also had a dreadfully sore throat, that was why she wanted the soup."

"Generally those symptoms sound more like a flu than poison," Eleanor replied calmly.

Mrs. Murray sighed with relief, and I shared her sentiment. "I can't say I was surprised that someone gave into the curse of the cold weather like that… Every year at first snow someone comes down with a horrible case of the flu," Mrs. Murray explained. "So, I gave her the soup and helped her back up to her room myself and tucked her right into bed. She was so grateful, Colonel! She sang my praises like I've never heard before from those ungrateful

Crowdens! I couldn't believe that such a kind woman could be married to such a brute! And can you believe her heartless husband cared so little about her that she had to come to the kitchen all by herself in that state?!"

"Did she say where her husband was?" Eleanor asked. I could hear the subtle excitement in her voice at the value of the unexpected intel.

"She said he was smoking cigars and drinking cognac with John! In the middle of the afternoon!" Mrs. Murray exclaimed. "Of all the poor excuses to ignore your ailing wife!"

"Do you think he was actually snorting cocaine with John?" Eleanor whispered into my ear in Gaelic. "Or conducting whatever their nefarious business is?"

"I don't know…" I murmured. "I suppose those are likely possibilities…"

"Perhaps Mr. Fitzgerald is the source of John's cocaine? Or vice versa…" Eleanor reasoned out loud. "That would explain a lot, actually…"

"We had better continue on straightaway," I whispered. "Mr. Fitzgerald is certainly a top suspect now, along with Mr. Kauter… but neither of them are likely to be straightforward in admitting their guilt. I think we should talk to Ralph and Anne to get more details, just like those that Mrs. Murray has shared with us, so that we can use them to corner our top suspects into telling us the truth."

Eleanor smiled encouragingly. "That is a very strategic suggestion, Colonel."

She stood up and made her way to the door. I stood up more slowly and pushed my chair in as I guiltily observed the dirty dishes I was leaving for Mrs. Murray. She followed my gaze and smiled kindly. "Leave that all to me, Colonel. You have more important things to attend to." She sighed sadly.

"Please, don't lose heart, Mrs. Murray," Eleanor reassured her. "We will get to the bottom of this and bring justice to Ingrid. And, in the meantime, I think that the colonel has already demonstrated his appreciation for your culinary skills. Perhaps you can get a position with him." Eleanor winked teasingly at me.

"I've always wanted to live in London," Mrs. Murray said expectantly with a sudden return of cheer.

"I will take the situation under consideration," I offered.

The idea of eating her delicious food every day was almost strong enough to overwhelm my fear of bringing in another member to my household of secrets, and so, acknowledging my unusually emotional state, I wisely decided to defer my decision until after the pressing issue of the unsolved murder was fully resolved.

"Do you know where Ralph and Anne are?" Eleanor asked as I followed her to the kitchen door.

"They rang from the Baron's office an hour ago for some tea. Perhaps they're still there? It's across from the library," Mrs. Murray suggested. A new enthusiasm had entered her tone, perhaps at the prospect of new employment.

"Thank you for your help. If you see anything suspicious, anything at all, please let us know. There is a murderer afoot," I said.

"Yes, Colonel. Thank you, Colonel."

"Shall we?" I asked as I offered Eleanor my arm.

"I'm quite impressed by your inquisitive tenacity, Colonel," Eleanor whispered.

I smiled at the compliment. "I will endeavor to keep it up."

"I hope so, Edmund. We both have a lot still to learn."

CHAPTER 19 – IN THE DARK

As we approached the office at the end of the hallway across from the library, Eleanor leaned in to offer me a gentle kiss on the cheek, and then whispered into my ear. "I think, Edmund, that we must keep top of mind that our murderer is devious. Whether Mr. Kauter is the culprit or not, this plot is much more complicated than I realized, and Ralph and Anne know more than they're letting on. I'm sure of it. We must get to the bottom of it."

I squeezed her hand and leaned down to sneak another kiss before taking a deep, calming breath, preparing myself for another round of inquiry.

I knocked lightly at the door, and then cracked it open and peeked inside. Together, Anne, Ralph, and Mr. Banning looked deeply enraptured in a hushed conversation. They all sat around an imposing mahogany desk covered in messy papers, and Mr. Banning's hand was covered in ink, indicating that he had likely been writing intensely for hours.

"Eh hem…" I called. "We are ready for those interviews you promised us."

"Ellie! Tell us what you've found!" Anne exclaimed as she jumped out of her seat and pulled Eleanor into a tight hug. Ralph, still looking as deathly ill as he had earlier in the day, only offered me a defeated nod.

Eleanor pulled away from Anne and looked at her with a hint of suspicion. "Mr. Rana was drugged last night with some sort of sleeping medication. His sword was stolen while he was trapped in an unnatural sleep."

"What?!" Anne exploded into awkward, inappropriate laughter. "How absurd! Why would anyone want to do that?"

"Undoubtedly so that they could frame him for murder," I replied as I took in the odd demeanors of all three of them. They were certainly guilty of something, but I couldn't believe that any of them had it in them to murder a young woman in cold blood.

"You don't think it could have been John, do you?" Ralph asked as he grabbed his inhaler from the desk and took in several long swigs. "He has harassed Ingrid since she was a girl, and he always threatened to ruin Mr. Rana, ever since our father whipped him on Mr. Rana's behalf."

"Yes, Mr. Rana told me about that incident… We considered the possibility that John was the guilty party, but he has a solid alibi. Lord Blakeney was watching him all day, and he has confirmed that John remained in his room throughout the afternoon." I looked carefully at each of their faces to observe their reactions. They gave away nothing.

"I don't like this Lord Blakeney character one bit," Mr. Banning muttered. "If he's such a good friend of the Baron's, I don't know why none of us have heard of him until today."

"He didn't claim to be a friend of the Baron's, did he?" I asked as I thought back to our initial conversation. "He claimed to be an acquaintance, hired by the Baron for a specific task. He gave the

218

details of his assignment to Eleanor." I regretted giving away the secret the moment the words came out of my mouth, as they all looked expectantly to her.

She sighed with subtle annoyance. "He only told me under the strict condition that I keep his exact assignment a secret, on the orders of the Baron himself. I will not break their confidence."

"Surely he didn't mean for you to keep the secret from us?" Mr. Banning argued.

"I'm most certain he did," Eleanor countered. "But the important point here is that John and Mr. Rana have alibis, which means that there is a murderer running loose on the property right now. We must find him before it's too late."

As if on cue, as Eleanor spoke her foreboding words, all of the lights went out at once.

"Bloody hell, you don't think he's here for us, do you?!" Anne said in a panic. "Maybe he's going to murder all of us!"

"Where's Mr. Rana?! Maybe he's going to take his revenge for us locking him in the library!" Mr. Banning exclaimed.

"That is enough, Mr. Banning," Ralph hissed. He exploded into a bout of coughs, but pushed forward anyway. "I have known... Mr. Rana... all my life. He has always... been a kind... and helpful man."

"I am certain that Mr. Rana has better things to do than to cut off the electricity and murder us in the dark." I was unable to hide my annoyance at Mr. Banning's continued ignorant insistence on Mr. Rana's guilt.

"I'm sure it's simply a result of the snow. It's a wonder the electricity lasted as long as it did in a blizzard like this." I noticed that Eleanor was using the exact same tone of feigned confidence that she had used with me in the stables.

I reached forward and turned the winding key of an antique oil lamp that I'd noticed in passing. It was strikingly similar to the ones I'd kept in my house across the village. I was certain that it had been procured by the Baron's father from the same shop that I had enjoyed perusing from time to time during my decades in Basingstoke.

"How lovely!" Eleanor exclaimed as the room lit up with the gentle light. "How did you know how it worked?"

"I am surprised myself." I deflected a direct answer to her question. "I didn't expect such an old lamp to still have fuel. Someone in this house must enjoy the old-fashioned ambiance."

"My father did," Ralph said as he took in another dose from his inhaler. "He always turned off the electric lights to spend the evening in his office with the old lamps. I could never figure out how any of them worked, though."

I stood up and scanned the room. I spotted two more old-fashioned lamps by the fireplace, and I quickly hopped up and wound their keys.

"Jolly good, Colonel!" Mr. Banning exclaimed. "Now Mr. Rana won't dare to pop in here for a quick stabbing!"

"Mr. Banning!" Ralph hissed. "That is enough!"

Anne rubbed his back while he wheezed.

I returned to the desk and squinted to observe the mechanism of the lamp. I pointed at the gilded golden barrel. "It is a carcel lamp. It is using clockwork to regulate the flow of the oil. Mr. Miller in the village used to import all sorts of unusual technologies from Europe. This one is probably from France. My grandfather had many in his home, as well. He too preferred the old-fashioned oil lighting over the dangerous technology of electricity. He used quite a bit of paraffin as well, but it didn't produce exactly the same effect." I, of course, was referring to my own opinions on the matter.

"I hope he didn't spend too much time in the dim light. It's wickedly bad for the eyesight," Eleanor pointed out.

The connection between the dismal lighting of my studio and my eyesight's aged degeneration in the 1870s had not occurred to me until that moment. I had subtly noticed over the last few years that while my vision had become a bit blurrier than I was willing to admit, it was nowhere near as bad as I'd remembered it from the last time I'd been in my physical fifties.

"You know, I think you're right… I think he did spend too much time painting in the dim light, now that you mention it."

"Was that painting that we discussed this morning his?" Eleanor asked with sudden excitement. "No wonder you had such a strong reaction to it!"

"Yes… yes, as a matter of fact, it was…" I admitted. "But surely, we have more important things to discuss than the art."

"Quite right," Eleanor agreed as she realized the error of her distraction. "We have a murder to solve, and we're still in the dark about the culprit." She looked around at the dark room. "That was not intended to be a pun. The point is: Mr. Rana and John didn't do it. That leaves us a short list of suspects. Someone drugged Mr. Rana's tea last night, obviously with the intent of framing him. This person must have had a motive to kill poor Ingrid, and we must find out who it was and bring him to justice. What do you know about Ingrid's situation?"

"Nothing at all. I've never met the girl in my life!" Mr. Banning exclaimed.

"I meant Ralph and Anne," Eleanor said with an eye roll.

"She was a fine maid. I'm sorry she suffered," Anne said with a shrug. "What else is there to say?"

"What do you know of Mr. Kauter?" I asked, hoping not to give away too much of our secret suspicions. I suddenly realized that we were participating in a chess match of sorts.

"He has lived here for years and years. He has always been a fine farmer. He harvests the fruit on time, and it makes wonderful pies. What else is there to say?" I realized as Anne repeated the phrase for the second time, that it meant that she was hiding something. I congratulated myself on noticing the trend.

"Perhaps you can shed some light on some sort of deal that Mr. Kauter had with John. When we arrived at his cottage to break the bad news, he accused us of being an agent of the Crowdens, and said that 'the deal was off.' Do you have any idea what he was talking about?" I eyed each of them suspiciously again.

Ralph began wheezing, and as Anne rubbed his back, Mr. Banning looked down at his feet.

"Well?" I pushed. Their silence spoke volumes.

"I know nothing of a deal with Mr. Kauter," Ralph hissed.

"Nor do I," Anne seconded with a bit too much passion.

"Mr. Banning?" I used my most authoritative tone.

"Nothing!" he exclaimed. "I know nothing!"

"He who doth protest too much..." I whispered to Eleanor. She nodded her agreement.

"Annie, please. A girl who has devoted her life to the service of this house had her throat slashed less than six hours ago, only a few hundred meters from where we are standing right now. Mr. Kauter told us that Mr. Crowden had made too many false promises. If you know anything about what he meant, you must tell us!"

Anne looked to Ralph and then Mr. Banning. "I honestly don't know what he was talking about, Ellie. Clearly John must have tried to make some deal with him, and then he backed out. John has done the same thing so many times, there is hardly anything noteworthy about it."

"Except that a girl might very well have been murdered over it this time," I corrected her.

Anne shrugged. "I'm sorry for Ingrid. I really am. But I can't tell you anything else."

Eleanor squeezed my hand subtly, and then launched into our next line of questioning. "Was Ingrid afraid of her father?"

Anne was taken aback. "Why would Ingrid be afraid of Mr. Kauter?"

222

"You tell us," Eleanor countered.

I loved how she lobbed Anne's deflections right back at her.

"I don't have any idea!" Anne exclaimed.

"Then why, Mrs. Crowden, would you have given Ingrid a room in the manor last month after you temporarily dismissed her from service?" I pushed.

I felt a burst of secret satisfaction as Anne's expression morphed into genuine fear. Obviously, she had been trying to hide her involvement in that aspect of the plot, but why, I could not fathom. I could not understand why she would have any motive to protect Mr. Kauter. She seemed far more interested in protecting herself, and perhaps Ralph.

"Why, I... I... I..." Anne stuttered. Eleanor threw me a satisfied glance. "I felt sorry for the girl! We couldn't afford to pay her while the Baron's will was undisclosed, and we had plenty of room in the house. It was an act of charity!"

Ralph took two long doses of his inhaler in a row, and his color turned vaguely blue.

"Are you alright, Ralph?" Eleanor asked with sudden concern. "There isn't camphor in that, is there? You've had five doses since we joined you a few minutes ago."

"It's fine," Anne said haughtily. "I have my husband's medications under control."

Eleanor was taken aback by Anne's defensive response. "Annie, you and I both know that camphor is lethal in high doses."

"I said it's fine," Anne hissed.

Eleanor threw me a nervous look.

"Did any of you know that Ingrid was pregnant?" I threw the most scandalous detail right out into the open.

Horrified looks crossed all three of their faces.

"I didn't share that detail with them earlier at the crime scene," Eleanor whispered into my ear in Gaelic. "I thought we would be able to use it as an ace in the hand for our investigation. It looks like you've played our ace well."

I worked hard not to show my satisfaction at Eleanor's praise to our increasingly desperate audience.

"How do you know?" Anne whispered. "How do you know she was pregnant?"

"I inspected the body closely after we came upon it. She was already showing. About four, maybe four and a half months, which would date conception back to late June or early July," Eleanor replied. "Surely, Annie, you must have noticed she was showing if she was living with you in the house?"

"Her clothing wasn't well-fitted," Anne murmured. "She always preferred to wear empire-waisted dresses. She thought it was better for her strenuous work."

"But surely you must have seen the signs for yourself when you were out there with me at the crime scene?" Eleanor pushed.

"The snow was in the way..." Anne seemed sad for the first time since our interview began. "And the bloody corpse was too hard to look at."

Ralph exploded into even more violent coughs.

"This is too much for Ralph in his weakened state," Anne addressed us sharply. "If you don't mind, he needs some rest. I think we've told you everything we know anyway."

She helped Ralph up out of his seat and escorted him towards the door.

Eleanor rushed to stop them. "Just a minute, Annie! What are the Fitzgeralds doing here? What were you shouting about with John in the hallway during dinner last night? What were you threatening to tell the Baron? You have to help us fit these pieces together!"

A look of indignance crossed Anne's face, and her tone became genuine for the first time since the conversation began. "Those wretched hooligans are here for money. They are here to collect a debt, one of hundreds, I'm sure, in John's bloody name. They have been here twice before when John wasn't here, and this time they followed him in from the village when he arrived. I have no idea how long they were waiting for him, but obviously the debt must be worth their efforts. If you want to know more, you will have to ask them. John has so many bloody debts these days, we don't have the energy to keep track. I will tell you this, though: They won't get a penny from us. Now, I need to help my ailing husband to bed."

I joined Eleanor by the door to watch Anne and Ralph walk slowly down the dark hallway.

"They're hiding something," she whispered to me in Gaelic. "She's so desperate to escape from our line of questioning that she didn't even bother to look for a lamp to take with them."

"What do you think it is? You don't think it's possible that they did it, do you? I don't know Ralph particularly well, and I don't know what either of them are capable of in the right circumstances."

"Neither do I..." Eleanor murmured.

"Still, Mr. Kauter is a stronger suspect... Do you think that they are protecting Mr. Kauter for some reason? Some reason pertaining to that 'deal' he mentioned when we interviewed him?"

"Perhaps... yes, perhaps that's the connection..." Eleanor agreed. "But if they won't tell us what they were talking about, I'm not sure we'll be able to weasel it out of them. Perhaps if we get more evidence, we can use it to motivate them to disclose whatever truths they're hiding."

"You've really got a knack for this," I said with a hint of a swoon in my voice.

"Perhaps I'll moonlight as a detective," Eleanor winked.

"So, the Fitzgeralds, is it?" I grimaced as Mr. Banning interrupted us. "They seem like a devious lot!"

"Indeed," Eleanor agreed.

"What have you been up to all day, Mr. Banning?" I asked as I eyed the stacks of paper. Something about his demeanor struck me as especially dodgy. "What is so important that it must be done now, while the household is under investigation for murder?"

"That is privileged information! I can't say anything about it!"

I straightened my posture and prepared to use my most authoritative tone. "If you know anything about this household, *anything* that might be of relevance to this investigation, you'd better share it now. Someone is going to hang for Ingrid's murder, Mr. Banning, and you mustn't be complicit. I don't have to tell an educated solicitor such as yourself that aiding and abetting a murderer is a serious crime."

"I... I..." Mr. Banning looked back and forth between me and Eleanor, and a burst of spicy fear wafted off of him.

"Tommy, if you have something to confess, you'd better confess it now. I won't be able to help you if you don't help yourself," I pushed.

"I... I've done nothing wrong!" Mr. Banning declared. "Now, I'd better get back to work!"

Mr. Banning threw himself down in the chair where Ralph had been sitting and began haphazardly shuffling through the messy papers.

"Come on, Colonel. We have a devious lot to interview next," Eleanor said loudly as she eyed him suspiciously. "I'm sure they'll shed light on any dubious legal activities that they know of."

"Yes, I suspect they will," I agreed.

Mr. Banning let off a quiet, involuntary whimper, but said nothing.

As I eyed the pitch-dark hallway, an idea occurred to me, and I glanced around the shelves of the dimly lit room until I spotted what I was looking for.

"There you are..." I carefully collected an antique portable paraffin lamp from the shelf closest to the door. I inspected the

226

neighboring shelves, quickly landing on an elaborately carved matchbox that the Baron had undoubtedly brought back with him from India. "Yes, this is exactly what we need," I said to myself, enjoying a moment of secret nostalgia as I used one of the old matches to light the paraffin lamp.

"How did you know there would be a lamp there?" Eleanor asked curiously.

"Because that is where my grandfather kept his... Always by the door. He used them for wandering about at night without disturbing the rest of the household. It is curious, though..." As I thought about my own use of the lamps, I glanced down to the fuel tank.

"Yes? What is curious?" Eleanor pushed.

"My grandfather always kept the paraffin filled in his portable lamps. This lamp has been burned down quite significantly. If the Baron kept the carcel lamps filled, surely he would have kept this one filled as well."

"Maybe he used the lamp to wander about in the dark before he was bedridden, and then he forgot to refill it. The elderly often forget things," Eleanor suggested.

"Yes, perhaps... Or, perhaps someone else used the lamp... Perhaps someone used it last night to steal Mr. Rana's sword!"

"That means that whomever the culprit is, he must know how to use one of these... Ralph didn't seem to..."

"Ralph would have known. We used paraffin in the trenches all the time. This one is much simpler than the carcel lamps."

"Hrm. Alright... well, Mr. Kauter surely would have known––I saw a paraffin lamp hanging by the door in his cottage... and Annie would have known from her rural upbringing on the moors... and the Fitzgeralds are old enough that they probably used them as children..."

"It isn't the most useful clue," I said disappointedly. "But I suppose it gives us more questions to ask. If someone was wandering about the house with the lamp in hand, perhaps someone saw the light, or perhaps someone saw someone lingering in this room in the evening."

"We are making progress." Eleanor sighed. "I wish it was all over. I'm ready for a solid rest."

I smiled and offered her my arm. "Shall we make more progress with the Fitzgeralds?"

"We shall," Eleanor agreed.

I threw a look of warning to Mr. Banning, hoping that perhaps my influence might still help him come clean about whatever dubious activities he was managing with Anne and Ralph, and together we left him alone to his fearful mutterings in the gentle, old-fashioned oil light of the bedridden Baron's office.

CHAPTER 20 – A DEVIOUS LOT

"Do you know which room the Fitzgeralds were staying in?" Eleanor whispered as we made our way up the stairs to the corridor above the library.

"No. I didn't see them last night after we left the dining room. Did you?" I asked.

"No. Don't you think it's odd that we haven't heard anything from Mr. Fitzgerald this evening? He was more than enthusiastic in joining Mr. Banning and me to inspect the crime scene, but I haven't seen him since we all returned to the house... I don't like it."

"Does that mean that Mrs. Fitzgerald didn't join you?" I asked.

"Yes... I wondered about it earlier, but there was too much going on to really even notice her absence. But with Mrs. Murray's testimony, I don't think it's surprising that she didn't join us. People with the flu rarely hop out of bed just to follow a commotion, and I suspect that with her husband's brutish conduct, commotions are not particularly uncommon in her life."

"I hate to admit that Mr. Banning is correct—Mr. Fitzgerald does seem rather devious," I agreed. "It was utterly inexcusable that he joined John for that shooting session on the roof this morning. He knew full well what that would do to Ralph's temperament... and mine."

"Come to think of it, we don't know where he went after that," Eleanor pointed out. "Perhaps he had his adrenaline pumping, and he went looking for trouble elsewhere while Lord Blakeney wrangled John."

Eleanor grimaced as an unpleasant thought entered her head.

"What?" I asked nervously.

"No... no I don't think so..." she murmured to herself as she closed her eyes in deep thought.

"You don't think what?"

"I am quite sure she wasn't raped. I looked for signs of it as soon as we came upon the body. I was just considering the scenario of Mr. Fitzgerald stealing Mr. Rana's sword after his shooting session with John, coming upon Ingrid, chasing her through the orchards, and having his way with her, but she didn't have any bruises. In fact, I was quite surprised that she didn't have *any*, given how she was killed. I'm not sure what to make of it. It's like the killer didn't have to hold her down at all."

"How horrible..." I murmured.

"Still, perhaps Ingrid saw something..." Eleanor continued to theorize. "Perhaps Mr. Fitzgerald was doing something illegal, perhaps he was selling cocaine to John, and he caught Ingrid watching them. He might have killed her to silence her, and her pregnancy was only a coincidence."

"It is still a brutal story."

"It was a brutal murder," Eleanor shrugged. "Now, come on. Let's go catch a brutal murderer."

She squeezed my hand, and together we picked up our pace.

As we worked our way to the end of the dark hallway, a commotion in one of the bedrooms brought us straight to attention.

"Isn't that John's room?" Eleanor hissed.

An angry muffled voice resonated into the hallway.

"That's Mr. Fitzgerald," I whispered.

"It sounds like they're arguing," Eleanor whispered back.

My anxiety exploded. "I only hear Mr. Fitzgerald."

"Lord Blakeney, where are you?" Eleanor muttered.

At the sound of a loud crash, I pushed back my raging nerves and grabbed the door handle. Locked. I handed the paraffin lamp to Eleanor, and then squeezed the knob with all my strength until it broke off.

"These old doors could use some repair," I whispered as I placed the damaged loot on a narrow antique table in the hallway.

"Yes, I have found them flimsy myself." My heart skipped a beat as Eleanor glanced over at the evidence of my unusual Rakshasa strength. "I'm right behind you, Colonel." She squeezed my hand encouragingly.

I nodded my agreement, took a deep breath, and pushed open the door.

"The account you gave me last night was empty. Empty! Do you think I was born yesterday? That'll teach you to play games with me, Johnny Boy," Mr. Fitzgerald spat as we burst into the pitch-dark room.

Eleanor reached forward to shine the paraffin lamp on Mr. Fitzgerald, and he looked back at her with wild eyes.

"You meddling bitch!" he hissed. "You think you're any better than your scoundrel of a father? You're just as much of a whore as he was!"

Eleanor stepped back as if his statement had slapped her in the face. "I don't know what you're talking about." Her tone was resigned rather than indignant.

"You think anyone who spent time at Musselburgh wouldn't be able to recognize a rotten little MacLeod?" Mr. Fitzgerald laughed. "Robby MacLeod's fiery seed is impossible to miss!"

Eleanor was speechless, but I could sense her shaking silently.

"That is enough," I declared with my most authoritative tone.

"Do you need your white knight to protect you from the truth, Miss MacLeod? Perhaps the good colonel can give your father the beating he deserves… Oh, that's right. He can't. Robby MacLeod already ate a bullet."

"You will desist this instant!" I shouted as I straightened my posture and let my instincts take over.

I stepped in front of Eleanor, blocking her from the beast's line of sight. She didn't protest, and instead she kneeled down and collected the lamp, illuminating John Crowden's unconscious, bruised body sprawled out across the floor of his own bedroom.

Mr. Fitzgerald shivered, and then regained his composure and grinned diabolically. He lifted up his fat leg and slammed it into John's side.

"Are you going to stop me, Colonel? You? The delicate, damaged soldier who can't even bear to watch puppies chase foxes? John bloody Crowden deserves far less of your sympathy than those foxes did."

He kicked John again, but John's unconscious body didn't respond.

As the scent of fresh blood from John's new injury worked its way into my nasal cavity, my last fleeting desire to rein in my demonic urges vanished, and with one covetous whiff of Mr. Fitzgerald's spicy fear, I grabbed his sweaty, obese body by the shoulders and threw him across the room onto John's messy writing desk. I rushed to catch up with him and ripped his hands apart, slamming them down onto the wooden platform above his head. I squeezed his wrists until he whimpered with a delightful medley of fear and pain.

"Do I look like a delicate, damaged solider to you?" I hissed as I loomed over him. "I think those foxes deserved far more of my sympathy than you do."

Mr. Fitzgerald wet himself.

His fear only fed my dark pleasure more. "Would you like to know how it feels to be damaged?" I squeezed his wrists until he screamed with pain. "Join the club! Do you know how many men I've killed?"

Mr. Fitzgerald began shaking uncontrollably as tears poured from his eyes.

"I don't! I don't have any idea how many men I've killed. It was too many to count!" I exclaimed with giddy laughter. "What is one more? Those quivering German boys I killed in the trenches were far better than you are, you bullying bastard!"

Mr. Fitzgerald's silent tears morphed into loud wails. "Please! I didn't mean anything by it! I didn't mean anything!"

"You didn't mean to attack John Crowden in his own bedroom? Or you didn't mean to insult Eleanor's father? Or perhaps you didn't mean to provoke a soldier who spent four years bathing in blood on behalf of your bloody empire? Which of these reprehensible things did you not mean to do? Perhaps, Mr. Fitzgerald, you didn't mean to murder an innocent young girl and her unborn child in cold blood?"

"Her unborn child?! I didn't know that little Kraut whore was pregnant!"

I moved my right hand to his neck. "I vowed that Ingrid's killer would be brought to justice by any means necessary."

"I didn't do it! I swear it wasn't me!!! It was that foreign butler!!! Everyone saw his bloody sword there!!!"

"The killer drugged him and stole his karpan. You wouldn't know anything about that, would you? WOULD YOU?!"

"Drugged?!" Mr. Fitzgerald squeaked. "I don't know anything about it! I swear! I was with you at dinner, and then I was with John Crowden until after midnight!"

"Why should I believe you?" I tightened my grip on his neck. "Your only witness is unconscious by your hand. What do you have to say about that?!"

"He owes me! Fifty-thousand pounds! That bastard owes a bloody fortune, and if I don't collect, *I* will be the one on the floor with more than a few bruises! I'm the victim!"

My dark voice cackled with delight as he struggled to breathe.

"Ingrid Kauter is the victim," I hissed.

"I didn't do it!"

I leaned in to drink in another whiff of his delicious fear.

"Edmund, that's enough," Eleanor said calmly.

I noticed her for the first time since I'd engaged Mr. Fitzgerald in our interrogation, and suddenly a burst of shame mixed with anxiety at the reality that Eleanor was witnessing my depraved demonic demonstration.

Eleanor put the lamp down on the floor and approached us. She placed her hand gently on my shoulder. "Colonel, you must remain an unquestionable authority if we're going to save Mr. Rana from the gallows. We need Mr. Fitzgerald alive."

My logical mind considered her assertion, but my raging demon was not interested in logic.

She leaned in and whispered into my ear. "Edmund, let him go. Do not give into the darkness. You can control it. I know you can."

She shivered as she ran her fingers along my arm to my right hand that was holding his neck pinned.

"Let him go," she reiterated.

I let her warmth infuse my frigid being, and slowly I let go of his neck. She gathered my hand into hers, and then took my other hand that still held his hand against the writing desk.

234

"Good," she whispered as I struggled against myself to let go.

But, as she held both of my hands in hers, and I slowly released myself from my pumping adrenaline, Mr. Fitzgerald made a very unwise decision.

With all of the energy the fat slob had left in him, he grabbed a letter-opener in the shape of a dagger that lay by his right hand on John's messy desk, and threw it with all his might straight at Eleanor.

Faster than I had ever moved before, I flung myself in front of her. The letter-opener cut through my riding jacket and lodged itself solidly in my ribcage several inches above my heart.

My demonic rage mixed dangerously with my panic at being discovered not only by Eleanor, but by this brute who would certainly use my secret against me however he could.

"Edmund!" Eleanor screamed.

I rushed into the dark shadows beyond the dim light of the paraffin lamp in the vain hope that neither of them would see the letter-opener stuck in my chest.

"I'm perfectly fine. He needs to improve his aim," I lied. "Are you alright?"

Instead of answering me, Eleanor threw herself at Mr. Fitzgerald. A moment of terror on my part for her safety quickly morphed into pride as she kneed the bastard in the groin, and he collapsed right on top of John Crowden's unconscious body.

"You... little... whore..." he hissed as he wiggled himself off of John, into a fetal position.

"Don't make me put you in your place again," Eleanor declared as she positioned herself to kick the worthless brute in the stomach if he moved. "Now you'll stay where you are, if you know what's good for you." She looked over to my position in the shadows. "Edmund? Edmund, are you really alright?"

My heart almost exploded as she rushed towards me.

"Please, just give me one minute to catch my breath," I implored with the calmest tone I could muster. Eleanor mercifully agreed, giving me my space and keeping a looming eye over Mr. Fitzgerald's recovery.

I turned towards the wall to rip the wicked weapon from my flesh. I took a moment to breathe in a sigh of intense relief that the injury was not a few inches lower. Surely, if it had been, I would have re-set to a young man right there in front of her.

As soon as the weapon was out, I slipped it into the inner pocket in my jacket in case any evidence of my unusual composition remained on the blade. I took in a deep breath and worked my hardest to temper the pained noises that were itching to burst forth from me as the cold burning sensation of my Rakshasa plasma setting to work to heal my throbbing wound bombarded me.

"Edmund, please let me help you," Eleanor implored as she approached me slowly. I maintained my position facing the wall, and leaned up against it to brace myself through the height of the healing pain.

"Please, Eleanor, just give me one more minute."

"Edmund, you sound like you're in pain," she pushed. "I'm a nurse, remember?"

"I'm perfectly fine!" I exclaimed desperately. "Just give me one more minute!"

I listened as Eleanor shifted uncomfortably, but I could focus on nothing but the pain. The process was reaching its apex, and I couldn't stifle a whimper.

"*Mon dieu*, what happened?" Lord Blakeney exclaimed as he burst into the room. In the back of my mind, his presence set off another round of panic, but I simply did not have the capacity to focus on it.

"It's about time!" Eleanor exclaimed. "Where in the bloody hell were you?!"

236

"I was working on restoring the electricity!" Lord Blakeney exclaimed. "These modern technologies are so bloody complicated!"

He paused to observe the scene, and as I felt the healing process finish up, I turned myself around and leaned up against the wall to face them. I hoped the darkness would hide the obvious hole in my clothing where the weapon had penetrated, but how I would be able to get myself all the way back to my bedroom to change my clothes without Eleanor or Lord Blakeney noticing, I had no bloody clue. During the war, every soldier's uniform was torn so often in the line of duty that no one ever questioned my many required replacements, but here... here I had no excuse!

"Edmund, are you alright?" Eleanor exclaimed as she rushed towards me. I didn't have the energy to ward her off, and instead I gathered her into my arms.

She shivered as she kissed me gently on the cheek, and then she stepped back to assess me.

"I'm perfectly fine now," I reassured her, this time truthfully. Somehow, the earlier battle I'd been fighting against my dark urges had dissolved. My violent interrogation of Mr. Fitzgerald seemed to have subdued it. A sense of intense relief I had not felt since before the war washed over me, but as Lord Blakeney joined Eleanor to face me in the dark, my posture deflated.

"It looks like you properly disciplined those two scoundrels in my absence. Hrm. It would seem they fought back? Were you injured?"

I startled as Lord Blakeney took my hand into his to examine it in a gesture that felt a bit too motherly, but suddenly a sense of peaceful well-being infused me. A burst of warmth traveled up my arm through my body and into my gut. I'd felt something similar on occasion before, although I couldn't, for my life, place exactly where. Lord Blakeney inspected the cuff of my jacket, and then stepped away.

"Well, it looks like you had the final word, Colonel," he declared. "I can take control of these two men from here. Have you found the murderer yet?"

"We did not get more useful intel." The odd peace further subdued my raging nerves, allowing me to refocus on the original task, although I wasn't nearly as upset by the failure as I normally would've been.

"I wouldn't say that," Eleanor corrected me. "I'm quite sure you scared Mr. Fitzgerald enough that his testimony must have been truthful. Don't you?"

"Yes, I suppose you're right," I admitted sheepishly.

"Then that means that Mr. Fitzgerald didn't do it. That reduces our list of suspects further..." Eleanor turned to observe Mr. Fitzgerald and John Crowden again.

Lord Blakeney leaned down to observe Mr. Fitzgerald in the dim light. "This looks like your handiwork, Miss MacLeod," Lord Blakeney said approvingly.

"Yes... Mr. Fitzgerald threw a poorly-aimed dagger at me, and Edmund rescued me just in the nick of time. While Edmund was distracted trying to find the evidence in the dark, I helped Mr. Fitzgerald understand the error of his ways. Didn't I?" Eleanor sounded especially pleased as she taunted him. "Not so bad for a rotten little MacLeod, don't you think, Fitzy?"

Lord Blakeney kneeled down to inspect John's wounds. "Colonel, this does not look like something you would have done. These bruises are from extended contact. They look more like the result of torture."

"That is Mr. Fitzgerald's handiwork. He was trying to collect on a debt," Eleanor explained on my behalf.

Lord Blakeney took in a deep whiff, and at his cue, I did the same. I shuddered. I knew the scent too well. How I detested its putrid sweetness.

"Mr. Crowden is not doing well," Lord Blakeney declared. "Miss MacLeod, perhaps you can use your medical acumen to diagnose him?"

Eleanor nodded her agreement and joined Lord Blakeney, while I wisely kept myself relegated to the shadows.

"You're right," Eleanor said as she unbuttoned John's shirt and ran her fingers across his bruised ribs. "He has at least three broken ribs... although... hrm... Look here... He is suffering from cirrhosis of the liver, undoubtedly from his addiction to the bottle... and here... the area around his protruding liver is bruised... this could be quite dangerous. Edmund and I both watched Mr. Fitzgerald impart this blow. John might very well be bleeding internally right now. There is nothing any doctor or nurse could do for him without a proper surgery... even then, his chances would be bleak."

"It looks like we might have two murderers on the property by morning," Lord Blakeney said as he looked upon Mr. Fitzgerald with disdain.

As Eleanor ran her fingers across John's chest, he stirred and then moaned with the pain. Eleanor leaned over him.

"John?"

He weakly opened his eyes.

"Am I sufficiently wounded to garner your attention, Ellie?" he asked cheekily. I found it hard to believe that in his decrepit state he was still willing and able to taunt her, but this time, Eleanor's sympathy overwhelmed her annoyance.

"John, your condition is dire. You might not survive the night."

He chuckled once, and his laughter dissolved into a pained moan.

"You have three broken ribs, and you're bleeding internally from the wounds Mr. Fitzgerald inflicted on you," Eleanor continued unfazed. "John, you must tell us everything you know about Mr. Fitzgerald and Ingrid Kauter. Did Mr. Fitzgerald attack you to silence you? Do you know something that he didn't want you to share?"

The idea hadn't even crossed my mind until Eleanor spoke the words. I had to admit that she was far better suited to the investigation game than I was.

"I loved that little Kraut. I would have married her! I *wanted* to marry her! If my selfish, wicked father hadn't stolen all of the money that should have been *mine*, I would have married her! Her father said so! He gave me his permission, if only I'd had the land to give him!"

"Was that it, then? That was the deal that Mr. Kauter was talking about? A marriage pact? Ingrid for the farmland?" Eleanor pushed.

"I'm the next bloody Baron of Heathfield, for god's sake! The heir bloody apparent!" John cried. "I would have made her a bloody lord's wife, but was that enough? NO! That greedy Kraut wanted more! More, more, MORE! For himself, not for Ingrid!"

"You were in love with Ingrid Kauter?" Eleanor asked with her gentlest tone.

"I did not think you capable of love," Lord Blakeney scoffed.

"I loved her, dammit all to Hell!" John wailed. "I've loved her since she was a girl!"

"She didn't love you," Lord Blakeney informed him. "Whatever you did to show your affection scared her."

"They turned her against me! All of them!" John's exclamation morphed into a pained cough. "But I loved her anyway!"

Eleanor threw me a pained look. I hoped for poor Ingrid's sake that John did not mean that he *physically* loved her against her will.

"But Mrs. Murray told us that you weren't here in June or July," Eleanor pointed out.

"Why should that matter?" John asked meekly.

"Because that was when Ingrid's child was conceived," Eleanor replied.

A look of genuine horror spread across John's face. "Ingrid was pregnant? Who was it? I'll kill the bastard!"

"You most certainly will not," Lord Blakeney replied flatly.

John looked to Eleanor and then squinted to observe me through the shadows. "This house is cursed," he whispered resignedly. "I am cursed. Nothing else matters."

"What do you mean this house is cursed?" Eleanor pushed. "How? What does this house have to do with Ingrid's death? Please, John, if you loved her, you must help us! We must find her killer and bring him to justice!"

"There is no justice in this world, and there never has been," John muttered. "Nothing is going to change that now."

"You have done nothing of value in your life," Lord Blakeney reminded him. "You are being given one chance to change that. Are you really going to ignore it?"

John moaned with pain, and then closed his eyes. "Talk to the Baron. Every dark deed I've ever done in my life was his bloody fault."

Lord Blakeney humphed. "You control your own actions, mon chéri. Everything you've ever done in your life is your fault."

"Talk to my father," John whispered. "I have nothing else to say."

He turned his head to the side and refused to look at Eleanor and Lord Blakeney again.

"You go," Lord Blakeney suggested to Eleanor. "Both of you go talk to the Baron. I will stay here with these two scoundrels. They will go nowhere."

"How can we talk to the Baron if he can't even speak anymore?" Eleanor asked. "Can Edmund talk to him somehow?"

The question seemed like an odd one, but Lord Blakeney answered her without hesitation. "You can always write to each other. Ralph confirmed this morning that the Baron is still capable of writing." Lord Blakeney glanced over at me. "There may also be another option… Colonel, the Baron lived in India for many decades. Perhaps you can speak to him in Hindi. You will earn his trust. I do believe that the Baron's refusal to speak to his sons is not entirely a medical issue. Now, go. You may have more questions for these two men after you talk to the Baron, and they must both be alive to answer them."

Eleanor nodded her agreement, gathered the paraffin lamp, and joined me in the shadows.

"Are you ready, Edmund?" she asked as she held the lamp up and looked into my eyes.

My heart skipped a beat as she glanced down to the position where the weapon had penetrated my suit. I followed her gaze to observe with utter puzzlement that my jacket appeared perfectly intact. I was too overwhelmed by the helpful development to even consider questioning how it had come to be.

"Yes, I suppose I am," I agreed.

Eleanor glanced back at Lord Blakeney.

"Go," he reiterated. "Time is of the essence."

Without another word, Eleanor took my hand and escorted me by the waning light of the lamp towards the Baron's chambers.

CHAPTER 21 – THE BARON

As we reached the Baron's room, Eleanor stopped abruptly. I looked around, worried that perhaps she had noticed something that I hadn't, but I could not sense any sort of intrusion.

"Edmund..." Eleanor suddenly sounded nervous. "I need to tell you something."

My heart began racing. Certainly, a modern woman as observant as she was would have noticed my blatant display of superhuman abilities... I'd been secretly wondering about her silence on the matter since we'd left Lord Blakeney's presence, and now we were alone... This was it, I was certain. The axe was about to drop. Fear and excitement rushed through me.

"Edmund, what Mr. Fitzgerald said about my father... It was true. All of it."

I wasn't sure I was happy for the reprieve, in fact, I was rather disappointed.

"You don't have to explain yourself to me," I said as I took her hands into mine. "I am the last person on Earth who should be judgmental about such things. I grew up in an orphanage, for god's sake!"

"Edmund, I want to tell you. I need to tell you. I haven't talked about it in years and years. You told me about your orphanage, and now it is time for me to tell you about my family scandal."

I squeezed her hands reassuringly, thrilled that she was offering me the privilege of consoling her. "Eleanor, you can tell me anything."

"Yes... yes, I know..." She hedged as a burst of spicy fear wafted off of her. "You see... the thing is... my father was a thoroughbred trainer up at Musselburgh... the racetrack just outside of Edinburgh. He loved the horses. They were his life. I spent my early childhood following him around in the stables. He was very good at his job, and he was very well known..." I nodded encouragingly. "But then, when I was ten years old, one of the thoroughbred owners demanded that he participate in throwing a race... a big one... They wanted him to do all sorts of unethical things, and so he refused..."

"There is nothing shameful about that," I reassured her.

"Yes, well, you're right. We were all very proud of him, my mother especially. She told him she would support him, no matter how it affected us... but the next day on the front page of the Edinburgh Evening News, there it was for the world to see... My mother learned the news at the same time that the rest of the world did: 'Robby MacLeod, Famous Thoroughbred Trainer and Polygamist Unmasked.' It turned out that my wonderfully ethical father had been keeping a second family for *years* back on Skye. He'd even married that wife first, making his marriage to my mother illegal, and my sisters and I bastards in the eyes of the church."

"Good lord," I murmured.

Eleanor's eyes teared up, and I pulled her into my arms. I kissed her forehead while she let herself cry for a minute, and then she took a deep breath, wiped her tears, and pushed forward.

"I suppose it should go without saying that it ruined all of us. He was run out of town, and before the police could catch up with him, he shot himself in an alleyway in Edinburgh. It was all the newspapers could talk about for weeks. Everyone in Scotland knew our family's shame."

"I'm sorry," I said as I held her against my chest.

"He was the one who should have been sorry," Eleanor muttered. "Without his income, we lost the house, and my sisters and I all had to become seamstresses to afford the most meagre cottage in the village. I argued with my mother for years that one of us doing intelligent work would pay more than all four of us sewing, but she just wouldn't listen. 'Eleanor Mary MacLeod, bastards and whores don't get what they want in life,' she'd say bitterly each time."

I squeezed her tighter. "I beg to differ."

Eleanor finally broke a smile. "Me too, Edmund. Me too." I leaned down and kissed her. She melted into my arms for a delicious embrace, and then begrudgingly pulled away. "When I was thirteen, I took the money I'd saved and ran away, off to a spinster aunt up in Perth who took pity on me and my desire for an education. She paid for me to go to school, and it is only because of her that I became a nurse. But... you see, it defined me, Edmund. I've vowed since I was a little girl to never let my life depend on a man. I've told myself again and again that they're all wicked liars."

Suddenly her words stung. "I am a liar," I confessed. "I lie about so many things all the time."

"I know." Eleanor reached her arms around my neck and looked up into my eyes. "You are the first man I've ever met who was so transparent about your lies. They pain you, I can tell. It makes me feel much more comfortable, actually, because I can read you, Edmund. I know what is true about you, and the rest of the details don't matter."

Another urge to reveal everything washed over me as Eleanor stood on her tiptoes to steal another kiss, but as she pulled away, she grabbed my hand and took a deep breath. "We will have time for ourselves later, Colonel. Right now, we have a cursed baron to interrogate."

Without waiting for my response, Eleanor pushed open the door. The Baron stirred, and then startled as he observed us.

"We're sorry to disturb you, Baron. I am Colonel Edmund Marriner, and this is Miss Eleanor MacLeod. We are investigating the murder of Miss Ingrid Kauter, one of your scullery maids. We found her dead in the orchards earlier today, with her throat slashed by Mr. Rana's sword."

The Baron's eyes widened at the news, and I decided to follow Lord Blakeney's advice, switching into Hindi. "You needn't worry about Mr. Rana's guilt."

I pulled up an antique chair from the corner to sit beside him, while Eleanor took a seat in the farthest corner, bringing the lamp with her and leaving my position barely illuminated in dim, flickering yellow light.

"You were in His Majesty's service in India?" the Baron asked approvingly.

Lord Blakeney had been correct. The Baron had been *choosing* not to speak to his sons. I couldn't fathom a father making such a decision. I decided to hold off on discussing it until after I gained the man's trust.

"For twenty years," I confirmed. "I was the commander of His Majesty's special forces for the United Provinces."

"Colonel Edmund Marriner..." The Baron repeated my name more thoughtfully. "I've heard of you. Many of my colleagues spoke very highly of you, and your diplomatic solution to the Ayodhya scandal."

"Yes, well, someone needed to be a diplomat. Lord Curzon certainly wasn't going to do it…" I scoffed. "I'm sorry, old politics have no place in this conversation. We have much more important things to discuss, and time is of the essence."

The Baron smiled weakly. "I agree with you, Colonel. On all accounts. But tell me this: You must be related to our very own Edmund Marriner, yes? The great painter who lived in the old manor on the other side of the village?"

"He was my grandfather," I lied. "I hear the local newspapers made the connection on my behalf when I was awarded the Victoria Cross."

The Baron raised his eyebrows. "The Victoria Cross? Were you Ralph's commander, then? He's talked about you for years." I nodded my agreement. "So a great hero has come to my bedside?"

I worked hard to keep my posture from deflating. "It is not heroic to do what every man should. I could have saved far more men than I did if I hadn't been such a coward."

The Baron sighed. "Colonel, we all do what we can. I produced two worthless sons—one monster and one caitiff. I would be a far happier dying man if either of them had turned out remotely as honorable as you are. Your grandfather would have been proud."

So many details of his statement aroused my interest that I could hardly decide where to start. "You knew my grandfather?" I began, rather unstrategically, with the most personally relevant point.

"Everyone in Basingstoke knew your grandfather. He was our very own famous artist. Many of our visitors from London knew of him after he exhibited at the Royal Academy. I wanted very much to meet him, but my father believed that fraternizing with artists was beneath us."

His response surprised me, as I had never thought of myself as remotely famous.

"His work was rather mundane," I pointed out. "Although, someone in this house must have approved of it. I noticed one of his later pieces by the kitchen door."

The Baron smiled. "Yes, I bought that myself when I was a young man. It was the only piece of art I bought before I joined the civil service in India."

"Did you buy it from my grandfather directly? You said that you never met him in person?"

"I wasn't supposed to wander about in the village. That, too, my father saw as beneath our stature. I sent out my valet to buy the piece on my behalf."

"Huh…" I murmured, grateful that the Baron seemed to only know me by reputation.

"But, tell me, Colonel, what is this scandal involving Mr. Rana? I can assure you that he didn't murder anyone."

"Yes, I agree with you. The whole affair is dastardly unfortunate. Miss MacLeod and I have been investigating the murder, and we have compelling evidence that Mr. Rana was drugged yesterday evening after tending to your medications. His karpan was stolen while he was trapped in an unnatural sleep, and was then used to slash the throat of Miss Ingrid Kauter sometime between two and three o'clock this afternoon."

"John," the Baron hissed.

"We thought so too," I admitted. "But Lord Blakeney was watching him all day. John was… er… fully occupied at the time of the murder, locked away in his bedroom in the manor."

"Who is Lord Blakeney?" the Baron asked as he struggled to sit up in his bed. Eleanor rushed to his side to help him.

"Oh, I'm sorry. I don't know his real name." I closed my eyes and concentrated on returning the conversation to English.

"Eleanor, what was Lord Blakeney's real name? The Baron and I were just discussing John's alibi."

"Oh, it's really not important…" Eleanor hedged.

She threw me a desperate look, and I decided to take her cue, assuming that something about Lord Blakeney's mysterious revelation to her had included keeping me in the dark about the exact details of his mission.

"In any event, John appears to have a solid alibi, as does Mr. Rana. Mr. Fitzgerald insisted upon his innocence, as well…"

"That worthless scoundrel is in this house?" the Baron exclaimed. "He's not welcome here!"

"He claims that he's here collecting a debt from John," I explained. "One of many, it seems. He was rather violent in his pursuit this afternoon. John is not doing well, as a matter of fact. Mr. Fitzgerald gave him the beating of his life."

The Baron began wheezing, and Eleanor rushed to fetch him some water from a small table in the corner of the room. He accepted her help and then looked straight at me and switched our conversation back into Hindi.

"How much did he say the debt was?" the Baron asked.

"Fifty-thousand pounds," I replied.

"Bastard…" the Baron muttered.

"You can tell me what is on your mind, Lord Crowden. I will be discretion itself."

"Everything is falling apart… everything, Colonel. Do you know how painful it is to watch your life's work dissolve into ashes while you lie meekly in your bed?"

"I can imagine." I did, in fact, know quite a bit about the feeling.

He looked into my eyes and resigned himself. "I worked for thirty years to impart justice, Colonel. For the Empire. For the glory of Britain. Thirty years. I gave up everything for the cause, and what did my glorious empire do to repay my efforts? It forced me to resign after I found a young Mohameddan not guilty for the rape and murder of a young British woman. The evidence against him was not compelling. He was simply on the streets at the time that her body was discovered, one of too many victims of circumstance. The young woman's friends offered testimony that a British suitor, a well-connected one to be sure, had been threatening her after she rejected his advances. I thought that my title and my position would be enough to keep me safe delivering an unpopular verdict, but I was wrong. I was forced to resign the following week. It was the first great tragedy of my life, only to be followed up by the disappointment of having two worthless sons."

"I have some understanding of why John is a disappointment to you…" I shifted uncomfortably, "but will you share with me why you are so disappointed in Ralph?"

The Baron stared before him in deep thought. "That boy should never have been born, Colonel. Charlotte, my wife, didn't want him. She was so desperately afraid that he'd be like John that the fear killed her! I loved that woman more than I ever loved those boys."

"Surely it wasn't Ralph's fault that Charlotte died," I argued.

"But it was, Colonel. Ralph's and mine. We did it to her," the Baron said wistfully. "Intent was irrelevant. We were both her killers."

I looked to Eleanor who was patiently observing our foreign conversation.

"Is that all of it, then? You simply resent Ralph because Charlotte died in childbirth?" The tragedy of the idea overwhelmed me, and I vowed then and there that I would *never* in my life, however long it would last, blame an innocent child for the death of her mother.

"Ralph was a quivering, weak little thing," the Baron continued with disdain in his voice. "He needed constant coddling, and I was not in a position to give it to him. He tormented me from the day he was born, just as John did. I knew from the moment he was born that he would be just as worthless as John was, and I was right. Look at him now. Twenty-five years later, and he's still a quivering, scared little thing."

I worked hard to control my burgeoning anger at his callous tone. "You cannot hold Ralph's shell shock against him. I was in the trenches for four years. He and I both saw things... did things... that you can't possibly imagine. No one can."

The Baron looked apologetically to me. "It is not Ralph's shell shock that I blame for his state, Colonel. It is his excessive cowardice. He was a coward long before he submitted himself to the atrocities of that bloody war."

"Ralph was conscripted, was he not? He showed great courage, far greater courage than John, who lied his way out of it."

The Baron stared straight ahead. "I am to blame for that debacle, Colonel. I was a foolish, desperate man."

"What do you mean?" I could feel that finally we were working our way towards something of value to the investigation.

"I paid Mr. Fitzgerald thirty-thousand pounds to connect Ralph and John with a crooked doctor who would diagnose them with whatever was necessary to keep them out of those bloody trenches." I couldn't hide my surprise at the confession. "It was foolish and illegal, but I am a dying man, Colonel. Mr. Fitzgerald fulfilled his promise, and John took his excuse, but Ralph refused. He was afraid he would be caught and imprisoned. His choice to fulfill his duty to the Empire was not made out of honor or nobility. It was made out of fear. He was simply too foolish to realize that a British prison would have been far better than the hell he signed up for."

"That is an unusual opinion for a man who never saw combat himself."

"I knew plenty of men in India who'd been ruined by the Crimean War. That was not worth a single British life, and neither was the wretched world war."

"I agree with you, but I do not see how you can hold Ralph's refusal to commit a crime against him. Did it ever occur to you that defying you, his powerful father, to fulfill his duty was an act of courage? He spoke quite often about his duty to the Empire when he was in the trenches. It was his patriotism that made him stand out to our mutual friend, Captain Rutherford, whom I respect more than any other man alive today."

The Baron considered my assertion. "I suppose I may have been too harsh on him... but my feelings are irrelevant now. What's done is done. My foolishness rescued John from the trenches and ruined Ralph. In that way, I suppose it ruined both of them. John was so horrible to Ralph when he came home. Worse than he'd ever been to him, even when they were children. I could do nothing to stop him. He was a grown man, and the heir to my title. And so, I did all that I could, and I cut them both off from my finances."

"Yes... Ralph and Anne have been struggling to pay for all of the estate's expenses. They've let go of almost the entire staff now, including Mrs. Murray. They even sold all of the horses but two, and the two remaining were being kept in despicable conditions."

"That is absurd! I allotted a small fortune for the management of the estate before I locked up the rest of the money! Are you saying that they have gone through ten thousand pounds in two months?"

I looked to Eleanor, and she looked expectantly towards me. I concentrated on returning to English. "The Baron says that he gave Ralph and Anne ten thousand pounds two months ago to pay for maintaining the estate. Did Anne mention anything about that to you?"

"No. Nothing. I have absolutely no idea what they would have spent that money on… Perhaps they had secret debts? But Annie was always so careful with money, and Ralph doesn't strike me as a gambler."

"Do you have any idea what they might have spent the money on? Did Ralph have debts?" I asked the Baron.

"It shouldn't have mattered. I ordered Mr. Banning to manage the payment of all estate bills from that trust. Ralph should not have been able to spend the money on anything outside of the estate allocations, even if he wanted to."

I fought back a burst of frustration that we were still no closer to solving the case. I mulled over the details in my mind, finally landing on another useful question.

"Lord Crowden, if you paid off Mr. Fitzgerald for his… er… services… why is he here now?"

Rage crossed the Baron's face, and he switched back into Hindi. "That bastard demanded another payment for his silence after the fact. Fifty thousand pounds. I have no doubt that he has come to collect it from John. That is one of the many reasons I locked the money away, out of his control… that, and John's scores of other debts."

"So you are just going to let John pay for your error?" I asked with disbelief.

"If he weren't such a lazy lout, he would have built a respectable career just as I did. Instead, he flitted about England causing trouble and wasting my funds to do it."

I was shocked by how uncaring the Baron was, regardless of John's conduct, given that he was responsible for the debacle. I wondered secretly if some of the Baron's coldness towards John reflected his own guilt.

The Baron took my silence as disapproval. "Colonel, my son would certainly be dead if he'd gone into the trenches. He chose to take the excuse, and now it is his debt."

"John is lying barely conscious on the floor of his bedroom right now after the beating Mr. Fitzgerald gave him," I reiterated.

"My son's a monster, Colonel, and he always has been. If he dies from a beating, it will be a blessing that I wasn't the one who had to impart it. The world will be better off without him."

I couldn't believe that the virtuous man that inspired Mr. Rana's decades of service was the callous miser before me. I hoped desperately that I would never become as jaded as he was, and I vowed to do everything in my power to prevent it.

"Don't look so shocked, Colonel. If you ever have a son who destroys your family name, you will resent him just as much as I resent my worthless sons. My legacy is all but ruined now."

His comment reminded me of another mystery that had floated around during our interviews.

"Are you willing to share with me the contents of your will? Did anyone in the household know your will, including Mr. Banning? Who were the witnesses?"

"Mr. Banning is just a lemming," the Baron scoffed. "I had the managing partner of his firm, Mr. Williams, write the will. It was witnessed by two of Mr. Williams's associates. Mr. Banning should know nothing of its contents."

"Then why did you send for Mr. Banning yesterday morning?"

"Mr. Banning is in charge of paying the bills. I received a delinquent notice on the electricity bill, and I demanded an explanation."

"I see…" Certainly the lies Mr. Banning, Ralph, and Anne had told were coming to a head. They had obviously not anticipated the Baron's ability to speak to me. "Ralph and Anne certainly seem to believe that Mr. Banning is in charge of your estate."

The Baron became indignant. "The only way Mr. Banning would know anything about the contents of my will, is if he had opened the sealed document illegally. I would not put it past him. He has always struck me as a conniving little dwarf."

254

Suddenly, an idea occurred to me. "Tell me this, Lord Crowden: Is there anything in that will, if Mr. Banning had illegally spied on it, that might constitute a motive for anyone in this household to murder Ingrid Kauter?"

A pained look crossed his face. He lowered his voice, and continued the conversation in Hindi. "I left everything to the firstborn son of the next generation of Crowdens. To the next heir apparent. Do you understand, Colonel? It wouldn't have gone to Ralph or John, it would have gone to their firstborn son, whichever came first. The money was to be locked in trusts until the boy turned twenty-one, and for the boy to be qualified to inherit, he was to be sent away to the home of my cousin, Lord Coswarth, in the North and then to Eton and Cambridge. I did not want either of my sons to corrupt their sons as I had mine. Otherwise, the money was to go entirely into a charity to be run by Mr. Rana in India, to pay for legal representation of native Hindustanis in the British courts."

I understood his reaction to John, but I still could not understand in the slightest how the Baron saw Ralph as remotely similar to his wicked brother.

"Lord Crowden, is there something you are not telling me about Ralph? I simply have not seen compelling evidence of why you would disinherit him so completely. Certainly, it is clear why John is a disappointment, but Ralph? Do you really believe that he is so depraved that he doesn't deserve to raise his own children?"

"Colonel, if I produced such worthless sons with my disciplined approach to parenting, can you imagine what monsters Ralph would produce? In his entire life, he has never found the courage to say no to John. His sons will walk all over him and sully our family name even more."

I wanted desperately to argue with the man, but I glanced over to Eleanor and refocused on my primary responsibility, which was not Ralph's financial future.

Suddenly, a dark connection burst forth in my mind. "Ingrid Kauter was pregnant. If either of your sons were the father, and the other knew of the will, they would have had a strong motive for murder. John has an alibi…" The horrific thought occurred to me.

"Ralph doesn't have the spine," the Baron scoffed.

I wasn't sure I agreed with him. He had not been in the trenches. He had not seen what Ralph and every other innocent boy had been forced to do.

I stood up. "Eleanor, we need to talk to Ralph and Anne." I paused as I reached the door. "Baron, are you really so ashamed of your sons that you must pretend to be mute to avoid their company?"

The Baron shrugged. "All they ever wanted to talk about was the will. That is all they saw me as, in the end, a bag full of money. Speaking to them only made me more depressed at the dismal future of my legacy. I prefer the silence now."

"Then I am sorry for you, and for them," I declared. "By the way, John's injuries are truly dire. He might not survive the night. If you want to speak to him again, you'd best have Mr. Rana help you arrange it."

Eleanor joined me by the door, and with one final glance at the miserable old miser, swimming in a sea of loneliness of his own making, we left him alone.

CHAPTER 22 – UNSPEAKABLE

As soon as we were in the hallway, Eleanor stopped. "Talk to me, Edmund. Tell me what he said. What has you so upset?"

She reached up and caressed my face, and I gathered her into my arms. After a long, loving embrace, I took a deep, calming breath.

"Please remind me never to be like that man," I whispered.

"I don't think you are at much risk of that, darling," Eleanor reassured me as she caressed my face again.

I nodded my disagreement. "Eleanor, I think that he and I were similar once, but now he's completely consumed by pessimism and loathing. There is still an inkling of the man he was, but he is hardly recognizable. He said that he was glad that Mr. Fitzgerald almost beat John to death! His own son!"

"Well, I can't say that his loathing is totally unfounded there," Eleanor pointed out. "But, I agree, to say so about his own son…"

"It isn't just John! He hates Ralph too!" I exclaimed. Something about the injustice of the Baron's opinion of Ralph was burrowing under my skin.

"Really, why?" Eleanor asked with surprise.

"Please, Eleanor, promise me that you will remind me never to be like him."

She took my hands into hers. "I promise you, Edmund."

I nodded my thanks. "I think… I think that the Baron hates Ralph because Charlotte, the Baron's wife, died in childbirth. I can't see any other reason for him to be so uncaring towards his son. He resents him, utterly and completely, just as much as he resents John. But those two are not the same at all… at least I didn't think that they were, but now I'm not even certain about that."

"Why? What did he tell you? Did he tell you something incriminating about Ralph?"

"I'm not sure…" I hedged.

"Please, Edmund, we don't have any more time to dawdle!"

"He told me the contents of the will." I felt guilty revealing what the Baron had told me in confidence, but I was not willing to withhold anything that would stand in the way of the investigation.

"Well done, Edmund!" Eleanor exclaimed. "What did it say?!"

I looked down the dark hallway, lowered my voice, and switched into Gaelic. "Neither John nor Ralph are named. All of the estate is to go to their firstborn son, but only if the son is raised by some cousin in the north. The Baron does not trust John or Ralph to parent his heir, rather unfairly, in Ralph's case, I think."

"How horrible! They have to give up their child for the child to inherit! I'm glad I'm not an aristocrat…" Eleanor muttered.

"Yes, I'm glad that I don't have to worry about such things myself. Wills have torn apart too many families in my experience… But, the thing is that we *know* John didn't do it. If the will was a factor, Ralph and Anne would have to be the culprits! Even if they thought incorrectly that Ingrid was carrying John's child, it would have been a strong motive for murder."

"Good lord…" Eleanor murmured. "John said that he would have married her… What if he voiced that sentiment in the house? That would have made the child the legitimate heir, and you're saying that Ralph and Anne would have been cut out completely?"

"Yes, that is what the Baron said… But the Baron was certain that none of them should have known the contents of the will! Not even Mr. Banning!"

"Mr. Banning?! How could he possibly not know the contents of the will? Didn't he write it?" I could hear Eleanor's excitement growing.

"He didn't!" I exclaimed. I looked nervously around the dark hallway and returned to a whisper. "The head of Mr. Banning's firm wrote it! Mr. Banning wasn't even a witness. But, Eleanor, he had access to the document in the firm's office. He was their errand-boy, as far as I can tell. His only business with the Baron was to manage the payment of the bills for the estate. He was the one who was supposed to manage the ten thousand quid that went missing! What if they're all in it together?! Mr. Banning took an illegal peek at the will, Anne and Ralph learned of its contents, then Anne realized Ingrid was pregnant, and the three of them conspired to kill poor Ingrid! They were *each other's* alibis!"

"They were all so quick to blame Mr. Rana, but we never asked Mr. Rana if he saw *them* in the afternoon!" Eleanor slammed her hand against her forehead in personal castigation. "How could we be so foolish?!"

"Did we not ask Mr. Rana what he was doing in the afternoon?" I asked. "Surely, we must have?" I found it hard to believe that we'd made such an egregious oversight.

"He confirmed that he was tending to their meeting, but we didn't ask him if he was in the room with them the whole time! They were meeting for hours! Maybe he was waiting outside the door!" Eleanor exclaimed. "Certainly, one of them could have slipped out the window while the others continued on their conversation, and Mr. Rana wouldn't have thought twice about it! He would never have realized someone was missing! Oh, we must be better at this, Edmund!"

My posture deflated. She was right. We were utterly useless investigators. "Surely, if they were conspiring with Mr. Banning on something devious, even if it weren't murder, they would not have allowed Mr. Rana to be in the room with them... but then, why would they tell us that they saw *him* all afternoon? If *they* drugged him and framed him?"

Eleanor began pacing. "Certainly Ralph has sleeping drugs—he *must* with his chronic symptoms of shell shock. They could have easily used Ralph's medication to drug Mr. Rana's chai while Mrs. Murray was tending to John... Blimey! Maybe that's why Ralph has been so ill today! Maybe his condition was compounded by the stress of his guilt! But, Edmund, would they have benefitted from Ingrid's death? What happened in the will if neither Ralph nor John had a son?"

"It would all be left to a charity in India, to be managed by Mr. Rana. I suppose that might have been more fodder for them to frame Mr. Rana... but they wouldn't have gotten the money in any circumstance."

"You were right, Edmund. We must go talk to Ralph and Anne now," Eleanor declared as she grabbed my hand.

We ran as fast as we could down the dark hallway until we reached Ralph and Anne's room.

Without even a polite knock, Eleanor pushed open the door.

"Tell us what you were holding back!" she exclaimed.

She rushed to the opposite side of the room and held the paraffin lamp to illuminate every corner of the space, but it was empty.

"Blimey," she whispered. "I hope they didn't escape in the night!"

I grabbed her hand. "Let's check the office. That's where we left Mr. Banning. If they had something to finish together, they probably returned after we left."

"Now you're thinking, Edmund!" Eleanor exclaimed.

We ran down the stairs, through several dark corridors, and burst into the office through the unlocked door. A fresh explosion of spicy fear bombarded me as Mr. Banning, Ralph, and Anne all looked up guiltily from their positions around the Baron's desk.

Without stopping for any polite niceties, I rushed to the desk and confiscated the stack of papers before Mr. Banning. Eleanor rushed to my side to illuminate the writing.

"That is privileged information!" Mr. Banning squeaked as he tried to snatch them back.

I held them up above my head, out of his limited reach.

"Oh, is it?" I made no effort to rein in the angry timbre of my voice. "On whose authority? The Baron's? Which bill is this that you are late in paying, Mr. Banning? Is it, perhaps, the electricity bill that the Baron wrote to you about yesterday? Was that not your only responsibility to this estate? The fiduciary responsibility of keeping it running with the small fortune allotted by the Baron for that sole purpose?"

All of the blood drained from Mr. Banning's face.

"What is he talking about, Mr. Banning?" Ralph demanded. "Your only responsibility to the estate is to manage the bills? What about the bloody will?"

Ralph exploded into coughs and leaned forward to brace himself on the desk. For the first time since I'd arrived, Anne did not rush to soothe him.

"I... I... I..." Mr. Banning stuttered.

"Tell him, Tommy," I taunted. "Tell Ralph Crowden who has full responsibility for the Baron's will."

I loomed over him threateningly.

"Tell him!" I commanded.

Mr. Banning shivered. "It's Mr. Williams's responsibility. Mr. Williams wrote the will. It was sealed and placed in a safe in the office."

"But... but... but... that can't be!" Anne exclaimed. "You knew what was in it!"

I held up the papers to the light. "You are writing a counterfeit will for the Baron?" My rage and disappointment in Tommy became dangerously intertwined with my pounding adrenaline. "So you were planning on adding forgery to your list of crimes, Mr. Banning?"

"I... I... I... haven't committed any crime!" Mr. Banning exclaimed as he threw a desperate look to Ralph and Anne.

"Let's see... embezzlement, fraud, espionage, perjury, forgery, swindling, assault, *murder*!" I shouted.

"What? No!" Mr. Banning backed away from me.

"What is the colonel talking about, Mr. Banning?" Ralph demanded angrily. "You said everything was perfectly legal!"

"Yes! Explain yourself!" Anne added with disingenuous melodrama.

"Drop the act, Annie. We talked to the Baron, and he talked to us. Quite capably, I might add. We know that Mr. Banning is not the only guilt party here," Eleanor said flatly.

"What?!" Anne exclaimed.

"Where did the ten thousand pounds go that were in the Baron's trust for managing the bills of the estate?" I demanded.

"*Ten* thousand pounds?!" Anne exclaimed indignantly. "You said it was only five, you thieving little toad!"

She rushed towards Mr. Banning, and he scurried away from her, taking refuge behind Eleanor, who only watched their exchange with increasing disappointment.

"So you admit that you were a party to the embezzlement of funds from the Baron's estate?" I addressed Anne directly.

"I... I... I... No! No, never!" Anne exclaimed with less conviction.

"If you embezzled funds from the Baron's estate, why did you let go of the staff and sell all the horses?" Eleanor demanded. "What did you spend the money on?"

"Nothing! We know nothing about the money!" Anne protested as she threw a desperate look towards Ralph. "Wait... Who sold the horses? You were riding horses earlier today!"

"Colonel, please join me in the library," Ralph said resignedly. "I would like to talk with you privately."

"Ralph, no!" Anne exclaimed.

"You stay here. Both of you." He threw a commanding look at Anne and Mr. Banning. "Miss MacLeod, please stay here and ring all of the servants' bells if either of these fools attempt to leave this office."

"Ralph!" Anne hissed.

He ignored her.

Eleanor nodded her approval of the development, and I joined Ralph with the forged will in hand.

We walked slowly and silently across the hallway to the library, as Ralph wheezed heavily. We sat down in the leather chairs where Eleanor and I had enjoyed our cognac on the prior evening. It felt like a lifetime had passed since that moment.

I reached forward and turned another key to illuminate a carcel lamp on the small side table between us.

"I have done many horrific things in my life, Colonel." My heart began pumping as Ralph began his confession. "But I did not murder Ingrid."

A wave of relief washed over me.

"That does not undo the fact that I very well might be responsible for her death," Ralph continued.

"Tell me, Ralph. Tell me everything you know, truthfully this time," I commanded gently.

Ralph took in several wheezing breaths, and then nodded his agreement. "No one meant anyone any harm. We were desperate, you see... Poor Anne didn't know what she was getting into with a soldier as direly wounded as I was. She thought it was just my lungs that were damaged, but it was my soul, Colonel. You know? You must know!"

"I do," I agreed.

He relaxed a bit with my showing of empathy. "But she was ever so patient with me. She was so wonderful, but over the years she became so desperately obsessed with having a child. It just wasn't happening. We tried and tried and nothing happened. I couldn't give her anything she wanted. Not a real husband, not a child, and not even a real home. We were utterly at the mercy of my father's whims, but what work could I do in my state? Nothing! I had to give her a nice home, Colonel. It was all I could give. And so we stayed here, pretending that we were the worthy heirs of the Barons of Heathfield. But that's all it ever was! Pretending! We were nothing, Colonel. Nothing. And it was entirely my fault. I should not have married Anne. I ruined her, Colonel. I ruined her life."

"I think that a modern woman likes to make her own decisions," I reminded him. "She was a VAD girl, Ralph. She knew what she was getting into by marrying a wounded soldier."

"I'm quite certain she didn't," Ralph countered. "In fact, we'd only known each other for three weeks when we got married. She had no idea what a mess I was, and she had some sort of false hope that somehow I would inherit my father's title. I suspect now that she simply didn't understand how hereditary titles work."

"You would inherit the title if your father and John were both to die, would you not?" I regretted the callous nature of the statement as soon as it came out of my mouth, especially in the face of John's dire condition, however much I disliked him.

264

"I suppose," Ralph shrugged. "But it doesn't matter. My father made it abundantly clear my whole life that I wouldn't inherit the money, and there is nothing more dismal than an impoverished baron."

"So you were conspiring with Mr. Banning to forge a new will for your father?"

"No!" Ralph exploded into a bout of coughs. "Never! Banning... that snake... claimed that my father had *asked* him to do it! Six months ago, Banning told us that my father had updated his will, and that he'd been named as the executor. He told us that my father didn't want John to know about the changes, but that whomever produced a child first would inherit everything. It gave us hope, Colonel! Hope for the first time in years that my father was finally seeing the light! That he was finally going to do something about John's disgraceful behavior. We thought that Banning's visit today was related to his role as executor!"

"If this were true, why would your father not have just openly left everything to you?"

"We thought he was worried that John would hurt me!" Ralph exclaimed. "But a child! A child could be kept safe, somewhere far away from here! But then... but then we realized that our situation was just as dismal as it was before. Anne and I had tried for four years to have a child with no success... So we did something, Colonel... something shameful and wicked... Something unspeakable..."

Ralph paused to take another series of wheezing breaths.

"Ralph, you must tell me everything," I reiterated.

He nodded his agreement and took in a shallow, belabored breath. "Mr. Banning approached Ingrid six months ago on our behalf. She was the perfect age. She was beautiful and intelligent and ever so blonde. Her child... her child with me would have been a beautiful child, Colonel, a beautiful child..." Ralph paused to fight back tears. He wheezed, wiped his eyes, and then pushed forward. "So we offered her a small fortune if she would be the mother of my child. Mind you, we didn't even know if it would work! I thought the whole problem was me, not Anne! I'm broken in every other way, why not that one too! And so Ingrid agreed to... er... submit herself to me for six months, several times a week, and if she didn't get pregnant, she'd still have the money! She could leave her horrible father and return to Switzerland after the baby was born! She agreed to it, Colonel! She even signed a bloody contract that Banning drew up! She agreed to everything out of her own free will!"

"Good lord..." I murmured. His confession was not something that had even crossed my mind in the realm of possibility. "So Ingrid's child was yours?" I already knew the answer.

Ralph's eyes teared up as he nodded his agreement.

"Did Mr. Kauter know about this arrangement?"

Ralph snorted in a shallow breath before answering. "No. He didn't know. We knew he wouldn't approve. How could he? We approached Ingrid directly. We wanted it to be her choice. We aren't monsters, Colonel. We weren't looking to engage a father in selling his daughter to the highest bidder."

"No, you encouraged her to sell herself," I murmured. "Your standards of morality are shamefully low, Lieutenant."

Ralph nodded his agreement. "It gets worse, Colonel. Ever so much worse... Anne knew of the plan. She concocted it! It was her bloody idea! For Anne, it became all about the money! An investment in gaining the entire inheritance through a child presented as ours. She was willing to give up everything Christian about our marriage for the money! But as I spent more time with Ingrid... I... I... I fell in love with her! I didn't mean to do it! It was just supposed to be a business transaction. That's all it was! And... and... and... Ingrid loved me!"

"Good lord."

266

"I couldn't let Anne know! I couldn't let her down again! But as Ingrid started showing, neither of us wanted to stop! We knew the deed had been accomplished successfully, but we wanted to lie in each other's arms! It was our only time to be together, and my child... *our* child was there, Colonel. Right there! Growing inside of her! God, how I loved her!"

He burst into tears, and I waited many minutes while he coughed and wheezed and snorted with his sobs until he could pull himself together.

"It's my bloody fault she's dead!!!" Ralph wailed. "I was so bloody selfish, and she paid the price!"

I was intensely torn about what to do. Should I comfort the miserable bloke or chastise him? He was surely not wrong. Some aspect of his scheme had very likely caused Ingrid's death in one way or another. I waited for him to calm himself, and then I pushed forward.

"Do you think Anne killed Ingrid when she found out about the pregnancy? Do you think she killed her out of jealousy?" I asked with the gentlest tone I could muster.

"Anne was with me all afternoon," Ralph reiterated. "She couldn't have done it. No, she couldn't have done it." He sounded as if he was reassuring himself.

"Do you think that she might have had an accomplice?" I asked as the thought occurred to me. "Or, perhaps... Good lord... perhaps she noticed Ingrid's condition, realized that with the intimate time you've been spending together you must have already known, realized you'd been lying to her, and then told Ingrid's father about the whole thing? Could Mr. Kauter have done the deed with Anne's prompting?"

"I don't know!!!" Ralph exclaimed. "Colonel, I don't bloody know! Anne has been so desperate for a life better than the one I've given her, but through all of it, we always loved each other! Or, at least that's what we told ourselves. But I didn't know love,

Colonel! I only knew it when I was with Ingrid. I would have given up everything for her! We were going to move to Switzerland together!"

"You were going to leave Anne penniless and alone after all she did for you?" I couldn't hide my condescending tone.

"No! Never! That's why I stole the other five thousand pounds! Banning got ten thousand pounds from my father. I helped him create a scheme with a series of fabricated improvement projects for the estate to get it all out of the trust at once. The first five thousand went into an account in Ingrid's name. Anne knew about it! It was Ingrid's payment for our business transaction. But the *other* five thousand, that was for Anne! I lied to her. I told her there was only five thousand to begin with! But the other half is in a trust right now with her name on it, Colonel! Banning was to give it to her after Ingrid and I left the country! But I didn't realize how expensive this bloody castle would be to maintain! I thought we could pay for it with our savings, and Anne was ever so generous. She spent all of the money she'd earned as a nurse to pay the bills, but it wasn't enough! I had to sell the horses! I knew Anne would be devastated, so I didn't bloody tell her!"

I was at a loss about what to say. The story was so tragically littered with terrible ideas gone horrifically wrong, I didn't even know where to start admonishing him. Perhaps, I admitted to myself, Ralph's poor judgment was one quality that had elicited the Baron's disapproval throughout the years. Perhaps the man had picked up on a subtle form of villainy that even Ralph himself did not fully recognize.

"You created quite the web of deceit, didn't you?" I finally spoke.

"I dug my own grave, Colonel, but I didn't mean to dig Ingrid's! I didn't mean to! But when John showed up here on Wednesday, I knew we wouldn't be able to hide Ingrid's condition from him. He had always watched her with the eyes of a hawk. He'd been chasing her for years! So, I've thought all afternoon that John must have done it! I worked it all out in my head: He discovered her condition and killed her in a jealous rage! But if you tell me that he has a solid alibi, I don't bloody know!"

I paused for a long moment while Ralph wheezed and coughed, choking on his tears.

"Why did you invite me here? You were out of money and planning to skip off with the maid to Switzerland. I cannot fathom why hosting a weekend party seemed like a remotely reasonable idea."

"We were lying to ourselves!" Ralph wailed. "We were just pretending that everything was going to be fine! Anne had suggested the idea months ago, long before our troubles began, and when she brought it up last week, I couldn't admit that there was no money left! I couldn't admit that Ingrid and I were in love, or that I'd been lying to Anne for months! She'd been so bloody supportive, Colonel! *She'd* suggested that Ingrid move into the house. *She'd* thought our plan wasn't working, and that Ingrid's chances of conceiving would be higher under her constant care! *She'd* made it possible for me to see Ingrid every bloody night! So I just said yes! I pretended that everything was normal. That's what the doctors said to do! They said that if I pretended that everything was normal, then someday it might become that way!"

Ralph exploded into another violent fit of coughs. His unreasonable interpretation of the advice given by the army's doctors reiterated my earlier conclusion. Ralph had an uncanny ability, it seemed, to justify his unwise decisions. I paused for a long moment to consider his confession and gather my thoughts.

"What was Banning getting out of all this?" I finally asked.

Ralph chuckled facetiously. "He wanted to create his own firm. He told us that an account as famous as ours was all he'd need to establish himself. He told us that Mr. Williams's firm didn't appreciate all of *his* hard work managing the Baron's excessive needs over the years... the lying bastard. We thought all he was asking for was a professional courtesy!"

"Lieutenant, you conspired with Mr. Banning to embezzle a small fortune from your father's estate. He wrote up an illegal contract for a young woman to sell her sexual services to you. Did you really believe that he would be a responsible custodian of your financial and legal affairs?"

Ralph paused to think about my statement for a long time. "Love makes fools of us all," he sighed. "I was so bloody desperate to give Anne what she wanted, and then I was so bloody desperate to escape her and run away with Ingrid. Mr. Banning made it seem like those things could happen, Colonel. That was all I was willing to see. It wasn't supposed to end like this." He gave in to another round of tears. "Oh, and Colonel, there's something else..." I couldn't believe that the story could get any worse. "I am the one who was drugging Mr. Rana's chai. I've been doing it for months whenever Ingrid and I have been together, so that Mr. Rana would not discover us. I could tell he was getting suspicious, so I needed to be extra careful that he didn't catch us in the act. He is the only one who has a key to Ingrid's room other than her. Last night I was startled. Mrs. Murray was coming back down the stairs when I was in the kitchen, and I must have given him too much."

"Is that why you fired Mrs. Murray after forty years of service?"

"I wasn't sure what she saw! I couldn't have her tell you she saw me drugging him! Then you'd think that *I* was the one who killed Ingrid!"

"Telling a woman who has devoted her life to your household that she is too old to do her job is a very selfish way of going about your devious plan." I couldn't help but chastise Ralph for his methods, despite the fact that the deeds themselves were far more worthy of castigation.

270

"Yes… yes… You're right, Colonel. I wasn't really thinking straight… but I swear to you, with God as my witness, I did not intend for Mr. Rana or Mrs. Murray to be involved in this at all, and I most certainly did not frame Mr. Rana. Someone else must have used the opportunity that my error created to steal his sword."

"Anne?" I whispered. "Did Anne know you were drugging him?"

"Yes." Ralph burst into another round of tears. "It was her idea! You know, at the beginning, when we thought it was just about business!"

"Good lord…" I murmured. "Ralph, we must talk to Anne. We must get to the bottom of this before the police arrive. Do you understand?"

Ralph nodded his agreement, wiped his eyes, and awkwardly stood up from his position in the low chair.

As I made my way towards the door, Ralph put his hand on my arm. "Colonel, please don't tell Captain Rutherford everything. Tell him what you must, but if you can… I don't want him to be disappointed in me."

"I will do what I can, but I can't make any promises, Ralph. Captain Rutherford and I have no secrets between us. Perhaps you should have thought about what Captain Rutherford would think before you set out on this path."

Ralph sniffled and wheezed and nodded his defeated concession, and together we headed across the dark corridor to face his reckoning.

CHAPTER 23 – WICKED PLANS GONE HORRIBLY AWRY

When we re-entered the office, Mr. Banning was standing in the corner, refusing to face Anne and Eleanor, and Anne was sitting in one of the chairs at the Baron's desk, burying her face in her hands. Eleanor threw me a searching look.

"Anne, please tell me you didn't do it!" Ralph exclaimed.

Anne looked up at him with a moment of confusion that quickly morphed into primal rage.

"You spineless fiend!" She jumped out of her chair and flung herself at her husband. "You will not make me hang for this!!!"

Knowing all that Ralph had confessed, I hesitated for a moment to intervene as she pounded her fists against his chest until he collapsed onto the floor in a fit of coughs. Suddenly, the scent of fresh blood bombarded my overtaxed senses, and as Anne dissolved into sobs and lay down in a fetal position on the floor next to him, I noticed the source. Ralph was coughing up blood.

Eleanor rushed to his side with a glass of water from the Baron's desk.

"Breathe slowly," she whispered as Ralph's coughs dissolved into sobs. She handed him a handkerchief and helped him wipe the blood from his chin. "Do not use your inhaler again, Ralph. Whatever is in the compound is making your condition worse."

I watched with overwhelming melancholy as the two ruined lovers sobbed separately side by side on the floor in the dark.

Eleanor stood up and approached me. "Did Anne do it?" she whispered as she held the lantern up to look into my eyes. "Close your eyes, Edmund. Breathe in and out slowly." She reached up and caressed my cheek as I followed her instructions, and when I opened my eyes, she smiled. "Good," she praised. "You are getting better at forcing yourself under control. I'm impressed by your rapid improvement today."

I was still at a loss as to how she was so perceptive about my secret struggles, but with another infusion of her calm confidence, I decided not to question the beautiful truth in the face of so many ugly ones, and I pushed forward.

"She did not do it directly," I whispered. "But she and Ralph have been involved in a series of reprehensible endeavors, compounded by Mr. Banning's greed and incompetence." I kneeled down beside Anne. "Mrs. Crowden, I need you to be honest with me. Did you urge Mr. Kauter to kill Ingrid?"

"What?" Anne asked meekly. "No! Never! I loved Ingrid!"

"Good lord…" I murmured, unsure of her exact meaning.

"Ingrid was going to give me everything I ever wanted!" Anne wailed. "All I ever wanted was a child! And instead, my worthless, wheezing, weakling of a husband took that from me too!"

"I loved her!" Ralph wailed. "I couldn't help it!"

"What are they talking about?" Eleanor whispered into my ear.

"Anne and Ralph paid Ingrid to be the mother of Ralph's child. Ralph and Ingrid have been intimate for six months, but Ralph fell in love with her. They were planning on running away together. Half of the money Mr. Banning embezzled went to Ingrid, the other was to go to Anne after Ralph ran away with Ingrid to Switzerland."

"Good lord," Eleanor murmured. She kneeled down to comfort Anne.

"How could he do this to me?!" Anne wailed. "I devoted my bloody life to him! And for months I had to watch, Ellie! For *months,* I had to stand by and watch him fall in love with her! I lied to myself. He lied to me. It was all part of the bloody, wicked plan––we swore it to each other! But I knew it wasn't! He was always so calm and content when he'd been with her! I'd never, ever seen him that way! How *could* he!"

Eleanor threw me a searching look, but dutifully gathered Anne's head into her lap and began stroking her hair like a loving mother.

"I just wanted a child, Ellie. That's all I wanted! Damn the money! Damn the bloody Barons of Heathfield! But... but... but you know what this means! It means that *I* was the problem! Not bloody Ralph! It means no matter what, I'll never have a child of my own!"

"Annie... Annie, you must tell me this: Why have you been giving Ralph too much camphor in his inhaler? Have you been trying to hurt him?"

Anne and Ralph wailed in unison as Eleanor suggested the horrific plot.

"He wasn't supposed to use it so much!" Anne cried. "I upped the dose because it wasn't working! He was constantly in pain! But now he's using it as a pacifier! Every bloody time he feels stress he uses it. I didn't realize he'd become addicted! I swear, Ellie, I didn't realize it was addictive! None of the literature says it's addictive!"

"Sshhh," Eleanor whispered soothingly as she ran her fingers through Anne's hair. "Everything will be okay, Annie. You'll get through this. We'll get through it together."

That was the moment when I realized for the first time the vast depths of the burning love that I felt for Eleanor MacLeod.

As Anne and Ralph wept on the floor, basking in their self-inflicted misery, I noticed Mr. Banning watching them from the dark shadows.

"Do you enjoy ruining lives, Mr. Banning? Or is it simply a side effect of your exceptional negligence?" I asked as I approached him. He backed all the way up against the wall.

"I... I... I... didn't mean to do anything wrong!" he exclaimed. "I just wanted their business! I wanted to start my own firm! I'm sixty-five! I *earned* it! Half of Mr. Williams's clients were only with him because he did business with the Baron, and he hardly ever did anything at all! I did all the real work!"

"Why did you lie to them about the contents of the Baron's will?" I pushed.

"I... I... I... didn't lie!" Mr. Banning looked around the room for any options for escape.

I straightened my posture and loomed over him. "You most certainly did. Your lies will desist this instant."

Mr. Banning shivered and then gave in. "I... I... I... couldn't unseal the will without Mr. Williams noticing! So I held the envelope up to the light, and that was what it said! It said the money would go to the son with the firstborn child! I was helping! It was their right to know!"

"It was not their right to know." I shook my head as I realized the extent of Tommy's foolishness. "Your scheme didn't work, Mr. Banning. You misread the will. The Baron told me its contents, and under no circumstance was the money to go to Ralph or John, regardless of their parental status."

"Wait... but, how? One of them will become the Baron! One of them has to get everything!" Mr. Banning exclaimed.

I let my full disappointment out in a long sigh. "Perhaps you would have been a better butcher, Mr. Banning. My grandfather should not have encouraged you. He worried that your scheming imagination was too fruitful, but he hoped he could steer you in the right direction. Clearly, he was wrong."

"He told you that?" Mr. Banning asked meekly.

"He told me everything," I replied. "And I can tell you with complete certainty that he would be very disappointed in you."

Mr. Banning's posture deflated. "I was just helping!" he declared half-heartedly.

"Annie," Eleanor whispered. "Did you do anything that might have resulted in Ingrid's death? Even unintentionally?"

"I don't think so!" Anne sobbed. "I wanted her child so desperately! I would have done anything to keep her safe! That's why I kept her in the house away from her father! But then John showed up, and I was terrified for her! We both knew he was mad! We knew he would do something horrific if he found out! It must have been him, I don't care what that Lord Blakeney character claims!"

"Blimey..." Eleanor muttered. "That leads us back to Mr. Kauter... it has to be him."

As if on cue, a commotion broke out in the hallway as the back door of the manor by the kitchen burst open, and a powerful draft traveled all the way into the office, whipping up Mr. Banning's many loose papers into a frenzy.

A series of loud crashes echoed as the house shook.

Someone had just broken down a door.

Eleanor wiggled away from Anne's position and gathered the paraffin lamp, and without another word, she joined me in my rush to investigate.

"There! At the end of the hallway!" Eleanor exclaimed as we ran through the dark corridor.

"That's Ingrid's room!" I exclaimed.

The dim light of another paraffin lamp illuminated the doorway.

"My god, what is this?!" Mr. Kauter's voice echoed into the hallway.

"Mr. Kauter!" Eleanor exclaimed.

As we reached the doorway, I pushed Eleanor behind me as Mr. Kauter aimed his shotgun straight at my head.

"Where is Ralph Crowden?!" he demanded. "Tell me, Colonel. It's my right as a father to avenge Ingrid's death!"

"Mrs. Fitzgerald?" Eleanor asked confusedly.

I glanced at Ingrid's bed, where, indeed, Mrs. Fitzgerald lay watching us with glassy eyes, illuminated by the dim yellow light of Mr. Kauter's paraffin lantern. Her breaths were shallow and frequent, each one a belabored gasp, and the scent of imminent death wafted off of her.

I switched into Bernese. "Mr. Kauter, this is not the way. Please, put the gun down. We do not need any more tragedy today."

"No!" Mr. Kauter shouted. "There will be no justice for Ingrid in these crooked English courts! They would not dare to charge Lord Crowden's son with the murder of a Kraut whore!"

I felt Eleanor's silent panic. I took one long moment to consider my limited options, and then I rushed to Mr. Kauter's position and ripped the shotgun right out of his hands.

"How did you do that?" he whispered as he stared at me with shock. I pulled out the shells and dropped them onto the floor.

As soon as Eleanor saw that he was neutralized, she rushed to Mrs. Fitzgerald's side and began assessing her condition.

"Mr. Kauter, I vowed to bring justice to Ingrid's killer, and I will do so," I declared.

Mr. Kauter reached into his jacket, and I glanced over to Eleanor's position, ready to throw myself in front of her if Mr. Kauter were to attempt another violent attack. Instead, he ripped the locket he had stolen from the crime scene out of his pocket, threw it onto the floor, and spat on it.

"That bastard made my daughter into a whore!" he shouted. "He thought he could get away with ruining my beautiful Ingrid?! I will kill him!"

I quickly gathered up the locket and opened it. A lock of Ralph's sandy blond hair gently floated to the ground.

"Only one person in this house has that hair!" Mr. Kauter boomed. "Ralph Crowden! He used her. He ruined her. And then he killed her!"

"He did not," Mrs. Fitzgerald whispered. "I killed her."

CHAPTER 24 – CONFESSION

Mr. Kauter and I were both stunned, but Eleanor seemed unfazed by the shocking confession as she felt Mrs. Fitzgerald's pulse.

"Mrs. Fitzgerald, what poison did you take?" Eleanor asked with the same feigned calm tone I had come to notice throughout the day. "Your pulse is far too fast. Can you move your limbs?"

"It doesn't matter," Mrs. Fitzgerald gasped. "My life is over."

Eleanor looked around the bedside table, gathering up a small, unmarked bottle. I almost threw myself across the room to stop her as she brought it to her mouth and then her nose to sniff it, and then I gathered all of my wits to bring myself back under control as she returned it to its position on the nightstand.

The scent of death bombarded my Rakshasa senses.

"Hemlock?" Eleanor asked.

"Yes. Enough to kill a bull," Mrs. Fitzgerald whispered. "It was for John, but then I had a better idea. A more foolish idea. An idea that will send me straight to Hell."

Eleanor threw me a nervous look. Mr. Kauter remained stunned in position, and I decided to remain in his vicinity with his shotgun in hand to ensure that he maintained his civility (and Eleanor's safety), in the wake of the tragic news.

"Tell us what happened," Eleanor said as she took Mrs. Fitzgerald's limp hand into hers. "You do not have long before you won't be able to speak. Please, tell us what you did."

Eleanor reached into her pocket and pulled out another handkerchief. She dipped it into a glass of water by the bedside. She silently began dabbing the sweat from Mrs. Fitzgerald's forehead.

Mrs. Fitzgerald looked straight at Mr. Kauter. "You will not be able to forgive me. You should not forgive me. From one parent who has lost a child to another, you *must* not forgive me."

Mr. Kauter leaned back against the wall and whispered a quiet prayer as he made the sign of the cross, but did not respond to her.

Mrs. Fitzgerald addressed her confession straight to Mr. Kauter. "John Crowden was a wanton, soulless cad, and Jenny was a foolish, headstrong girl. I told her to keep her legs closed until she was married. 'No one buys what they can take for free,' I told her from the time she was a girl. But she didn't listen, the silly little tart. She thought that a baron would want to marry her? The daughter of Harry Fitzgerald, a debt-collector of the most violent variety? I told her it would never happen, and she ignored me. 'Love is blind,' she told me, that little fool…

"She came home in a panic three months later. I knew it the moment she couldn't stomach her supper. I told her we would do nothing to help a worthless little whore. I told her that if John bloody Crowden loved her so much, she should secure his proposal by the end of the week to rescue her from her dire straits.

"She disappeared. For three weeks, she disappeared, and when she returned to our door with the evidence of her shame presented for the world to see, we turned her away. The next day she was found dead in an alleyway. Bleach, the coroner said. She'd consumed a hearty serving of bleach..."

Mrs. Fitzgerald began choking, and Eleanor silently soothed her until she got herself under control. Tears dripped from the corners of her drooping eyelids.

"She had a note in her pocket. John bloody Crowden had refused her. He'd called her a whore just as we had, and insisted that a whore like her couldn't possibly know who the father was. He sent her away in shame, and then we did the same... It was his bloody fault. Jenny died alone in a pile of rubbish because of that bastard. And so, I vowed to avenge her.

"When Harry was sent here to collect the debt, I came with him. All my husband ever cared about was the money. He would have slept with the devil himself for the commission on a fifty-thousand quid bounty. So I harvested the hemlock in the garden. I made it into the tonic. I contrived the perfect scheme. No one would have blinked an eye if that alcoholic, cocaine-snorting bastard had overdosed. But then I saw them together. I watched them in the hallway. John bloody Crowden stood on one knee, proposing marriage to a scullery maid.

"Ingrid refused to answer him. She ran away. But I caught up with her. I cornered her in the hallway and listened as she sang the praises of her perfect Mr. Crowden. Her knight in shining armor who was going to rescue her from a lifetime of servitude. He was going to make her into a lady after all she had suffered. He *loved* her, and she loved him. Before the month was out, they were going to run off and get married in Switzerland where no one would ever find them. That poor girl was so desperate to share her joy that she told a perfect stranger everything rushing through her optimistic young mind.

"So I improved my plan. John Crowden was going to watch his beloved little cinder girl die, and only then would he die himself. He would know the pain I felt at the loss of my daughter. The only girl he had ever truly loved would be ripped from his arms. My revenge would soothe the seething wounds that he had imparted on my Jenny.

"It took almost no effort to execute. The idiot foreign butler had fallen asleep with the door to his room wide open. He'd left the keys to every room in the house in the pocket of his uniform, right there on the floor of his room for all to see. They would be useful twofold. I would use them to kill Ingrid, and then later to kill John without producing a hint of evidence of struggle.

"I stole the keys, but as he stirred, I noticed his sword on the floor by his bed, and I took it, just in case. It was clear that he was fiercely loyal to that crooked Baron—he had threatened Harry once before on the Baron's behalf—and I would not let him get in my way or Harry's. I stashed the sword under the bed in my room, and while my husband drank with the man who ruined our daughter, I went to Ingrid's room and fed her the poison. I rationed just enough for the sickly girl so that I'd have the mortal dose remaining for John bloody Crowden. But when I got to Ingrid's room, I didn't even need the stolen keys. It was too bloody easy! The girl was still awake!

"'Mrs. Crowden sends this tea for your health,' I told that gullible little girl. Her world was so upside down that she thought that a guest of the house would bring *her* tea before bed. And so, I watched her drink her death. I turned out the light for her and left her alone to die in the dark.

"I waited patiently for the news to spread through the household in the morning. Surely, someone would notice that the girl had died in the night. I waited and I waited, but the selfish fools didn't pay her any mind. I couldn't believe it, and so under the guise of my ill-health, I checked with Mrs. Murray, who was utterly unconcerned about her absence. She doted upon me like no one I had ever encountered, certainly nothing like my cruel mother, and then she tucked me back into bed. I waited and waited, and still there was no commotion. Nothing that indicated that Ingrid had been found dead in her bed, and so I had to check on her myself. I waited for Mrs. Murray to leave the house to gather the eggs in the chicken coop, and then I scurried through the empty hallways to Ingrid's undiscovered tomb, but when I entered her room, she was still alive. The dose I'd given her hadn't been enough. I went to her bedside and felt her warm forehead. It was too warm, as if she had a fever.

"'Has John left yet?' she asked me. I startled as she opened her eyes. 'I don't want to go out if John is still here. I don't want him to see me like this.'

"I began to panic. This girl now knew that I had given her the tea. She was awake. She was ill. I didn't have the rest of the poison with me. In a moment of foolishness, I grabbed the pillow beside her and tried to smother her, but she fought me off. She kicked and screamed, and I knew the entire household would hear her, so I stopped. She was still alive.

"I stood up and ran to the door. The hallway was empty. The kitchen was silent. There was no one to hear her screams, but Ingrid was not going to let me do her in so easily a third time.

"'You are an evil lady!' she rasped. My efforts had injured her vocal cords. She knew as well as I did what it meant—she wasn't going to be able to scream. Like a trapped animal, she pushed past me and ran right out the back door and into the snow. She ran in her nightgown, with bare feet, out into the frozen courtyard. She knew. She knew I'd tried to kill her. The Crowdens were people of influence. I would not let John bloody Crowden or his little whore ruin my plan! So I ran back to my room, grabbed the sword, and chased that girl out into the fields.

"As she ran, she called for her father to save her, just as my Jenny had called for me. Her pleas echoed into nothingness, just as Jenny's had.

"I followed her into the orchards, and with the agony of Jenny's death the only thought in my mind, I slashed Ingrid's throat. As soon as the deed was done, I was covered in her blood. I dropped the sword beside her. I looked at my gruesome carnage. It was too bloody... There was blood everywhere... And then I saw it. I saw the bump. I saw that poor Ingrid was pregnant, and suddenly she looked exactly like Jenny! Jenny was lying by that tree, and her blood was all over me! I was swimming in my daughter's blood!

"The silent snowflakes began to cover her in a blanket of white. They covered my footsteps and all the evidence of my crime. I ran back to the house, straight to my room. I burned my bloody clothes in the fireplace, and I tiptoed to the bath. When no evidence of the blood remained on me or in the bathroom, I dressed myself for a relaxed afternoon 'resting up' as Mrs. Murray had kindly suggested and placed the bottle of poison in the bedside drawer in one of the scores of empty bedrooms on the other side of the house. No one in the household disturbed me.

"But as the colonel began asking questions, I used the stolen keys to sneak back here, to Ingrid's room, to make sure that no evidence of my guilt remained. I rifled through her bedside table, and there it was—one of the same bloody inhalers that Ralph Crowden had been using all day. I began to panic. I rifled through the rest of the drawers. There, in the back of her linens, was a stack of love letters from *Ralph* bloody Crowden. I realized then the grave error I had made. The image of Ingrid running away from me, begging for mercy, overwhelmed me. I had done far worse to her than what Jenny had done to herself, but she was *innocent*. She and Jenny were the same, and they were *both* dead by my hand!

"I went straight up to the room where my last dose of hemlock was hidden. Ingrid's pleas echoed through my mind. I listened from outside the door of John's bedroom as my husband beat that bastard until he begged for mercy, and then I returned to the scene of my damnation to finish what I had started. I drank the entire dose."

"You don't have long," Eleanor whispered. "Maybe only a few minutes."

"Soon enough I will be in Hell where I belong. Jenny and I will burn together," Mrs. Fitzgerald said as she closed her eyes. "Mr. Kauter, do not ever forgive me."

The floorboards in the hallway creaked, and I turned to observe Ralph Crowden standing in the shadows with silent tears streaming down his face. Behind him, Anne and Mr. Banning stood, watching the confession with their own wide eyes.

Eleanor measured Mrs. Fitzgerald's pulse. "She doesn't have long. Her organs are shutting down. Her breathing is very light."

Mr. Kauter collapsed onto the floor and exploded into wailing sobs. Eleanor looked searchingly to me, and I kneeled down beside the poor man to do what I could to console him. He grabbed onto me and leaned in, like a child in his father's arms, sobbing into my chest. I held him tighter. I couldn't quell my own tears at his palpable despair, and when I finally looked up at Eleanor, she was watching me with a look I will never forget. That, I believe, as I think back on it, was the moment that Eleanor began loving me as much as I loved her.

And so together, in the flickering light of a dying oil lamp, under the tragic roof of a cursed baron, we waited for Ingrid's murderer to be brought to justice.

CHAPTER 25 – MOONLIGHT

We waited in Ingrid Kauter's bedroom for almost an hour until Mrs. Fitzgerald took her last breath. Eleanor reached forward and stopped the clock by the bedside, and then pulled the sheet up to cover her head.

"What do we do now?" Anne whispered wearily.

"I suppose we must prepare ourselves to make statements when the investigators arrive," I suggested as I stood up from my position on the floor, leaving Mr. Kauter to lean up against the wall on his own. I was ready for the entire ordeal to be over.

"There is no need, Colonel," Lord Blakeney said as he joined us from the dark hallway. "I will see to everything. I am a member of His Majesty's Secret Service, and I will do what is necessary to clean up this mess."

"The Secret Service?" Ralph asked as a fresh batch of fear wafted off of him.

"Yes. I cannot reveal my primary mission," Lord Blakeney replied. "But I will be taking statements from all of you and discussing with my superiors what to do about the numerous other crimes that you have each committed in recent months. Now, Mr. Crowden, your father is with your brother upstairs. Your brother will be dead by morning. You had best go say your goodbyes."

"John? John is dying?" Ralph asked with panicked confusion.

"Yes, there will be another murderer on the property by morning. Mr. Fitzgerald beat John to the brink of death. Now we are waiting for the inevitable," Lord Blakeney replied.

"I will go help out," Eleanor offered.

"That will not be necessary, Miss MacLeod," Lord Blakeney argued. "I can take it from here. There is nothing you can do for him now."

"Where is Mr. Fitzgerald?" I asked. "He needs to be contained until the authorities can get here."

"Mr. Fitzgerald is locked in his room until I hear back from my superiors about his fate. My methods are flawless. There is no possibility that he will escape. I will go inform him of his wife's dismal fate now," Lord Blakeney said resignedly. "Mr. and Mrs. Crowden, and Mr. Banning, you will wait in the office for my return. Mr. Kauter, do what you must to grieve, but we have had enough death on this property for one day. Please find it in your heart to control yourself, for Ingrid's sake."

Mr. Kauter didn't look up at him.

Ralph, Anne, and Mr. Banning slinked obediently towards the office, while Eleanor stood up and joined me to address Lord Blakeney in the hallway.

"Are you sure there's nothing we can do?"

"You two have done more than enough," Lord Blakeney reassured her. "I must thank you for your tenacious support of this investigation." He looked to me.

"We didn't even solve the crime," I shrugged. "Mrs. Fitzgerald completely slipped my mind as a suspect. I hardly even remembered she was here."

"You uncovered many other crimes that the members of this household will have to face," Lord Blakeney reminded me. "Both of you did. From the destruction of their lies, there will come a new era of truth for them. You two have made that possible."

"Their ending was so tragic," Eleanor murmured. "Everyone in this house is ruined."

"Greed, war, and love, ma chérie—everyone is destined to be ruined by one of them. It is the way of the world," Lord Blakeney sighed. "But, you two have had a thoroughly taxing day. I anticipated that you might need a place to rest and relax, and so, I hope you don't mind, Colonel, but Mr. Rana gave me the key to your house on the other side of the village, and I've had my people air it out and prepare it for your arrival. You should be able to make it over there in what? A half hour? With the help of those two enthusiastic thoroughbreds I found waiting patiently for you by the stables."

"I'm sorry, what?" I asked with utter confusion.

Every aspect of Lord Blakeney's statement filled me with dread. The implications of a troop of strangers invading the unopened house I had kept for decades rushed through my mind. My only consoling thought was the knowledge that I had wisely hidden the evidence of my past before I shut it up and left for India almost three decades earlier, and the photographs of my former exploits were locked away in the cellar. Certainly, Lord Blakeney's staff would not dare to intrude to such a degree…

"If you were able to have your staff invade my house on the other side of the village, how are the investigators unable to make it through the snow to attend to the Crowdens' criminal catastrophe?"

Lord Blakeney smiled and threw a look of distinct approval to Eleanor. "Colonel, I think you are finally catching onto the investigative line of inquiry. Please, keep asking such useful questions."

"You didn't answer my question," I pointed out.

Lord Blakeney's smile only grew wider. "You are right, Colonel. I didn't. I have friends in high places and a very skilled staff. They arranged everything for your little sojourn. I will remain here to deal with the fallout of the Crowden's tragic mess. My people will likely have questions for you tomorrow, but it is important that we keep this whole affair hushed up. I'm certain the Baron will agree with me. I will see to the dirty details, and you two must free yourselves from the tragedy that ensnared you today."

Eleanor took my hand into hers. "Let's go, Edmund. I can't wait to get out of this cursed house."

"Oh, and I already had your things taken over there," Lord Blakeney added.

"How in the world did you do that?!" I exclaimed. "My trunk was atrociously heavy."

Lord Blakeney grinned. "You wouldn't believe me if I told you, Colonel. My point was that you have no need to rush back over here. My skilled staff will be dealing with this, and we will come to you when we need your testimony. Oh, and Mr. Rana thanks you for your generous offer. Here is your key back. He has decided to stay by the Baron's side until the very end."

Lord Blakeney handed me back the key I'd given to Mr. Rana and closed it into my hand.

"Go, Colonel. Enjoy the rest of your weekend in peace," Lord Blakeney reiterated.

"Come on, Edmund," Eleanor said as she offered Lord Blakeney a friendly smile and a nod. "I think Lord Blakeney can take it from here."

I let Eleanor guide me to the back door.

"I hope to see you again in better circumstances," Lord Blakeney called. "Both of you."

I offered him a simple salute as Eleanor led me into the yard. The snow was slowly melting, and the temperature of the air was outright balmy.

"I suppose the storm has passed," I said as I looked up at the bright full moon, illuminating the snowy landscape with an array of beautiful pale blue hues. The fine ice crystals glittered in the moonlight.

"It's beautiful," Eleanor whispered as I squeezed her hand.

My contentment at sharing the moment with her was unlike anything I had ever felt before, despite all of the witnessed misery that still infused my being.

"Greed, war, or love, is it? One of those will ruin us?" I philosophized.

"One of those three poisons tastes a lot better than the others," Eleanor quipped.

"Yesterday I would have said that war had ruined me," I said pensively. "But now... now I think perhaps I'm not entirely ruined yet."

Eleanor smiled and leaned into my arms. "Are you going to join me in choosing the sweetest poison, then?"

I leaned down and licked her lips teasingly. She melted into my arms, and we both let out satisfied sighs as our passion mounted, until Eleanor pulled away.

"We must vow, Edmund, never to be ignorant or desperate enough to end up like any of them. We must always remember to be true to ourselves and to each other. Together, we can avoid a tragedy like this one."

"Yes... yes, I suppose..." I murmured.

"Now, shall we enjoy the beauty of this snowy, moonlit night by horseback as we scamper across the village to your grandfather's mysterious old house?" Eleanor changed the subject cheerfully.

My heart raced with excitement and anxiety, as all that had come to pass washed over me. The idea of bringing Eleanor into the house that I had loved so dearly, to be with her in the place that felt most like my home in the world, was so overwhelming that it pushed back the many unanswered questions in the back of my mind left by Lord Blakeney's web of half-truths.

"Eleanor, I have a lot of secrets…" I hedged as I thought about how I was going to prepare her for all that I desperately wanted to tell her.

"Sshh," she whispered as she placed her finger on my lips. "We've had enough questions and answers for now. Tonight, no matter what happens, let's just be, Edmund. Alright?"

I gathered her into my arms again, and as I kissed her, a lifetime's worth of love in my heart burst forth from somewhere deep within me, and I felt like I was swimming in light.

After many moments of sheer bliss, Eleanor took a step back to catch her breath.

"Are you alright?" I asked concernedly.

"I am more than alright." She grabbed my hand. "Let's go, Edmund. It is time for us to fully explore the unique pleasures of getting to know each other."

And so, on a magical, snowy night in October of 1922, I rode through the sparkling moonlight with Eleanor MacLeod by my side, past the haunted orchard, across the sleeping village, beside the babbling brook I had painted hundreds of times, and up the winding, tree-lined path to the house where I had lived for forty-seven lonely years. And together, for the first time in either of our lives, we discovered the unequaled pleasures of loving one another completely.

CHAPTER 26 – IN THE LIGHT OF DAY

As the bright sun passed its midday apex, Edmund looked around at his audience and sighed with relief.

"And, that was that, I suppose. Eleanor and I both returned to our separate homes for a bit to gather our wits about us, and I joined her for a weekend in Scotland a few weeks later. I wanted to follow her about like a lost puppy in need of a home, but Eleanor wisely suggested that we take some time apart to be sure that we knew what we wanted. It was only then, for the first time in a century, that I fully understood what Ovid meant with his suggestion: Let her miss you, but not for too long. That was when I realized that the suggestion did not need to have a manipulative connotation, as I had always assumed it did. It was simply a technique for understanding oneself in the face of becoming thoroughly entranced by love, and a rather wise one, I think. We wrote each other letters, and Eleanor came down to London several times, and by January, I had revealed all of my deepest, darkest Rakshasa secrets... at least the ones I knew about at the time.

"We were married by March at my house in Basingstoke, and then set off for our honeymoon in India, where we ended up staying for almost two years."

"I didn't know that," Ellie murmured. "I thought you lived in Basingstoke the whole time you were together."

Edmund swallowed hard. "We actually didn't live in Basingstoke for very long before... before she died. Most of our blissful life together was in India, with some time in Western Australia for good measure."

"Western Australia?!" Neha exclaimed. "You really got around in the 1920s, didn't you?"

"Travel back then for people like us was not so difficult to manage. We had money and tenacity and we enjoyed exploring. We made such good friends together." Edmund sighed nostalgically, and then he glanced over to Debbie in the back row, who'd sat silently the whole time. "We only returned to England after some MacLeod family tragedies necessitated the move. Even then, though, our life together was more blissful than I thought life could be." He looked to Ellie. "Your mother taught me what love was in every sense of the word."

"And you taught her," Supriya added. "Ovid would have approved."

Supriya stood up from her position on the couch and helped Ellie to her feet. Edmund joined them and engulfed them both into a tight hug. "I love you both so much, and love hasn't ruined us yet."

"I was a bit pessimistic on the topic," Mélusine admitted sheepishly. "I must admit now that some people do not have to be ruined at all. It is a phenomenon I'm still trying to fully comprehend for myself."

"You'd better!" Neha laughed. "We're getting married in just a few months!"

"*C'est vrai, ma chérie, c'est vrai,*" Mélusine agreed as she pulled her fiancée into a gentle embrace.

"Ooo, Melly, wait!" Neha pulled away excitedly. "The story isn't over yet! Tell us what Lord Blakeney ended up doing with the cursed Crowdens!"

"Yes, I was always curious about that myself," Edmund seconded. "Eleanor and I were called in to offer testimony as to Mr. Fitzgerald's guilt, but we never heard a peep about Ingrid's murder. I did see Ralph out and about in the village every so often after Eleanor and I moved back to Basingstoke, but he was not particularly keen on catching up."

"I can see why!" Neha interrupted. "He turned out to be quite a villain, didn't he? A tragic villain who didn't mean any harm, I suppose. Although, I suppose it depends on your definition of morality in the case of the contract with Ingrid Kauter... She did sign it willingly, exercising one of the only aspects of free agency a woman had at the time, which is certainly better than the plan John and Mr. Kauter had concocted to basically sell her as a wife to a man she feared for some farmland... Although, she may have been under mental and physical duress when she signed the contract... Never mind. We have much more pleasant things to discuss. So, Melly, what did you do with them?"

Mélusine nodded her approval of her fiancée's unusual showing of conversational self-control. "As soon as Edmund and Eleanor were out of the house, I went to Vibhi for advice. I had to come clean about my meddling, since I was never good at lying to him, even before I thought he might end up as my father-in-law."

"Mélusine took all of the blame," Kuveni interjected to clarify for the group. "She didn't even mention my name, the blessed girl. I'm still grateful that Lord Vibhishana never found out that I was at the root of that disastrous plan."

"I'm sure he knew. Dad knew everything." Neha put her arm around Mélusine's shoulders and kissed her cheek. "Well, almost everything."

"He knew about us too, ma chérie," Mélusine informed her.

"He did?! Since when?! When did he find out?!" Neha exclaimed. "I was stewing for *years* about when to tell him. Decades even!"

"It is a story for another time, ma chérie." Mélusine glanced around at their attentive audience and changed the subject. "Now, as I was saying… I didn't want to make decisions about so many humans' fates without consulting our wise leader. In the case of Ingrid's murder, we all agreed that there was no need to create more pain with Mrs. Fitzgerald and John both dead. Under the guise of Lord Blakeney's supposed Secret Service position, Kuveni and I helped arrange the funerals for Ingrid and John, although we were careful to conduct them at separate times and bury them far away from each other, at Mr. Kauter's request. Mr. Kauter returned to Switzerland after that with a small pittance provided by the Baron for his loss and his silence."

"How horrible!" Ellie exclaimed. "As if money would do anything to relieve him of the pain of losing his only child!"

"He did try to sell her to John," Neha pointed out.

"I don't think he saw it like that." Mélusine thought carefully about the assertion. "I do believe that Mr. Kauter thought he was doing something good for Ingrid with his meddling. In his eyes, she would have become a respectable wife, a *baron's* wife. Her station in life would have been solidified, and no other English man was willing to touch her. In his mind, marriage, even to a man she hated, was the ultimate goal. He told me later, after Ingrid's funeral, that the land was a test for John. He wouldn't let John marry her until he could prove that he had legal rights over the family's land, otherwise, he worried that John would leave her penniless, even if they were married, to seek greener pastures elsewhere."

"I guess," Neha remained unconvinced. "I'm glad I wasn't around back then. It sounds a lot more dismal for women than I realized. Weren't the 1920s supposed to be super progressive?"

"It's all relative, ma chérie," Mélusine shrugged. "Why do you think I came as Sir Percy Blakeney? I made that persona because for hundreds of years, human societies were so backwards that I simply could not conduct my various exploits in my feminine form, and believe me, I *tried*. No one would give me the time of day. If I'd shown up that morning as a woman, even in 1922, I would not have had the authority to wrangle anyone as I did. None of the Crowdens would have allowed it, and they certainly would not have believed that I was a member of the Secret Service."

"What happened to Ralph and Anne?" Charlie asked. "Did they go to jail?"

"Ralph and Anne escaped all of the charges in the end, but their punishment came in other forms. The Baron pressed charges against Mr. Banning for embezzlement and fraud, and Mr. Banning ended up losing his license and serving a jail sentence. The Baron died a few months later, before Mr. Banning's trial even began, making Ralph the new Baron of Heathfield. His counsel managed to keep him and Anne out of the embezzlement charges by arguing that the entire scheme was concocted and executed by Mr. Banning, and that Mr. Banning's false legal counsel led them into believing that all of their activities were perfectly legal."

"A jury believed that?" Neha scoffed.

"Juries back then were not in the habit of convicting barons of idiocy," Mélusine shrugged. "They were all quite happy to pin everything on Mr. Banning. But, Ralph and Anne didn't escape unscathed. They spent their last penny on legal counsel, and Ralph ended up the dismal impoverished baron he had always feared he would be, living in a one-room cottage in the village on his pension from the military. He and Anne divorced, and she ended up going back to work as a nurse at a veteran's hospital in Yorkshire. I believe she re-married a widower who already had a troop of children for her to mother, but Ralph never married again. The title died out when he died in 1935 from complications from his war injuries."

"It really was a tragic story, wasn't it?" Ellie murmured. "They all ruined each other in the end."

"Not entirely," Mélusine smiled. "Anne really got what she'd always wanted, Mr. Rana returned to India to run the charity with the Baron's money, and Mrs. Murray soon entered the employ of one Colonel Edmund Marriner in his growing marital household a few months later. And from the ashes of the incredible disaster, Edmund and Eleanor found each other. As stories go, it has quite a happy ending in my book."

"Mine too," Edmund agreed.

He pulled Ellie into another hug. "I love you, Ellie. Happy birthday."

"I love you, Dad."

They embraced for a long moment as their large familial audience watched happily.

"Now, shall we go outside and play in the snow?" Edmund suggested.

"Yes!" Charlie exclaimed as he hopped off the couch and ran for the door.

"Let's make a snow castle!" Neha exclaimed as she whooshed to join him. "Come on, slow pokes. I'll show you how!"

The rest of the party followed them at a more grown-up, human pace.

"I've always loved the snow," Ellie sighed.

"Me too," Edmund smiled.

"But, I think I'd rather stay inside for the moment. Supriya, I think you have a letter for me from my mother."

"I have her memories too," Supriya reminded her.

"I think I'd rather wait on those," Ellie said as Supriya handed her the note. "I don't want to rush. Getting all of her memories at once seems rather daunting, now that I think about it."

"I will be here when you're ready," Supriya said as she offered Ellie a supportive hug.

Ellie squeezed Supriya tighter than she ever had. "Thank you for everything."

"Do you want us to stay with you?" Edmund asked.

"No, I think I'd rather read it alone," Ellie decided.

"As you wish, Ellie-bean," Edmund agreed as he pulled her into a final hug. "Kuveni," he called into the seemingly empty room, "Ellie requested that she read the letter *alone*. Perhaps you can join us in the garden for a game of snowplay."

A disembodied humph accompanied a begrudging agreement.

And so, as the many loving relatives of the gentle English soldier followed him out into the mid-afternoon sun to celebrate the many beautiful benefits of the Age of Truth, Eleanor Ariadne MacLeod Marriner sat down on the edge of the fireplace of her freshly re-acquired ancestral home, and finally, after ninety long years, she met her mother.

~TO BE CONTINUED~

SNEAK PEEK: ANGELS IN DISGUISE
The Glorious Victories of Eleanor MacLeod – Book Two

CHAPTER 1 – THE MORNING AFTER

January, 1923 – London

Eleanor stirred in the cold arms of her sleeping fiancé as a beam of sunlight landed on her face through the frosted window pane. The pounding headache of an epic hangover almost sent her right back into a disjointed dream, but as her foggy memories of the prior night flowed into her brain, a sudden excitement wrested her from her physical plight.

It had happened. The confession she had waited three long months for Edmund to make had finally happened. An entire web of deceit was now mercifully in tatters, and now Eleanor only had to worry about that other web... her web... the web Edmund's divine guardians had sucked her into within twenty-four hours of their fateful introduction.

At the request of Mélusine—whom Eleanor saw as Edmund's mysterious, shapeshifting auntie (for lack of a better term)—who had hastily revealed herself to Eleanor during their harrowing quest to solve the gory murder of a young scullery maid, Eleanor had patiently waited as her gentle, shell-shocked, half-human soldier bumbled his way through months of half-truths about his long, secret past and his plethora of otherworldly abilities until their rendez-vous with his oldest friend, Edward Rutherford (the only friend he'd ever had who knew his secret), pushed him right over the edge.

Even with everything she knew about him, her beloved soldier still had a knack for surprising her. She hadn't expected in the slightest that he would demonstrate his superhuman healing ability right there in a public cocktail lounge! And without the excuse of giddy intoxication that she and Edward could claim! She had already seen plenty of evidence that Edmund was never affected by alcohol, and despite his hasty revelation, she did not believe that the excessive amount of cognac they'd consumed throughout the evening was the culprit. Now, the hours they'd spent in the company of Edward Rutherford's grotesquely shrewish wife before they'd retired without her to the cocktail lounge in peace… that perhaps had more to do with it.

She had barely been able to contain herself as the woman hemmed and hawed over the most minor mishaps, and so she assumed that observing the contrast between the irrational, controlling relationship that Margaret Rutherford had with Edward, and the friendly, mutually-respectful one that she herself had with Edmund must have been as impactful for him as it had been for her.

With a completely sober mind, in the dark corner of the smoky bar, Edmund had squeezed his cognac glass until it shattered and cut open his hand to reveal the utterly alien violet metallic plasma that served as his body's primary healing mechanism. She had to admit, it was a bit more alien than she'd anticipated.

She'd expected some sort of unique self-healing ability in her gentle English soldier ever since Mélusine had casually dropped the interesting factoid that she herself was two thousand years old. After all, Edmund had managed to survive four hellish years in the trenches of Belgium without a single, miniscule scar to show for it. She knew this for certain, as she had already spent many delightful hours on many separate occasions inspecting every lovely crevice of his naked body.

Then, of course, there was that moment in the dark, in the Baron of Heathfield's cursed home during their wretched murder investigation, when Edmund had pushed her out of the way and taken on the full brunt of an ill-conceived dagger attack. The power outage had conveniently allowed him to hide in the dark shadows while his Rakshasa plasma completed its work on his human flesh. She'd worked ever so hard to contain her curiosity as she'd respected his wishes and kept her distance, listening helplessly to his pained whimpers until the agonizing healing process was complete, and ever since then, she had wondered from time to time what the strange process would look like.

But, the intelligent movement of the bizarre foreign substance that disappeared right back into Edmund's body when it had completed its task—*that*, Eleanor hadn't expected. She was glad, in the end, that she'd had three months to prepare herself. She'd managed to hide the temporary discomfort his revelation had evoked, and now she was already reaping the rewards.

She'd had no idea how much more pleasurable their intimacy could be with Edmund basking in the novelty of their newfound honesty, and now she was thoroughly entranced. She was glad, in some ways, that she hadn't known it sooner; it would have made the wait feel that much more interminable. But now there was another problem. A new problem. The problem of the secrets that *she* would be forced to keep on behalf of Edmund's guardians who had given her far more information about his unique origins than he knew himself.

She wished for a fleeting moment that Mélusine had not revealed herself. Then she reached over to stroke the soft cheek of her sleeping soldier, and she let the thought go. They were engaged now. They were going to be together. She knew exactly what she was getting herself into, perhaps even more than he did, and she was grateful. If Mélusine hadn't revealed herself, Eleanor knew that her tenacity would have pushed Edmund too fast. She might have lost him completely. But now... *now* they were going to revel in the joys of fully knowing each other until death they do part. Or, at least until she died. The Grim Reaper would surely knock on her door before he knocked on Edmund's, if he could even get close to Edmund. She'd already noticed Mélusine's careful deflections on the topic of Edmund's mortality more than once.

Her mind wandered as she contemplated the other revelation of the evening that had truly surprised her—Edmund's centennial.

She knew he was special the day that they met, but somehow through all of his half-truths and all of Mélusine's nuggets of useful information, she had not let herself acknowledge the possibility that he was already much older than he looked. Mélusine had called him 'Young Edmund' for god's sake! She had assumed that he was at the beginning of a very long journey, not already in the middle! She smiled as she realized her human logical folly. To someone two-thousand years old, one century on Earth *was* still young.

She wondered how exactly it all worked. Mélusine had perfectly emulated a variety of human forms during their revelatory conversation… Would Edmund someday be able to do the same? Would he be able to make himself entirely into someone else? What would happen as he continued to age? Would he simply wake up one morning and be a young man again? Or even a young woman! The idea seemed utterly absurd, and a bit disconcerting. She loved him exactly how he was.

She relegated the thought to the back of her mind as he began to stir. She wiggled into the nook of his cold arm and waited for him to open his eyes.

"Good morning, old man," she said as he took in a deep, awakening breath.

He looked down at her and smiled. "I was afraid last night that you might not remember what happened. You and Edward drank more cognac than I've ever seen anyone drink… anyone other than me, of course."

"There is a footie match being played with my eyeballs," Eleanor admitted. "But I remember everything, old man. You're stuck marrying a wild Scottish thistle now. There's no way to weasel your way out of it."

He kissed her forehead, and then worked his way down to her lips. "I couldn't be happier, my dearest thistle. It is like the weight of the world has been lifted from my shoulders."

"I'm glad." Eleanor returned his embrace.

She fought back a pang of sadness that she didn't feel the same. Happy, yes. Unburdened, no. Alas, she was grateful that one of them could feel that way, and there were ever so many benefits that balanced out the great burden of the unusual destiny she had accepted…

As she leaned in for a deeper kiss, her headache's pounding exploded, and she pulled away.

"Are you alright?" Edmund asked concernedly.

"Perfectly fine," she lied as she reached over to the bedside table and drank down an entire glass of water. "The cognac is catching up with me, that's all. I suppose I should be more careful from now on not to pace you. My meagre human temperament isn't up to the task."

Edmund was startled by her reference. "Do you really think that I'm not human then?"

Eleanor struggled for words as she noticed the subtle expression on his face that indicated she'd given herself away. She knew him well enough already to recognize when he smelled her fear. It was a rather annoying ability of his, if she was going to be honest. It made the years she'd spent perfecting the art of hiding her emotions utterly useless.

"Darling, you have violet metallic blood that heals you within moments of injury. I don't think that my medical background is necessary to diagnose that you aren't entirely human. Do you think that you're human?"

He paused for a long moment as he considered her assertion. "There are many things about me that aren't human… You have experienced most of them now, but not all of them. I suppose without more context about the source of my abnormalities, I must think of myself as mostly human."

Eleanor leaned in and kissed him gently on the lips. "I love you, Edmund. I love all that you are. Human and whatever else you happen to be. The violet blood does seem rather alien, don't you think? If I didn't know any better, I'd guess you were part Martian, but that is a rather silly thought."

It suddenly occurred to her as she spoke the words that Mélusine had not, in fact, told her anything about the original homeland of the Rakshasa people, only that they had been on Earth longer than humans had existed.

"Martian is better than demon," he murmured. He startled as he realized he'd voiced the thought out loud.

Eleanor became serious as she took his hands tightly into hers. "I do not believe for one second that you are a demon, Edmund, and you should not let yourself even entertain that possibility. Demons are superstitious creatures made up by religious zealots to trick humans into being afraid of anyone or anything different from them. Do not ever let their ignorance change the way you see yourself."

"I love you so much, Eleanor. After a hundred years, I finally know what love is," Edmund whispered as he kissed her again.

He gently invited her to settle back into his arms, and he sighed contentedly as she began running her warm fingers across his cold chest in gentle patterns.

"A hundred years..." Eleanor murmured. "It actually makes sense now that I think about it. I assumed that each of the adventures you mentioned over the last few months had been rather short, but it makes more sense that they were spread out over an extra fifty years."

Edmund shifted uncomfortably. "I'm sorry I lied to you about so many things, Eleanor. I hope you can forgive me."

Eleanor continued on with her soft, soothing strokes. "There is nothing to forgive, darling. You told me that you were lying to me practically as soon as we met, remember? That was rather honest of you when you think about it."

"Yes... I suppose... but still... It has been very painful keeping things from you. I know how much you detest men lying to you."

310

"I love that you have thought so much about it. You are nothing like any other man in this world, Edmund, and I love you so dearly for it." Eleanor moved her gentle attention to his nipples until they hardened, and a fresh round of goosebumps exploded across his skin. "Someone once told me that it is a most profound act of love to withhold information until the appropriate time. If you'd revealed all your cards to me the day we met, we wouldn't have been able to enjoy the slow unraveling of your web of lies together."

She hoped that her forgiveness would be returned to her if ever he discovered the ugly web of lies that she was spinning.

"You are a bastion of understanding, my dearest thistle," Edmund said as he sat up and gathered her into his arms.

After a few minutes of licking each other's tongues, Eleanor straddled her gentle soldier, and as a fresh burst of desire exploded deep within her, she set about enjoying another round of the new sensual pleasures afforded by Edmund's unburdened happiness.

"There is one thing that I haven't been able to figure out," she said as she nestled into the nook of his arm for a post work-out rest. "If you are over one hundred years old, why do you look like you are only middle-aged? Do you age slower than humans do? Or is there something else happening entirely? If you aged slower than everyone else, then certainly your old army acquaintances would have noticed by now."

"Are you sure you want to know?" Edmund asked with a fresh batch of nerves in his tone.

"I already know your deepest, darkest secret, darling," Eleanor reminded him. "Unless... unless the process is gruesome..."

Edmund shifted uncomfortably as he struggled to decide how exactly to describe the painful details.

"Good lord, you don't have to kill anyone, do you? Like a creature out of a Penny Dreadful?" Eleanor asked as she felt a pang of anxiety about Edmund's foreign nature for the first time. "That would be just my luck… proving my mother right for kissing on the first date…"

Edmund smiled as he brought the palm of her hand to his mouth to kiss it. "No, I don't have to kill anyone."

"You see, my imagination is always worse than reality." Eleanor sighed with relief. "It's best just to tell me straight, Colonel, on this and every other shocking secret, before my mind has a chance to wander too much."

Edmund took a moment to choose his words carefully. "When I am mortally wounded, the healing process returns my body to its strongest state. All of a sudden, I end up looking and feeling as if I'm a spring chicken, and then I age normally until it happens again."

"Good lord… That means that you have been mortally wounded? You poor thing! That must have felt wretched!"

Edmund gently intertwined her fingers with his. "I have re-set twice. Once in 1840 and once in 1895. Both times I was stabbed through the abdomen with multiple swords."

"Good lord." Eleanor worked to push the horrific image from her mind, and then another thought occurred to her. "What horrible luck! It happened the exact same way twice? What were the chances of that?!"

Edmund smiled. "The first time it was an accident. Two drunken soldiers were aiming for someone else, and I stepped in the way. The second time I did it to myself." She gasped, but he was unfazed by her predictable reaction. "I was grotesquely old and dreadfully uncomfortable. I was afraid I might die of old age, so I… er… catalyzed the process myself. Luckily it worked, but it was far more painful than the first time. Stabbing oneself with two swords at once is extremely unpleasant."

"I can imagine…" Eleanor murmured. She fought back the mental image. "Does that mean, then, that you were never mortally wounded in the war? You'd look much younger if you had been?"

Edmund nodded. "I was shot six times, but never so badly that it caused my body to re-set. I was rather lucky, I think. I don't know what those wicked army scientists would have done if they'd discovered my secret. Their chemical weapons were ghoulish enough, and I hate to fathom the experimentation that must have gone into those..." He grimaced. "I was more terrified of being captured by our own bloody doctors than I was of death itself. Who knows how many more men I could have saved if I hadn't been so bloody afraid of revealing my secret, but I just... couldn't. So many men died because of my selfish fear, Eleanor... too many to count."

"You were right to be afraid. I'm sorry, Edmund. You must have felt very alone in your fear."

That was the first time that Eleanor truly understood the complicated source of Edmund's unique brand of guilt-ridden shell shock.

"Yes... yes, I did."

"You are not alone anymore." Eleanor kissed him gently on the lips.

"There was something else..."

She felt his heart race as he prepared for his confession.

"You can tell me anything, Edmund. *Anything.*"

Edmund's grimace grew as he let himself give into the memories that he'd avoided for so long. "The mustard gas... it infused me with power, and I hated myself for liking it, but I couldn't help it. It brought pain and death to my men. It caused such horrific injuries. I dreaded its consequences, but I craved it all the same, Eleanor! Sometimes I still dream about it, and my stomach growls with hunger."

Eleanor squeezed his hand. "The way you are describing it, it sounds like how humans respond to certain drugs. Perhaps your unique body chemistry has some sort of special compatibility with the substance."

Edmund brought her hand to his lips and kissed her fingers. "I've never considered that possibility. It sounds so mundane when you put it like that... almost natural."

"I'm sure that it was natural, darling. Everything in the world is. The things we think of superstitiously only seem that way because we don't know enough about them yet... your unusual talents included."

"But over time, Eleanor... over time the mustard gas made me hungry for other things. For ghoulish, monstrous, unspeakable things. I never acted upon the urges, but they were there more and more, taunting me at every turn. I don't know how much longer I could have held out if the war hadn't ended when it did. It was those urges I was fighting the weekend we met. The smell of the bloody corpse brought them back for the first time in four years. It was like nothing had changed. It made me terrified that I would never outrun it."

Eleanor thought for a long time before choosing her response. "In the trenches you were practically bathing in blood, Edmund. You were constantly faced with unimaginable gore. You were starving and malnourished, and all the while, you were taunted by a euphoric substance that made you feel good while those you loved were dying. Those are horrific circumstances for the strongest of men."

Edmund looked away. "I am not a man, Eleanor. It awoke something evil within me, something that now I have to control at the slightest provocation. There is no telling how dangerous I could be if I fully lost control."

"Darling, you are many things, and I can attest to the highest court that you are certainly a man." She winked, but he did not find her facetious comment funny. She hunkered down and returned to seriousness, noting for future reference that the inappropriate humor that worked so well with her other patients was not a useful tool with her own shell-shocked soldier. "Edmund, I have treated several soldiers over the years who didn't have the self-control that you had. One even tried to eat another soldier. When he realized what he'd done during a psychotherapy session at the army hospital afterwards, he killed himself the same evening." Edmund cringed at the image, and Eleanor took both of his hands into hers. "You have known a darkness that no one else can truly comprehend, but you triumphed. You didn't give in! Even when you were trapped in the thick of it, you didn't give in! And in Basingstoke, all it took was some focus and determination on your part, and you got over your urges, didn't you? Have they troubled you again since then? Since you escaped the stimulation that triggered your war memories?"

"No," he admitted. "I haven't struggled with them since."

Eleanor smiled. "You are mostly human, darling. And these struggles are entirely human. They may be compounded by your unusual composition, but they are not unique to you. You are strong enough to overcome them, and I have already seen you make great progress since we met. I couldn't be prouder, really."

Edmund kissed her on the forehead as he fought back tears. "I love you, Eleanor."

She let him give in to his joyful melancholy for a few more moments, and then a mischievous grin spread across her face, and she forcefully pulled him out of his misery and attacked him with tickles. "So, you'd better stay on the up-and-up, Colonel, because I am too much of a wild Scottish thistle to become a glorified nurse-wife. Got it?"

He burst into involuntary laughter, and she continued her light-hearted offense until his face turned red and his eyes teared up.

"Now, what should we do today, my dashing, mostly-human fiancé? I'm down here for two more days before I have to return to Scotland to settle my affairs. There's a lot to do when a modern woman agrees to be married, you know. And don't even get me started on the mess of trouble I'm going to face trying to get anyone to employ me down here in the land of sassanacks. But whit's fur ye'll no go past ye."

"I'm sorry, what?"

Eleanor laughed. "It is an old Scots phrase, I think. My father used to say it when I was just a wee lass. But, Colonel, we have just reached a milestone! I've just reached the boundary of your superhuman linguistic talent!"

She tickled him playfully again, and he returned her jab with his own until they were both rolling on the bed with laughter. She couldn't remember the last time she'd laughed so hard that her stomach muscles hurt. In fact, she wasn't sure it had ever happened before in her life.

As he wiped the happy tears from her eyes, Edmund sighed with contentment and returned to their conversation.

"I often have trouble with idioms, unless I use a language often enough to understand them in context. I've never heard that one before."

"I suppose it's a bit like *que sera sera*. I'll have to leave my fate and my career to destiny, because the British Army isn't going to help."

"You can't just request a transfer?" Edmund asked naively. "With your experience? There are five veterans' hospitals in London alone."

"Darling, it is strictly against army policy to employ a married woman. I will be lucky if anyone on Earth will employ me after the deed is done. But, I'm a rather tenacious thistle in the side, so I am going to assume that somehow I'll manage. *How* is not something I'd like to think about at the moment."

Joy and sorrow battled fiercely in Edmund's expression.

"Please, darling, don't let it get you down. We are both very resourceful. I'm sure we'll be able to make something work. I've never been able to sit around and wait for fate. I'll start coming up with a whole mess of plans before I pop back down here in a few weeks. I'm sure by the time we're married, I'll have everything all worked out."

"I can't believe you'd agree to marry me knowing that it would cause you such problems!" Edmund exclaimed. "You love your work!"

"And I love you, darling," Eleanor said as she hopped off the bed and pulled him up into her arms. "I'm not willing to concede on either of my great loves. I will find a way to make both of them work."

Edmund twirled her around and pulled her into a passionate embrace, and Eleanor couldn't stop herself from giggling giddily at the romance of the moment.

"What shall we do today, old man? We've already danced naked in each other's arms. That's a fine start!"

Edmund snuck another kiss, and then grinned as a bewitching idea that he had only ever fantasized about in his wildest dreams entered his head. "Would you like to see what I looked like as an old man? Would you like to know what's in store for you in twenty years?"

Eleanor's heart began racing as she contemplated whether or not Edmund had already managed to stumble into some ability that Mélusine didn't know he had.

"Show me, Edmund!" Eleanor agreed with anxious excitement. "I'd love to see!"

"The pictures aren't here. They're at my house in Basingstoke. It's mine, by the way, and it has been since I bought it in 1848. Every reference I made to my 'grandfather' when we were there before was really to me. I lived there for forty-seven years in the nineteenth century, making my living as an artist."

"Forty-seven years! Yes... yes, of course... Many more things make sense now!" Eleanor exclaimed. She couldn't believe she hadn't put that obvious reality together in her head sooner.

Edmund pulled her into one final, delicious, naked embrace and then naughtily slapped her bum. "Come on, my wild Scottish thistle. More revelations await!"

GLOSSARY OF HINDU REFERENCES

Hinduism, the world's oldest continuously practiced religion, is an exceptionally diverse collection of philosophies and rituals practiced by over one billion people globally. There is no single institution and no single written text that defines the 'rules' of Hinduism, and thus it varies widely in practice and belief across the world.

While there is a pantheon featuring a plethora of gods and goddesses with various regional names and stories, there are also numerous sects who worship Vishnu (Vaishnavism), Shiva (Shaivism), Shakti (Shaktism), and combinations/permutations of these major gods and goddesses, and their manifestations (including avatars), as representations of the one supreme being.

The vast and fascinating complexity of Hinduism cannot be captured in a short glossary, and it is not the author's intent to do so. This glossary is meant to give the uninitiated reader some basic context for references throughout the Ashley Mayers universe. Further research is recommended for those interested in digging deeper.

Agni (uh-**gnee**) – 'Fire' in Sanskrit, Agni is also the god of fire and the conveyor of sacrifices to the gods. It is Agni's role in the Hindu pantheon that is invariably linked with the many rituals, both daily and for special occasions, that require a *yajna*, or sacred fire.

Artha (**ahr**-tah) – One of the four aims of human life in Hindu philosophy, sometimes 'meaning, sense, or purpose,' *artha* generally focuses on the 'means to live the life you want,' including but not limited to wealth, career, and financial security. It can perhaps be thought of as 'why you do work.'

Asura/Asuri (ah-soo-ruh/ah-soo-ree) – Originally a term used to describe divine, powerful beings, good or bad, the term later came to represent primarily darker powered beings in Hinduism and is sometimes (but not always) synonymous with demons. Rakshasas are sometimes described as one type of *Asura*. *Asuri* is the feminine form of *Asura*.

Avatar (**ah**-vuh-tuhr) – In Hinduism, an avatar is a deliberate descent of a deity to Earth. The term is most commonly used to describe incarnations or manifestations of Vishnu, but has been used with other deities, including Shiva, Ganesh, and Shakti. The lists of avatars and consensus around them is dubious. Some sects believe that Shiva, as a formless entity, will never have an avatar, while others believe that Hanuman is an avatar of Shiva. The lists of Vishnu avatars range from ten to twenty-five avatars, and some characters in epics are referred to as 'partial' avatars, such as Rama's brother, Lakshmana, sometimes being considered 'one-quarter Vishnu.' One major thematic element throughout the Ashley Mayers universe explores what exactly it means (and doesn't mean) to be an avatar.

Ayodhya (ah-**yoh**-dyuh) – An ancient city located in Uttar Pradesh in Northern India that remains inhabited today, Ayodhya is considered to be the birthplace and ancient kingdom of Rama. In modern times, tragedy and controversy, fuelled by Hindu/Muslim animosity, have plagued the city after a violent uprising in 1992 that led to the destruction of the 16th c. Babri Mosque, which many people believed was built upon the site of Rama's original temple.

Bhoomi (**boo**-mee) – The embodiment/personification of 'Mother Earth.' Bhoomi is referred to as the mother of Sita, and at the end of *the Ramayana*, when Sita's suffering becomes unbearable, she returns to her 'mother,' being swallowed by the earth.

Ceylon (say-lon) – The historical, British colonial name of modern-day Sri Lanka, Ceylon is a key setting in *the Ramayana*, as the home of the Rakshasa king, Ravana, who kidnaps Sita and takes her back to Lanka to woo her (while she is imprisoned).

Chiranjivi (chee-ruhn-**jee**-vee) – Seven immortals in Hinduism who remain on Earth to lead humans in various paths of righteousness. In this series, we have two: Vibhishana, Hanuman.

Dasara (**Duh**-suh-ruh) – Otherwise known as *Dussera*, *Dushera*, or *Vijayadashami*, depending on the region and language, Dasara is a holiday at the end/culmination of Navaratri, the nine-night autumn festival devoted to the Goddess. Dasara traditions vary across India, ranging from sacred dances of Garba and Dandiya in the north, to a candlelight vigil and elephant parade in Mysore in the south, a city that considers itself the namesake of the Goddess in her defeat of the demon Mahishasura (sometimes referred to as *Mahishasura-Mardini* from the Sanskrit holy mantras). It coincides with the culmination of Durga Puja in Bengal, and always involves great cheer, festivities, and often fireworks and light shows.

Devi/Deva (deh-**vee**/deh-**vah**) – 'Heavenly' or 'divine' beings in Hinduism, *Devi* can be synonymous with 'god' or 'deity' but primarily refers to powerful beings who are 'good,' and can sometimes be contrasted with the 'evil' *Asura*. However, the designations of 'good' versus 'evil' are far less clearly defined in Hinduism compared to Judeo-Christian religions, and so, for example, Kartikeya, the god of war, is still considered a *Deva*. In Hinduism, an *Asura* can ascend and become a *Deva*, with Vibhishana being a prime example, demonstrating that birthright is less important than actions on Earth to define one's character and virtue.

Devi Mahatmya (deh-**vee** muh-**hat**-myuh) – The *Devi Mahatmya* is a religious text (from the *Markandeya Purana,* one of eighteen primary religious texts in Hinduism) devoted to the Great Goddess (Shakti). It recounts her manifestation on Earth in the warrior form of Durga to protect the innocent by defeating the shapeshifting buffalo demon Mahishasura, and her subsequent return of balance and virtue to the world. A text revered by Hindus across many sects, the *Devi Mahatmya* serves as a primary text for Shaktist Hindus, who believe that the Goddess is the Supreme Being. It serves as the inspiration for the festivals of Navaratri, Durga Puja, and Dasara/Vijayadashmi.

Dharma (**dahr**-muh) – One of the four aims of human life in Hindu philosophy, with many meanings, *dharma* is roughly translated as virtue, morality, righteousness, obligations, and correct conduct. The Hindu epics, *the Ramayana* and *the Mahabharata,* both demonstrate that there is often no single clear path to *dharma,* as various 'right' paths often conflict and need to be prioritized, with each difficult choice producing complicated consequences and satisfying drama.

Diwali (Dih-**vah**-lee) – Also known as Deepavali in many South Indian languages, Diwali is one of the most important festivals across Hindu tradition, and celebrates the triumph of light over darkness, knowledge over ignorance, and hope over despair. Based on the Hindu calendar, the festival of lights typically falls between mid-October and mid-November each year, and its observance dates back to ancient times. The rituals vary across the many cultures who celebrate the holiday, but it is generally consistent that people light candles and offer prayers to Lakshmi.

Durga (door-**gah**) – A principle form of the Goddess (Shakti), who manifests physically in many different forms depending on the task at hand, Durga is also called Maa Durga or the Holy Mother (not to be confused with the Christian/Catholic Holy Mother Mary). The primary hero of her own epic, the *Devi Mahatmya,* Durga is most famous as a warrior for justice who wields the power of the entire pantheon, coming to Earth with many arms and weapons to defeat the shapeshifting buffalo demon, Mahishasura. Her triumph in defeating an insidious, ever-changing manifestation of evil can be viewed as a model of perseverance that can be applied in everyday life. Every year her triumph is celebrated during the festivals of Navaratri ("Nine Nights," each celebrating a manifestation of the Goddess), Durga Puja (five nights celebrating her defeat of Mahishasura, primarily celebrated in Bengal), Dasara (the culmination of Navaratri celebrated across India), and Diwali (the Festival of Lights, celebrated across the Hindu world and by other related religions). As the Great Goddess, she is sometimes referred to interchangeably with Parvati, wife of Shiva, and she is sometimes said to manifest as Lakshmi and Saraswati in their roles as the primordial energy that animates the universe. Across most sects, Durga is worshipped as the underlying creative, preservative, and destructive energy of the universe (Shakti), who exists as a formless entity always, and sometimes takes form within the gods or goddesses, to fulfill tasks on behalf of the universe.

Durga Puja (door-**gah poo**-ja) – A five-night festival primarily celebrated in Bengal, Durga Puja coincides with the festival of Navaratri in other parts of India, all in celebration of the Great Goddess (Shakti), manifested as Durga for her defeat of the shapeshifting demon Mahishasura. Known for its *pandals* (elaborate temporary altars to the Goddess), Durga Puja is celebrated with costume, dance, food, special rituals, and bright firecrackers, making the streets of Calcutta one of the liveliest (and most crowded) places in the world to experience the frenetic energy of the Devi in one of her most beloved forms.

Garuda (**guh**-roo-duh) – The 'mount' of Lord Vishnu, Garuda is a large bird, sometimes a humanoid bird, who flies Lord Vishnu around. Sometimes represented as a large phoenix, eagle, or kite, Garuda also exists in Buddhist mythology.

Hanuman (**hahn**-oo-mahn) – Rama's right-hand man and a beloved star of *the Ramayana*, Hanuman is a Vanara, a monkey-like humanoid race who fought by Rama's side in his attack against Ravana in Lanka. In *the Ramayana*, Hanuman uses his flying ability to track and eventually make contact with Sita while she is incarcerated by Ravana, but she refuses to go with him back to Rama. Various interpretations of this interaction range from it exemplifying Sita's purity through her refusal to be in another man's arms, even to be rescued, to a valid observation that had Sita agreed to go back to Rama with Hanuman, the entire war between Rama and Ravana might have been avoided. Hanuman is consistently referred to as one of the *Chiranjivi*, representing loyalty, courage and devotion.

Harihara (**hah**-ree-**hah**-ruh) – A combined form of Shiva and Vishnu (Transformation and Preservation), Harihara is sometimes used to explain/describe the complementary nature of the two gods as aspects of one supreme being. The symbolism evokes the necessary balance (and tug-of-war) between the two primary aspects of existence, each keeping the other in check.

Hiranyakashipu – (**hee**-ran-**yaak**-shih-poo) – A demon evil enough to warrant the Preserver of the Universe coming to Earth (as Narasimha, the fourth avatar of Vishnu), Hiranyakashipu gained a boon from Lord Brahma so that he couldn't be defeated by man or beast, thus requiring Lord Vishnu to take a more clever form, in his case, as a half-man, half-lion, to defeat him.

Lakshmi (**luhk**-shmee) – The female aspect of the Preserver of the Universe, often referred to as the goddess of prosperity (material and spiritual), and the wife of Lord Vishnu, Lakshmi (or Laxmi), is one of the principal goddesses of the *Tridevi*, or 'Trinity of Goddesses.' She is said to be the life-force of Lord Vishnu and is worshipped during the major festival of Diwali every autumn. As the wife of Rama, seventh avatar of Vishnu, Sita is an avatar of Lakshmi.

Kali (kuh-lee) – Hinduism's primary apocalyptic demon—not to be confused with Kali, a fierce incarnation of Shakti (spelled the same in English but not in Sanskrit)—this demon is often depicted with a dog's head. He is said to fan the flames of human greed, violence, and iniquity during *Kali Yuga* ('The Age of Vice'), an era that many Hindus believe describes the modern world. It is sometimes said that Ravana is an incarnation and/or devotee of the demon, Kali, and that Lord Vishnu will incarnate in his ultimate avatar form, Lord Kalki, to defeat Kali and bring the worlds into *Satya Yuga* ("The Age of Truth").

Kali/Kaali (Kah-lee) – A fierce incarnation of the female life-force of the Transformer of the Universe, Kaali (often spelled Kali in English, but too easily confused with the demon Kali), is one of the most misunderstood incarnations of the Goddess. Often referred to as the goddess of time, and represented with blue or black skin, her tongue out, standing on the dead body of her husband, Shiva, wearing a skull necklace and holding a severed, bloody head, she is often thought of as a ghoulish character by those who don't know any better. However, the symbolism of the imagery of her standing on Shiva's body is meant to represent that she is his life-force, and without her, he is lifeless. The life-force of change is fierce, and the ravages of time often frightening, which are two reasons why she is depicted in such a monstrous style. She is, however, a natural manifestation of the destruction required for our ever-changing universe to exist.

Kalki (**kuhl**-kee) – Lord Kalki, 'Destroyer of Filth,' the tenth and final avatar of Vishnu (the Preserver of the Universe), is believed to be the only avatar who has not already been on Earth. Legends tell of him being born in Shambhala, a mythical place of great spiritual power north of Tibet, a place of great interest to the sages when the stories were written, due to its association and proximity to the homeland of the invading Khans. While references to Lord Kalki can be conflicting, it is consistent in texts that Lord Kalki will come to Earth to defeat the demon, Kali, and restore balance and order, bringing humans back to the path of virtue, and ushering in the Age of Truth.

Mahagauri (**Maa**-huh-**gau**-ree) – A manifestation of Maa Durga (considered her eighth of nine manifestations by some sects), Mahagauri is worshipped on the eighth night of the festival of Navaratri in some parts of India. She is said to be "the fair one," with a fair complexion, who offers forgiveness and protection to all of her followers.

Mantra (**mahn**-truh) – Words or sounds, often repetitive, that are used in prayer.

Moksha (**mohk**-shuh) – One of the four aims of human life in Hindu philosophy, meaning 'release' or 'liberation,' *moksha* primarily refers to release from the reincarnation cycle of birth and death on Earth.

Naraka (nah-**rah**-kuh) – In Hinduism, Naraka, or the underworld (somewhat similar to Christian purgatory), is a temporary place for expiation of sins to be endured between a soul's mortal death and its return to Earth. There are many different forms of Naraka, each featuring colorful punishments that are related to a person's sins, such as murderers being eaten alive by Rakshasas. As positive and negative actions do not 'cancel each other out' in Hinduism, a soul can repent through their punishment in Naraka and enjoy the peace of *Svarga* (a heavenly place), both before their return to Earth.

Narasimha (**Nur**-sim-**haa**) – Regarded as the fourth avatar of Vishnu, Narasimha is a manifestation of the Preserver of the Universe who comes to Earth as a half-man, half-lion to defeat the demon Hiranyakashipu, who has immortality against "all men and beasts." He is considered a protector of the innocent and warrior for justice, as well as an example of one of Lord Vishnu's many clever responses to the inconvenient ancient boons held by his enemies.

Navaratri (Nuv-**rah**-tree) – Otherwise known as "Nine Nights," Navaratri is the primary festival of the Goddess and takes place at the beginning of autumn, typically three weeks before the festival of Diwali. Traditions and details of each night's symbolism differ across regions and sects, with fasting and the wearing of special colors to honor various manifestations of the Goddess being common across regions. In Gujarat, sacred dances known as Garba and Dandiya, enact Durga's battle and defeat of the demon Mahishasura.

Parvati (**pahr**-vuh-**tee**) – The wife of Shiva and one of the three chief goddesses of the *Tridevi* or 'Trinity of Goddesses,' Parvati is the benevolent female aspect of the Transformer of the Universe, and is often referred to as the goddess of power, love, fertility, and devotion. She is also sometimes referred to as an aspect or alternative name of Durga (the root form of creation, preservation, and annihilation), Shakti (the cosmic energy that underlies all life in the universe), and 'one thousand' other names/personas. In the Shaivism sects, Parvati is considered an inextricable force, without which, Shiva (and therefore God) would cease to exist, for it is her life-force that gives them both power and energy. Parvati is the benevolent form of Shiva's wife (a complementary aspect to the fierce form of Kali), and the mother of their two sons, Ganesh and Kartikeya.

Puja (**poo**-ja) – A prayer or offering, puja describes the manifestation of worship and reverence in Hinduism. Often involving offerings of light (candles or diyas), flowers, water, or food, along with prayers (often in the form of mantras), puja rituals are an important aspect of religious life for most practicing Hindus, and are particularly common and elaborate on holy days, during festivals, and to celebrate major life events such as weddings, funerals, and baby-namings.

Rakshasa (**raahk**-shuh-suh) – Shapeshifting demons in Hindu mythology, Rakshasas have been referred to with various characteristics throughout Hindu and Buddhist literature. Ravana, Vibhishana, Surpanakha, and Kumbhakarna are Rakshasas in *the Ramayana*. Due to the varying (and often conflicting) representations of Rakshasas throughout the literature, this series has expanded on the mythological depictions with far greater detail than has been generally used in the past. While there has been a parallel drawn between some vampire representations and Rakshasas, they are not considered to be the same, in the mythology or in this series. The origin of Rakshasas on Venus was entirely invented by the author, upon the suggestion of Neha, as she was writing her own story.

Rama (**raah**-muh) – The main protagonist of *the Ramayana*, Rama is generally considered to be the seventh avatar of Vishnu. Often referred to as 'the ideal king' and 'the ideal husband,' despite the miserable ending of his wife, Rama is still a beloved figure in modern Hinduism. While there is significant debate about whether Rama should be considered infallible, this series explores the dichotomy between the divine and human aspects of his character, in line with major historical representations across the Hindu world, including the iconic version by the ancient Sanskrit poet Valmiki, that demonstrate his crooked path to virtue in great detail. The festival of Diwali, one of the most popular Hindu festivals celebrated by hundreds of millions of people every autumn, celebrates the triumph of light over darkness, as embodied by Durga's triumph over Mahishasura, and Rama's triumph over Ravana.

Ramayana, the (**raah**-mah-yuh-nuh) – One of the most well-known and beloved of the ancient Hindu Sanskrit epics, *the Ramayana* follows the many triumphs and tribulations of Rama, the seventh avatar of Vishnu, and Sita, his wife and the avatar of Lakshmi. While the epic covers a range of stories and characters, the primary conflict centers around Rama's battle with Ravana, the Rakshasa King of Lanka, after his capture and incarceration of Sita. While there are many versions of *the Ramayana* referenced across Southeast Asia including in India, Nepal, Thailand, Cambodia, and more, the most famous version is credited to the storyteller Valmiki. *The Ramayana* of Valmiki contains seven *kandas* or 'books.' The seven-book structure of *The Sita Chronicles* is meant to be a nod to the original epic.

Ravana (raah-vuh-nuh) – The main antagonist of *the Ramayana*, Ravana is the Rakshasa King of Lanka. He is said to be a devotee of Shiva, and to have received the 'nectar of immortality' as a boon from Lord Brahma that allows him to withstand any injury from any creature, other than a human. Lord Vishnu comes to Earth as the human, Rama, to take advantage of this epic loophole.

Sanskrit (sahn-skrit) – The primary sacred language of Hinduism, it has many forms and served as the foundation for many modern languages in Southeast Asia. Its role in spreading Indic culture throughout the region can generally be compared to Latin's role in disseminating and communicating literature, religion, and secular education throughout Europe for the two millennia spanning the Roman Empire to the end of the 18th century AD.

Saraswati (sah-ruh-svuh-tee) – The female aspect of the Creator of the Universe, Saraswati is also considered the goddess of knowledge, music, arts, learning, and wisdom. Saraswati is the wife of Brahma, and one of the principal goddesses of the *Tridevi*, or 'Trinity of Goddesses.'

Satya Yuga (saht-yuh yoo-guh) – 'The Age of Truth,' *Satya Yuga* is said to be the peaceful era that will return to Earth after the Preserver of the Universe vanquishes Kali, ending Kali Yuga (the 'Age of Vice').

Shakti (shuhk-tee) – The Great Goddess, the primordial cosmic energy of the universe, and the personification of the 'divine mother,' Shakti has many manifestations, including the *Tridevi*, Durga, Lakshmi, Saraswati, and Parvati. She is said to manifest on Earth as the embodiment of creative power and fertility, and of life itself. Some sects believe that Shakti is responsible for all creation and is the agent of all change, as it is her energy that animates everything in the universe, including the gods. In Shaktism and Shaivism, Shakti is worshipped as the animating energy of the Supreme Being.

Shiva (shih-vuh) – One of the primary deities of Hinduism, and one of the *Trimurti*, or 'Trinity of Gods,' Lord Shiva is considered to be 'the Destroyer,' 'the Transformer,' and 'the Regenerator.' He is represented by hundreds, possibly thousands, of different epithets. He is often represented as conflicting personas: He can be 'fierce' or 'benevolent,' and he is portrayed as a 'householder' with his wife, Parvati, and their sons, Ganesh and Kartikeya, but he is also portrayed as an ascetic yogi (chaste and focused on solitary prayer)— two lifestyles that are mutually exclusive in traditional Hindu society. Shiva's wife, Parvati (also referred to as Durga, Shakti, Kali, and many other names), is considered to be his life-force. In Valmiki's *Ramayana*, Ravana is a follower of Shiva, and Shiva is said to have given him a divine sword with the stipulation that if he uses his sword for unjust purposes, it will be returned to 'the three-eyed one' (Shiva himself). Shiva is often considered to be 'formless,' and it is common to worship him through the formless idol of a 'lingam' (internet image search recommended).

Sita (**see**-tuh) – The main female protagonist of *the Ramayana*, Sita is Rama's wife and an avatar of Lakshmi. Often referred to as 'the ideal wife' for her desire and ability to make the deepest personal sacrifices on behalf of her husband, Sita's tragic suicidal ending is controversial in modern academic discussions of the ancient epics.

Sugriva (soo-**gree**-vuh) – The king of the Vanaras (non-human intelligent primates who can fly), Sugriva's support is crucial to Rama's defeat of Ravana in *the Ramayana*. It is with Sugriva's army that Rama attacks Lanka. Many discussions around historical validity of *the Ramayana* have centered around the assertion that Rama led Sugriva's army over a formerly existing land bridge from mainland India to the island of Sri Lanka, as NASA images show that a series of lightly submerged sandbar islands do appear to have, at some point in the past, connected the two land masses.

Surpanakha (**soor**-puh-nuh-khuh) – The sister of Ravana, Vibhishana, and Kumbhakarna, Surpanakha is a primary female antagonist in *the Ramayana*. She is often considered the catalyst of the main events of *the Ramayana* (often taking the blame for Ravana's despicable actions). Surpanakha's story is also complex, as one of her primary scenes in the epic is when she falls in love with Rama. When she is rejected and humiliated by Rama, Rama's brother, Lakshmana, permanently maims her by cutting off her nose with a divine weapon. Surpanakha's hatred of Sita and her anger at Rama's rejection is a driving force of her character's antagonistic actions later in the story and in this series.

Tridevi (tree-**deh**-vee) – The 'Trinity of Goddesses': Saraswati ('the Creator'), Lakshmi ('the Preserver'), and Parvati, ('the Transformer'), serve as the female aspects and underlying energy of their male, godly counterpart husbands. Together they create balance between the three main aspects of existence. Each one individually, and the group as a whole, manifest Shakti's energy as is necessary to participate in worldly endeavors on behalf of the gods and goddesses, usually to support the cause of righteousness and restore balance.

Trimurti (tree-**moor**-tee) – The 'trinity' of Hindu gods: Brahma ('the Creator'), Vishnu ('the Preserver'), and Shiva ('the Destroyer' and 'the Transformer'). Together, the trinity complements each other, representing a descriptive model of various aspects of life on Earth.

Valmiki (**vahl**-mih-kee) – The most widely attributed author of *the Ramayana*, he is credited with inventing the poetic structure of epic Sanskrit literature, somewhat akin to Homer's role in codifying ancient Greek verse. In Valmiki's *Ramayana*, he participates as a character in his own work, being said to have taken Sita in after her trial by fire when Rama banished her to the jungle to raise their twin sons alone. Valmiki's own voiced admonishment of Rama's behaviour in the final chapters serves as a valuable, if controversial, reminder of the story's main point of demonstrating the complex and imperfect paths to *dharma* (virtue), along with its tragic consequences.

Vanara (**vaah**-nuh-ruh) – An ancient race of nonhuman, intelligent primates, the Vanaras are supporters of Rama and serve as his primary troops in his battle against Ravana. Sometimes referred to just as 'monkeys,' other times referred to as 'half-man, half-monkeys,' the literature is not consistent in its depiction of Vanaras. Hanuman and Sugriva are the most famous Vanaras, from their important roles in *the Ramayana*.

Varuna (vuh-**roo**-nuh) – The god of water and the celestial ocean, Varuna was the original chief god of the Vedic pantheon and later appeared throughout Sanskrit literature, primarily as the ruler of the sea. He plays a secondary role in *the Ramayana*, and is often referred to as a symbol of *rta*, an ancient vedic concept believed to encompass cosmic order and divine balance or justice.

Vibhishana (vee-**bhee**-shuh-nuh) – The youngest brother of the villain demon king, Ravana, Vibhishana is an important ally of Rama in *the Ramayana*. In *the Ramayana*, Vibhishana attempts to convince Ravana to return Sita to Rama, but his efforts are not successful. He then joins Rama and provides important intel that leads to Ravana's eventual defeat. Rama crowns Vibhishana the King of Lanka after Ravana is dead. Vibhishana's role in *the Ramayana* is a complex one, as he betrays his family and his race in order to follow a path he considers to be more dharmic. Still, there is no perfect path towards *dharma* (righteousness), and so, he is also considered a traitor. Vibhishana is one of the *Chiranjivi*, one of the seven immortals of Hinduism, who are said to remain on Earth to this day to guide humans on the path of righteousness.

Vishnu (**vihsh**-noo) – One of the primary deities of Hinduism, Lord Vishnu is considered to be 'the Preserver of the Universe.' Lord Vishnu is one of the *Trimurti*, or 'trinity' of Hindu gods, along with Brahma and Shiva. Together with his wife, Lakshmi (or Laxmi), who is considered his life-force, Lord Vishnu is mentioned throughout numerous Sanskrit texts and is worshipped as the supreme being by the Vaishnavist sects of Hindus. Rama is generally considered the seventh avatar of Vishnu among the *Dashavatara* ('ten avatars of Vishnu'). Some Hindu texts/sects refer to more avatars of Vishnu, including Mohini, a female avatar.

Vishrava (vihsh-**rah**-vuh) – The father of Ravana, Vibhishana, Kumbhakarna, and Surpanakha, he is described as a powerful rishi or 'seer.' He is said to have left his wife, Kaikesi, the mother of his four Rakshasa children, to return to his first wife after he became unhappy with Ravana's conduct.

Ya Devi Sarva Bhuteshu (yah deh-**vee** sar-vuh **bhoo**-teh-**shoo**) – The beginning of the *Devi Suktam,* one of the primary prayers/mantras to the Goddess (often sung in worship), these Sanskrit words celebrate the Goddess's embodiment of power, peace, knowledge, and many other necessary and beautiful aspects of existence in the universe, allowing the worshippers to feel the Shakti, or energy, of the Goddess within themselves, while bowing (figuratively or literally) to the greatness of all that is.

Yajna (**yahg**-nyuh) – 'Sacrifice, devotion, worship, or offering,' it refers to any ritual done in front of a sacred fire, often with mantras.

Yaksha/Yakshini (**yahk**-shuh / yahk-**shee**-nee) – A powerful nature spirit with shapeshifting abilities, generally considered to be the caretakers of Earth. The feminine form of a Yaksha is a Yakshini.

Yama (**yah**-muh) – The god of death, lord of justice, and the gatekeeper of the underworld, Yama is one of several deities who participates in the management of the afterlife. The gatekeeper of Naraka (roughly Hindu 'purgatory'), Yama is said to be one of the judges of human life/morality and 'the first mortal to have died.'

Pronunciation Key:
Rather than using the international phonetic alphabet that is not commonly used by the average reader, these pronunciation notes use references to common sounds in American English, more similar to a foreign language guide for casual travelers. Note that an "h" does not represent an aspiration in this transliteration; it is used to demonstrate various vowel sounds in English. Also note that the consonants have been simplified for an English speaker and do not fully represent the nuanced differences in the Sanskrit alphabet, such as aspirated v. non-aspirated consonants, that a native Hindi speaker would recognize.

Ah – as in "car" and "hard"

Aah – hold "ah" as in "car" and "hard" longer

Uh – as in "under" and "bus"

Ih – as in "in" and "interest"

Eh – as in "extra" and "**e**xcellent"

Oh – as in "over" and "ornate"

Ee – as in "cheese" and "beast," note that this does not indicate an elongation

Oo – as in "choose" and "I do," note that this does not indicate an elongation

This series is dedicated to the Goddess who resides in all of us.

May she give us the energy, inspiration, and perseverance to triumph over all that holds us back, no matter what forms our enemies take.

"We are told too often what we can't do."

May we do it anyway.

Jai Mata Di.

~Ashley Mayers

www.ingramcontent.com/pod-product-compliance
Lightning Source LLC
Chambersburg PA
CBHW030924260626
47169CB00002B/367